# Defeat, Resist and Rescue

Joyce W. Hahn

iUniverse, Inc.
New York   Bloomington

# Defeat, Resist and Rescue

*iUniverse books may be ordered through booksellers or by contacting:*

*iUniverse
1663 Liberty Drive
Bloomington, IN 47403
www.iuniverse.com
1-800-Authors (1-800-288-4677)*

*ISBN: 978-1-4502-2965-4 (sc)
ISBN: 978-1-4502-2966-1 (ebk)*

*Printed in the United States of America*

*iUniverse rev. date: 5/20/2010*

# Acknowledgments

I want to thank several people who helped me write this book: My husband, George, a counter intelligence agent in World War II, whom I consulted frequently; Lester Gorn, who read my manuscript and offered expert criticism, and to members of my writing group, Joan Condon, Natalya Dabrunsky, George Hahn, Beverley Paik, Evelyn Smart and Nick Souza.

For absent friends

Aux armes, citoyans
Formez vos battaillons

*La Marseillaise*

# PART ONE

## DEFEAT

# Chapter One

## On the Road

*June 23, 1940*

Jean was tired, hungry and angry. His legs ached as he pedaled the bike along the rough track. He thought of the French infantry officers he'd seen racing south on the highway—in staff cars—and his blood boiled. The bastards had turned tail and run, abandoning their men to the Germans. Suddenly, the whine of an airplane engine brought Jean to a jolting stop. He leaped from his bicycle and bolted into the wooded field, dragging his bike as he ran. From his hiding place under a pear tree he peered up at the sky. Through the blossoming branches he watched the plane disappear—a German Messerschmidt 109. He knew the type well. On the beach at Dunkirk he had dodged bullets from planes just like it. He recalled the terror those beasts invoked, engines screaming, machine-guns rattling as he'd crouched, curled up in the sand—or swam to the boats—with hundreds of other desperate, bloodied soldiers.

Now as Jean rose from the dirt, he brushed off his grimy French army uniform. He listened for sounds of machine guns or bomb blasts, but all he heard was birdsong and the rustling of leaves in the pear orchard. He climbed on the bike and continued down the dirt track. It was so quiet. The day before he had biked on the main road south of Angers, and the bombing and strafing had been continuous and deadly. Abandoned cars blackened by fire or riddled with bullets were scattered along the roadside. Disheveled refugees on foot, some swathed in bloodied bandages, were heading south, fleeing from the advancing German army. Paris had been taken the week before. Families were burdened with heavy bundles and crying children. Trains weren't running, the tracks having been destroyed by bombs. It was then that Jean had bitterly noted the only moving cars on the road were jammed with French army officers in flight. Only they could obtain petrol.

He'd taken this narrow track through the orchards yesterday afternoon, avoiding the major roads. The June weather was warm and the sky clear, and last night he'd wrapped himself in his army-issue blanket and slept on the ground under a pear tree. He hadn't yet obtained his discharge papers, and until he possessed that document he could be picked up by German soldiers and taken prisoner. He was looking for a fighting unit—or resistance fighters—if they existed—and was determined to continue the war against fascism. He'd fought in Spain, he'd fought here in France and he would continue fighting.

He recalled the frustration he'd felt these last weeks after the defeat at Dunkirk. He'd been evacuated from the beach, taken to Dover and then shipped back to France with the remnants of his regiment, the 147th Infantry. They'd landed in Cherbourg and were dispatched by train from one town to another. At each stop the soldiers believed they would be organized into a fighting unit, but instead they'd be shuttled off in another cattle car to yet another station. Then their officers disappeared. They were left leaderless and the division disintegrated. The word was débrouillier, to slip through the cracks, to manage—each man for himself. He'd found the bicycle abandoned next to a bombed car. Luckily, the bike hadn't been damaged. He reflected only briefly about its former owner, hoping he was still alive, but not hesitating to take the bike.

The silvery sound of rushing water now caused Jean to stop. He was thirsty and needed to fill his canteen. He wheeled the bike to the side of the road. A few yards beyond a row of poplars a flow of water tumbled over rocks. At the edge of the stream a man in a gray cap was leading a horse toward the water, still hitched to a wooden cart. The man touched his cap and called out a greeting. Jean responded with a wave. He fished his canteen from his musette bag and trudged through the meadow grass toward the stream.

"Good morning, soldier," the man said. "On your way home?"

"Home? Not yet, sir." Jean was troubled by the question. Did the man assume he was a deserter? He stooped to fill his canteen.

"Too bad. My wife and I are hoping our son will walk in our farm door soon—now that the war is over, now there's an armistice."

Shocked, Jean stared at the man. "Armistice?" Had the French surrendered? "When did you hear of an armistice?"

"Yesterday evening. Maréchal Pétain spoke on the radio. Our French generals and the Prime Minister signed an agreement with the Germans. Hitler was in Paris. They met in the same railroad car the Versailles Treaty was signed." He tugged off his cap and gave Jean a sharp glance. "We've been beaten this time. I thought it could never happen. I fought in the last one. Three of my brothers were killed." He replaced his cap, pulling it low on his brow, shading his tired eyes. "My son was at Sedan. He survived, thank God. Those Boches came right through the Ardennes with their beastly tanks."

"Did Pétain say what he agreed to?"

"I'm not sure, but it seems that only part of France will be occupied by German troops. The French government will move to Vichy. South of Tours will be under French control. The north of France will be occupied—and the west coast. They're in Paris, of course." He shrugged, his mouth turned down as if he'd bitten into something bitter. "Alors, soldier, you'd better head south-east. I'm pretty sure this region is in the occupied zone. You can't trust those Germans. They might take you prisoner. I worry about my son." The horse had stopped drinking and the farmer led the horse and cart toward the road.

"Well, good luck to him. If he could survive Sedan he'll find his way home, I'm sure." Jean tried to sound reassuring, but doubted his own words. The boy was probably already behind barbed wire.

"And good luck to you, too, soldier." The farmer climbed onto the driver's seat, flicked the horse's reins, and plodded away.

Jean took a long swig of water from the canteen and re-filled it. His head throbbed with anger. Those bastards! Those lily-livered, right-wing fascist generals and politicians. They wanted Germany to win. They went belly up. Caved in. Then he thought about the farmer's son returning home. Would he ever see his own home in Genoa again? Would he become Gino Baroli again, not Jean Barrault? He felt the carefully buttoned pocket of his khaki shirt for the identity card the Comintern agent had procured for him. So much had happened since escaping from Mussolini's prison: Spain, the detention camp on the beach at Argelés, Dunkirk. It had been a little over three years, but it seemed like centuries. He was no longer the same man. He'd abandoned his Italian persona and become a bona fide Frenchman. It hadn't been too difficult. His mother was Parisian and he had spoken French since he could walk.

Now he must find a French army official who'd sign his discharge papers. And he needed civilian clothes. He mounted his bike and took off down the dirt track, determined to avoid the German army.

Fléré la Riviére, twilight the same day, June 23, 1940. Twenty-two year old Danielle Berger and her fourteen-year old brother, David, were perched on the grass-covered bank overlooking the wide Indre River. The sun had just dipped below the horizon, and robins and sparrows had flitted into the branches of the willows lining the river bank. Danielle's pale arms hugged her drawn up knees, her blue cotton dress pulled down to reach her ankles. She stared out at the wide, flowing river. "How can it be so peaceful here when our world is falling apart?"

David picked up a stone and with a fast throw sent it flying into the river. "If only we could do something. Fight. I wish I had a gun. What if the Germans get here before we leave tomorrow?"

Danielle pushed a blonde curl behind her ear. "They won't. There's an armistice, remember? The war's over."

"But the war's not over for us. Hitler's in Paris." He threw another stone.

Danielle sighed. The war was most certainly not over for their family. They could not return to Paris. She could not return to the Ecole de Beaux Arts nor her parents to their teaching jobs at the university, nor David to his Lyceé. They were Jewish. The fact that they were secular, assimilated, didn't matter. They knew what the Nazis did to anyone with Jewish blood in Germany and the countries they'd invaded. But where would they go? Danielle put her head on her knees. She was so tired, so discouraged. The trains and buses weren't running and it was imperative they get as far south as they could. Papa wanted to get to Marseilles. They'd had to leave their car at a farm north of Tours. No petrol. They'd been lucky to find a place to sleep tonight. They'd left Tours early this morning on foot. Eventually, a farmer had given them a lift in his wagon. He'd suggested they come to this farm on the edge of the village, Fléré la Riviére. "The Frindels take in guests." he'd said. "Their son is in the army and they have an extra room."

And he'd been right. The Frindels took them in—for a price. Maman and she could have the son's room and Papa and David could sleep in the barn. Mme Frindel said she'd cook for them. "Soup and sausage," she'd said, "but no bread. We have no flour."

Papa had money to pay the farmer for their lodging. Several weeks ago he had drawn cash from his bank and their mother had sewn it into the linings and pockets of their clothing. M. Frindel had scrutinized the cash Papa had placed in his hand with a sharp eye.

Danielle peered at her gold watch, the watch her parents had given her when she achieved top scores in the Bacs. Mme Frindel would be serving dinner in half an hour. Reluctantly, she rose from her perch. "It's almost time for dinner, David. Let's go."

"Good. I'm starved. And I saw those sausages hanging from the ceiling in the kitchen. And I could smell the soup on the stove."

As they approached the Frindels' cottage, Danielle noticed a bicycle leaning against the yellow plastered wall—propped under the green window shutters. Had it been there when she and David walked to the river? The door to the house was open to the mild June evening. A curtain of beaded strings hung over it to keep out the flies, but the aroma of simmering onions and thyme wafted through the opening. Inside, in the center of the room, a large rectangular table was set with bowls and glasses—and pitchers filled with red wine. At the far end of the room Danielle noted her parents, M. Frindel, and a strange man in the uniform of the French army. They were deep in conversation. She heard the words demarcation line.

Jean rose to his feet when M. Berger's daughter and son entered the farmhouse. He found himself staring at the girl as she moved into the room. She was lovely. When her father made the introductions, Jean noted her long delicate fingers when she reached out her hand. He bent over it and gave a soldierly bow. "Enchanté, Madamoiselle." He shook hands with the boy, David, who with his dark hair and long narrow nose looked more Spanish than French. The blonde, blue-eyed Danielle had the same coloring as her mother.

David was eying the soup pot steaming on the stove. "I'm famished."

M. Berger touched the boy's shoulder and smiled. "Soon, David. Mme. Frindel will call us."

Danielle was giving him a questioning glance. "M. Barrault, when we walked in the door I heard you mention the demarcation line. Have you heard where it will be?"

"Not exactly. But I can tell you this. Earlier today I was given a lift to a French military installation just outside Tours, a bit north. The soldiers there were striking camp, preparing to move south. In fact, they were demobilizing many of the men. The officer who signed my discharge papers told me he'd been informed that the French Zone would start forty kilometers south of Tours—more or less. If that's true, this village, Fléré la Riviére, would be beyond German control. The main road south was jammed with army vehicles and people on foot. You probably saw it yourselves." He turned to M. Berger. "But I didn't encounter any German checkpoints."

"Nor did we. But even so, tomorrow we want to leave early and get as far south as we can. Our host, here, M. Frindel, promised to take us in his wagon to the next town, Chateauroux. He says one can catch a train there for Marseilles. The tracks have not been badly damaged. The problem, of course, will be buying tickets."

Jean nodded. "I was told that we might need a special permit to travel."

Berger swore under his breath, "merde!"

Jean gave a wry laugh. "D'accord!"

# Chapter Two

## To the Train

### June 24, 1940

True to his word, the next morning M. Frindel harnessed his two horses and helped the Bergers into the wagon. They sat next to the two large containers of fresh milk and a wicker hamper containing wheels of cheese. It was market day in Chateauroux and M. Frindel intended to sell his milk and cheese there. "Now I don't have to watch out for Messerchmidts. The first time in a month. The bombing and strafing wasn't as bad here as I heard it was in the north, but we all stayed home. Today I think the market will be full. Villagers will be stocking up, then hiding their supplies from the Germans—if they come."

Jean rode beside the cart on his bike. Other horse-drawn carts were on the road, and from time to time an army truck or a car would pass them by. The road followed the Indre river. Black and white cows grazed in the green fields that stretched out along the banks of the wide meandering river. Clouds were gathering overhead, and Jean gave the sky a wary glance. He now wore the corduroy pants and cotton shirt belonging to M. Frindel's son. He had paid the farmer for the clothes and his lodging from the demobilization packet of francs he had received the day before. His army rain coat and uniform were rolled up in his musette bag along with his blanket, toilet articles and eating utensils—and his precious passport and demob papers.

As they approached the town, he noted the ancient stone houses that lined the road. The fields between the cottages contained small vineyards or kitchen gardens sprouting with tender shoots of lettuce, tomatoes or carrots. So bucolic. So peaceful. The air smelled of early summer, of greenery, of promise. Jean stared. It would be more appropriate to the situation if the land were brown and arid and smelled of decay.

As he trailed after the wagon on his bike he caught Danielle's glance. She gave him a warm smile. He reflected on their conversation the evening before after dinner at the farmhouse. They'd strolled to the bank of the river, and although it was almost nine in the evening, it was still light. He couldn't keep his eyes off her lovely, heart-shaped face as she spoke. Her eyes were a deep blue like the sea. She talked about the family's need to escape Paris and the Nazis, the fact that they were Jewish. Then on a lighter note she had told him she'd attended the Sorbonne the year before.

Jean had also studied at the Sorbonne. In fact, on his forged identity card he had given his student address in Paris as his home. Although it had been five years since he had attended classes there, when he mentioned the name of his French literature professor, M. Colombier, Danielle exclaimed, "I had him too!"

Jean laughed. "I detested that man!"

"So did I!" Danielle's face lit up. As she laughed the fear that had shadowed her eyes disappeared for the moment.

Jean didn't mention to Danielle that he had been in Paris only for the four years he was at the university. The Comintern agent had told him to keep his background story as close to the truth as possible, and that's what he'd done. When she asked him about his family he told her half-truths. "My parents are both dead. They died in a boating accident in Italy five years ago." He reached for a willow branch and snapped it off, avoiding Danielle's glance. "My father was a shipping agent in Le Havre. My mother was raised in Paris, but her family came from Brittany. I have cousins there, but I've lost touch with them."

"So you have no family?" she asked, her eyes expressing sympathy.

He gave Danielle a direct look. "I have a sister. She's married to an Italian schoolteacher in Milan. I haven't seen her for years." He had just told her the truth. His sister really did live in Milan and was married to a schoolteacher. He wanted to be honest with Danielle, divulge his true past. Her expression was so open, so trusting. But lie he must. His life was at stake. If the police discovered he was Italian—not French—a fugitive with forged papers, and had escaped from a detention camp for soldiers who had fought for Republican Spain, he would be turned over to the Italians and thrown back into one of Mussolini's prisons—like the one he had escaped from to go to Spain. And he most certainly couldn't admit to being a Comintern agent. But some of what he told her was true. His father had been a shipping agent—but in Genoa not Le Havre. His parents had died in a boating accident, his mother had been raised in Paris, and he'd lost touch with his cousins in Brittany.

Danielle had wandered to the edge of the bank overlooking the river. A cool breeze had sprung up and a strand of her blonde hair had blown against her cheek. She looked up at him, smiling. "So what were you studying at the Sorbonne—beside French literature?"

"Economics, philosophy. After the Sorbonne I went to England and took classes at the London School of Economics for a year." He picked up a flat stone and sent it skipping into the river." He turned to her again. "I learned English, but not much economics. I decided I wanted to be a journalist, but then the war in Spain began. I volunteered for the International Brigade." What he omitted to tell her was that before Spain, he had first written for a Socialist paper in Milan and had been arrested and jailed by Mussolini's police, accused of subversive activity. "When we were withdrawn from Spain I joined the French army. After the fiasco in Spain I knew it was inevitable the fascists would attempt to conquer all Europe."

The breeze grew stronger and Danielle hugged her chest with folded arms. "But you're cold," Jean said, resisting the impulse to put his arm around her shoulders, "we'd better go back." They turned their backs on the river and found the path to the farmhouse. "But, Danielle, what about you" Jean said, peering into her eyes. "Do you paint, do sculpture? Which artists do you admire?"

The light faded from her face, and she glanced away from him. "All that is over. I don't know when I'll paint again—or study paintings— or where I'll live. Or whether we can escape the Germans."

"Your father believes you might find a ship in Marseilles."

"But where would it take us? Algeria? Morocco? And then what?"

Now as Jean pedaled his bike behind M. Frindel's wagon he asked himself what were his own plans? He wasn't sure. He wanted to fight Germans, join a group of resisters, if there was such a movement. A communist organization might be the place to find out, although the communists were keeping a low profile these days. Anyway, the less he had to do with them the better. He kept expecting to suddenly see Paul, his Comintern agent, the one who had recruited him, the one he promised to report to in exchange for his forged papers and help to escape the camp on the beach at Argelés, his Faustian bargain.

Or should he try to flee the country, find his way to England. To hell with the communists. He could join the British army—or the Free French. The officer at the military camp he'd talked to the day before spoke about General de Gaulle, who'd escaped to England. "I hear de Gaulle's organizing a French army in exile," he'd said, offering Jean a Gauloises.

Jean slid the cigarette from the pack. "Have you heard how men will get there? Me, for instance."

The officer lit both their cigarettes. "No, unfortunately. In fact, it's going to be damned difficult. The Armistice agreement states that anyone planning to leave the country must have an exit visa—and any man of military age will not be granted one."

"Terrific. So, somehow I'd have to cross the frontier avoiding the French officials."

The officer nodded. "Right. And to make matters worse, anyone who travels anywhere within the country will need a travel permit."

"Merde! Anything else?"

"It doesn't affect you, of course, but the French police must surrender on demand any individual the Gestapo wishes to question. They're particularly anxious to round up German anti-fascists who fled here to France."

Now M. Frindel guided his horse and wagon to the side of the road. Jean peered at the scene around him. They had entered the market area, where vendors were selling their wares from lines of kiosks and farmer's carts and was teaming with women, children and old men carrying shopping baskets. M. Frindel pointed to a street going off to the right from the central square. "The gare, the train station, is two blocks in that direction. You should get out here. The street is blocked by the market. It will be easier for you to walk."

Maurice and Danielle jumped down from the wagon bed, and David from his perch next to M. Frindel They adjusted the straps of their backpacks and reached for their suitcases. They all called out to M. Frindel. "Many, many thanks, Monsieur." Jean, who had only his bike to push along the street, balanced Danielle's case on the handlebars. Now they had to surmount the next barrier: the train station and acquiring tickets to Marseilles—and most difficult of all, perhaps—travel permits. As they crossed the square Jean stared at the monument in its center. A bronze statue of a soldier in the uniform of the last war stood on top of a large block of marble. A long list of names was etched in the stone. The war dead. The war to end all wars.

Danielle eyed the Memorial and its distressing list of names. She thought of her close friends, Jules, Marc and Charles—especially Jules, with whom she'd been in love. Almost all the boys in her class at the Sorbonne had been called up to join the French army. Would their names be written in stone when this war was over? She'd heard that Charles had been killed at Dunkirk; Marc and Jules had been taken prisoner. She'd received a letter from Jules the week before she left Paris. She'd wept when she read it, picturing sensitive, talented Jules behind barbed wire. Marc was tougher. But at least they were alive. She found it impossible to believe that Charles was dead. She stepped close to the stone of the Memorial and touched it, imagining Charles' name inscribed there. He'd been so wickedly funny, so full of life— and so intensely political. She imagined his deep voice shouting out from the stone. "We must fight those fascists. To the death!"

As she turned away from the Memorial, she reflected on those three boys. All three had been leftists, flirting with communism, although they weren't Party members, and they didn't broadcast their political beliefs. The Deladier government arrested communists they considered dangerous. The boys had been too young to fight in Spain, but had longed to join the International Brigade. She remembered their furious arguments, their cries of anguish when they first heard the shocking news of the Nazi/Soviet Pact. It was if they'd been stabbed in the gut, betrayed. Charles had yelled back that Stalin was just biding his time. "He's stockpiling weapons, manufacturing airplanes, preparing for war with Germany. Stalin has not betrayed the class struggle!" All the same, they had been troubled by the Comintern's new Party line— appeasement! Then they became officers and were eager to fight for France.

Danielle shook off her troubled thoughts and caught up with her mother. Monique was limping as she walked. Danielle held out her arm. "Here, Maman, let me help you."

Monique grasped Danielle's arm and sighed. "I think my blisters are infected." Both Monique and Danielle wore espadrilles, rope-soled peasant shoes. They'd started their journey in high-heels, and Monique hadn't changed into espadrilles soon enough.

By now their progress down the street was impeded by a logjam of people shoving their way into the gare. Danielle groaned. "So many people! What are we going to do?"

Maurice grasped her shoulder. "We join the queue. Like the rest of the refugees. We might as well get used to it." His expression was grim. Clinging together, the Bergers shouldered their way into the cavernous structure.

Jean zigzagged his bike through the crowd, still balancing Danielle's suitcase on the handlebars. He scanned the throng, the ashen, sweaty faces, men and women loaded with crying children and large bundles. Some with dogs or cats stuffed in bags. Frantic voices echoed from the high glass roof covering the gare. He searched for police and counted six at their posts by the entrance and the train tracks. They shot a sharp look at each person who entered the gare, but did not demand to examine documents. Perhaps the government hadn't had time to print the forms for the travel permits. For once he was thankful for the bureaucrats' inefficiency.

Against the far wall in the station were four ticket windows. Long lines of travelers waited at each one. Setting down the two suitcases, David took a position at the end of one of the queues. "We could take turns holding a place. We will need five tickets, right?" He glanced at Jean. "You're going to Marseilles, too?"

Jean nodded, handing him money for the train. "I'll scout around and look at the schedule. Find out if we need travel permits—and if so where to get them."

Maurice stepped to Jean's side. "I'll go with you." He then fished out his wallet and handed David a few francs for their tickets.

As another family took it's place behind them, David moved the suitcases. "I'll stay here. Maman, Danielle. Look, there's a café over there in the corner. Maybe you can find a place to sit down." The café was overflowing with women and children. All were surrounded by bags and bundles. Solemn-faced children hugged toys to their chests.

Danielle reached for Jean's bike and wheeled it toward the café. "I'll look after this for you."

Jean gave her a nod of thanks and the two men maneuvered through the crowd to the train tracks. They peered up at the large board announcing the trains' arrival and departure times and to and from which city and on what track. Maurice pointed to the board. "We could take the train to Toulouse and change trains from there for Marseilles."

"It leaves in two hours. But can we get tickets?"

A puffing, hissing train had just arrived from Vierzon Ville, a town north of Chateauroux. The passengers poured off the train and rushed into the station and out the door. Jean watched their progress to see if the police were demanding a show of papers—specifically, travel permits, but the six gendarmes in the station stood watchfully at their posts, but did not stop anyone.

Returning to the ticket window queue, Jean and Maurice took David's place in line and David returned the ticket money to his father. Jean eyed their fellow purchasers. They shuffled nervously as they stood in place. Their clothes were rumpled and they smelled of sweat. Watching the travelers, a man in a pale gray suit and a dark fedora stood at the end of the ticket counter. He scrutinized each person as he or she approached the windows. A prickle of fear crept up Jean's spine.

Who was this man? An agent of the French police or of the Gestapo? Was he searching for someone in particular? Or merely anyone who looked suspicious, who he could arrest and throw into one of the many detention camps. Jean patted his shirt pocket that contained his wallet and forged identity card. His passport and demob papers were in his musette bag on his back.

At last there was only one person in front of them. Jean held his breath, praying that tickets were still available, turning to glance at Maurice, who stood next to him. And les voilá, there they were. Five tickets for Toulouse. As Maurice paid for the tickets, Jean knew that the man in the fedora was watching them closely. He made sure to avoid eye contact with the man.

An hour later found the Bergers and Jean squeezed into a compartment with five other rumpled passengers. The bicycle and luggage were in the baggage car. Dispirited travelers filled the corridors outside the compartment. Some sat on the floor leaning against their bags, while others stood staring blankly out the window. Jean looked across the compartment at Danielle. She was trembling, breathing hard. He gave her a smile which he hoped would be reassuring. "We should be in Toulouse in five hours." He wanted to add that they would be far away from the German army—and Paris, but he felt the need to watch his tongue. France was no longer free. One didn't know who was listening.

The train finally began to move away from the station and enter the open countryside. Green meadows stretched out to rows of willows and poplars. Glimpses of the silvery Indre flashed between the trees. Suddenly, the door to their compartment slid open and two officials stood at the entrance—one a train official, the other a gendarme. "Documents, please!"

The passengers reached into their pockets and bags for their tickets and cartes d'identité. Jean was the last to hand the gendarme his card. His heart skipped a beat. He had never become used to showing his forged document, always expecting the official to notice it's falseness and arrest him. The gendarme stared at the card and raised an eyebrow. "You're American?"

Jean frowned. "No, but I was born in America when my father was working there for a French firm, a shipping agency. I'm French. I have a French passport." He reached for his musette bag.

The gendarme handed the identity card back to Jean. "No problem," and went out the door. Jean shot a quick glance at Danielle who was staring at him strangely. He had not been born in America, of course. The forger had decided upon America as his place of birth so that it would be more difficult for the police to check on his document's authenticity. Damn. He would need to lie again to Danielle when she asked about his birthplace—which he could tell by the curiosity her eyes expressed, she would most surely do.

Danielle had been watching Jean during this exchange with the officials. She had noticed his sudden slight nervousness, a tightening of his mouth, a wary expression in his eyes. He had beautiful eyes; dark gold, flecked with green, edged by long, dark eyelashes that sometimes made shadows on his cheeks. His skin was tanned and his hair was thick and black. And he was born in America? He hadn't told her that bit. At that moment she decided she must find out more about Jean Barrault.

# Chapter Three

## Marseilles

### June 26, 1940

The tired travelers waited on the platform of Gare St Charles for their luggage to be unloaded. Danielle tugged at her blouse, which clung to her skin damp with sweat. She felt miserably unwashed and sticky, but thank God they had finally arrived in Marseilles. Their jammed compartment on the train from Toulouse had been as hot as a steam bath. The train had been even more crowded than the one from Chateauroux—and so slow. It had taken six hours instead of its scheduled four. Furthermore, they'd had to wait two days in Toulouse, since the trains to Marseilles were fully booked.

It seemed as if all of defeated France had descended on the town. Frantic men and women were searching for husbands, wives, children. Hotels were completely full. She and her family had to sleep on the floor at a refugee center, a former movie house. The seats had been taken out and straw scattered on the floor. She still itched and hoped it wasn't fleas. Jean had chosen to sleep in the public park. He'd told her it was a warm night, and he was used to sleeping outdoors.

They'd spent some time together in Toulouse. He'd taken her to a sidewalk café on Place de Capitale where they sat under an awning quietly sipping glasses of wine. She'd noticed the tension in his body as he scanned the tables nearby. How wary he was. She recalled how nervous he'd appeared when the train conductor checked his identity card and asked him if he were an American. She'd wanted to question him about it. And why not? She plunged. "Were you really born in America?"

He shifted in his chair. "Yes, I happened to be born there. I'm French, of course." He'd abruptly changed the subject and spoke about his time in Spain. "I really believed we could stop Franco, stop fascism from spreading like an ugly fungus. We all knew Hitler and Mussolini wanted to divide Europe between them." He gave her a penetrating look. "The Nazis are cruel, brutal, demented with their Aryan nonsense. Their treatment of Jews is despicable, criminal. Franco and Mussolini aren't any better. They don't persecute Jews—unless they're socialists or communists—but they run a repressive, dictatorial, unspeakably vicious government." He paused as if to catch his breath and fished a pack of Gauloises from his shirt pocket. He held the pack out to her.

She shook her head. "I don't smoke."

Jean lit his cigarette with his dented lighter, his eyes flickering with anger. He gestured to the people around them. "The French wouldn't even sell weapons to Spain so we could fight the fascists—even though civilians were being bombed by German planes with swastikas on their wings. We had no ammunition, no guns. The only country who helped was Russia—and the Stalinists came with strings attached!"

Now standing by the train Danielle glanced at Jean who was watching his bike being unloaded. She found herself fascinated by the intensity in his green-gold eyes. He was different from the other young men she'd known. More complex. Although he was passionate about finding a fighting unit or a group of resisters, she found herself hoping he wouldn't leave Marseilles for a while. It didn't seem likely that she and her parents would be escaping from France soon. They were surrounded by refugees desperate to leave—especially the German Jews and anti-fascists. As her father had said, they'd just have to join the queue.

The baggage handler was now loading bags and Jean's bike onto the handcart. A few minutes later they were at the main door of the gare. Two gendarmes were checking documents. When she held out her identity card the gendarme scrutinized her photo, then her face, and quickly returned it to her. She turned to watch Jean hand over his papers. Once more, the skin around his eyes became tense. He immediately relaxed when the gendarme returned the documents.

Soon they were out the door at the top of the grand stone staircase leading down into the city. Marseilles lay below, dazzling in the sunlight, the spire of Notre Dame de Garde rising up from the cone-shaped bluff overlooking the bay. "And there's the Mediterranean." Danielle, cried, turning to her mother. "I had no idea Marseilles was so beautiful." Taking Monique's arm to steady her, Danielle stepped carefully down the hundred steps or so to the street below. Jean carried his bike and Maurice and David hauled the heavy suitcases. A tram rumbled by, crammed with riders. Danielle, still holding her mother's arm, maneuvered her through the crush of people hurrying along the sidewalk. Bicycle riders whizzed by, but there seemed to be no taxis.

Maurice turned to Jean. "At least you have wheels. Have you decided where you'll go next?"

"Not really. First I need to find a cheap place to stay. But look, let me help you get settled."

Once more Jean balanced one of the Bergers' bags on his bicycle handlebars as the group trudged down the street searching for a place to stay. They stopped at four hotels, but all were fully occupied. Each time a solemn-faced concierge would shake his head. "Sorry, Monsieur, Madame. No rooms." Hauling their luggage, the discouraged family proceeded slowly down the street in the burning southern heat.

Jean glanced at David and Danielle, who were darting solemn looks at the buildings, the trolleys and the streams of people walking by. Jean studied their faces. They both looked hot, exhausted and somewhat bewildered—and so very vulnerable. Danielle was lifting her hair up from the back of her neck. Even exhausted, she was beautiful. It was essential the Bergers leave France, but it might not be soon. He'd be sorry to see Danielle go. Of course, he had no idea where he himself would be. Perhaps he could help them escape. At least he could help them find a place to stay here in Marseilles.

Jean turned to Maurice. "I think you might have more luck finding a place off the main street, nearer the port. The baggage handler told me to turn off on Blvd Canebiére. We should get there soon. He'd said Canebiére leads to the port—then to take the narrow streets that cross it. We'd find small hotels there."

Eventually, the family found a small hotel with two rooms, Hotel Ventoux. It was still too expensive for him, Jean decided. "I'll look for a place nearer the port. But I'll see you later. D'accord?"

"Oh yes,"Danielle said, giving him a tired smile. "See you later!"

And Jean did call on her later after he'd found a cheap hotel on a dark alley near the port. It was now sundown and a cool breeze blew from the sea. He wanted to show her the Vieux Port, the old section of the city and its seaport. David insisted upon coming along, but Maurice and Monique were content to stay in the café next to their hotel. Monique needed to rest her blistered feet.

The city swarmed with worried-looking, tired refugees. The sidewalk cafés were jammed. At the end of a narrow street in the old quarter the trio spied the blue Mediterranean. Fishing boats and a few large ships were anchored by the docks, but the wharves were quiet. Facing the harbor Jean noted the ruins of a brick building, evidence of the German and Italian recent air raids. The interior was open to the sea air, the same doll house effect he'd seen in Madrid.

Determined to remain cheerful, Jean pointed to an empty table at a café opposite from the pier. "Let's see if we can get something to eat."

David happily agreed. "I'm starved. And Papa gave me some money."

They sat at a tiny table placed in a row facing the bay. Jean noted a group of tall, blond young men sitting at a table inside the café. British soldiers? He'd heard a group of escapees from Dunkirk had been detained by the French at the fort up on the hill. They were allowed out on a pass during the day. Next to them were tables of unsavory looking men speaking in low voices, as if plotting something illegal or criminal. Marseilles was well known for its gangsters.

Their nearby neighbors nodded polite greetings as Danielle, David and he squeezed into rickety chairs. A constant chatter continued around them. Jean heard the middle-aged woman at his elbow talking about a ship that might be sailing to Casablanca in a few days. Her ruddy-faced companion laughed. "Where did you hear that bit of gossip. The port is blockaded. British war ships don't let anything through. Didn't you know that?"

The woman shrugged. "We'll see."

Jean and Danielle exchanged glances. "Why have we come here?" Danielle murmured. "If the port is blockaded."

The woman gave her a sympathetic look. "I hear some sturdy refugees are climbing over the Pyrenees to Spain—then to Portugal. Ships are sailing from Lisbon. But I really did hear a ship would leave for Casablanca soon."

"But," said her companion. "You need transit visas for both Spain and Portugal and for Portugal you also need a visa for somewhere else—America, Cuba, South America—wherever. They don't want you filling up their country like bedbugs."

Danielle sighed, then turned to Jean. "Tomorrow Papa is going to Montredon to the American consulate to apply for a visa."

The man snorted. "Bon chance, cherie!"

# Chapter Four

## Documents

*June 27, 1940*

The seats on the trolley were filled with solemn, shabbily-dressed men and women. Danielle and her father stood in the aisle, holding on to overhead straps. They were heading for Montredon, the suburb of Marseilles where they would apply for an American visa. Danielle peered out the window of the trolley as it rattled out of the city. Soon it traveled along the edge of the Mediterranean. They passed gray limestone hills dotted with beach houses, umbrella pines and tall palm trees that were lit by the early morning light. She glanced at her watch. It was now ten past six.

The passengers surrounding her were subdued. No one spoke. Some were reading newspapers, others peered out the windows, eyes dark with fatigue. When the trolley arrived at Montredon the entire carload poured out the doors and rushed to join the long queue that stretched in front of a huge brick villa. A sign announced that the building housed the visa section of the American consulate. Three other handwritten signs stated in tall black letters, APPLICATIONS FROM CENTRAL EUROPE CLOSED, QUOTA TRANSFERS FROM PARIS DISCONTINUED, and PASSAGE FOR LISBON SOLD OUT FOR MONTHS.

Danielle stood next to her father reading the signs, then read them again and again. That the applications from central Europe were closed and that passage for Lisbon was sold out was clear enough, but the one about Paris? She turned to her father. "What does the one about a Paris quota mean, father?"

Maurice's olive skin had taken on a greenish tone. "Nothing good, cherie. The Americans choose which nationals they prefer as immigrants. I'm not sure how many French are permitted on the quota. If in Paris I had put our family's names on the quota for U.S. immigration at the Embassy, it would not be valid here." He took hold of her arm. "But I did no such thing." He led her to the end of the queue. "That's exactly what we must do now."

Danielle stared at the long line of people ahead of them. Some slumped against the brick wall, others sat on the slate walkway or on the steps of the villa. She could hear a multitude of languages. The blonde woman in front of her was carrying an umbrella. Danielle looked up at the clear blue sky. There was no sign of rain. The sun shone low on the horizon. It was still only a little after six and was still cool. Perhaps the umbrella was to provide shade later in the heat of the afternoon. Danielle winced. Obviously, the woman was experienced at standing in queues.

Jean drank from his cup of café au lait at a café in the Vieux Port. He gazed out at the view of the city to the north across the water. The spire of Notre Dame de la Garde poked up into the sky on its hill, and red-tiled roofs zigzagged down the slope. Jean drained his coffee cup, considered ordering another and then mentally counted his supply of francs. The room he'd rented on the next street cost only five francs a week, but he still had to eat. The one thousand francs he had received in his demobilization package wouldn't last forever.

He glanced around the café at the men in a variety of French uniforms. Marseilles had been designated as a demobilization center and every day trains had been arriving packed with soldiers. Next to him was a group of colonials with bright red fezzes on their heads. On the other side of the room were cavalry officers dressed in khaki tunics and beige riding britches. At least these soldiers had escaped becoming

German prisoners of war. He'd heard that well over a million French soldiers had been taken prisoner and shipped to Germany.

He still hadn't heard any news of a resistance group. After he left Danielle the night before he had roamed the bars and cafés listening to rumors, refugee chatter—the underground telegraph. The truth was that not many refugees were escaping France. A few managed to go over the Pyrenees, others had taken the rare ship to Casablanca. The people who were most desperate were those without passports, the stateless German anti-fascists who were pursued by the Gestapo.

Jean slid a Gauloises from his shirt pocket and lit it with his dented cigarette lighter. He thought about Danielle and her family. From what he'd heard, obtaining a visa to America was impossible unless the applicant had some connection there—relatives, a job or influential friends. Would they be willing to go to Cuba, Dominican Republic or some of the other obscure countries that might allow them in? From what he'd heard, it wasn't too difficult to get transit visas, and there was a thriving market for forged documents of all types but they were expensive.

He gazed out at he docks, noting the fishing boat that was chugging into the bay. A flock of seagulls swooped over it, crying raucously. Then from the corner of his eye he spied two gendarmes threading their way amongst the café tables. They stopped at one nearby where two gray-haired men sat drinking coffee. "Documents," one of the gendarmes snapped. The two men handed over their papers, and the gendarme examined them carefully. "En regle!" he said, and they strode off, eying the customers as they left. Jean noted how one of the gray-haired men's hands shook as he thrust his papers into his pocket.

Jean felt his own pulse racing. He had been sure to avoid eye contact with the gendarmes. They were in the unoccupied zone, but for how long? The French police seemed quite willing to cooperate with the Germans. He thought again of Danielle. She must leave France, of course, but he found himself not wanting to see her go.

But what were his own plans? How could he be part of a resistance, if there were none. Could he escape France? Should he try to get to London and volunteer for de Gaulle's free French—or the British army? Would his fake passport and identity card be accepted as genuine? He was Italian, had fought in Spain for the Republicans. He had been an agent of the Comintern. Could he continue to keep that a secret? Not get caught in a lie? If it were known in England he was Italian he would be locked up in a detention camp. If it were known he'd been an agent for Comintern he would be labeled as a spy.

He thought of his Comintern handler, Paul. When Russia and Germany became allies after the Stalin/Hitler non-aggression pact and during the first year of the war the French Communists had gone underground—along with Paul. The government considered them enemies and Communist leaders were imprisoned. Their members were in a state of shock. He had only made contact with Paul twice. He hadn't had much information to give him. Comintern had wanted tactical information—battle plans, details about weapons, troop movements and so on. During the phony war he had almost nothing to report. New weapons were non-existent. Soldiers in his battalion near Le Havre had lounged around playing cards. Then when the Germans attacked Belgium and invaded France all hell broke loose and he hadn't seen his handler since. He hoped never to see him. But he did want to make contact with the Resistance.

It was only one week since the Armistice, perhaps too soon for resistance movements to become organized. He would keep his ears and eyes open. In the meantime, he'd try to help the Bergers—especially Danielle. The image of her lovely face kept intruding on his thoughts. He hoped he could be alone with her this evening. He smiled to himself—without little brother, David.

That evening Jean managed to extricate Danielle from her family alone. He took her to the café in the Vieux Port. They sat at a small round table facing the docks. Lights shimmered in the velvety black water and the night sky was a mass of stars. Danielle was peering upward. "No moon, tonight. The stars are so sharp and clear. Look, there's Cassiopia."

Jean glanced briefly at the stars but found himself fixing his eyes on Danielle. He reached for her hand. "It's good to have you to myself. I've missed you today."

Danielle didn't reclaim her hand. "It was a terrible day, Jean. Father and I stood in line for hours and hours and never really spoke to anyone who knew anything."

The waiter interrupted her and placed a carafe of wine and two glasses on the table. Jean removed his hand from Danielle's and poured the wine. His eyes lingered on her tapered fingers encircling the stem of the wineglass. She continued her tale. "The woman whose desk we finally reached was horrible. She thrust an application form into each of our hands and snapped, 'fill them out and bring them back next week.' Then she said, next! and turned to the woman behind us. So we left. Exhausted. After waiting all that time. Come back next week!"

Jean leaned forward. Danielle's eyes were flashing with outrage. He felt sympathetic, but he knew what she had experienced today was only the beginning of her trials. "So what's your father's plan, Danielle? Does he really think he could get an American visa?"

"He thinks it's possible. He has colleagues in America. He's writing letters to everyone he knows. His best bet, he says, is University of California. The one in Berkeley. They have a good Physics department there."

"But will the mail get through?"

"He's thought of that. He's going to send cables as well. He's also cabled our concierge at our apartment in Paris. He talked to some people in the queue today who've arranged for their belongings to be shipped here. Apparently, the barriers between the occupied and unoccupied zones are still open. The Germans and Vichy have set up checkpoints, but they allow people and baggage through after a thorough search. Anyway, Father asked the concierge to contact our maid and get her to pack our clothes, linens, silver—things like that and ship them here. Then he wants to rent an apartment in Marseilles. It looks as though we'll be here for a while."

Jean wondered how Maurice would be able to afford to rent an apartment. Had he carried that much cash with him? Maurice had told him that months ago, during the phony war, he had opened a bank account in America and had withdrawn cash from their Paris bank. Maurice had heard too many ghastly stories from Jewish refugees from Germany and Austria. He'd figured the odds. "Europe is doomed," he'd said.

As Jean and Danielle sipped their wine, the table next to them was suddenly engulfed by a flock of laughing Italian officers. Silver wings glittered on their tunics and the patch on their shoulders said GA. Jean knew it meant Regia Aeronautica, Italian royal air force.

"Scusi," one of them said. Then he asked Jean politely in Italian if he minded if he took the extra chair at Jean's table. Jean waved for him to take it, speaking French.

"Grazie," the officer answered, giving a polite bow and flashing a radiant smile at Danielle.

"Prego," Jean replied.

Danielle was giving Jean a curious stare. In almost a whisper, she said, "Italians? Jean do you speak Italian as well as English?"

Jean nodded then took another sip of wine, thinking up a story, part truth, part lie. "Yes, I speak Italian pretty well. My father was a shipping agent, remember? He worked for two years in Genoa. I went to school there when I was eight years old."

Danielle glanced at the Italian airmen. She leaned closer to Jean, whispering again. "I wonder if any of these good looking boys were shooting at us when we were escaping from Paris?"

Jean gave a wry laugh. "No, that was the German Luftwaffe. But these boys might have bombed Marseilles last week. I heard that raid killed 150 people. Danielle, let's get out of here. It's getting crowded."

# Chapter Five

## New Tasks

*August, 1940*

Over a month had passed since Jean's arrival in Marseilles. His fingers now tapped rapidly on the JAPY upright typewriter he'd placed on the rickety wooden table in his rented room. A bare light bulb hung from a wire above his head, which hardly lit the corners of his cramped space. The sun was shining outside, but the one window to his room faced a brick wall which blocked the light. He was writing a piece for the Bulletin, the one-page newspaper of the infant resistance organization, Mouvement de Liberation Nationale.

Two weeks earlier Jean had been recruited by the French army captain, Henri Frenay, the officer who had organized the movement. Jean had met the captain in his favorite café in the Vieux Port close to the officers' headquarters. Jean guessed that Frenay would be in his mid-thirties. He was straight-backed and sharp-eyed.

When Frenay had heard Jean's veiled questions about how to get in touch with fellow resisters, and then learned that Jean had been a journalist, he put him to work on the Bulletin. Jean's task was to contribute pieces that would counter the German propaganda published in the daily newspapers. Frenay believed the French in the free zone needed to be prodded into action. They had become complacent, believing Pétain would keep the Germans from punishing them. They needed to be told the truth. Jean was one of his first recruits.

Now a knock on the door of his room caused Jean to jump from his chair. He snatched the paper from the JAPY and slid it under the tablecloth, quickly rolling another half-written page into the machine. Only then did he call "who is it?"

"Just me, Danielle."

His breathing returning to normal, Jean unlocked the door and drew her inside, giving her the three-time kiss on the cheek he'd learned in Paris. He held her at arms length, noting her pale skin and wide-open, frightened eyes. "Are you OK? Any problems getting here?"

"Not really." She gave a nervous laugh. "Although I felt like everyone on the trolley had x-ray eyes and could see what I was carrying." She indicated her artist's portfolio.

He kissed her again and held her close. Reluctantly he released her and looked directly into her eyes. "It's frightening at first, I know." Then he indicated the typewriter. "I haven't finished the piece yet, but I won't be long." He pulled out a chair opposite his at the typewriter. "Assez-toi, ma chére."

Danielle sat and placed the portfolio on the table. She pointed to the typewriter. "What's the subject this week?"

"The German annexation of Alsace Lorraine, that it violated Pétain's Armistice agreement." He slid the paper he'd hidden from under the tablecloth and switched typewriter sheets, rolling the original into the cylinder.

Jean glanced up at Danielle, noting that the rosy color had returned to her face. She was watching him type. "I feel so sorry for those Alsatians. Hundreds are here in Marseilles. And most are penniless." She pulled off her straw hat and shook out her hair. "This morning at the bakery a woman from a village near Metz told me how they were forced to sell their farm house to a German family for a pittance."

Jean nodded, continuing to type rapidly. "And our muzzled press doesn't print a word of it. And I'm reporting what we heard on BBC last night—about the RAF downing hundreds of Luftwaffe planes and bombing German factories."

Jean typed for a few minutes then turned the cylinder of the JAPY and removed the sheet of paper. "OK. It's done. Will you show me your drawing?" He jumped up from his chair and moved around the table to where Danielle had placed her portfolio. He had been reluctant to involve Danielle in the project, but when she had discovered the Bulletin inserted between the pages of Le Temps she begged him to help her find who was producing it. She wanted to be part of the Resistance. After first checking with Frenay, he told her he was writing copy for the Bulletin and that if she wanted to help she could draw a masthead. He also refused to permit her to meet Simone, his contact. The fewer members she knew, the better.

Danielle opened the portfolio and held up the drawing for Jean to examine. "Perfect," he said. He slid the drawing and his copy into a large envelope and placed it into his musette bag. He then turned to her, placed his hand on her smooth cheek and fastened his eyes on hers. "Danielle, does Maurice know you're doing this?"

"No. He's too busy writing letters, applying for visas—all that. And Maman is so worried about her sisters in Paris—trying to persuade them to leave she doesn't notice what I'm drawing. And she's tacking up notices on kiosks about her English lessons. And I've been out sketching. I've even sold one of my watercolors."

"Danielle, please be careful. Beware of the police. They can turn up anywhere, as you know."

He slung the musette bag on his back, Danielle put on her hat, picked up her portfolio and the pair left the dismal room. Jean locked the door and shoved the key deep into his pocket. They descended the four flights of stairs and emerged from the tenement into the dark narrow alley, which was barely wide enough for two people to walk side by side. Dark walls of blackened brick rose up like coal-covered bluffs. Jean shifted his bag on his back, his right hand grasping the strap on his shoulder. Tenement doorways were flush with the wall. His glance shifted from side to side, scrutinizing each doorway, watching for thieves—or plainclothes police. Finally they reached the broad sidewalk along Canebiére where Danielle could catch the trolley to her family's apartment. When the tram arrived, Jean kissed her on the cheek. "I'll drop in at your apartment this afternoon, OK?" The family's rented modest apartment was near the shore beyond the Vieux Port.

"Good. And Jean, be careful. Watch your back!"

"Don't worry. I will." His eyes followed her as she stepped lightly onto the trolley. Her blue cotton dress fluttered about her knees as she climbed the steps. Her slender ankles were crisscrossed by espadrille ribbons. He sighed. But now he must get to work. He shifted the bag on his back and turned toward the Vielle Ville. Again he remained alert, scrutinizing the dark alley with sharp eyes, but feigning a relaxed demeanor. He thought of Danielle's comment about her fears on the trolley. He'd been through Spain and Dunkirk, but still, at this moment his musette bag felt as if it were jammed with grenades about to explode.

He was on his way to the apartment of a close friend of Frenay, a tall, handsome middle-aged woman Jean only knew her by the name, Simone. Simone lived on the upper edge of the Vielle Ville, the ancient port city built on the side of a hill leading to the docks. The district was made up of a warren of narrow medieval paths, caves and tunnels, and was notorious for its thieves, smugglers and gangsters.

Jean arrived at Simone's apartment building and before pushing the buzzer that would open the door to the building, shot a quick glance down the street and out toward the red-tiled rooftops and rocky outcroppings below. He took a deep breath, opened the door and climbed the stairs to the second floor.

When Danielle entered her family's apartment, she found her mother bending over a large black trunk. On the floor surrounding the trunk were stacks of sheets, dishes and a pair of antique wooden candlesticks. "You're packing?" Danielle exclaimed. The trunks had been unpacked two weeks earlier when they had arrived from Paris by rail.

Monique stood and pushed her hair back from her smudged face. "Only the things we don't need here. I want to be ready to leave at a moment's notice."

Danielle stared at her mother. Why was she feeling so optimistic? At that moment, David burst into the room from the tiny kitchen. "Danielle, have you heard about the American?"

"What American?"

"The guy who's helping people get American visas!"

Danielle slowly removed her hat and hung it on a hook by the door. "And who is this man? Tell me. What gossip have you heard this time?"

"Everyone's talking about it. He just got here a few days ago. He's at the Hotel Splendide and he has a list of names the Americans want to help. It's a rescue organization. Maybe like the Jewish Relief, or the Quakers, or Unitarians."

"You mean the American government actually wants to help refugees emigrate!"

"Not the government. Certain individuals. They donate money to help artists and intellectuals get out of France."

"And who told you about this American?"

"I heard it at the café by the fish market. Everyone is talking about him. His name is Fry, or something like that."

Monique had finished placing the stack of sheets in the trunk. "Your father left an hour ago to investigate. He said it was worth trying. He's determined to leave France. And he says physicists are certainly intellectuals." She gave a wry smile. "I'm not sure what he thinks about English professors."

"But David, didn't you say there was a list?"

"That's what I heard."


Later that evening, as Jean hauled his bike down his four flights of stairs, he pondered over the problem of the Bulletin's distribution. He had typed his report on the stencil and Simone had traced and etched Danielle's drawing of the masthead onto it. They then had run the printing. Simone harbored an ancient mimeograph machine, another JAPY typewriter and a stock of stencils and paper. The equipment had been obtained from an elderly former printer, another volunteer recruited by Frenay. Soon they hoped to find someone with a printing press who would print more than the fifty copies they were able to produce on the mimeograph machine.

Simone had given two others the task of slipping the single sheet into newspapers and magazines. It had to be done secretly and randomly, so none of the news agents or delivery boys would be accused of cooperating with the Resistance. Frenay had suggested the distribution take place just before dawn—after the papers had been delivered to the various news kiosks but before the kiosks had opened. It would be tricky.

Now Jean took a deep breath of the cooling air. It was early evening. He could relax. The Bulletin was now in circulation. He would no longer feel the need to watch his back. He mounted the bike and pedaled down the Canebiére, where he had only to avoid the clanging trolleys and horse-drawn carts. An occasional police or army vehicle would pass him, but no civilian cars or trucks were on the street. No gasoline. Instead, it bustled with bicycles and pedestrians. Long lines of people emerged from bakeries and food shops. The previous day announcements had gone up on posters and broadcast on the radio that rationing would begin next Monday. Ration books could be acquired at the Prefecture.

He rode by Vieux Port and continued south along the docks several blocks until he arrived at a residential neighborhood overlooking the bay. The Bergers' apartment building was one street beyond the water's edge. They were on the second floor, which was easier for lugging his bike up the stairs than his own building. Marseilles' famous thieves meant it was impossible to leave a bike on the street or with the concierge—even locked and chained.

The Bergers greeted Jean with a barrage of words. After the hugs and kisses and confusion Jean held up his hand. "Wait! What's happened? You all look so happy!"

Maurice laughed. "Actually, Jean, nothing concrete has happened, but for the first time since we left Paris I can see a glimmer of light."

"So?"

"I went to see the American, Varian Fry. I stood in line for three hours, but finally was able to talk to him. My name is not on his list, unfortunately, but he is willing to look at my scientific papers and my letters from colleagues in the States. He made no promises, but he said he'd see what he could do. He will see me tomorrow at 11:30 in the morning."

Jean reached for Maurice's hand and shook it vigorously. "Congratulations! What great news. But who is this guy, this Varian Fry?"

Maurice's lined, narrow face was wreathed with smiles and his brown eyes shone. "He seems a rather contained quiet man—very serious, intelligent, kind, conscientious. His French is good, but we spoke English. He told me his organization is funded by donations from concerned Americans who want to save talented people from German and French concentration camps. They're aware of Hitler's persecutions of Jews and anti-fascist intellectuals. President Roosevelt's wife, Eleanor, is a sponsor."

Monique linked arms with her husband, but the worried frown on her forehead had returned. "But the American immigration department has not been issuing visas to Jews. They don't like us. They don't want us in their country."

Jean shrugged. "Maybe there are enough smart people in America who'll pressure the government to drop their prejudices."

Maurice poured them all glasses of wine. "Who knows! But let's drink to Varian Fry."

They all held up their glasses. "To Varian Fry!"

# PART TWO

## RESCUE

# Chapter Six

## Frenay and Fry

*August, 1940*

The next morning morning Jean was flicking through the stack of Le Temps at the news kiosk on Canebiére. Finding one in which he recognized a certain sheet of paper, he quickly closed it, handed the vendor a coin and shoved the newspaper under his arm. He hadn't yet had his morning coffee and headed for a café next to Hotel Splendide. He noted the cluster of weary-faced people gathered outside the hotel, obviously refugees waiting to talk to the American.

He glanced at his watch. Eight o'clock. Later, at ten, he was supposed to be at the café next door to meet Frenay and to receive instructions for the next Bulletin. Most of the time Frenay used a spy's tradecraft. His usual method was to slip his message inside the pages of a newspaper, which he would leave on the table next to the one where Jean was sitting. He would walk away without speaking to Jean. Jean would casually pick up the paper and begin to read it. Today would be different. Frenay had left the message they needed a few minutes to talk about publishing methods.

But now Jean wanted coffee. Jean had also promised to meet Maurice and Danielle after their interview here in this café around noon. Maurice wasn't sure whether the authorities would grant visas to his entire family. Danielle was over twenty-one, which in America meant she was no longer a minor. He had suggested she come with him.

As Jean threaded his way between the café tables, he heard a voice call out to him from a corner of the café. "Baroli, Hola!" Jean froze. Turning, he saw a familiar figure waving to him, striding toward him. It was Johann Hirsch, who knew him as Gino Baroli when they both fought in Spain. Shocked to the core, Jean quickly scanned the café. Had anyone heard his Italian name? The two men gave each other a hearty abrazo. In a low, intense voice Jean spoke into Johann's ear. "My name is now Barrault. I'm French, not Italian. Jean Barrault." He spoke in French.

Johann snorted. "I can't believe it! And in Jean's ear he also said quietly in French. My name is now Jean Valleron. I'm French, not German. My friends call me Val."

Jean clapped Val on his back, and the two men put their heads back and laughed. They then walked arm in arm to the table where Val had been sitting. "Come have some coffee with me." They both sat and Val beckoned the waiter. Jean gave his order and laid his newspaper carefully on the table.

"So, Jean, did your shoulder heal well?"

"Yes. Well enough. And yours?"

Val nodded, smiling broadly. Jean scrutinized his friends' tanned face, his sharp blue eyes. There were a few more lines around his mouth, but he looked healthy and well—better than when they had first met when they were both being treated in the hospital in the Palace Hotel in Madrid for shrapnel wounds. They both had fought for the International Brigades.

While the waiter set the coffee cups on the table, Jean glanced again at his friend, remembering that before he came to Spain Val had been involved with anti-Mussolini activities while doing graduate work at Torino University in northern Italy. He was Jewish and had left Germany in his teens—first to go to school in France, then England, then Italy.

The waiter departed and they began to exchange stories of what had happened to them since Spain. Jean was surprised to hear Val had been in the French army and had fought in the Ardenne. "So how did you escape from the camp at Argelés?"

"When I jumped off the truck that took us there I was lucky enough to slip away. The guard wasn't looking. What about you?"

Jean hesitated, but when he looked into Val's questioning blue eyes he decided to admit most of the truth. "A Comintern agent helped me. And he provided my French identity papers—so that I could join the French army. But how did you get your papers?"

"I made my way to Paris, staying with farmers, sleeping in barns. Then my old school friends from the Sorbonne collected enough money for me to buy forged documents." Val sipped his coffee and gave Jean a quizzical look. "So a Comintern agent helped you? If I remember correctly, you were pretty pissed with the Communists—just as I was. We'd witnessed those executions."

Jean felt the blood rush to his face. His voice rose defensively. "But, Val, I just had to get out of that death trap. And by now the agent has disappeared. Another of Stalin's victims, probably."

As if to change the subject, Val fished a pack of Gauloises from his shirt pocket and held it out to Jean. "So, Jean," and he pronounced the name with a grin. "What are you doing in Marseilles? Anything interesting?" He held out his lighter to Jean's cigarette.

"Not much." Jean leaned into the lighter, took a deep drag of the cigarette, and glanced at the neighboring tables. At the closest table, three men were arguing excitedly, their voices raised. Jean lowered his voice. " I'd hoped to continue to fight fascists. And what about you?"

"At the moment I'm working for Varian Fry, the American—next door at the Splendide."

"For Varian Fry! God God, don't tell me!" He slapped his hand on the table and gave a hooting laugh. "Incroyable! My girlfriend and her father have an appointment with him later this morning. They're Jewish and want to leave France." He cocked his head to one side and grinned. "So you son of a bitch, what do you do for Fry?

"Many things. He'd only been here a week when I met him. I queued up to see him because I also need to leave France. As a German Jew it's not healthy for me here either, but while I wait for an American visa I want to help Fry. He's doing great work and he has jobs for people with certain skills. In fact, if you're not "engaged" you might like to meet him. You have the experience and languages he needs. I can introduce you right now. He opens his room to clients in half an hour. He might want to interview you."

"I'd like to. And I need a job." He looked at his watch. He still had time before his meeting with Henri Frenay. He would tell Frenay about Fry's organization and that he hoped to work for him. He was almost certain Frenay would not object.

"OK. Allons-y." They each drained their coffee cups and rose to go. Val dropped some coins on the table and they walked out onto the street. Before Jean left the café he casually placed the newspaper on an empty table. Someone would find—and read—the inserted Bulletin.

Fifteen minutes later Jean and Fry were descending the stairs of the Splendide and entering the café next door. Fry headed for a table in a quiet corner of the room. "We can talk here without being overheard, I believe." A waiter promptly approached and took their orders for coffee. Fry sighed, removed his glasses and cleaned them with the immaculate handkerchief he plucked from his breast pocket. "This work is not easy, believe me. So many people beg for our help and much of the time all we can do is give them a few francs for food and lodging—to keep them out of the dreadful detention camps."

As the waiter brought the coffee cups and set them on the table, Fry replaced his glasses and tucked his handkerchief back in his pocket. "My instructions from the New York office are strict. They only want us to obtain visas for exceptionally talented people. It's heartbreaking to turn people away. Val is good at trying alternatives—other countries—Mexico, Dominican Republic, Cuba. They all have their difficulties."

Jean noted the troubled expression in Fry's eyes as he spoke. "From what Val has told me about you I believe you could be useful, but I need to know more. He told me you both fought in Spain and were anti-fascist and that you were unhappy with the communists. He said you are fluent in English, French, Italian and have some Spanish and German. But I want to hear what you hope to do here. Tell me about your background and skills."

Jean shrugged. "I think my major skill is as a débrouillard, one who slips through the cracks, as the French say. I've made many escapes." He scrutinized Fry's face. It was a trustworthy face, somehow. He would tell him much of the truth about his past—perhaps not about his bargain with agent Paul—and most certainly not about his work with Henri Frenay. Frenay's work was dangerous and should not be jeopardized.

Jean took a deep breath as if he were about to dive off a cliff into deep water. He spoke in a rapid but accented English. "OK, you want to know my background. I was born in Italy and my true name is Gino Baroli. My mother was French and she made sure I was bilingual from my infancy. We lived in Genoa. My father was a shipping agent. When I finished secondary school I went to Paris to study at the Sorbonne. While I was there my parents were killed in a boating accident. After that I spent a year at the London School of Economics where I discovered I wanted to be a journalist. I returned to Italy, got a job with a newspaper in Milan whose staff were anti-fascist, anti-Mussolini. I was arrested, thrown in prison as a subversive. I escaped and managed to get to Spain where I volunteered with the International Brigade. When the Brigades were withdrawn I ended up at the detention camp at Argelés. Since I was a fugitive I was unable to return to Italy. I escaped and obtained forged French papers under the name of Jean Barrault. I then volunteered for the French army and survived Dunkirk. I escaped again and found my way to Marseilles, hoping to do some sort of resistance work." Jean took another deep breath. He felt depleted, needing oxygen, as if he'd been swimming a long-distance race.

Fry had listened closely. He picked up his coffee and sipped, his eyes focused on Jean's face. "That's quite a story, Jean Barrault. You and Val have a lot in common."

He set down his coffee cup and hesitated a moment. Then he reached to shake Jean's hand. "Welcome to our strange organization, Jean. I believe you are uniquely qualified for our work. You will be paid a small salary and any expenses incurred on your assignments. At first I want you to work in the office, filling out forms for our clients—and so on. After that will come other tasks." He rose and dropped a few coins on the table. "Now I must get back to work. I'd like you to report in tomorrow, please—at eight?"

Jean stood and the two men shook hands again. "I'll be there M. Fry."

"Varian, please. Call me Varian." He put on his hat, gave a nod and strode purposely out of the café."

As Jean watched Varian depart, he was thinking that he also needed to discuss Fry's offer with Henri Frenay, who he would be meeting at ten o'clock. He would tell him he'd still write for the Bulletin, and from what Frenay had said earlier, he would not object to his working with Fry's organization. Helping people escape from France was a legitimate resistance activity. Frenay might be more interested in helping young men escape to join the French freedom fighters or the British army, but who knows? Perhaps that could be done.

Jean suddenly felt a wave of relief as well as excitement. He had finally been able to tell the truth—almost all of it. Now he wished he could tell Danielle his true story. And why not? This town was jammed with people with forged documents and invented names and nationalities, their noms de guerre. He still could not tell her about his bargain with agent Paul—and it hardly seemed important now. Paul had disappeared. Perhaps forever.

Danielle gripped her portfolio tightly as she entered room number 307 at the Hotel Splendide. It was 11:25 A.M. Her palms were damp with sweat, and she felt stiff with apprehension. Maurice held her arm. A thirtyish-looking man in horn-rimmed glasses peered up at them as they approached his small table. Two other men sat at another table before stacks of documents.

"M. Fry?" Maurice said, politely to the man at the small table. "I have brought my documents, as you asked. And this is my daughter, Danielle."

Fry nodded, and shook Danielle's hand. "Please, sit down." He indicated the two chairs that faced his table. They both sat as they had been bidden, and Maurice reached into his briefcase for his sheaf of papers. Danielle couldn't keep her eyes from Fry's face. It was a kind face, she decided. And intelligent. Perhaps he could really help. She then took a quick glance at the other two men at the second table. They were younger than Fry. Perhaps in their late twenties. And good looking. One was blond, the other red-headed. The blue-eyed one caught her glance and gave her an encouraging smile.

Fry shuffled through the documents Maurice had given him. He skimmed one of the scientific papers and then shot Maurice a wry smile. "I'm afraid this is beyond my college physics. My field is Foreign Policy, but you've produced quite a body of work," and he shuffled the stack. And I'm also impressed by your letters from colleagues in the States. I believe you and your family could be considered eligible for emigration, although you must understand I can make no promises. Our immigration department is unpredictable."

"Maurice's face had become flushed and his breathing quickened. "You can't know how overjoyed I am to hear your words. . ." He spoke in English.

Fry smiled, answering in English. "By now I think I know. So many of you have come here. But now we need more information. My assistants here, Val or Marcel will need to talk to you."

Danielle tapped her father's arm. "My age?"

"Oh, M. Fry, yes, my daughter, Danielle is twenty-two and worries she would not be considered eligible as one of my children."

"That shouldn't be  a problem. Generally, the Department has a policy of keeping family members together. But again, no promises." Fry turned to the men at the table next to him.  "Val could you or Marcel please work with M. Berger on his visa request?"  He then picked up his fountain pen and scribbled a few words into a notebook. And M. Berger, Mlle Berger it was a pleasure to meet you. We'll see what we can do.

# Chapter Seven

## The Centre

*August, 1940*

As Jean hopped off the trolley at the corner near the Hotel Splendide, he glanced into the sidewalk café next to the hotel. He was pleased to note a neatly dressed man reading a sheet he recognized as yesterday's Bulletin. Good! It was being read.

At his meeting the day before with Frenay he had told him about working for Fry. He described Fry's organization and his efforts to help refugees escape from France. Frenay's deep-set, flinty eyes had scrutinized Jean's face. For a moment Jean couldn't guess from the captain's expression whether he approved of Fry or not. "Excellent," Frenay said, finally. A worthwhile effort. Good for the Americans. Maybe they're finally coming to their senses. But I assume you'll continue to write for our Bulletin."

"Of course. I can write late at night, if necessary, and deliver the copy early in the morning." Frenay nodded with approval, shook Jean's hand and departed, leaving his newspaper on the table with the instructions for the next Bulletin inserted between its pages.

Now Jean took a deep breath and walked into the Splendide, feeling a surge of excitement as he rushed through the lobby and ran up the three flights of stairs. Writing for the Bulletin was important, but this work of Fry's, helping people escape concentration camps or death seemed even more crucial. When he reached room 307 there was already a queue of anxious-faced people waiting in the hall. He knocked at the door, then entered. "Jean Barrault reporting to work," he said, grinning. Varian was seated at the same document-covered table he'd manned the day before. He rose, reached across the table and shook Jean's hand. "Welcome, Jean. And good morning."

Val was at the other small table that held stacks of papers. He gave Jean a broad smile and pulled out a chair for him. "OK, pal, let's put you to work! You can have Marcel's place. He's not in yet."

Val's first move was to show Jean the list of 200 artists and intellectuals the Emergency Rescue Committee in New York had prepared for Fry. Jean was familiar with most of the names: Konrad Heiden, the writer, an outspoken critic of Hitler, novelist and screenwriter, Franz Werfel, his wife, Alma Mahler, the writer Leon Feuchtwanger, Heinrich Mann, André Breton and many, many more. Many were German or Austrian and they were all famous writers, poets, and artists.

Val pointed to the names on the top of the list, some which had been crossed out. "These names," pointing to the ones with the line through them, "have already left Marseilles headed for the Pyrenees. We are waiting to hear from New York to know if they made it."

Val gave Jean a direct look, his blue eyes showing concern. "We have given priority to the people who are in gravest danger of being picked up by the Gestapo—those who have written or spoken openly against Hitler and the Nazis. Most of these have been stripped of their passports, are apatrides—stateless."

"So how do they get a visa without a passport?"

"U.S. Immigration gives them a visa en lieu of a passport. Many of these people already have U.S. visas, but need documents to get transit visas for Spain and Portugal. Exit visas are impossible for them because to get one they must apply to the office in Vichy. If they're on the Gestapo black list, Vichy must surrender them on demand. Safe conduct travel passes are impossible for the same reason."

"So they hike over the Pyrenees?"

"Correct—to avoid the border police." Val tapped his pencil on the table as a kind of exclamation point.

"But without passports how do they get transit visas?"

Val laughed. "Hah! Now listen carefully. Come with me." After first glancing at Varian, who nodded his approval, he drew Jean into the small bathroom and turned on the noisy shower. "We can't be sure if we're bugged." He then slid three pink passports from behind the mirror. "Czechoslovakian. We have a super friend in the Czech consul, Vladimir Vochoc. He detests the Germans. The pink passports are supposed to be temporary—but they seem to work. Many of our clients are famous and recognizable and are on the Gestapo list. Vochoc issues the documents with false identities. We provide photographs and descriptions of the client—age and so on." He opened the passport to show Jean the picture, name and information, then turned to a visa page containing a red Chinese stamp. "So far this stamp in Chinese from the Chinese Consul is being honored. Of course we haven't the faintest idea what it really says, but its accepted as a genuine visa by the Spanish and Portuguese consulates to get transit visas. When our refugees board the ship to the States they show their true papers, which they've hidden carefully, we hope, while they travel. So far it's worked for twenty or so people on our list. And we've been in operation for only ten days!"

Val pushed pink booklets back behind he mirror. "Now we interview prospective clients. Later this afternoon we'll confer and make recommendations about who should be added to our list. Then Varian cables the New York office with the information. The Committee takes it from there. If we know the Committee won't consider the clients talented enough to be blessed with a U.S. visa, we try to help them in other ways—a little money, search for alternate countries—whatever. "

Jean thought about Danielle and her family. Had their names been wired to the States? "What about the safe conduct travel pass? And where do they cross the Pyrenees?

"Cerbére. You know that town, I'm sure. The camp at Argelés is on the beach nearby. They go to Perpignan then change trains for a short ride to Cerbére. The clients leave St Charles station here at 5AM, before the police go on duty. At Cerbére they get off the train and head up the mountain. An Austrian gave us a map of the route, and I checked it out. It's steep, but not bad. The mountain isn't very high at that spot. When they get to the Spanish border at Port Bou they ask the officials for an entrada stamp on their passports and take the train to Barcelona. Then to Lisbon."

Jean was impressed. Varian Fry and company were clever. He followed Val into the hotel room, sat in the chair indicated and gave his full attention to a trembling man who had just sat in the chair opposite him.

The sun had dipped into the bay and Danielle was waiting for Jean at their favorite café in the Vieux Port. The doors to the café were folded back, open to the sea air. As the twilight darkened, the dock lamps flashed on. They had been painted blue to be less visible in air raids. After the armistice the air raids had stopped but the lights were still blue.

Sipping the house wine the waiter had brought her, she watched a fishing boat approach the pier. When it nudged the wooden boards, a man in a striped shirt leaped onto the dock, hemp rope in hand, and secured the boat. She wasn't able to watch a boat land or sail away without wondering about her own departure from Europe. Would Jean learn anything today about her family's visa applications? Jean had asked her to meet him today for dinner, his first day working for Fry, as a kind of celebration.

She felt a rush of pleasure when she thought of meeting Jean. Was she in love with him? How would she respond to him? He hadn't made any direct moves to get her into bed, but she knew he would soon. She sighed, gazing out at the bay. Tiny flickers of blue light reflected in the darkening water. A soft breeze touched her face.

Should she let it happen? Was this the time to start a love affair? Jean could be killed in the Resistance. She could be sailing away away from France, perhaps forever. They might never see each other again. She thought of her first love, Jules. When she heard he had been taken prisoner and sent to Germany she had wept for him, picturing him behind barbed wire, fearing she'd never see him again. She'd believed she would never love anyone else—but look what was happening. She couldn't stop dreaming about Jean. And she had barely thought about Jules since coming to Marseilles. Was she shallow, lacking in depth? Heartless? And was Jean in love with her?

She looked at her gold watch. Jean would be here any moment. From her banquette, she craned her neck over the heads of the men who sat at the table blocking her view of the promenade facing the docks. In the distance she recognized Jean's figure striding toward her. She caught her breath. How happy it made her to see him. He carried his musette bag easily over one broad shoulder, and his dark hair shone in the bluish lamplight.

When he caught a glimpse of her he waved and quickened his pace. She noted how gracefully he moved. He zigzagged around the tables and bent down to kiss her. "It's so good to see you, ma chére Danielle," he said. He kissed her again as he sat close to her on the banquette and slid his arm around her waist. He smelled of sweat and ink, which she didn't find unpleasant. "So, Jean, how did it go? Did you like your new job?"

"I think it went well. And I most definitely like the job." He placed his free hand over hers. "You're looking lovely, Danielle." He was giving her a long, admiring look with his astonishing eyes.

She felt her cheeks flush with pleasure. "Thank you! And you look like you've had a productive day!"

"I have. At least I hope I was productive." He frowned. "But this work won't be easy. So many people need help. But Varian is fantastic. He pulls rabbits out of hats to solve problems. He's made contacts all over town." Jean beckoned to the waiter. "And he has money—I don't know yet how he gets it, but he says the donations in the States are pouring in."

"Jean, did you her anything today about our family's visa application?"

Jean's green-gold eyes became solemn. "It's much too early, Danielle. Varian submitted your names but he says it could take months to process them." He laughed. "At least Varian has concluded that scientists are intellectuals. He told me that at first he wasn't at all sure if the Committee would not insist upon sticking to the original 200 names of artists and writers who they called intellectuals. They hadn't considered naming physicists like your father—or for that matter, economists like Val as intellectuals."

The waiter approached, and they were forced to concentrate on their menus for a moment. They both ordered bouillabaisse, the popular fish soup of Marseilles. While the waiter took their order and their ration stamps Danielle thought about her father's problems with money. The cash he had brought from Paris was dwindling away, and the American embargo on transferring money to wartime Europe was a disaster for them. He couldn't withdraw money from his bank account in New York.

The waiter then brought a carafe of wine and a glass for Jean. Danielle lifted her glass. "To your new job!

"Santé!" Jean responded.

Danielle set down her glass. "Jean, is there any chance that I could get a job with the organization? I need to earn some money to help out at home—and I'd also like to do something worthwhile. Now that I've finished the art work for" and she lowered her voice "the Bulletin, I'd like to do more."

Jean took hold of her hand. "I don't know, Danielle. Maybe we can think of something—something that isn't dangerous. I'll ask Varian—or Val. I'd like you to meet them both, anyway. I'll arrange something." He kissed the tips of her fingers.

At that point the waiter set down their bowls of bouillabaisse. Jean grinned. "I'm starved."

Danielle breathed in the fragrance of garlic, tomatoes and fish. "Mmm smells heavenly. Bon appetit!"

Later, walking arm in arm with Jean along the promenade under the stars, Danielle concluded she wasn't heartless. She would always remember Jules, but he was in the past. It seemed that from one moment to another life could change. All their lives had been turned upside down by Hitler and this war. And here she was in Marseilles, walking along the glittering docks, Jean's arm around her, speaking of love.

Accordion music echoed over the water and her heart pumped with excitement—at the warm night air, with Jean's touch, even with the exotic sense of danger—the thieves and smugglers she knew frequented the neighborhood. When Jean stopped to kiss her yet again and murmured in her ear how much he wanted to make love to her, she found herself nodding. "Moi aussi!" she said, laughing, feeling giddy and more than a little wild. "Est-ce que nous allons a ta chambre?"

"OK!" he cried, hugging her hard. "Allons-y!"

Much later that evening, lying close together on Jean's narrow bed, his arms wrapped around her, he told her his true life story. She wasn't at all shocked, or disturbed at his tale. She had been aware that he was avoiding opening up to her about his past, but she knew she loved him whatever his name was—Jean Barrault or Gino Baroli—or whether he was French or Italian. It just didn't matter. The future was so terribly uncertain. What was important was being alive. At this moment.

# Chapter Eight

## More Tasks

*Late August, 1940*

For the first week in room 307 Jean worked on strictly above-board "relief" tasks—interviewing, providing stipends to people in need, and preparing visa applications. He also wrote his piece for the weekly Bulletin at night. He had moved Frenay's JAPY typewriter to Simone's, carrying it in a cardboard box tied onto the rack of his bicycle. He felt it was prudent to keep the two jobs separate. If he were caught writing the Bulletin he didn't want Fry's organization to be implicated.

The activity at the now-called Centre Américain de Secours, CAS, the American Center for Relief, had grown so that it was necessary to look for larger quarters. In their search for a new site, Val happened upon a French-Jewish businessman who wanted to sell out as fast as possible, before the Pétain government expropriated his store. The man strongly suspected the French would pass laws similar to those in Germany, which would force Jewish traders to sell out for a fraction of its value, which Vichy did two months later. The property was near the American consulate.

The staff settled in to the new quarters quickly. They bought typewriters, desks and chairs but needed to expand the staff. Jean introduced Danielle to Fry, describing her abilities to speak English,

French and some German—and how she could type and do any art work necessary. Fry hired her. Danielle was delighted and went to work immediately. When Val heard that she was an artist, he raised his eyebrows and exchanged meaningful looks with Marcel, the auburn-haired muscular, ex soldier. Jean caught the glance and shook his head. "No, Val. She's not a forger."

Until now Jean's work had been strictly legal. Both Fry and Val decided that Jean was now ready to take part in activities that were illegal and possibly dangerous.

One hot afternoon in late August, Val suggested Jean take a walk with him. "Varian and I think its time you met Dmitri."

Jean had heard this name mentioned but he had heard nothing further. "Dmitri?"

"Yes, and Jean you can refuse. He's a black marketeer and a crook. We're dealing with a shady character and using him to obtain cash for CAS. And if we're caught we could be in big trouble. Are you willing?"

Jean grinned. "Do you need to ask?"

"Yeah." He clapped Jean on the shoulder. "And this is just the beginning." Val picked up a scarred briefcase from behind his desk, and they left the office. Val indicated they'd be walking toward the Vieux Port.

"OK, Val, you better explain. What's the deal?"

Val kept his voice low as they walked along the narrow street. "Dmitri and Varian have figured out a system to provide cash to CAS. Apparently plenty of people in Marseilles want to deposit money in American bank accounts they don't want the police to know about. Dmitri provides a certain amount of cash in francs to the Centre Américain at a black market rate and the same day Varian wires the New York office to deposit that amount in dollars into a numbered bank account."

"Clever! So the donations given to the Committee that can't be transferred here because of the embargo go into the sub-rosa accounts, but we get the cash we need to help people survive!"

"Right. It's a black market deal, gangster money, but it works like a charm."

"So much for the U.S. financial embargo."

By now they had arrived at a small restaurant in a narrow alley near the Vieux Port. Val took hold of Jean's arm. "There he is, that little guy in the corner—sitting on the banquette. The other two guys with him are gangsters, too." Val held his briefcase under his arm as they maneuvered toward Dmitri's table.

The room was dark and smelled sour with spilled wine. Jean's nerves tensed when he eyed the three men's shadowed faces. They had a wily, crafty look, eying him with shuttered eyes. One of them had a scar above his eyebrow. When Jean and Val approached, the small man stood up and shook hands—the other two remained seated but made a brief gesture of welcome. Dmitri was barely five feet tall and looked rather like Peter Lorre. "Have a seat." he said, pointing to two chairs opposite him. "Would you like something? Some wine, coffee?"

Jean and Val asked for coffee. Jean noted the bulky package wrapped in newspaper and tied with string on the banquette under Dmitri's right hand. The waiter brought their coffee and Val pointed to the package. Dmitri handed it to him along with a white envelope. Val opened the envelope and fished out a sheet of paper containing figures which he quickly scanned. "OK," he said. "We'll take care of it." He slid the sheet of paper back in the envelope, closed it, then stuffed it and the package into his briefcase. It took him a minute or two to close the bulging briefcase and fasten its buckles, which he did carefully. He then held it on his lap. He drank his coffee in one gulp and looked at Jean. "Dmitri, I've brought Jean here today because he'll sometimes be the courier who will contact you. We'll continue meeting once a week. if that's OK with you."

Dmitri nodded. "Sure. Whatever. I'll call your office to set the appointment."

They all shook hands again and Val and Jean left the restaurant and walked quickly down the dark alley. Val shot glances behind them and into shadowed doorways and held the briefcase in the hand closest to Jean. Jean listened for footsteps behind them and peered at each passerby with a sharp eye. He was accustomed to watch out for pickpockets and thieves, but he'd never played bodyguard to so much cash. Now he needed to watch for the police. Dealing with a black marketeer could land them in jail. "Some operation! How much are you carrying?"

"$1,500 worth of francs. He's giving us a rate well above the official one. 70 francs per dollar. Around 105,000 francs. He takes a cut, of course. So do the other two guys."

"And you can trust the guy? No signing for it. No signatures?"

Val grinned. "Honor amongst thieves. Dmitri says he doesn't normally do deals with Americans. He says gangsters in America are crooks!"

"Some character! You're not going to count it?"

He laughed. "Later!"

Jean remained vigilant, considering what he would say to the gendarmes if they searched the briefcase. How would they explain carrying that much money? Jean breathed a sigh of relief when they arrived at the Centre Américain. With a ceremonious gesture Val placed the briefcase before Varian on his desk. "Voila!"

Varian acknowledged Val's gesture, but was smiling broadly, holding a postcard in his hand. "Val, Look. It's from New York."

Val read what was on the card and whooped. "Heiden made it. He arrived!"

"Who?" Jean asked.

"Konrad Heiden. See, all he says is Thanks. David." Val handed the postcard to Jean. "Our route is working! David Silberman was his name on his documents. It's a postcard of the New York harbor."

Varian stood up, his face wreathed in smiles. "Congratulations everyone. At least one of our clients is safe. Let's hope we help many more." He picked up the briefcase Val had placed on his desk. "But I'd better take care of this. Thanks, Val, Jean, for fetching it. It's rather important."

Danielle glanced up from her typewriter. She could hear the happy commotion the men were making in the next room. She exchanged looks with Marian Dolan, the amber-eyed young woman who worked at a desk next to hers. Marian had joined the Centre Américain staff the same time as Danielle. She was an American art history student from Philadelphia and had been studying at the Sorbonne, and was only a year older than Danielle—twenty-three. She'd left Paris but was yet unwilling to go home. She and Danielle were now roommates. Marian had suggested Danielle share a small apartment with her when she heard Danielle complain about the dangers of her trip home at night—even with Jean. Now working at the Centre Américain, the staff often stayed late. And of course, there were times when Danielle stayed with Jean. If the trolleys had stopped, he would take her home sitting sidesaddle on the bar of his bicycle. Marseilles was not a city to be out on the streets late at night. Her parents agreed it was better for her to move in with her fellow worker, Marian. For a few francs she would be safer. She hadn't told them she was staying with Jean some nights, but figured they suspected.

A smiling Jean came into the room. Walking behind Danielle's chair, he put his hand on her shoulder and gave it a squeeze. She shot him a questioning glance. He then explained the merriment about the postcard. "Fantastic," Danielle cried. "Did he have one of those pink passports?"

Jean grinned. "You're not supposed to know about those."

"But I do. So does Marian."

Marian gave Jean a sideways look. Her eyes sparked with amusement. "It's hard to keep anything secret in this office," she said in an American-accented English.

Jean frowned. "The fewer secrets you know the better when the gendarmes come nosing around."

Marian shook her head, "What I don't understand is how there can be so many working consulates from countries that have been taken over by the Germans. Poland, Czechoslovakia, Belgium? They just keep on going?"

Jean laughed. "You might ask! But it's lucky for us they do!"

"I guess I really don't understand why the Europeans are so obsessed with passports, visas, transit visas, exit visas. It's insane!"

"Danielle sighed and turned to her typewriter. "Excuse me but I need to finish THIS visa application before we go to lunch. And you're right, Marian. It _is_ insane."

"Jean grinned. "Insane is the word, all right. See you later," and he returned to Varian's office.

The form Danielle was typing came from the Cuban consulate. She had been pleased to discover that the staff had gathered forms from various consulates in Marseilles. If a U.S. visa was impossible, Varian allowed them to help clients apply to some other country. She'd arranged visas for other desperate refugees: to Dominican Republic, Mexico, Haiti. It just meant the bookkeeping for the Committee had to be tweaked a little. The funds that would help this Polish couple flee to Cuba would be written as living expenses instead of travel expenses. Danielle grinned to herself. Another little secret that they all knew.

When Jean returned to the main office, Varian called him to his desk. "Jean, I'm about to ask you to do something difficult, but important."

"OK. Shoot."

Varian adjusted the nose piece on his glasses and cleared his throat. "I'd like you to accompany our clients when they travel to the Spanish border. Some of our clients—well, they need help maneuvering the obstacles on that journey. I need Val here. We're looking at other means of escape. We don't know how much longer the Pyrenees route will be viable."

Jean's heart beat a little faster. Val had told him the logistics of the Pyrenees route, but he was well aware of its pitfalls. "Of course, Varian. When do I start?"

"Tomorrow. The client is a friend of Val's, Henry Ehrlich, a young economist Val knew in Paris. He persuaded me to put his name on the list. Val says Henry's in danger of being picked up by the Gestapo. He needs to leave as soon as possible and, of course, can't apply to Vichy for an exit visa. It's been only two months since the Armistice and the Vichy government and police are still disorganized—but it won't be long that they'll be obeying the Gestapo's commands to surrender on demand anyone on their black list." Varian shuffled through a stack of papers on his desk and picked up a telegram. "Two days ago the Committee wired us that approval for Ehrlich visa had been granted and sent to the Marseilles consulate. He's picking up his visa at this moment. He has a Czech passport and transit visas for Spain and Portugal in the name of Henry Enterman. His passport has a Chinese visa stamp."

Varian unlocked a drawer in his desk and took out a carton of Lucky Strikes. He handed it to Jean. He then slid a dog-eared sheet of paper out from under a panel at the bottom of the drawer. "This is the map we've been using of the Pyrenees route. You should copy it.

Get Danielle to help you. But keep it hidden. Henry will come here to the office later this afternoon to meet you. Give these cigarette packs to him to sweeten the Spanish guards at the frontier—and Jean, Val and I think Henry is a good client for you to start out with. Val says guiding him should be easy. He's smart and in good physical shape. If it works out, I'd like you to take clients once or twice a week for a while. OK?"

"OK!" Jean took a deep breath and left Varian's office, the carton of cigarettes in one hand, the map in the other.

# Chapter Nine

## Escapes

*September, 1940*

The compartment was stuffy and becoming hotter. Jean and Henry Ehrlich had been traveling for three hours and were now approaching the gare at Montpelier. The two men sat across from one another next to the window. They did not acknowledge they were traveling together and refrained from speaking to one another. Three other men were in the compartment, all wearing well-worn French army uniforms. They smelled of sweat and grime. They had been demobbed, they said, and were returning home. As the train slowed for its stop in Montpelier, the former soldiers reached for their musette bags and left the compartment.

Jean and Henry exchanged nervous glances. Henry's mouth had tightened. Jean held his breath, watching for gendarmes. Two women then entered the compartment carrying suitcases. Jean rose to lift the cases onto the racks above their heads. "Merci beaucoup," the women murmured and sat next to Jean. The scent of a light perfume filled the compartment.

The conductors' whistles blew high-pitched blasts, the engine hissed and the train chugged out of the cavernous glass-covered station. Jean eyed the corridor, his palms sweaty. No gendarmes. Yet. As the train picked up speed a conductor entered the compartment carrying a hole punch and leather pouch. The two women handed him their tickets, which he punched and returned to them. He gave Jean and Henry a perfunctory glance, checked his passenger list, and turning on his heel left the compartment. Jean's breathing slowed, but his shoulders remained tense. Henry, who had kept his eyes on his magazine while the conductor was present, sighed audibly. He raised his eyebrows and shot a quick look at Jean. Jean returned the look and shifted in his seat. If Henry were arrested he'd be turned over to the Gestapo, and if the police knew that Jean was helping him escape, Jean could could be executed. Anyone aiding a male under the age of forty-two to escape France could be condemned to death. Varian had not been kidding when he had said this would be a dangerous undertaking. Jean fingered his papers in his shirt pocket. Along with his forged carte d'identité he carried his army discharge papers, which were genuine, definitely en regle.

Henry was well provided with documents: a Czech passport with Spanish and Portuguese transit visas, U. S. visa en lieu of passport, and a forged carte d'identité. He'd hidden his passport under the lining of his beret and carried his identity card in his buttoned shirt pocket. Henry's name on the identity card was Henri Elger. The identity card had been manufactured by Bill Frier, another refugee, an artist. Jean and Val had watched Frier at his work. "The forms for the cards can be purchased at any tabac," Frier had said as he pressed a small glass into an ink pad and gently set it on the card, twisting it a little so that it blurred. He then took a tiny paint brush and with delicate strokes created a stamp. "As place of issue, I'll write in Villejean, a village near Metz. Difficult to check now it's annexed to Germany."

Val had picked up the card. "Good work, Bill." He'd then turned to Jean. "Ehrlich is only thirty-two, but was a judge in Berlin, an anti-Nazi, when the Gestapo arrested him. They sent him to the Oranienburg concentration camp. He's never told me the details, but he escaped to Prague—then to Paris. He knows how to slip through the cracks!"

Now Jean glanced briefly at Henry, whose keen eyes were fixed on his magazine. He had a full head of wavy brown hair, straight nose and a narrow face. He'd taken off the jacket of his dark suit and hung it on the hook next to him. Earlier Jean had watched Henry place his beret carefully in the jacket pocket. His dark blue shirt was slightly frayed at the collar, but his tie looked almost new.

Jean allowed himself to relax a little, his body rocking with the rhythm of the train as it rolled along the tracks. There were no more stops until Perpignan. He gazed out the window at the vineyards spread on the gentle slopes, their branches heavy with purple grapes. It would be harvest time soon. The vines were bright green against the gold of the late-August grass. The scene dazzled his eyes. He was in the beautiful south of France—Languedoc—but could not enjoy it.

After a numbing, stifling three more hours they arrived at Perpignan. Cautiously, they lifted down their musettes, grabbed their jackets, donned their berets and left the train. There would be a two hour wait before the train to Cerbére departed. Jean looked up at the big board over the rows of train tracks. Engines were hissing and snorting ready to depart. The voie for the Cerbére train had not yet been posted, and the two men waited on separate wooden benches in the noisy center of the station. Jean bought a newspaper and held it up before his face. Henry pretended to read his magazine. Jean watched for gendarmes without moving his eyes. His peripheral vision was acute.

The Cerbére train chugged into its voie and the two men boarded. Soon after the train left the station and picked up speed, a weary-faced conductor entered the compartment and asked to see their tickets. Once again Jean held his breath. The conductor checked their tickets and quickly moved on. Henry and Jean exchanged glances but remained silent. One more hurdle surmounted, Jean thought. He peered out the window at the position of the sun. It was now mid-afternoon. Too late to begin the hike over the mountain. Val had given him the name of an inn in Cerbére, which he said was owned by a sympathetic man, a Socialist. They would stay there for the night.

At Cerbére Jean and Henry, their musette bags on their backs, descended from the train. They both stared at the dark tunnel into which the train to Port Bou would take its lucky passengers the short distance to Spain. Leaving the station, they walked side by side down the hill into town, keeping a sharp eye out for gendarmes or Armistice Commission police. They both were wearing their berets and carrying jackets over their arms. The Pyrenees' rocky peaks loomed above them, white stuccoed houses with red-tiled roofs anchored on their slopes. Jean could see the cemetery at the foot of the mountain, the cemetery that was so clearly drawn on his map. The town's shutters were closed against the afternoon heat, but a few passersby turned to stare at them as they walked by. The air smelled of fish. At last Jean spied the sign, Auberge sur la Mer. "There it is, the inn Val told us about. Thank God! We can hide for a while."

Jean paid the innkeeper when they registered, explaining that they would be leaving before dawn the next morning. "So will you be doing a little hiking?" the innkeeper asked, smiling. As Val had told them, the man seemed sympathetic.

"Yes, before it gets too hot."

"Good idea." The innkeeper then showed them to a room with two single beds and a view of the sea. He smiled again, handed Jean the room key and left them alone.

Henry let out a loud sigh. "So far so good!" He gave a grim laugh. "Now I can breathe." He took off his beret and placed it carefully on the heavy oak dresser.

Jean clapped him on the shoulder. "And now we just have the mountain to climb!"

Reaching into his musette, Henry fished out a pair of espadrilles. "Val told me about the shoes. And not to look too cityfied." He then dragged out a sweater, folded his jacket and stuffed it into the bag.

"Val's right." Jean dug out his own rope-soled sandals and removed his tie. He was wearing his old army pants, which he thought would seem suitable for a trek in the mountains. "I'll go see if I can find something for us to eat—and food for our hike. I have a few ration stamps. Did you bring a canteen for water?"

Henry nodded and held up the canteen.

"Good. You stay in the room while I'm gone. Lock the door. I'll knock four times when I return. See you later."

At 4:30 the next morning the two men quietly left the inn. Except for an occasional farmer on a horse-drawn cart rumbling over cobblestones, the town had not yet awakened. It was still dark when they reached the cemetery. They walked quickly along a path between the rows of headstones until they came to the ancient wall fencing the graveyard. Above it rose the steep slope of the mountain, which was barely visible in the pre-dawn light. Nimbly, they climbed over the shadowed wall, protruding stones providing footholds for their rope-soled shoes.

Jean removed the map from his inside jacket pocket, and crouching behind the wall, lit his cigarette lighter. Henry squatted beside him and they both studied the map. With his finger Jean traced the ink drawing of the path. "It looks like we go straight up until we get to that row of pines." They both stood and stared at the steep, slate slope that rose above them.

Henry grinned. "Now we'll test our special shoes. That's a slippery slope up there, but if the smugglers can do it, so can we."

Jean settled his musette on his shoulders and tugged his beret snuggly on his head. "When it gets light we'll be visible from below until we reach the trees. So let's go! And watch out for police. Arriba!"

The two men scrambled up the mountain, sliding, holding on to jutting rocks and plants, but steadily climbing upward. When they finally reached the pine trees, Jean felt a certain exhilaration. The silvery Mediterranean lay below, the cool air was fresh and the sun was rising—and they had covered the most dangerous section of their climb. But when he fixed his eyes on the summit, his mood darkened. In another hour or so they would cross into Franco's Spain.

They carefully followed the map, zigzagging amongst trees and around sharp rocky outcroppings, avoiding the trail clearly drawn on the map that led to the French frontier station. Suddenly, they spied the Spanish flag waving over the Port Bou border crossing below. "We're here! We're in Spain already." Jean cried. "And I have to get out of here. I'll wait half an hour back on the French side—just in case they won't let you in without an exit visa." He opened his musette and fished out the cigarette packs for the border guards. "And here. The cigarettes. And take the tomatoes. That's all we have left, but you might not get much to eat for a while. And when you get to Lisbon don't forget to go to the Unitarian mission. Like Varian said, Charles Joy will help you find a safe place to stay and your passage on a ship to America."

Henry shot Jean an indulgent smile. "His name is etched on my brain! Don't worry." He stuffed the cigarettes into his pocket and the tomatoes in his musette. The two men then gave each other a hearty embrace. Jean grasped Henry's arm. "Good luck, man, good luck and—one more thing—for Christ's sake don't forget to ask the border guards to stamp your passport with the *entrada* stamp!"

Henry saluted then patted his shirt pocket where he'd placed his pink passport. "Believe me, I won't forget. And Jean, good luck to you—and what can I say—thanks! I owe you—and Varian!" He turned, gave a quick wave and strode down the slope toward the border. Guarding the frontier shelter, Jean spied two dark figures looking like vultures in their three-cornered hats and long black capes. Civiles. Jean shivered. He took one last look at Franco's flag, at Henry's retreating figure, and turned his back on Spain.

# Chapter Ten

## Collaboration

*September, 1940*

Danielle and Marian clattered down the two flights of stairs from their apartment. It was not quite eight o'clock in the morning, and fog shrouded the tops of the plane trees planted along the sidewalk. Danielle put her arms into the sleeves of the yellow sweater she'd thrown over her shoulders. She thought of her sleepless night and her visions of Jean behind bars or barbed wire. She turned to Marian. "Ehrlich should be in Spain by now. Maybe Jean is on his way back." Danielle's voice wavered.

"Danielle, they'll both be fine. None of the others had problems on that Pyrenees route."

"I wonder if they needed to show their papers when they boarded at Cerbére."

"They were en regle except for their travel pass, which the police on that route don't seem to care about. Jean will be OK, Danielle," Marian took hold of Danielle's arm. "Both he and Ehrlich are smart and experienced. Val told me Henry Ehrlich escaped from a concentration camp in Germany, no easy feat."

They were now a block away from the Centre Américain office. As they stopped at the curb waiting to cross the street, Danielle glanced at a poster pasted on the trolley stop shelter.

"Oh my God. Look, Marian. Look at that poster." The poster showed pictures of two houses. One, dilapidated and shabby and the other sturdy and new. The shabby one had a star of David and a hammer and sickle on its roof—the sturdy one was topped by a tricolor. At the foundation of the rickety structure the words for the former regime were written: Radicalism, Capitalism, Demagoguery, Laziness, Democracy, Parliament, Jewishness, Avarice, Disorder, Wine. Under the sturdy house the words written were: Order, School, Artisanry, Peasantry, Discipline, Order, Thrift, Courage.

Danielle felt the blood drain from her face. She'd listened to Pétain's rightist speeches on the radio, but hadn't wanted to believe he would become an outright fascist. "Oh, Marian, France is going to be just as repressive as Germany."

Varian was already at his cluttered desk when Danielle and Marian entered the Centre Américain quarters. He glanced up from the letter he was reading and gave Danielle a sharp look. "Danielle, are you OK? Is it Jean?"

She shook her head, leaning her hands on his desk for support. "No, it's not Jean. I'm fine, just shocked. There's a poster on the trolley kiosk. Have you seen it? A Vichy announcement?"

Varian sighed. "Yes, unfortunately. Vichy is showing its true colors, I'm afraid. You have every right to be disturbed. This is not good news for you and your family—or our clients."

Danielle raised her chin. Her head cleared. She has been dreaming here in Marseilles, naïve, so happy in love, denying her family's danger—and her own. "Varian, has there been any news from America about our visas? It's obvious that Vichy's collaboration with the Nazis means disaster for us Jews. Even if we're French."

"No, Danielle, I've had no news about your visas, but I will wire them again tonight. Actually, I'm considering accompanying our next group of refugees to Lisbon. When I'm no longer in France I can send a report to the Committee without Vichy censors reading every word. And I need to talk to the American and British consuls there."

The door opened and Val rushed into the room. "Varian, have you seen the Vichy poster? We have to get our Jews out of here!" He swept off his gray fedora hat and jammed it on the coat rack.

"Yes, I've seen the poster. And I've read this morning's' Le Temps. It reports that In occupied France Jews have been ordered to register. The persecution begins, I'm afraid. You're quite right. Our Jewish clients must leave as soon as possible." Varian's tone was calm, controlled. He opened a folder on his desk. "The Werfels have received their American visas but are waiting for their exit visa from Vichy, which does not arrive. Franz is Jewish. Alma is not, but she's an outspoken critic of Hitler. Then there are the Mann's, Thomas Mann's brother and his wife—and Golo Mann, Thomas' son. They're not Jewish, but they've been vocal anti-Nazis. Heinrich went into exile after his publications were banned—and burned. The Gestapo would be delighted to catch him in their net. At the moment, as you know, the Manns are staying with Consul Harry Bingham. It's time they all left."

Danielle had remained next to Varian's desk, listening carefully. When—and if—her family's visas were granted, they would also need to leave—quickly. "But Varian, if the Werfels and Manns don't have exit visas will they take the Pyrenees route? Jean told me Franz has a bad heart. And Heinrich Mann is no youngster."

"We will try to slip them through on the train, but if that's not possible, they'll have to go on foot. Jean and Golo will have to assist Franz and Heinrich. Alma and Nelly shouldn't be a problem."

Danielle smiled to herself, remembering Alma Mahler, Franz Werfel's wife, when she marched into this office like a royal empress. Imperious, was the word that described her—intrepid, and undoubtedly she would conquer the Pyrenees just as she had conquered so many of her famous lovers and husbands— Klimpt, Mahler, Kokoshka, the architect, Gropius—and novelist, Franz Werfel.

Val snorted. "It should be an interesting trip. Varian. are you serious about going with them?"

Varian nodded, shuffling through the stack of papers on his desk. "It's an opportunity to communicate with the Committee without resorting to code. They need to know how desperate the refugees are. Vichy has had four months to organize its bureaucracy. Obviously, Pétain is collaborating with the Nazis. The police roundups of undocumented refugees are increasing, and the detention camps are little more than death camps. We've got to get more people out." Varian removed his glasses and polished the lenses with his handkerchief. He peered up at Val. "And, Val, you also must leave soon."

Val was half-sitting on the surface of his desk. "I know—and I've been meaning to tell you—some friends of mine, colleagues at University of California, Berkeley, have recommended me for a Fellowship there. I should hear from them soon. When—and if—it comes through I would be eligible for an American visa."

Varian settled his glasses on his nose and sighed. "It will be a sad day for me when you leave—but a joyous one when I know you've arrived in New York. Let me know as soon as you hear from Berkeley. Please!"

Danielle eyed the two men, thinking how close they all became doing this work of saving lives. Slowly, she left Varian's office and went to her desk. She glanced at her watch. The office was about to open for clients. When could she expect to see Jean? If her visa came through soon they wouldn't have much time together. And if it didn't come?

Jean heard the Cerbére church bell ring nine times. He climbed over the cemetery wall and trudged along the path skirting a row of headstones. It had taken him less than an hour to descend the mountain. He'd waited half an hour for Henry, as he had promised, but Henry hadn't been turned back, nor had there been any disturbing noises from the border—shouts, whistles, gunshots. By now Henry should be on the train to Barcelona.

Jean headed for the railway station, a glass-roofed structure a little smaller than the grand gares of Perpignan and Marseilles. Along the main street of the village shopkeepers were raising their awnings to shade their windows, and the market was in full swing. Jean eyed the bright red tomatoes, his stomach rumbling. He was hungry and yearned for coffee and something to eat.

He had only half an hour to wait for the train, just enough time for a cup of coffee and a piece of bread, which he exchanged for one ration coupon and a few francs. He also bought the morning Le Temps. Next to the news stand three Customs officials eyed travelers as they descended from the Perpignan train. One of the men glanced at Jean, but then looked away. Jean speculated that his musette wasn't assumed large enough to carry contraband. Two gendarmes stood by the entrance to the station. Twice they asked for passengers' papers, but waved them on after a brief examination. To his relief, they did not confront Jean. He wondered if his grubby army pants, worn beret and espadrilles made him invisible.

He settled on a wooden bench on the platform where the Marseilles train would depart, briefly eying the tunnel to Port Bou and Spain. He opened Le Temps. The headlines announced that the Luftwaffe had initiated a "blitz" on London. Jean read the story, his heart sinking. Massive air strikes had devastated London, Birmingham, Southampton and other major cities. England was in flames. Hundreds of Spitfires had been shot down. Jean took a deep breath. Was it possible that England would lose the war, that Hitler would take over all of Europe? Were they all doomed? He turned the page, reflecting that he must be sure to listen to BBC tonight, to hear the report from London. Le Temps printed what the Germans dictated. Their propaganda could not be trusted. He would report on what he heard in the next issue of the Bulletin.

As Jean scanned the paper, he was jolted into attention. A short paragraph on the second page announced that all Jews in occupied France had been ordered to register at their local prefectures. It also reported that government officials in Vichy were preparing new laws, the Statuts de Juifs, which would address the question of Jews in the professions and in the work place. Jean jumped up from his bench, crumpled the newspaper and slammed it into the garbage can. "Merde!" he said aloud. Jews would be denied the right to earn a living!

A woman who sat waiting on the bench next to him stopped knitting and stared at him, a perplexed expression on her face. When Jean's fierce eyes connected with hers, she returned to her knitting. Jean paced the platform, deep in thought. The persecution of Jews was beginning. The Nazis would spread their unspeakable poison, their cruelty, their Aryan ideology to all of France. Danielle and her family must leave France soon.

The noise of an approaching train stopped his pacing. He watched as it steamed and snorted to a stop. The conductors blew their whistles, passengers boarded, and Jean climbed up the steps into the car. By mid-afternoon he would arrive in Marseilles. He needed to talk to Varian about Danielle and her family—and their other Jewish clients, of course. Jean slumped in a corner of the compartment in a cloud of gloom.

# Chapter Eleven

## More Escapes

*September, 1940*

Jean's return trip from Cerbére was without problems, except for his feeling exhausted, depressed and apprehensive. He couldn't stop thinking about Vichy's new Jewish edicts—and Danielle. How could he protect her? And how could he bear her absence when—and if— she received her visa and left for America?

When he walked into the Centre Américain, Varian and the staff hailed him like a returning hero. Danielle greeted him as if he'd returned from the dead. Jean assured them that the trip had been successful as far as he knew. "Nobody stopped us on the train or on the mountain, and Henry crossed into Spain without difficulty."

Later, when Varian suggested that Jean assist the Werfels and Manns to escape—and told him what he'd heard and read about Vichy's move toward political and racial repression, Jean agreed they needed to spirit their foreign Jewish clients away immediately. He would provide escort for the Mann/Werfel group as soon as it could be arranged.

Later that evening, Jean and Danielle stopped at a Vieux Port café for dinner. Danielle's worried eyes were fixed on Jean's face. She leaned forward and lowered her voice. "Did the police ask you any questions? Did the conductors look at you suspiciously?"

Jean eyed the neighboring table and spoke quietly. "We had no problems, Danielle. Our papers were en regle. The police passed us by, the conductors barely looked at us. No one asked for a travel pass. They just took our tickets and moved on. Henry arrived at the frontier without a hitch."

Suddenly, a clamor of voices caused them to look toward the entrance to the café. At the same time, the two couples at the table next to them leaped from their chairs and dashed out the back of the café through the swinging door into the kitchen. The clattering of pots and shouts of alarm rang out. Three more men ran by, disappearing through the kitchen door. In the front of the café, four gendarmes were moving from table to table, demanding to see documents. One of the gendarmes was hustling a middle-aged couple out the front door. The woman was wailing, the man struggling and shouting.

Jean glanced at Danielle and pressed her hand. Her blue eyes were dark with fright. "You have papers, Danielle," he said, leaning toward her, speaking quietly. He tried to be reassuring, but had to force himself to sound confident. "You're French, you have a residence permit, a job, a carte d'identité. When they ask for your documents, just hand them over and smile."

The police slowly made their way through the café. One other couple were hauled off. When the gendarme asked for Jean and Danielle's papers, he took their proffered documents and examined them closely. He gave them each a long, searching look, handed them back, and moved on. Jean gave Danielle a quick glance. Her cheeks had paled, but she had maintained her composure. He grinned at her. "Well done, Danielle."

The gendarmes swooped out the door and after a moment's absolute silence a buzz of angry, excited voices filled the room. Danielle gave a wan smile. "I'm not hungry anymore. Can we get out of here?"

"Yes, let's go." He tossed some francs on the table and took hold of Danielle's arm. In his room a short while later, Danielle stood by the window looking out at the blackened brick wall. Jean stood behind her, his hands on her waist. She suddenly turned and stared at him with frightened eyes. "That raid was terrifying. I knew we"re both en regle, but those gendarmes. . . Vichy is changing—collaborating with the Nazis. They'll persecute Jews—even if we're French. And yesterday when you escorted Henry I was so afraid for <u>you</u>. And I'm afraid for myself and my family. Sometimes. . ." and she burst into tears.

He put his arms around her and held her close. "We'll have to get you out of France—as much as I don't want you to go!" That night they made love as if their hours together were numbered.

A week later, It was still dark at 5 A.M when Jean approached the Gare St Charles. He wore his beret, a warm jacket and his old army pants and carried his weather-beaten musette bag. His documents were carefully buttoned into his inside jacket pocket. Varian had told Jean to meet him and the Werfel/Mann party at the ticket counter. They would catch the train that departed for Perpignon and Cerbére at 5:30.

Jean strode into the cavernous station, scanning the glass-roofed structure for police. None were in evidence. He glanced toward the ticket counter and instantly recognized the six people waiting beside a mountain of luggage. Jean was alarmed. He knew that Varian had been clear in his instructions about bringing only the luggage that could be easily carried. If they had to hike over the mountain there would be no way they could carry those bags.

After the initial greetings Jean pointed to the baggage. "What will we do with these?"

Alma Mahler lifted her chin and glared at him. "They must go with us. These cases contain holograph music scores of my former husband Gustav Mahler. Also, the original manuscript of Bruckner's Third Symphony. I couldn't possibly abandon them to the Nazis." Her tone was imperious, unrelenting.

Varian and Jean exchanged exasperated glances. Varian sighed. "I'll say the bags are mine and send them through to Port Bou on the train. That might work." His lips twitched into a small smile. "I just hope the customs officials won't open you cases and question me about your woman's clothing, Mrs Werfel." Varian then left them for the ticket counter, soon returning with seven first class tickets. "The police might not bother us if we're traveling first class. We won't look like refugees."

Jean eyed the group, judging their ability to avoid confrontations with the police and to climb the mountain. Varian hoped that the American visas would be impressive enough to the French border officials to issue the group exit visas, but if they refused Jean would have to guide them up the steep mountain slope. Varian was the only one who had been issued an exit visa. At least the Werfels had a travel pass. Jean's eyes fixed on Heinrich Mann, who was 69 years old. Unfortunately, he was also fat and not in good shape. Jean's scrutiny then moved to Franz Werfel, who was in his sixties and had suffered a heart attack a few months earlier. He, too, was overweight. Next he gazed at Alma Mahler Werfel who was sixty-one, but stood straight and looked sturdy. She was a handsome woman. Her strong will would propel her over the mountain, he was sure. He just hope her manner wouldn't anger the police. Nelly Mann stood next to her. Heinrich's wife was a young thirty, with large breasts and vacant blue eyes. He'd heard she'd been a cabaret singer in Germany. Her French was not good, which meant she'd need to keep her mouth shut as they traveled. At least Golo Mann was a young and strong thirty-one. He had been an ambulance driver in the French army and seemed sensible. None of them had exit permits, but they all had American visas and Czech passports stamped with Spanish and Portuguese transit visas. The problem would occur if he had to guide them over the Pyrenees. The two older men would need help. And what would he do if Werfel had another heart attack?

Before Jean climbed the steps into the first class car he bought a newspaper and carried it aboard. He followed his charges into the compartment, which was ample enough to provide seats for all seven. They quickly stowed hand baggage, hats and jackets and took their seats. When Jean opened his newspaper he was surprised to see a copy of the Bulletin fall onto his lap. He knew that the piece he'd written after hearing the BBC version of the Battle of Britain two nights earlier would be its lead story. He'd written that the young RAF Spitfire pilots were holding their own, that they suffered many casualties, their planes going down in flames, but while they fought they were shooting down countless numbers of German bombers. The English populace was putting up a fight. They had organized teams of volunteers who drove ambulances, fought fires, rescued trapped victims. Churchill vowed they would not surrender.

Now Varian, who sat next to him, was peering at the sheet. Jean met his glance, then quickly slid the illegal sheet into the back pages of the paper. "For later," Jean murmured in English. He'd never told Varian about his Resistance work. The next time Frenay was in Marseilles he intended to ask him if Fry should be told.

Jean glanced across the compartment at Nelly Mann, who was straightening her silk dress around her knees. She began to chatter in German. Varian leaned forward, holding up his hand and spoke quietly. "Madame. Ne parle pas en alemán ici, je vous en prie."

Alma glared at Nelly. Nelly frowned and bit her lip. Heinrich, who sat next to her, patted her hand and mumbled something in French which she obviously didn't understand. Jean smiled to himself. This was going to be a long, long trip. At least he knew their papers were all en regle.

After a tiresome, hot journey of six hours and a four-hour wait in Perpignan, they at last arrived at the Cerbére station. Until this moment they had been ignored by officials except for handing over their tickets. Now they descended from the train, damp with sweat and pale with exhaustion. Alma peered down the tunnel that led to Spain. "We are close," she said, in a wilted, most uncharacteristic voice.

Jean eyed the French police and border officials who loomed at the end of the arrival platform where passengers tickets and documents were being scrutinized for the connecting train to Port Bou. Jean could see the panic surge in his charges faces. Werfel's hand went to his chest. Heinrich Mann was breathing heavily. Varian touched Jean's arm. "I think under the circumstances," and he shot a look at the group, "we should collect the passports and present them to the officer in charge. I will explain that these passengers all have American visas and have been waiting for exit permits which have never arrived."

Unfortunately, the officer could not cooperative. "C' est imposible!" he said firmly, thrusting the passports back at Varian.

After discussing this obstacle to their plan to take the connecting train through the tunnel to Port Bou, they decided to go to a quiet inn and try again the next day. Jean returned the passports to the official and explained that his companions wanted to stay in Cerbére for the night. The official accepted the passports and slid them into his drawer. "Return for them tomorrow morning." His tone was brusque but not unfriendly.

Jean guided his charges to the same inn he had stayed before with Henry Ehrlich. As they walked down the hill he told them that since they might need to hike over the mountain the next morning, they should dig out the espadrilles he had told them to bring. He glanced at Alma and Nelly in their white dresses. "Please wear something darker, and bring a jacket or sweater. At the top the winds can be icy. And put your purses into your shoulder bags. You'll need your hands free to climb the steep slopes."

Alma shot him an arrogant look.

Jean pointed to the mountain that rose above the cemetery. "Madame, tomorrow there's a good chance that you will be climbing over that cemetery wall and scrabbling your way up that rocky slope. Be prepared."

The next morning all but Varian were standing in front of that wall. The official had refused to provide exit visas and had returned their passports. Varian had boarded the train with all seventeen pieces of luggage, promising to meet them when they crossed into Spain at Port Bou. Jean and his charges had pocketed their papers and left the station.

Golo Mann and Jean boosted Werfel and Heinrich up and over the wall and gave the two women a hand. At the bottom of the steep slope that rose from the cemetery Jean gathered the group around him. "We will need to get up to the pine trees you can see at the top of the slope. Until you are into the trees you will be visible to the police. First Golo and I will help the Werfels up the slope. Manns, you stay here, hidden behind the wall. We will come back for you as soon as the Werfels reach the pines."

Franz glanced upward, his glasses glinting in the early morning sunlight. "Let's go," he said, stepping forward. Jean took hold of his left arm, Golo his right and they lifted him step by slippery step up the slope. Werfel panted for breath. They stopped a few seconds at a time, then resumed pushing and pulling, grabbing for hand-holds as they carried him toward the trees. Alma scrabbled up the mountain behind them, groaning, breathing hard, but needed little help. At the top, the Werfels rested while Golo and Jean returned for the Manns. Nelly was able to assist the two men heave the heavy, sixty-nine year old Heinrich up the mountain. As they climbed, Jean's sharp eyes combed the trail below for police, but none appeared.

Finally they all reached the crest where they looked out at the Mediterranean below. Jean pointed down the mountain toward Spain. "Now we go down. It's not far."

A half hour later Alma let out a cry. "Look, the Spanish flag!" She pointed to the hut with the flag flying over it.

Jean gave them each an embrace. "I must leave you now." He emptied his pockets and musette bag of cigarette packages and handed them around. "Gifts for the guards. And don't forget to get your passport stamped with a Spanish entrada."

They thanked him warmly. Werfel was breathing hard, but his cheeks were no longer flushed a bright red. Heinrich's blue eyes behind his glasses were clouded with fatigue, but he was smiling. "We did it!" he said with a certain pride.

Jean waved them off and waited in the shadow while they trudged down the mountain. He watched them step into the border station. He waited another half hour until he was certain they were not being turned back. He then slung his musette over his shoulder and hiked quickly down the mountain to Cerbére.

# Chapter Twelve

## Changes

*September-October, 1940*

Jean slid down the crumbling shale, relieved to be on his own but pleased that his charges crossed into Spain. As he eyed the terrain for footholds, he continued to scan the bare slope and the cemetery below for police. Just as he reached the cemetery wall, he stopped with a jolt, his heart pounding. He spied an open German army car rumbling along the road next to the cemetery—occupied by eight men in gray officer's uniforms. Automatically, Jean threw himself on the ground behind the wall and remained motionless until the sound of the car engine faded away.

Cautiously, adrenaline pumping, he peered over the wall at the road, listening intently for the roar of heavy vehicles driving along the road. Birds sang, crickets chirped, but no engine noises marred the bucolic scene. After waiting what seemed a lifetime, but was only ten minutes, he scrambled over the wall and strode toward the town. He maintained a steady pace, but behaved as if he'd been on a morning stroll on the mountain. He forced himself to control his breathing. What did this mean? The presence of German officers? What were they doing here? He walked through the town on his way to the railway station, expecting to smell some whiff of change in the air, but, as usual, people were on the street shopping, children were walking to school with book bags on their backs. All seemed normal.

At the gare café he drank a cup of coffee while he waited for his train to depart. Two men sat at a table next to him. He wanted to ask them what they knew about the German officers, but didn't want to attract attention to himself. He speculated that since it was a rare occasion for German army officers to be in this part of the country, the men might gossip about the event. Soon enough they did, and what he heard filled him with dread. "Ricardo told me he'd heard that German troops in the occupied zone are massing at the demarcation line," one of the men said. "They've seen columns of panzars and motorized troops on the move toward the frontier with Spain. They think the Germans plan to invade. They want Gibralter, and If the Germans take Gibralter they could control shipping on the Mediterranean—like the Brits do now. They'd win the war, for sure."

"Christ, let's hope they don't decide to take a detour through Cerbére! Do you suppose that's why those German officers were snooping around?"

The noise of the train steaming down the track drowned out the rest of the men's conversation. Jean quickly paid for his coffee and boarded the train, pondering over this latest bit of information. If he hadn't seen the German officers on the road he would have discounted what he'd heard as a foolish rumor, but he was shaken. Was the Pyrenees escape route in danger? And worse, would the Germans take over Spain and Gibralter? They'd win the war, that was certain.

Clients and the rest of the Centre Américain staff had left for the day. Carefully, Danielle locked the front door to the agency. Danielle had hoped Jean would have returned from Cerbére by now, but she knew another train would be due in an hour. Val called to her from inside Varian's office. "Danielle, is the front door locked?"

She held the keys in her hands. "Yes, Val. All clear." She stood in the doorway to the tiny back room that served as Varian's private domain, watching as Val dumped out the contents of his briefcase onto a table next to the wall. Val began to stack bank notes into piles, mumbling to himself as he counted them. He checked a sheet of paper, nodded, then twiddled the combination lock on the safe that had been dug into the wall and stashed the cash away. He slammed the safe shut and re-hung the framed poster that had covered it. "One more time!" he said, sighing. "I keep expecting that crook to cheat me—or set me up. On the street with this stuffed briefcase I wait for the tap on my shoulder or the blow to the head. Police or gangsters, who will it be?"

Danielle remembered how it felt when she helped Jean with the Bulletin. "So far, Val, you've been lucky. And you know how important it is—what you're doing."

Danielle knew about the black market money and most of the other clearly illegal methods they employed to save clients' lives. Varian had tried to keep the legal, humanitarian aid work separate from the illegal activities, He'd employed Danielle and Marian as interviewers, while Val, Jean and one of the new employees, Frederique Chardin, were involved in clandestine activities—like acquiring false passports, forged signatures, carrying black market money and guiding refugees illegally into Spain. In spite of Varian's desire to protect Danielle and Marian from knowing about the illegal work, it had been impossible to keep it from them. They all knew they would be implicated if the police became aware of the true nature of the work.

Now Danielle glanced at Val. "Val, have you heard anymore about your visa?"

"No, but my American friends have contacted the immigration people about me."

"You've heard that Vichy has ordered foreign Jews to register. It won't be long that they'll order us French to register, too."

"I hope I'll be long gone by then—or underground with the Resistance!"

Danielle picked up the copy of Le Temps on Varian's desk, opening it to the front page. "My parents are worried sick about my aunts and uncles in Paris—trying to persuade them to find a way to leave France." She pointed to the photo on the front page of the paper. "Did you see this picture? Of Pétain and Hitler?"

"Yes, indeed. Scary as hell. But not surprising. I feel the screws tightening. The Nazis will have their way! The truth is we all have to get out of here."

"Go over the mountain? Find a ship?"

"If Vichy would start sending out exit visas, French citizens wouldn't need to go over the mountain. A few ships leave port and actually arrive at their destination—in spite of the British blockade. For German Jews and Communists . . . well . . . that's another story."

Danielle leaned against the desk and gave Val a troubled look. She knew that Val was a German Jew, that his French identity was forged. "Yeah, I know." She also knew Val and Varian were trying to find a way to get the imprisoned British soldiers here in Marseilles back to England, which would be extremely dangerous. And which most certainly was not an action the Emergency Rescue Committee in New York would condone. Almost every day she saw tall, blonde young men sitting in the back of cafés in the Vieux Port. They were detained in the fort that perched on top of the hill next to the port, but were granted passes that allowed them to leave for the day. "Val, I keep seeing those Brits, those soldiers. They're so conspicuous. They don't speak French and they're so much taller than everyone else. I don't see how we can get them back to England."

Val closed the door to Varian's office and reached for his hat on the hook by the front door. "Well, we have to try. If we send them one or two at a time, maybe. And yesterday I heard of another route over the mountains that's working—from Banyuls. It's not far from Cerbére. It's a little longer than the cemetery route, but the German couple who are helping refugees say it's safer. The Socialist mayor of Banyuls is cooperating. I'm going there as soon as Varian gets back—to talk to the couple, Hans and Lise Fittco."

He opened the door for Danielle, took the keys from her hand, and locked it behind them. Danielle looked at her watch. Jean's train should be here in fifteen minutes. "Val, I'm going to the gare to meet Jean. He should be on that train. I can't wait to hear about his trip with that gang of primadonnas. It couldn't have been easy. See you tomorrow."

When Danielle spied Jean striding down the platform she ran toward him and threw her arms around his neck. "You made it! Thank God. Are you OK?"

"Now I am," he said, kissing her warmly. They then walked arm in arm through the station toward the door to the front stairs. Jean stopped. Four police were checking people's documents at the door. He sighed. "Let's go the other way."

They turned to the right and went through the door marked Hotel Terminus. Danielle knew the way through the lobby of the hotel to a door that opened onto the street. She'd taken it many times. It was here they met with the Czechs to pick up the pink passports. Soon they were on their way to Jean's room in the Vieux Port. She could breathe again.

On his first day back from Spain and Portugal, Varian met with Val, Danielle and Jean over breakfast at a café across the street from the Centre Américain. Before they all entered the café Val had first checked it out for police. He led them to a table in the back of the room where they would not be overheard by other patrons. Jean immediately asked Varian how his charges, the Werfels and Manns had fared.

Varian stirred his coffee while he spoke. "The last I heard they were all in Lisbon waiting for their ship to sail. I met them in Port Bou as they came through Spanish migración and aduana—as we had agreed. They were nervous, but they'd had no problems with the officials. We all then took the train to Barcelona and I put them on flights to Lisbon."

Jean grinned. "With all their luggage?"

Varian laughed. "With all their luggage. And, by the way, the officials in Port Bou didn't examine my seventeen pieces of luggage, or even show surprise. It was all very easy. I told the Werfels and Manns to stay in their hotel rooms in Lisbon until their ship sailed. That city is swarming with Gestapo."

At the mention of the Gestapo, Jean hurried to tell Varian about his sighting of the German officers in Cerbére and the rumors circulating about the massing of German troops at the demarcation line.

Varian listened carefully to Jean's tale, slowly sipping his coffee. He set down his cup and nodded. "I heard similar stories in Spain." He lowered his voice. "There's talk of a possible meeting of Hitler and Franco, but nothing concrete. Hitler wants Gibralter, of course. The French bombed it at Hitler's insistence, but that rock is impregnable. American embassy staff I spoke to speculate that unlike the French, Franco won't cooperate with the Germans. They say he'll wait to see who wins. They say Hitler has postponed his invasion of England until May."

Val fished a pack of Gauloises from his pocket and held it out to the others. He then lit their cigarettes with his lighter. He leaned closer to Varian, speaking quietly. "Varian, whether it's a rumor or not—or whatever Franco decides to do with the Germans, we need to find another route for our refugees. There's a couple in Banyuls, Hans and Lise Fittco, have you heard of them?"

Varian nodded. "I have." Again, he peered around the café for eavesdroppers. "They're taking people over the path that Spain's General Lister used evacuating his Republican soldiers into France. I'd like to meet them."

"I was hoping you'd say that. Jean and I could go down there and check it out. Maybe we could persuade them to come to meet you. They need funds, I'm sure. The mayor there is helpful, apparently, but the refugees still need money for food and lodging—and rail and ship passage."

Varian agreed. "OK. See what you can do. Maybe we can join forces. But now let's get back to work. I have a stack of wires to go through."

"One more thing," Val said, "glancing around the room. "Our Czech passports. There are so many of them around I'm afraid the officials will find them suspicious. I think we should contact Frederic Drasch."

Jean remembered that Drasch had shown them Danish and Dutch passports that looked genuine, but Varian didn't trust him. Varian sighed. "Val, let's talk about it later."

# Chapter Thirteen

## Winter Chill

*November, December 1940*

The mistral was blowing from the northwest, and Jean and Val bowed their heads into the dry, icy wind. They were returning from Banyuls after having met with Hans and Lise Fittco. They had hiked the Fittco's trail to the border. As Jean hurried down the Gare St Charles open stairway, holding his beret to his head with one hand, he thought about the Pyrenees and the cold wind on the mountain. Winter approached. At least the police might hesitate to be out in the wind. Here at the gare the police hadn't been checking documents at the exit. Were they huddling in some cozy café somewhere?

Varian greeted the two men warmly when they burst into the Centre Américain. Danielle jumped up from her chair at the typewriter and gave Jean a tight hug. "It's always such a relief to see you walk through that door after a mission."

Jean put his arm around her waist and grinned. "For me, too. Believe me."

Danielle could feel her cheeks flush with excitement. "The last of our clients just left. Every time the door opened my heart jumped, hoping it would be you."

The newcomer to the group, Frederique Chardin, whom they called Fredi, stepped forward and shook Val and Jean's hands. Varian then ushered the four of them into a back room that contained a large, scarred oak table and several mismatched chairs. It was their conference room where the staff met to discuss which clients to recommend for American visas—or to help in other ways. The Centre Américain staff now consisted of twenty people, most whose task was interviewing clients, acquiring legal visas or dispensing small amounts of money to desperate refugees for food and lodging.

The conference table was also where Varian met with Jean and Val—and now Danielle and Fredi—concerning their clandestine tasks. Danielle attended these meetings, although Jean had been reluctant to involve her. She had pleaded with Varian to include her. "I know what Val and Jean are doing. I'm already involved, and I can be useful. I can carry messages, passports, visas, I can draw maps, type false documents."

The newcomer, Fredi, took a chair opposite from Danielle. As the others took their seats, Danielle fixed her eyes on Fredi. She didn't know him well yet. He'd only been on the staff two weeks and this was the first time Varian had suggested he join their underground section. She did know that he was twenty-seven years old, a chemical engineer from Alsace Lorraine and detested the Germans. He'd fought in the French army in the Ardenne and was captured by the Germans, but escaped. He spoke English and German as well as French, was tall, blond, broad-shouldered, and was wily enough to have escaped prisoner of war camp and find his way to Marseilles. Both Val and Jean had persuaded Varian to put him to work at clandestine tasks. Now Fredi was listening carefully to what Val reported about the new Pyreneean escape route. His keen blue eyes were focused on Val's face.

"So, how did it go?" Varian said, "Will the Fittcos work with us?"

Val nodded. "Maybe. At least they agreed to meet you. They'll come to Marseilles next Friday—if they make it without travel permits. They need to renew their Spanish and Portuguese transit visas. They're apatrides, stateless, and they're Jewish."

"Did you tell me they're from Berlin?" Varian asked.

"Right. And they were active in the anti-Nazi German resistance."

"Do they have papers?"

"They have the usual pink Czech passport and Chinese visa. And as soon as they get their transit visas renewed they plan to take their Pyrenees route themselves. We'd have to convince them to stay a while longer."

Varian removed his glasses and cleaned the lenses with his handkerchief. "Let's hope we're successful. OK, Val, let me know where and when we will meet." He rose, picked up the stack of telegrams he'd placed on the table, and headed for his office. "See you all tomorrow. Get some rest."

Danielle stopped him before he went out the door. "Varian, I hate to keep bothering you, but have you heard anything about my families' American visa?"

Varian sighed and held up the stack of wires. "Not yet, Danielle, but I hope we'll hear very soon. I sent a strong recommendation for your father when I was in Lisbon. I also complained to the Committee about the State Department officials here and in Washington. I needed to write to them without needing to resort to code because of the Vichy censors. I told them I thought the State Department's attitude toward refugees in France was criminal. And stupid, of course! My letters will have been received by now. We should hear soon, Danielle."

"I hope so. My parents are frantic. Thanks, Varian, and I'm sorry to bother you."

He shook his head. "No problem, That's what I'm here for." He gave her a warm smile and went out the door. Slowly, Danielle left the conference room and headed for her desk. Jean and Val followed, slinging their musettes over their shoulders. Fredi trailed behind, his hands in the pockets of his worn woolen pants. A shout from Varian caused them all to glance in the direction of his office. "Val, there's a telegram for you! It's from the American immigration department!"

Danielle held her breath. Were they granting Val his visa? Varian handed the wire to Val. In an instant Val had torn the envelope and allowed it to flutter to the floor. He held up the half-sheet of yellow paper. "It says I'm to go to the consulate to pick up my visa in lieu of passport! Fantastic!"

Danielle and Jean caught Val in bear hugs and Varian pumped his hand. in congratulation. Fredi, too, shook his hand.

Val was breathing rapidly. "I'll go tomorrow to pick it up, but I'm not ready to leave for Berkeley just yet, Varian. There's still so much work to be done. So many people who need help."

Varian's expression became solemn. "Val, I'm not sure how we can continue without you, but you must save your own life. Take care. The moment you feel you're in danger you must flee. Do you understand?"

"I do understand, Varian. You can count on it." Val shoved the yellow piece of paper into his pocket and turned to go. "I'll see you all tomorrow, with my visa!"

Danielle watched him as he shouldered his musette and went out the door. How will she feel if she receives such a telegram? Will she be willing to leave? Her father had been offered a teaching job at U.C. Berkeley—like Val. If she goes to California with her family, at least Val's presence would be a connection to her life here. But life without Jean?

A week later the Fittcos met with Varian, Val, Jean and Fredi in the café across the street from CAS. Val entered first to check it out for police and any suspicious individuals who might be members of the Armistice Commission. Jean always wondered how Val thought he could identify Armistice police. Val claimed he could smell a Nazi from twenty feet away. After Val signaled his all clear, Varian, the Fittcos, Val and Jean entered the café, heading to a table in the corner of the room. Fredi remained by the door as lookout.

After ordering coffee, Varian described the work in which the Centre Américain staff was engaged. "As Val and Jean told you, the route they have been using from Cerbére has become known by the police—and perhaps the Germans."

Hans fixed his dark eyes on Varian. He asked questions about procedure, funds, and documents. After giving Lise a questioning glance and waiting for her murmured assent, he spoke with energy. "OK, we'll guide your clients—until it's no longer safe for us or for them. We just hope you can help us when it's our turn to escape."

As Jean listened to the Fittcos he was filled with admiration for them. Their own lives were in danger, but it was obvious that their commitment to fighting Nazis was so intense they would take that risk. He eyed Lise, who was small, slender and agile. He figured she'd be no more than thirty years old. Hans was tall and sturdy, and about the same age. They'd both been involved in underground, anti-Nazi activities since they were in their teens, they'd said.

It was agreed that most of the time either Val or Jean would accompany the clients in groups of two or three. If the clients arrived on their own, they would present the Fittcos with a small piece of paper with a code written on it which had been torn in half. The Fittcos would possess the other half of the paper with the code—which had been left with them by Jean or Val on their previous trip.

Hans added, "there's a hotel in the village where your clients can spend the night. The owner is a friend. We begin our hike before dawn as if we were workers in the vineyard. Your clients must wear espadrilles and old clothes so they look as if they were field workers."

Varian assured the couple that Centre Américain clients would be carefully briefed. "And their luggage?"

Jean grinned, remembering the seventeen pieces Varian escorted belonging to the Werfels and Manns.

Lise set down her coffee cup. "On the mountain they can carry a musette, but nothing larger. But . . ."and her face lit up with a smile, "we can send luggage on the train with a railroad engineer we've befriended—for a tip, of course."

"Well," said Varian, rising from the table. "I'm impressed with your work—and deeply grateful you're willing to stay in the country a little longer. Val and Jean will take care of the finances and documents you will need. How much money do you want?"

Hans' eyes suddenly flashed in anger. He turned to Val and said in German, "what does he mean, how much do we want? Is he trying to buy us!"

Jean knew enough German to realize Hans had misunderstood Varian's question. He glanced at Varian, whose eyes expressed puzzlement. He spoke haltingly in German. "Mr. Fittco, I think you have taken offense at my question about money. I merely want to know what your expense needs will be—for our clients and yourselves."

Hans expression softened. "Sorry, I didn't understand. I should have known."

Varian gave a wan smile. "I speak French with an American accent—and my German is rudimentary. With all these languages, it's easy to be misunderstood. But now I must get back to work. Val and Jean can take care of the arrangements. Good luck to you both." He put his hat firmly on his head and strode from the café.

Later, Val and Jean escorted the Fittcos to the train station, keeping a sharp eye out for Armistice police. Val and Fredi walked a few paces ahead of the couple and Jean trailed behind. To avoid the gendarmes posted at the main entrance to the gare, they entered through the Hotel Terminus. The Fittcos' train arrived promptly and they quickly climbed aboard. Jean, Fredi and Val mingled with the crowd a few minutes, then separately left the station through the hotel exit. As Jean walked along the Canebiére, he pondered over this new chapter in the Pyrenees crossing challenge. It ought to work, he decided. Hans and Lise Fittco were not only brave, but competent. He was impressed.

# Chapter Fourteen

## Vielle Ville and the Villa

*November-December, 1940*

Early that evening Jean headed to the Vielle Ville for his appointment with Simone about the Bulletin. Danielle was dining with her family and he hadn't told her about the meeting. Simone had hinted that Frenay might attend. As he strode down the narrow alley to Simone's place he listened carefully for footsteps behind him. His sharp eyes scanned doorways and barred windows as he passed by. Except for four or five scrawny cats, their ribs poking from scarred fur, Jean was the path's sole occupant. The alley was curved, conforming to the hill on which this section of the old city was built. Some of the ancient stone buildings were crumbled, in ruins, covered with debris. Beyond, he could catch glimpses of the darkening sea and the red tiled roofs of the buildings below.

Before pressing the buzzer at the door of Simone's building, Jean made a quick surveillance in both directions of the alley—and of the windows above. He buzzed, pushed the door open, and climbed the two flights of stairs to Simone's apartment. Simone responded to his knock, asked him to identify himself and opened the door. Seated at a table in the center of the room, Captain Frenay raised his hand in a greeting. When Jean approached, Frenay rose and embraced him. "Good work, Jean," he said. "I've read your pieces."

Simone gave him a welcoming smile and pointed to the table. "Please, sit down. And let me take your coat."

Jean removed his hat and overcoat and handed them to her. He watched as she hung them on a hook by the door. She wore a warm, bulky blue sweater, a navy skirt and sensible brown walking shoes. She was in her forties, Jean knew, but moved like a much younger woman. Frenay must be ten years younger, Jean speculated. He wondered if the pair were lovers. Frenay's straight dark hair was combed back from his high forehead and his brown eyes peered sharply under well-defined brows. He, too, wore a thick sweater over civilian clothes. His back was straight as he settled in his chair, his bearing definitely military.

Frenay held up a copy of the last Bulletin. "Jean, I'm pleased with your work. I'm counting on you to continue. We've found a printer who's willing to put out a twice monthly paper, a proper newspaper. I'm trying to organize a staff." Frenay then held out a pack of Gauloises to Jean, then lit both his own and Jean's cigarette with a silver lighter.

"I'm certainly willing to continue, Captain Frenay. As you know, I'm working for Varian Fry. I've been escorting people to the Spanish frontier near Perpignon about once a week, but I keep my eyes and ears open for information. I write at night."

"Good," Frenay said, tapping his cigarette on the ashtray Simone had brought them. "I'd hoped you'd say that. Now I would like you to recruit a cell of five people to work with you here in Marseilles. Would that be possible?"

"A cell?"

"Yes, And I'd like you to lead it. I'm trying to organize a structure that will keep you more or less safe. I envision three sections. Propaganda, Intelligence, and Armed action. Each district will contain five man cells within a circle of thirty."

"A circle of thirty?"

"Yes. The person in charge of the group of thirty would meet only with the leaders of the cells. This structure should prevent the destruction of an entire district when one of the members is arrested and tortured."

Jean listened carefully to Frenay. Frenay's plan was practical, of course, but chilling. He tried not to think about being arrested—and tortured. The Gestapo were the torturers. Supposedly, the Vichy police were not so vicious.

Frenay crushed out his cigarette. "I'm expecting you to recruit workers to help you—the young woman who drew the masthead, for instance."

Jean took a drag on his cigarette. Danielle? He couldn't bear to think of her being tortured. He thought of Franco's henchmen in Spain. He exhaled the smoke. It was best not to go in that direction. He must stick to business. "What about printing and distribution?"

"At this point I can see the printer being in your cell. That could change later if the newspaper becomes multi-district. A separate cell should handle distribution. But we'll work out the details. For the moment, Simone has agreed to be the leader of the circle of thirty. She will be your contact."

Jean shot a glance at Simone, who sat next to Frenay, but who hadn't spoken. "And the editorial content? Will there be guidance from you or your lieutenants?"

"I will make suggestions—and hopefully, provide intelligence. And from time to time write an editorial. Simone will let you know. Your section will aim to inform the people here in unoccupied France of the truth—to arouse them to resist the Germans."

Jean fixed his eyes on Frenay's face as he listened to his words. Frenay spoke with force and his eyes shone with fervor. He was a charismatic leader, that was certain.

Frenay continued. "In the occupied zone Frenchmen hear the sound of German boots on French streets. They witness Nazi brutality. The resistance movement is organizing rapidly. Here people believe their beloved Maréchal will keep them safe. They are complacent. We must convince them they are mistaken." Frenay rose and reached for his briefcase. "Now I must go. I've been posted to Vichy."

Jean felt a jolt of dismay. "Vichy?"

Frenay gave a crooked smile. "Don't be alarmed. I will use the opportunity to dig up intelligence. I've been assigned to the Deuxieme Bureau."

The Deuxieme Bureau was the army secret service, Jean knew. "Congratulations, sir. I wish you luck. And I will do the best I can running my cell!"

As Frenay was buttoning his overcoat, Jean remembered the question he had planned to ask Frenay. "Captain, I have one more question. Should I inform Varian Fry of my work on the Bulletin?"

Frenay frowned. "My first response is to say no." He reached for his hat, which Simone held out to him. "On the other hand, Fry's organization is already involved in clandestine activities to save refugees. It appears he is trustworthy, but I think it would be safer for him and for his organization—and for us—if he doesn't know. Unless you decide it's necessary. That will be your decision. But now I must go." He put on his hat and tugged the brim over his right eye. He embraced Jean, then Simone, wished them both luck, and went out the door.

On a Monday morning a week later Danielle was riding a tram taking her to Villa Air Bel, the house that Varian shared with some of the Centre Américain staff and one or two of their clients who waited for visas. Varian had telephoned that he had a great deal of work to do and decided he could get more done at home, but he needed more help. Marian was already there, but he needed to get the reports for New York finished that afternoon. As Danielle peered out the window, she was alarmed to see several police wagons roar by—filled with what she assumed were refugees. How lucky she was to have a job and a place to live.

She thought of the client she had interviewed before Varian's telephone call, a woman, a Belgian Jew with two children and a sick husband, who had shown Danielle her portfolio of charcoal drawings. "I am an artist, she said, and I heard America is giving visas to artists."

Danielle had wanted to weep. The drawings were amateurish. "These drawings are very nice, Mme, but you are not well known. You are not on the list of famous artists. But we can give you some help." She then had explained that they could give her a stipend for food and lodging while she applied for visas elsewhere. Danielle then led her to Marcel, who handled the accounts and petty cash. Before the war

Marcel had been an accountant in Brittany. He and Fredi were the only other staff members who had turned up this morning.

Gazing out the tram window, Danielle thought about Val. He had left the day before to visit a friend in a nearby village. "I want to get out of here for a few days," he'd said. "Pétain will be passing through here on his way to inspect the port at Toulon. The police will be rounding up anyone they decide looks suspicious."

Jean had left yesterday also, guiding three British soldiers to Banyuls. He'd promised her he'd be particularly careful, since as she knew, anyone aiding men of fighting age to escape France could receive the death penalty. Jean would lead the soldiers to the Fittcos and then return. The Fittcos would then guide the men over the mountains. To her relief, Jean had been able to persuade the officials to give him a travel permit for the month of December, which meant he was entirely en regle. Varian had introduced Jean to Captain Dubois, the chief of police, whom Varian had befriended and who was sympathetic to the plight of the refugees. In fact, Danielle suspected that Dubois was aware of the agency's illegal activities, but chose to look the other way.

She wasn't so sure Dubois would be so tolerant of Jean's work for Frenay. Jean had told her about his meeting with Frenay, how he had suggested she could be recruited to help with the Bulletin. She felt a surge of excitement thinking that she would be a bona fide member of the new resistance movement. She wasn't sure what she'd be doing. At least she could type copy or draw illustrations. Jean would be working on his pieces next week.

Danielle descended from the tram and walked along the rural road to Varian's villa. It was a large house surrounded by a flower-filled garden. A maid answered the door and told her that M. Fry was expecting her and was working in his study upstairs. As Danielle mounted the stairway, she admired the paintings on the wall. André Breton, the artist, was living here—as was Victor Serge, the Russian writer.

Varian greeted her from behind a stack of papers. Marian stopped typing for a moment to say hello. Suddenly, the sounds of angry shouts and sharp cries from below caused all three to freeze. Danielle shot a look at Marian—then Varian. "What's going on?" Varian cried, jumping up from his chair, venturing onto the stair landing. At that moment the maid was running up the stairs. "Police," she cried. "They demand your presence! They're going to search the house!"

Varian quickly picked up a few papers scattered on his desk and threw them into the fire. He then tugged at his tie, straightened his jacket and marched down the stairs. Danielle and Marian crept behind him. When they entered the salon they found three burly men in plain clothes opening drawers, peering behind paintings, lifting up sofa cushions. The largest of the men, who identified himself as Inspector Cardon, thrust a mimeographed paper in front of Varian's nose. "We're authorized to inspect the premises of suspected communists!"

"This is outrageous! I'm an American citizen. And so is this young lady here," and he touched Marian's arm. "We are not communists!" As Varian spoke, one of the police holding a pearl-handled pistol in his hand, escorted Victor Serge into the room, "Sir, this man had a gun in his possession. And no papers for it."

Danielle's eyes were fixed on Serge's trembling form. She had met this middle-aged refugee in the Centre Américain office, but had never seen him under duress. She knew he was a Russian writer who had spent three years in Siberia because of his anti-Stalinist position. He'd been a friend of Trotsky but now disavowed communism. He'd spent months here in France in detention camps.

The second policeman rushed into the room holding a drawing in one hand and the arm of André Breton in the other. "Look, sir, a cartoon of our Maréchal Pétain!" When Danielle glanced at the drawing she could see Pétain's profile superimposed on the image of a rooster. At the bottom of the page was written Le terrible cretín de Pétain.

The burly inspector snapped his fingers. "That settles it. You are all under arrest!" He beckoned to his men. "Put them in the wagon."

Varian's face had turned bright red. "You can't arrest me! I demand to speak to my American Consul. Where is Captain Dubois?"

"I can arrest you, M. Fry, and Captain Dubois is in the field, preparing for the Maréchal's visit. You can speak to the judge at the Evêche."

After permitting them to fetch their coats, the police shoved Varian, Danielle, Marian, André Breton and Victor Serge out the door and into the waiting police wagon. The servants watched as the vehicle raced away, its siren blaring.

# Chapter Fifteen

## Vive le Maréchal

*December, 1940*

The next day when Jean was returning to Marseilles from Banyuls after escorting his charges to the Fittcos, he was shocked to see the cordon of uniformed police lined up along the voie. Dozens of sharp eyes watched him as he strode into the Gare St Charles. Besides the uniformed police, men in dark suits and hats sat on benches scrutinizing each passenger as he or she walked by. Jean tried to be nonchalant, relaxed. And why shouldn't he be? He was en regle. He had his precious travel permit and carried his army discharge papers as well as his carte d'identité. Even so, he decided to duck into the Hotel Terminus and exit onto the side street.

He walked down the Canebiére toward the Centre Américain and was puzzled to see that crowds of people stood along both sides of the boulevard, but the shops and cafés were closed and shuttered. What was going on? Then he remembered that Val had said something about about Pétain's expected visit to Toulon. Maybe Pétain was coming by train, which would explain why Gare St Charles was crammed with police.

When he arrived at the Centre Américain, the stairs were empty. No refugees were waiting to see Varian. Fredi called out to Jean as he entered the office. "Jean. You're OK. Thank God!"

"And why shouldn't I be?" Jean peered around the office and saw only Fredi and Marcel. The other desks were empty. "And where's Danielle?"

"We're not sure." Fredi glanced at Marcel, as if he needed encouragement to speak. He spoke slowly. "All we know is what the maid at Villa Air Bel told us. And André Breton's wife. They said that yesterday when Danielle and Marian were working with Varian at his home, the police barged in, searched the house and arrested Varian, the two girls, Breton and Victor Serge."

"Arrested? Danielle? And Varian and Marian? But why?"

"It's hard to know. Victor was carrying a pistol and had no papers for it, of course. And they found a disrespectful cartoon of Maréchal Pétain in Breton's room."

"A cartoon! They were arrested because Breton had drawn a cartoon!"

"Breton's wife, who wasn't at home during the raid, told us that André had a police record. A few years ago he was arrested as an Anarchist—unjustly, of course, she said. But that may be the reason. And the police decided to pick them all up."

Jean's heart was racing. Had the police found out about Varian's underground activities—or Danielle's connection with the Bulletin? "Are they in jail at Evêche?"

Marcel fixed Jean with a sympathetic glance. "Jean we don't know where they are exactly. Apparently, they were all hauled away from police headquarters in trucks—along with hundreds of others—refugees, gangsters, people on the street. The police have cleaned up the town. They're scared shitless someone will throw a bomb at their beloved Maréchal. They've arrested anyone at all suspicious."

At that moment, from outside the building, a roar of hundreds of voices could be heard above the blare of a military band. Fredi moved to the window overlooking the street below. "He's arrived, our Maréchal! The parade has begun."

Jean and Marcel joined Fredi at the window. The clatter of artillery men on horseback, the rattle of horse-drawn caissons, and the tramping of boots filled the air. Next, three black limousines, tricolors attached to the front fenders, rolled down the boulevard. The crowd burst into frenzied yelling and shouting, waving the tricolor, calling out to their hero, vive le Maréchal! The white-haired, eighty-five year old soldier, with a wool muffler around his neck, waved to the crowd as he passed by.

Jean stared at Pétain, watching the Maréchal's upraised hand, thinking of that hand shaking Hitler's. The thought sickened him. And for this traitor, Danielle had been arrested. He turned to Fredi. "How long will Pétain be here in Marseilles? Do you know?"

Fredi shook his head. "All I know is he's on his way to Toulon— to inspect the mothballed fleet and confer with the Admirals. If he returns through Marseilles on his way back to Vichy they'll keep their prisoners under lock and key until he's on the train home."

"But where are they!"

Fredi was staring out the window. "I'm going to look up a guy I knew in the army. He's a policeman here. He might know where they've been taken."

Marcel pointed below. "Good God, look at the bicycle troop!"

Fredi shook his head in disbelief. "The emasculated French army! Mounted artillery, horse-drawn caissons, a bicycle troop? Remember the German tanks in the Ardenne? And the Messerschmidts at Dunkirk? What is Pétain thinking of?"

"Betrayal!" Jean said firmly.

Danielle and Marian were huddled in a ship's cabin where they were ordered to remain. Five other women shared the cramped, stuffy space, smelling of unwashed bodies. Danielle's stomach growled with hunger and she hadn't washed or changed clothes for over twenty-four hours. There was no water to wash in and the toilet they shared with three other cabins was already overflowing. The stench made her gag.

And why were they being kept here? After spending ten hours at Evêche, the police station, they had been loaded into a truck and taken to the commercial docks where this rusty old ocean liner was moored. She had noted the name as they were herded up the gangplank, the SS Sinaia. The women were housed in third class cabins, and the men in the hold. Until an hour ago they all had been allowed on deck where they could breath clean, cool air. Nobody would tell them what they were charged with or when they would be released. Varian had asked to speak to the American Consul, but had been refused. In fact, the guards wouldn't answer any questions, and nobody seemed to be in charge.

As Danielle slumped on a lower bunk squeezed between Marian and a woman from Alsace, named Jeanette, she thought about her parents and Jean. Jean would have returned from Banyuls by now. Would he find out they were on this ship. Maybe he could help them somehow. Danielle turned to Marian. "My parents will be frantic. They won't know what has happened to me—or where where I am. Do you think the police will let them know? I asked them to."

Marian's face was drawn and the skin under her eyes looked bruised with fatigue. "There are too many of us. The police don't care." She took hold of Danielle's hand. "You know, if we ever get out of here, I've just decided it's time for me to go home. My parents don't even know I've disappeared!"

Danielle squeezed Marian's hand. She didn't know how to respond. It was time for them all to flee France. And Marian was an American. She had a magical American passport in her very own name. She didn't have to be here. She had just been trying to help people. Marian really must go home. How she'd miss her. Danielle gave a deep sigh. They didn't even know <u>why</u> they were prisoners.

At the police station nobody had told them anything. Breton was interrogated repeatedly, but his questioners didn't inform him of why they were all arrested. Hundreds of people. Maybe thousands. Why! At least the Jews among the prisoners had not been segregated. The police had looked only briefly at her documents. They'd all been loaded like cattle into the trucks and then the ship.

After a long day shut up in their cabin, the women were allowed out on deck. The men were also released from their dismal, stinking captivity in the hold. Both men and women walked in the cold air, peering at the shore, bewildered, frightened, some muttering angrily. Danielle and Marian found Varian gripping the deck railing, staring out at the city. A sharp wind blew from the north. Danielle shivered, but breathed deeply of the clean air. She gave Varian a hug, which he awkwardly returned. She noted that Victor Serge had found a spot under a lifeboat where he huddled. Breton sat on the deck leaning against the bulkhead, hugging his knees for warmth. But how long would they be held here?

A gaunt, middle-aged man standing next to Varian, his brow furrowed, murmured quietly, "I've heard they're going to take us to North Africa. Forced labor. That's why they've put us in a ship."

Danielle's heart shrank. Varian shook his head. "Surely, not."

But Danielle caught the stricken expression in Varian's eyes. The man might be right. Why else would so many people be rounded up?

Varian suddenly touched Marian's arm. "Marian, we must try to reach Vice Consul Bingham. And somehow we have to get to the captain. Inform him we're American citizens. They have no right to treat us this way."

Danielle eyed the deck, searching for a guard or a sailor they could approach, but none were in sight. She counted three police on the dock below. The gangplank had been removed. There was no way to escape this huge ocean liner.

Marian pointed to an empty wine bottle next to the bulkhead. "I have an idea!" she said, picking up the bottle. "We'll write a note, stuff it into the bottle and drop it over the side. Someone might find it!"

Varian gave a wry smile. "Marian, you're a romantic."

"Well, in the story books it works!"

Danielle stared at the bottle. Clear glass. She picked it up, removed the cork and shook out the remains of the wine. Then she laughed. "Why not? Let's try it. Varian, you write the note."

Varian shook his head, muttering that it most certainly was a futile gesture, but reached into his shirt pocket for his pen. "What do I use for paper?"

"Newspaper," Danielle cried. "Look." She pulled a scrap of newsprint from the pocket of her coat. She didn't mention that she'd kept it as toilet paper.

Marian turned her back to Varian. "Write on my back, OK?"

"OK, Marian. I'll address it to Harry Bingham. He's the only official at the American Consulate who might help us."

Varian scribbled onto the newsprint, then rolled the note into a tube. "I'll wrap a hundred franc note around it. Maybe someone will notice. And actually deliver it. Probably not, but it's worth a try!"

He inserted the wrapped note into the bottle, replaced the cork and dropped it over the side of the ship into the water. All three stood side by side at the railing, watching the bottle bob on the surface of the water and inch toward the dock. Danielle grinned. "I guess we should make a wish!"

At nightfall they were herded once more into the cabins and hold. Varian yelled at the guards who shoved him down the companionway. "I demand to speak to the American consul! And the captain of this ship. You have no right!" but the guard merely shoved him harder down the stairway to the hold. Breton and Serge followed more slowly.

The next afternoon on the deck Danielle heard someone calling Varian's name. As Varian stepped forward a man in maritime uniform approached him. "Are you Varian Fry?"

"Yes," Varian said, hesitantly.

"And Marian Dolan?"

Marian held up her hand.

"You're both American citizens?"

"Yes! We are!" Varian's tone was firm.

"You are to come to the captain's cabin. A M. Bingham is here to see you."

Marian gave Danielle a quick hug. Varian touched Danielle's arm. "I'll see if I can get us all released, Danielle. Wait here." He and Marian followed the officer up the stairs to the Bridge. Danielle's eyes followed them until they disappeared. How lucky they were to be American, she thought. Here she was, French, on a French ship in a French city and had nobody who could help her. And now she was alone. Jean would be looking for her—as would her father—but they had no clout. So she waited, finding it difficult to keep back her tears. She eyed the deck for André and Victor, but they were not in sight. Varian had told her to stay here, and that's what she would do. She tugged her coat close to her body and sat on the cold metal deck, leaning her back against the bulkhead opposite the railing where they had dropped the bottle.

After an hour, a laughing Marian came running toward her, lugging a loaded wicker basket. Two baguettes poked up from its opening. Varian appeared with wine bottles clutched to his chest. "Danielle, look. Food. Wine. A boy actually found the bottle, read the note and took it to the American consulate."

"Will they let us go?" Danielle asked, stiffly rising from the cold deck, a puff of hope lifting her heart.

"I'm afraid not, but the captain doesn't think it will be too much longer. But he told us why we're here. We've all been rounded up because Maréchal Pétain came through town on his way to Toulon to inspect the fleet, After he returns they'll probably let us go."

She heard the word probably. "Did you ask M. Bingham to tell my parents where we are?"

"Yes. He'll call the Centre Américain and request them to inform relatives and friends where we're being held."

Danielle gave Varian a hug and then put her arms around Marian. "What a relief. That bottle really worked. Marian, you're a genius!"

By now André and Victor had appeared. Varian pulled a wine bottle opener from his pocket. "Courtesy of Harry Bingham" he said laughing. He opened the wine and handed it to Marian. "No glasses, but we'll just pass it around!"

Danielle eyed Varian. She had never seen him so loose. The tightness had vanished—for the moment at least. They sat on the deck and drank wine and feasted on bread and cheese, sharing it with others. Soon it was gone, but they continued to sing bawdy French songs until they were forced to go back to their quarters.

They were held on the creaking old ship two more days. On the next to the last day they were forced to remain the entire day locked up in the cabins and hold once more. The next morning they were all processed and released. In the midst of the horde of former prisoners trudging down the gangplank, Danielle walked behind Varian, hungry, dirty, and disheveled. Varian was muttering to himself. "Searched without a warrant, arrested without a warrant, never informed of our charges, kept incommunicado, released without an explanation. What a country!"

Before they reached the quai, Danielle heard her name being called. Jean was waving to her standing next to her parents and brother David. Then she spied Harry Bingham pushing his way through the crowd, waving at Varian.

Bingham was apologetic. "Varian, I tried hard, believe me, to get you released, but the whole affair was a bureaucratic mess. And all the top officials were with the Maréchal." He then touched Marian's arm. "I'm so sorry you had to be subjected to such barbarous treatment."

Varian gave him a weary look. "Barbarous is the word. But the wine and food helped, Harry. We're grateful."

Bingham then shook hands with Danielle, who introduced him to her parents.

Maurice was frowning. "If only the officials had told us where they'd taken the prisoners. So many people were rounded up. And we heard hundreds of horror stories. Then Jean told me where you were—but we knew your wouldn't be released until Pétain returned from Toulon."

Jean encircled Danielle's waist. "Fredi found out where you were held—before the message got to M. Bingham."

Bingham shot Jean a strange look. "Good for Fredi. I couldn't find anyone who would talk to me. The officials in charge were all in the field."

Varian was moving along the quai to the street. "Well, it's over. Now I want a bath."

Bingham took his arm. "I have my car. Let me give you a ride to your Villa."

"Thank you, that would be most kind. But I see Breton and Serge coming toward us. Do you have room for them too?"

"Of course," Bingham said with a troubled smile.

Danielle and Marian embraced Varian and watched as the four men walked toward Bingham's waiting car. Monique then insisted that Marian and Jean come with Danielle to their apartment for lunch. "And we'll heat some water so you girls can bathe." As they trudged wearily toward the tram, Danielle looked over her shoulder at the rusty ship. It was over! Or was it? Was it just the beginning?

# Chapter Sixteen

## Val

*Marseilles, December, 1940, January, 1941*

A week after Pétain's disruptive visit, Jean and Val were proceeding cautiously along the docks of the Vieux Port. Although it was early evening, not more than eight o-clock, it was as dark as midnight. The blue-painted street lights cast a ghostly glow on the black, oily water below. Cracks of light edged café windows facing the dock but did little to illuminate the quai. Jean and Val had just left Frederick Dasch's apartment, and Val was carrying a briefcase stuffed with Dasch's forged Belgian and Danish passports. Nervously, one or the other of the two men shot glances behind them.

After Jean made sure there was no one near enough to eavesdrop, he glanced at Val and spoke quietly. "Has Varian come up with any ideas about where we should hide these passports—and the money we get from Dmitri?"

Val shrugged. "Not yet. Certainly, the Centre Américain is no longer safe—unless we invent a clever hiding place. Varian's Villa is out—not after the police raid."

"Varian told me Captain Dubois warned him he was under surveillance. He wants us to keep checking for bugs and watching what we say on our phones. They've picked up Frier, caught him while he was working on his forgeries."

"Yeah, I know. It's that Inspector Cardon. He despises us all. And he's violently anti-semitic."

Jean gestured to the briefcase in Val's hand. "What are we going to do with these?"

"I'm thinking. Let's go over to the office. I have a key. We'll figure something out."

As they continued toward the commercial docks, Jean heard a clamor of men's voices and the drone of machinery ahead of them in the darkness—and then an eerie chorus of cries. As they drew closer, light from the ship illuminated the scene. Bleating sheep were being lowered from the hold of the ship by a crane, then herded up a ramp into freight cars by German soldiers. A long train stretched out on the tracks by the quai. A French flag was painted on the prow of the ship.

Jean touched Val's shoulder and whispered. "Stay here. I want to get a closer look at what else they're loading." Jean crouched low and crept forward in the shadows, making sure his own shadow wasn't visible. When he reached the spot on the quai where the boxes were stacked, he could see they were filled with wine, dates and figs—from Algeria, Vichy's north African province, he speculated. Sheep and God knows what else were being loaded on that train headed for Germany. French food and wool was being consumed by the enemy. Jean felt a volcano of rage surge through his blood. Those fucking bastards!

Cautiously, Jean darted back to where Val was hiding.

"Let's get out of here," Val whispered, and the two men backed slowly away from the ship. At a safe distance, they turned and walked rapidly away from the port.

Later that evening Jean began to type pieces for the Bulletin. He'd bought his own JAPY portable typewriter at the flea market the week before. He worked at the scarred green-painted table under the electric light bulb that hung from the ceiling. Since Frenay appointed Simone head of the Marseilles resistance movement, Jean felt it was no longer appropriate for him to use Simone's apartment as his headquarters. His own tiny room would have to do. It was time he organized his own staff, his cell, for this district. He smiled to himself. So far his only recruit was Danielle. He'd asked Val, but Val had put him off. "I might have to run at any moment. And I have my American visa, remember?"

He was considering Fredi—or maybe Marcel. In the meantime, he'd do most of it himself. The Bulletin was only three pages, after all. But now he must get to work. The scene at the dock was what he wanted to write about first.

His fingers tapped rapidly on the keys. He described what he and Val had seen at the dock that evening. The people of Marseilles, he typed, had little to eat and wore threadbare clothing, while German soldiers would be dining opulently and dressed in warm woolen uniforms.

Jean stopped typing and leaned back in his wooden chair. He reached for his pack of Gauloises, which was almost empty. Cigarettes were difficult to find and he was rationing himself. He thought of those bleating sheep and their pelts of wool. Hitler had postponed his invasion of England, although the bombing was continuing—but Hitler's soldiers would need winter uniforms. German troops had just entered Romania. Were they preparing to invade Russia? A Russian invasion was speculation, of course. A herd of sheep didn't necessarily imply Hitler would attack his supposed ally.

He lit the cigarette with his lighter and picked up the typewritten pages he'd finished the night before. He'd written accounts of news events that had occurred in the last two weeks. He'd described the incarceration of people during Pétain's visit—20,000 of them—that they had been locked up for three days on rusting ships, sports arenas or barracks without being charged with a crime.

He'd also reported news of the Italians' defeat by the British at Tobruk and the re-election of Franklin Roosevelt in the United States. It was hoped Roosevelt would lead America to join the fight against Nazism.

Jean sighed. Tomorrow evening Danielle had agreed to come and type a clean copy of his work and help him with the layout before he delivered it to the printer. When he thought of the danger he was exposing Danielle to, he felt a stab of remorse. He shouldn't have listened to her pleading to join the movement, but he couldn't resist.

He stubbed out his cigarette. There was nothing he could do about it now. They would just have to be vigilant, watch every step, be smarter than the police or the Germans. He gathered the typewritten papers together and slid them under the false bottom he'd fixed in the drawer of the table. He then packed the JAPY into its case and stowed it into the back of the heavy armoire. And now to sleep!

Two days later Danielle was at her desk interviewing a new client when the sound of raised voices at the entrance to the office caused her to pause in mid-sentence. She glanced around the room. Fredi and Marcel were at their desks and Varian was going over some work with Marian at the table in the center of the large room. Danielle knew that Jean was on an errand picking up money from Dmitri. Suddenly, blond Charlie, the newest and youngest member of the staff, an American, burst into the room. He rushed to Varian's side, his eyes frantic. "The inspector is looking for Val!" he whispered. Behind Charlie, Inspector Cardon swaggered into the room, his short, stocky form looking bear-like in his brown overcoat and gray fedora. He was followed by three uniformed gendarmes. Danielle shivered, pulling her blue cardigan close to her body. Inspector Cardon was the officer who arrested them at Villa Air Bel during Pétain's visit.

Varian rose from the chair and adjusted his glasses. "Well, Inspector, we meet again. What can I do for you? What is it this time?"

The Inspector scowled and thrust an official-looking paper under Varian's eyes. "I have a warrant for the arrest of Jean Valleron. He works here at your agency, does he not, M. Fry?"

Varian shot Cardon an icy look. "I'm sorry, Monsieur Inspector. M. Valleron left our employ two weeks ago. I don't know where he is. I'm afraid I can't help you."

The Inspector stared at Varian then glanced around the room. He beckoned to the three uniformed police. "My men will inspect the premises," and he gave Varian a crooked smile. "To make sure that unknown to you he didn't return."

"I assure you, Inspector, Jean Valleron is not here. But go ahead. Look for him. You won't find him."

The three police quickly went through the three other rooms and returned, shaking their heads. "Not here," the tallest one said.

The inspector shrugged. "I will find that Gaullist traitor, never fear. A bientot, M. Fry."

"Au revoir, M. Inspector," Varian answered, his face impassive.

The Inspector turned on his heel and marched out the door.

The entire staff remained speechless until the pounding of footsteps on the stairs receded. The refugees who had avoided eye contact with the dread policeman gradually stopped trembling. Varian whipped his handkerchief from his breast pocket and dabbed at his brow. Without a word, he strode briskly into his office.

Danielle quickly finished the interview with her client. She found it impossible to concentrate. Her hands were shaking. She knew that Val had left the day before for Banyuls with four clients—all who carried forged passports. He would be due back this afternoon. She thought of Varian. How smoothly he had lied to the Inspector. Did the Inspector believe him? And why was Val being arrested? Had Dmitri betrayed him? Or had Frier, the forger, divulged his name under interrogation? Or torture?

Then she thought about Jean. Jean would be bringing back his musette filled with francs. She knew he and Val had fixed up a new hiding place for the cash and the passports. A reasonable amount of money or gold could be kept in the safe behind the poster, but the police could force Varian to open it. They had bought two large paintings, seascapes, at the flea market and made cardboard backs that could be removed and replaced easily with metal clips. Between the canvas of the painting and the cardboard they taped envelopes of francs and passports. They'd hung the two paintings in Varian's office.

At that moment Jean was pedaling down the Canebiére with his musette on his back stuffed with francs. As he approached the Centre Américain he saw a police wagon pulling away from the curb. Sitting next to the uniformed driver, he recognized Inspector Cardon. Jean quickly continued down the boulevard and turned onto a side street. Feigning nonchalance he dismounted from his bike and wheeled it into a small café. He bought a newspaper, ordered coffee—and pretended to read. He slid the musette from his back and rested it on his lap. He remained in the café for twenty minutes or so, watching the street over the edge of his newspaper. When he considered it safe, he finished his coffee, slung his musette over his shoulders, and wheeled his bike onto the street.

Keeping alert for police, he cautiously rode again to the Centre. He left the bike with the concierge and ran up the stairs into the office. His eyes sought out Danielle, who had risen from her desk. She didn't speak, but took hold of his arm, gave him a warning look, and guided him into Varian's office. Varian shut the door, then quickly removed the poster on the wall and opened the safe. Silently, Jean placed his musette on Varian's desk and deposited it's contents in Varian's hands. Varian separated one of the bundles of francs, stuffed it in his pocket and placed the rest in the safe. He then reached into the back of the safe for an envelope which he placed on his desk. Giving both Jean and Danielle a meaningful glance, he switched on the radio on the shelf behind him and turned up the volume. Orchestral music blared from the set. Jean was familiar with the maneuver, knowing the sound of the radio music would mask their conversation. "I'll store the cash in the paintings after we close," Varian murmured.

Not until he had locked the safe and re-hung the poster, did he lean close, and in a low voice, describe Cardon's visit to Jean. "We've got to get hold of Val. His train should arrive from Perpignon in about an hour. Jean, will you go to the gare and warn him?"

It took a moment for Jean to recover from shock. He shot a glance at Danielle and saw the fright and pain in her blue eyes. "Yes, of course I'll go. Do you want him to come here?" Like Varian, he spoke softly.

"It would be wiser if he doesn't. He has his American visa in lieu of a passport. He needs to get out of Marseilles as quickly as possible. Tell him I'll see him in New York—or California. And here. Give him these." And he reached into his pocket for the packet of francs. For expenses—bribes, tickets, whatever." Then he handed Jean the envelope he'd placed on his desk. "Dollars for when he gets to the States. He's a client, after all—as well as an employee. And wish him luck!"

Jean was dazed by Varian's words, stunned. But what had happened? Who had betrayed them? "Did Cardon tell you why Val was to be arrested?"

"Unfortunately, no. But he didn't ask about any of the others on our staff. Perhaps the Gestapo caught up with him somehow." He glanced at the radio and lowered his voice to almost a whisper. "He's German, after all, an anti-Nazi, and has been surviving with a forged French identity for months."

The phrase, forged papers caused Jean's heart to jump. He'd grown so used to being Jean Barrault he'd almost forgotten his true identity, Gino Baroli. Gino Baroli had become a stranger to him.

Varian peered at his watch then opened the door to his office. "Jean, you should get to the gare—just in case he comes in on an earlier train. We've got to stop him."

Jean nodded, picked up his musette and touched Danielle's shoulder. "I'll meet you here later, OK?" He fixed his eyes on hers.

"I'll be waiting." Danielle said quietly.

Jean raced down the stairs. He walked to Gare St Charles and found a bench on which to wait where he could keep his eye on both the door to the station and the big board that announced which voie where the trains would arrive. He didn't want to believe what was happening to Val—or to himself. Somewhere in his center he was feeling a hollowness. He'd always known Val would have to leave, but obviously he hadn't truly believed it. The same was true for Danielle. She must go soon. Cardon and his buddies were clamping down on them all. Soon they'd be interning Jews. Pétain and Laval were bending to the Germans' will. He shook his head. He wouldn't think about that at the moment. Now he had to concentrate on Val.

A half hour later the Perpignan train chugged onto voie six. Jean scrutinized the passengers as they descended from the cars. Finally, he caught sight of Val's tall, sturdy form. He strode toward him and took hold of his arm. Val peered at Jean, his light blue eyes alert. "Somethings wrong? What is it!"

"I'll tell you in a minute," Jean murmured into his ear. He then led Val into the Hotel Terminus to a sofa in the lobby where they sat side by side. After checking to make sure nobody could hear him, he blurted the bad news into Val's ear. "You've got to leave Marseilles," he murmured. "Cardon has a warrant for your arrest. Do you have your papers, your visa?"

With a sharp intake of breath Val nodded. He tapped his right shoulder. "Sewn under the lining of my coat," he said, quietly. "The U. S. visa in lieu of a passport."

"Good." Jean surreptitiously handed him the roll of francs and the envelope of dollars. Val quickly shoved the francs into his pocket and the envelope into his backpack. Jean locked eyes with Val. "Where will you go? The Pyrenees? You'll need transit visas. You can't get them here. They'll be watching for you. Is there anything I can do?"

Val shook his head. "I've got to think. I'll go to Toulouse. They don't know me there. And somehow I'll get transit visas." He indicated his pocket where he'd stowed the francs. "Then back to Banyuls." He grinned. "I guess I know the way!"

"I guess you do!" Jean gave him a wan smile. "But take care. You know that Madrid and Lisbon are crawling with Gestapo and Abwehr agents."

"Have no fear. I can smell them a mile off!"

Within an hour Val had boarded the train for Toulouse. Jean stood on the platform, a stone in his heart, watching the train back down the track. "Good luck," he whispered as the train disappeared, "God be with you."

# Chapter Seventeen

## Corelli's

*Marseilles, February, 1941*

It was a Sunday afternoon, and Danielle and Jean hurried along the quai of the Vieux Port where they would meet Varian and some of the Centre staff for lunch. Although the sun was shining in a brilliant blue sky, the wind was cold and Danielle tugged the collar of her old camel hair coat against her neck. The air smelled of seaweed and fish. Jean walked close beside her, holding tightly to her bent elbow,

Danielle was curious about the restaurant where they were to meet Varian. It was owned by a gangster named Corelli. Varian had moved to the Beaumont Hotel, which was also owned by Corelli. As they approached the restaurant, Danielle turned to Jean. "Did Varian ever tell you why he chose the Beaumont?"

Jean grinned. "For the food. Corelli deals in the black market and gets supplies for his restaurant. And fake ration stamps. He and Dmitri are buddies—or rivals—I don't know which. Also, I wouldn't be surprised if Corelli has some arrangement with the police. Most of them are corrupt. Maybe Varian feels protected."

Danielle was puzzled by Varian's ability to deal with gangsters like Corelli and Dmitri. Varian's manners were so proper, his character so upright, it was odd, indeed. She'd decided he was so dedicated to saving his clients he could bend his rules. She smiled to herself. She supposed he also appreciated a good French meal. "I was surprised Varian left the Villa Air Bel. It's such a beautiful house."

"I think after his arrest he was nervous about his tenants. André Breton is charming, but he does have a police record and is under surveillance. Victor Serge is a well-known Trotskyite—and even though he's left the Party, the police consider him a potential terrorist. Varian needs to distance himself from them for a while. He's already in enough trouble."

A seagull swept over her head and landed on a post on the pier they were passing. It stared at Danielle with beady eyes, reminding her of Inspector Cardon. "You mean trouble with the police or the New York Committee?"

"Both. Besides the police, it seems that Consul Fullerton reported the Sinaia incident to the State Department, which then got back to the Committee. He hinted that Varian was arrested because of his illegal activities."

Danielle gave a wry laugh. "Which he is, of course,"

"Fullerton would love to get rid of Varian. Get him recalled. That guy does everything in his power to prevent refugees getting to to the U.S. Especially Jews, by the way. Or suspected Communists."

Now they were now at the door of Corelli's restaurant. The air was redolent with the fragrance of garlic, thyme and lavender. Suddenly, Danielle felt famished. She wouldn't think about American visas for a while—or consuls. They were about to have a truly good lunch.

They entered and immediately spied Varian at a corner table. Fredi and Marian were sitting on either side of Varian, and Charlie was hanging up his coat. Varian had told her he'd decided to meet with them here at the restaurant instead of their conference room. He was afraid the police would bug their office or put informers on his staff. Charlie, another American, was the newest member Varian trusted to take on some of their underground maneuvers. Charlie was younger than Danielle, only twenty-one. He was tall and athletic and had a thick shock of blond hair that fell over his brow. He greeted Danielle and Jean with a broad grin and mischievous eyes.

After hearty salutations they all settled in their chairs. Varian peered at Jean with a pleased look. "Jean, you're back, I see. Any problems?"

"None. The Brits took off from the Fittcos at 3:30 in the morning with Hans, as usual. Hans had returned before I left for Perpignan. He said they made it to the border in three hours and he watched the boys turn themselves in to the Spanish officials." Jean's face lit up. "But Varian, I have good news about Val. Hans told me Val made it to Port Bou and got through without a hitch. Hans was watching from above."

Varian beamed. "Thank God. He should be on a ship to the States by now."

"Let's hope so. Apparently he got his transit visas in Toulouse and then took the train back to Banyuls. The next morning he crossed into Spain!"

The waiter appeared at the table with a bottle of Bordeaux and poured a portion into Varian's glass. Varian tasted it and nodded. "C'a va." While the waiter poured wine for the others, Varian glanced around the table. "I hope you'll approve, but I've already ordered our lunch." He lifted his wine glass. "Santé"

They all responded and sipped their wine. Marian then spoke up. "I have an announcement to make. I've already told Varian, but I have to tell the rest of you that my papers are in order and I'll be leaving for Lisbon in two weeks."

"So soon!" Danielle exclaimed. She knew Marian was preparing to go home, but had tried not to think about it. First Val. Now Marian.

Varian touched Marian's hand. "I'm not sure what we'll do without you, Marian."

Tears filled Marian's eyes. "I don't know what I'll do without all of you! I'll miss you all terribly. But it's time for me to go home. The police. . ." She shook her head with an angry gesture. "And my parents have been after me for months to come home. They sent me a ticket to fly home on Pan American from Lisbon. So I'm going."

With solemn faces her co-workers offered her their best wishes. Danielle forced a smile. "You'll be able to look up some of our clients. Maybe Val."

Marian gave a wan smile. "He'll be in California. I'll be in New York. "Danielle, I don't think you realize just how long 3,000 miles can be on a train."

"Maybe you can fly?"

"I'd have to rob a bank!"

By now the tension had eased and they all sipped their wine and welcomed the first dish the waiter brought, plates of paté de compagne and a basket of fresh bread. Fredi whooped. "I can't remember the last time I saw paté!" He turned to Varian. "Our M. Corelli must know the right people!"

Varian shot Fredi a wry smile. "I'm afraid he does! But while we're enjoying this largesse I want to tell you my incredible news. I was just informed yesterday that our local prefecture is now issuing exit visas! Our clients no longer have to apply in Vichy—and suddenly, they are readily available—for almost everyone."

At Varian's words, the staff cheered heartily and lifted their wine glasses.

"Before we become too euphoric I must tell you that the police are refusing a few people, but I've managed to. . ." and he lowered his voice, "to get that list. So we'll know who still must go the Fittco route."

Danielle glanced around the table at her colleagues. Their serious expressions showed they understood the meaning of Varian's words. The Fittco route meant forged passports, transit visas and a freezing climb over the icy mountain trail to Spain.

Varian set down his wine glass and cut a piece of paté and spread it on a chunk of bread. "And I have other news. Our friend, Peggy Guggenheim has donated 50,000 francs to our agency, which means we can purchase tickets for the passenger ship that sails to Martinique. From there our clients can get to America, Cuba and Mexico."

An expression that almost looked like shock appeared in the faces around the table. Suddenly, a new escape route had opened up. Danielle knew that most of their clients in danger of arrest by the Gestapo had already left France. A few remained, but Varian would find a way for them, also—she was sure of that. She thought of her parents and herself. They had French passports and if they ever received their U.S. visas they would have no problem getting exit visas—or transit visas if they decided to leave from Lisbon.

The waiter then appeared carrying aloft a large platter containing a baked fish. "Bass", he said, "with garlic sauce." Another waiter brought a large bowl of ratatouille and set in on the table. They all watched as the first waiter skillfully de-boned and served the fish.

After the waiters departed, and they all forked morsels of bass into their mouths, Varian paused and glanced at Danielle. "In spite of our good news, we know that we are facing very rough times ahead for our Jewish clients—and staff. Police raids and arrests of Jews are increasing. Vichy is cooperating with Hitler."

Fredi set down his wine glass. "Varian, I'm concerned about the Chagalls. Can't you persuade them to leave?"

Varian shrugged. "I hope so. Two days ago M. Chagall was picked up by the police. I called Inspector Cardon and told him in no uncertain terms that to arrest such a famous artist would bring on an international deluge of criticism and shame on the city. Chagall was released."

"So is he now willing to leave France?"

"I repeat, I hope so. André Breton has also decided the time has come to leave his beloved country. Both the Bretons and the Chagalls have U.S. visas. Victor Serge will sail to Martinique, but he's been refused an American visa. He's agreed to go to Mexico—and we obtained him a visa."

Varian paused to spoon a serving of ratatouille from the bowl the waiter had set before him. "It would seem we'll have our work cut out for us—and without Marian here—or Val. We need to recruit more staff. People trustworthy and dedicated. If you know anyone please let me know. But now, let's enjoy our meal!"

Danielle savored her bass and the eggplant and garlic ratatouille, consuming every scrap on her plate. She and Jean exchanged happy glances and the conversation amongst the diners was lively. When they were ready to leave, Varian asked Danielle and Jean to stay a moment.

After the others had left, Varian resumed his seat at the table. He removed his glasses, whisked his handkerchief from his breast pocket and polished the lenses before he spoke. He replaced the glasses and adjusted the nose piece. "Danielle, I have news for you. Both good and bad."

Danielle's pulse quickened. Had he heard about their visas? She stopped breathing a moment. "Is it about our visas?"

"Yes," Varian replied, quietly. "Your parents' and brother's visas can be issued at the consulate Monday."

"My parents? And David's—but..."

"Unfortunately, they refused your application. They didn't say why. I will try my best to get them to reconsider, but I'm no longer popular with the State Department. . . I'm so sorry Danielle."

Danielle felt as if an icy wind had blown through the room. Jean grasped her hand and fastened his eyes on hers.

Varian slowly folded his handkerchief and tucked it into his pocket. "Or, Danielle, we could apply for Cuban or Mexican visas—or to the the Dominican Republic."

Danielle straightened her spine. "I must go and tell my parents their good news, And Varian, I will stay and work with you until it's no longer safe for me to do so. Like Val. When it's time for me to get away from Marseilles I'll find a village somewhere—in the mountains perhaps." She lifted her chin.

Jean rose from his chair and pulled Danielle to her feet. "And I'll be with you."

# Chapter Eighteen

## Visas

*Marseilles, February, 1941*

Danielle hesitated before opening the door to her parents' apartment. She locked eyes with Jean. "You'll need to help me, Jean. Help me stay calm. A storm is about to hit!" She'd been trying to decide whether to blurt out the news about the visas in one fell swoop—the good and the bad—or to proceed in stages. She knew her parents wouldn't want to leave her here alone, that they would want to wait for Varian to ask again about her own visa, but she would be adamant. They must leave the moment they acquired all the paperwork.

She pushed open the door and walked briskly inside. Maurice was working at the table under the window he used as a desk, and her mother sat in her usual chair mending a shirt of David's. Sprawled face-down on the floor, David was reading. All three looked up with surprise as she entered.

"We didn't expect you!" Monique cried. She jumped up from her chair and they all exchanged hugs and kisses. "Have you eaten? We've just finished our lunch, but can I fix you something? Would you like something to drink?"

"No, Maman, we just came from lunch with Varian—at Corelli's."

"Well then, sit down and tell us about it." Monique picked up the shirt she was mending and they all sat around the small room. Danielle perched on the edge of the sofa, unable to relax. Jean sat close beside her.

Maurice raised his eyebrows. "Corelli's did you say? Alors, you ate well, I imagine."

Danielle forced a smile. "Yes, we certainly did. But we have news, Papa, and I'm bursting to tell you."

Monique gave Danielle a sharp look. "News? What kind of news?" Then she glanced at Jean, which Danielle realized meant that her mother was thinking the announcement had something to do with her relationship with Jean.

"It's news about your visas. Varian has heard from New York. Papa, tomorrow you must go to the American consulate and get your American visas!"

Monique jumped up from her chair, dropping her mending, and pulling Danielle from her chair, hugged her tightly. "At last! We can leave!" She then hugged Jean. Maurice embraced them both, shouting with joy. David was hopping around crazily. "We're going to America!" he chanted repeatedly.

Danielle watched them, feeling a tempest of conflicting emotions sweep through her. She could hardly breathe. Her family would be safe. They could start a new life, but she would be left behind. She would be alone.

Maurice was staring at her quizzically. "Danielle, what's wrong. Is there something you're not telling us?"

Danielle exchanged looks with Jean. The words stuck in her throat. She couldn't tell them. She gave Jean a pleading look. "Jean will you tell them, please."

Jean took a deep breath. "What Danielle is having so much trouble telling you is this. Her application for the American visa was refused. Varian said no explanation was given for the refusal. He was going to send another request to the Committee to apply again, but he doesn't believe they'll respond to his request."

Maurice and Monique stared at Danielle with stunned eyes. Abruptly, Monique slumped onto the chair and burst into tears. After a moment she lifted her head and stopped crying. "I'll stay here with you, Danielle. I can't leave without you."

"Maurice moved to her side. "We'll both stay. Until we find a way out for you. We can all try for Cuba or the Dominican Republic. But David should go to America. He's old enough. Our friends in Berkeley will help him."

David shook his head. "No!"

Danielle stamped her foot. She shouted in anger. "You will go! You will go to America and make a life for us there! I will join you when I can. I'm no longer a child. I want to stay in France and fight the Germans."

Jean put his arm over her shoulders. "And I'll be with her. We'll be together. I'll look after her."

Maurice stared at Jean—then Danielle. "You don't know what you're talking about. Do you truly know what the Nazis are doing to Jews in Germany. And now in Vichy. They're commanding us to register. In the occupied zone Jews are being rounded up and thrown in detention camps—where they die. No, Danielle, you must leave— go to Cuba—anywhere but here. If you want to fight the Germans go to America or Canada."

"Papa, please. Please go tomorrow to the American consulate with your passports. Then get your Spanish and Portuguese transit visas. The prefecture of police is issuing exit visas and travel passes. You could go by train to Port Bou. You don't need to cross the Pyrenees on foot. You would be completely en regle. Think of Maman, of David."

Maurice paced the room. No one spoke. After a few moments Maurice turned and faced Danielle. "Danielle, the American State department won't give visas to known Communists. Think carefully, do you have some connection with a communist group? That boyfriend of yours in Paris? Or anyone at the Centre Américain?"

"No, Papa. The boys in Paris were not members of the Party. And as far as I know none of the Centre staff is communist. Varian certainly isn't"

Jean stepped forward. "Maurice, I doubt if the State department has investigated her background." He hesitated. "Unless it has to do with the arrest when Pétain was here—but that seems unlikely. It must be a fluke, a mistake."

Maurice sank onto a chair and put his head in his hands.

"We'll keep trying to get her a visa. Jean continued. "She could join you later, And once you are there you would be in a better position to plead with the State Department to reconsider her case."

Monique rose and stood behind Maurice. "Maurice, maybe they're right. Once we are in America, as Jean says, out friends—your colleagues—will help us get her a visa. They are well-known physicists." She moved toward Jean. "And Jean, somehow I trust you. I believe you will do your best to protect Danielle."

"You can be sure of that!" Jean said firmly. "I love your daughter."

"And I love Jean, but really, Maman, Jean, I'm perfectly capable of protecting myself. I'm a modern woman. This is the twentieth century."

Maurice stared at Danielle with an expression of disbelief. His voice was thick with sarcasm. "Yes, this wonderful twentieth century." He then shouted at her. "The only way to protect yourself is to escape from this cursed continent."

He turned away from her, then suddenly threw up his hands in a gesture of defeat. "Danielle," he said, not meeting her eyes, "it's possible Jean is right. We could fight from within the United States to extract you from this inferno—with the help of our American colleagues."

He moved toward her and placed both hands on her shoulders, holding her at arms' length, looking directly into her eyes. "I will go tomorrow to the blessed American consulate with our passports. Your mother, David and I will leave this cursed country and abandon you to your fate."

Danielle threw herself into her father's arms and he held her tightly. Tears streamed down their cheeks. Monique stood sobbing quietly while Jean and David each stared down at the floor.

As they rode the crowded tram to Danielle's flat, the couple barely spoke. Jean gripped Danielle's hand in his, but he kept replaying the scene he'd just witnessed. It had been heartrending. And there had been Maurice's questioning Danielle about her past involvement with communists. Could he, Jean, be to blame? For the last few months his own connection with the Comintern agent, Paul, had vanished from his mind—almost as if it hadn't happened. He had convinced himself that Paul had disappeared or had been killed like so many other victims of Stalin's terror. But was there the slightest chance that this connection could be the cause of the American State department refusal of Danielle's visa? No, he thought. Impossible. Who would know? Who had he told? Not Danielle. Only Val. And Val was somewhere in transit.

He kept hearing Monique's words repeating in his head—I believe you will do your best to protect Danielle, she had said. He gave Danielle's hand a squeeze and turned toward her. She met his gaze with tear-filled eyes, but didn't speak. And what could he say to her? How could he protect her? They could marry, but he wasn't French. His papers were forged. With a false name a marriage wouldn't be legal—or would it? Instead of protecting her, he'd involved her in his work with the Resistance. And in this war who knew what would happen from one day to the next. He could be killed. Or thrown in a concentration camp. Or prison.

By now they had reached Danielle's trolley stop. They pushed their way through the passengers standing in the aisle and descended to the street. The wind was cold and Jean put his arm over Danielle's shoulders and held her close as they walked briskly to her door. He wasn't going up to her flat with her because he had an appointment with Simone about the Bulletin.

Danielle reached up to kiss him. "I'll see you later, Jean. I'll be helping Marian pack."

"I'll be back in an hour or so." He held her in his arms for a moment. "And cheer up. Your parents and David will be safe. Your visa could come through—and anyway, you have ME! And I must admit, Danielle, I was dreading your leaving—and I know we can go somewhere safe if Vichy starts rounding up Jews. And anyway, you're not going to register! Right!"

Right!" and she gave him a wan smile. "A toute a l'heure, mon chere."

# Chapter Nineteen

## Departures

*February-April, 1941*

Jean watched Danielle disappear behind the heavy door of her apartment building. He didn't know how to relieve her distress, her conflicting emotions. He had his own mixed feelings to deal with. He loved her. He wanted her to stay with him. But how could he deny the facts: As a Jew she was vulnerable. His own identity was forged, illegal. Marrying him would not save her from the Nazis. He should help her leave France.

He hurried down the narrow, rubble-strewn path to Simone's, careless about watching his back, pondering over Danielle's plight, thinking about the Bergers visas. Suddenly, the sound of footsteps behind him penetrated his thoughts. He slowed, then stopped and pretended to tie his shoe. As he glanced down the path, he grinned. It was Fredi. He laughed. "Fredi! I thought for a minute you were the flics."

Fredi pushed back the brim of his fedora and gave Jean a long look with his sky-blue eyes. "No, it's just me. So, Jean, what are you doing in this lovely part of town?"

"I could say the same for you, Fredi. An assignation?"

Fredi laughed. "Not the kind you mean. But I am meeting someone."

They walked side by side down the winding path. Now Jean kept alert for sounds of footsteps or the sight of faces in upper windows. He noticed that Fredi, likewise, darted glances right and left. When Jean arrived at Simone's apartment building he stopped. "I'm going to visit someone here," he said quietly. "So I'll see you tomorrow, OK?"

Fredi stared at him. "Who, Jean? A woman?"

Jean hesitated a moment, trying to think of a plausible answer. "One of our clients. An older woman—in her forties."

Fredi thrust his hands in his pants pockets. "It may be a coincidence, but I'm also meeting a woman here—one in her forties, but she's not a Centre Américain client."

The truth slowly beginning to dawn, Jean pushed open the door to the building and held it for Fredi. Could it be possible that Fredi was also involved with Frenay? That he was here for a meeting with Simone? Had they both been with the new resistance movement and been able to keep it secret? The two friends trudged up the stairs without speaking. When they reached Simone's door, they both stopped, exchanged looks and broke into laughter. "Is your friend's name Simone?" Jean sputtered.

Fredi nodded, continuing to laugh. Jean knocked and called out his and Fredi's names. Simone opened the door and gestured for them both to enter and be seated at the table in the center of the small room. She smoothed her tweed skirt as she sat at her place at the head of the table as their group leader.

"So," she said, "I decided it was time you joined forces." She exchanged looks with them both, her blue eyes glinting with humor. "Sooner or later you would have discovered you were both involved in Frenay's organization."

She then went on to explain to them that Fredi was in charge of Intelligence-gathering in Marseilles and Jean propaganda. She commented on the last articles Jean had written, especially about the sheep and supplies being loaded onto a train by German soldiers. "I realized that you two could work together. That story is the type of information Fredi here needs to transmit to London."

"If only we had a reliable way to do that!" Fredi exclaimed. He turned to Jean. "Actually, Jean, I've discovered other train loads of supplies going to the Reich. I've steamed bills of lading off the sides of the cars. The cars contained not only food, but also potash—which is used to make explosives. Varian has written up this information and given it to the American Consulate—hopefully to transmit to Britain. But we don't know if they cooperate. We need a radio to transmit to de Gaulle."

Jean was shocked to hear that Varian was involved in Fredi's ventures. An amazing man! Frenay had advised against informing Varian of Jean's connection with the movement, but obviously Fredi had considered it OK.

As the evening progressed the two men agreed to cooperate. They both needed to recruit people. Fredi told Jean that one of his informants was the gendarme who had told him about the ship where Varian and the others had been imprisoned. He'd also recruited two men who worked for the railroad and he knew a printer who had a printing press and might be willing to print the Bulletin.

On their way back to town they discussed the problem of finding people to work for Varian. With Marian leaving Varian would need an efficient secretary. He or she would need to speak English, French and some of the other European languages. As Hitler expanded territory the numbers of languages spoken in Marseilles had multiplied.

"I have someone in mind for Varian," Fredi said. "He's a communist, and since the Hitler/Stalin pact he's been pretty quiet, but he hates fascists. He studied in England, so his English is pretty good. He wrote for Humanité for a while, so maybe he could help you with the Bulletin. He's also a photographer."

"Good. I'd like to meet him."

"OK, I'll get in touch with him. His name's Alain Montret. Varian might want to hire him, too. And I know another couple we could trust—who are competent, Jaques and Lili Duchamp. They both worked for the government in Paris, the foreign office, but are strongly anti-Nazi, anti-German. He was in the army with me. I'll give their names to Varian." By now they had reached Danielle's street, and the two men parted, first giving each other a comradely embrace.

126

For the next few weeks the staff at the Centre worked day and night to secure passage and arrange papers for their clients to sail to Martinique from the Marseilles docks. Jean carried fake passports through the streets and money to purchase ship tickets. Danielle had thoughts only of the imminent departure of her parents. They had decided to leave from Lisbon. With mixed feelings, Danielle helped her parents obtain their transit visas, exit visas and travel permits from the Spanish and Portuguese consulates and the local prefecture. There were moments when she felt like an abandoned child and others when she thanked the gods her parents and David would be safe.

The day finally arrived when her family had assembled all the necessary documents and had packed their belongings. Danielle insisted upon traveling with them to the border, where they would take the train through the tunnel to Port Bou, Spain. Jean would be their escort. Varian had given Maurice funds for their ship passage to New York. Maurice promised to write a check from his bank account he'd established in California and send it to the Emergency Committee in New York.

Danielle sat next to her mother in their compartment gripping her hand. Although no other passengers shared their space, they spoke rarely, occasionally mentioning the rainy weather, the clouded sky, trying to remain calm. Monique clutched a crumpled handkerchief in her free hand, and from time to time dabbed at her nose. Danielle held back her tears. David stared out the window. Maurice sat opposite from Danielle holding a newspaper in front of his face, but his eyes stared straight ahead. Jean sat next to him, watching the rain fall against the window.

When the conductor opened the door to their compartment and barked out his order, "tickets and documents, please," they all stiffly handed their tickets and papers to him, avoiding eye contact. The conductor punched the tickets, gave the papers a quick glance, returned them to their owners and swept out the door. Danielle's tense shoulders relaxed. They all exchanged looks, but did not speak.

At last they arrived in Perpignon, where they were forced to sit on benches and wait an interminable two hours for the train to Cerbére. Jean had guided them to the voie that he knew so well from his many journeys with clients. Danielle recalled his tale about guiding the

Manns and Werfels over the Pyrenees, dragging and pushing them up the mountain. She had caught a glimpse of the snow-capped mountains as their train pulled into the gare.

Finally, their train arrived and they traveled the short distance to Cerbére. They descended from the train and proceeded slowly toward the line of officials who would examine her parents' papers and luggage before they boarded the train for Port Bou. Danielle could no longer hold back her tears. She threw herself into her mother's arms, kissed her on both cheeks, then was enveloped by her father's strong embrace. Finally, he released her and held her at arms' length, tears filming his eyes. "I will contact everyone I know to help us get your visa, Danielle. I will not rest until it's issued."

"Papa, don't worry about me. I'll be fine. Jean is with me. Varian Fry will help me. Now you must go." She gave a tearful laugh. "You don't want to miss this train!"

David gave her a quick hug and the Bergers turned and stiffly walked toward the officials. Jean held her close as they both watched Maurice hand over the family's documents to the gendarmes. The official peered carefully at the passports, glanced up into all their faces to verify the photographs, and beckoned them through the barrier toward the Customs officials. When their luggage had been opened and investigated the official stamped their papers and motioned them on.

Monique turned, her face streaming with tears, gave Daniele a long, last look. Maurice held Monique's arm, lifted his fedora in a gesture of farewell, and with a brave smile hurried Monique and David toward the steaming, whistling train. David waved, gave a thumbs-up sign, and took his mother's other arm. All three climbed up the steps onto the train, which immediately let out a cloud of steam and chugged into the dark tunnel that would take them through the mountain into Spain.

Danielle buried her face in Jean's shoulder and wept. She felt like a small, lost child. When would she ever see her parents or David again?

# Chapter Twenty

## Exits

### April-May, 1941

During the next few weeks Danielle spent every moment of the day working for her clients, trying not to think about her parents' journey or her own sense of doomed orphanhood. Whenever images of disaster crept into her mind, she pushed them away and concentrated on her work. When she wasn't at the Centre she was with Jean, who did his best to comfort her and ease her worries about her parent's safety at sea.

The entire staff continued to slave night and day to take advantage of Vichy's easing of the exit permit regulations. They all knew that the rules could be changed at any moment, and they should process as many of their clients as possible. In a two week period over 1,000 refugees came through their office asking for help.

They were especially proud of their arrangements for the high-profile clients, the Bretons and Victor Serge, who had papers and tickets to sail from Marseilles to Martinique on the French ship, Capitaine Paul Lemerle. The day they were to depart the entire Centre staff trooped to the port to say goodbye to their famous clients.

As Danielle stood on the quai, Jean at her side, she scanned the queue of passengers lined up at the gangplank. She nudged Jean. "I see them. There they are behind that woman holding a baby."

Jean nodded. "From the way that André's wife is clutching his arm, I'd say she's scared to death."

Danielle gave a wan smile. "She needn't be. Their papers are in order. They have their exit visas. I wonder if they both still think of America as barbaric."

"Probably, but after André's arrest, he figures he'd rather face American barbarism than that of the Nazis and Inspector Cardon."

Danielle now fixed her eyes on Serge. "Victor is fidgety, too. And I don't blame him." She knew that his passport was one of the forged ones with a visa for Mexico. He was Russian and a former Party member and the Americans wouldn't accept him.

As Danielle's eyes scrutinized the passengers, she recognized two other famous Frenchman, Claude Levi-Strauss, the anthropologist. and André Masson, the surrealist artist. Danielle turned to Jean. "All that talent! All those brains. Lucky America and Mexico. God keep them safe."

"D'accord!" Jean murmured.

At that moment the Bretons and Serge were approaching the officials at the bottom of the gangplank. The officials first examined the Breton's passport, then beckoned them on. When Serge handed his papers to the official Danielle gripped Jean's hand. The official said something to Serge she couldn't hear. Serge then gave a brief nod of his head. The watching staff let out a collective sigh of relief when the official handed the documents back to Serge and then turned to the next passenger in line. When all the passengers had boarded, a crewman untied the ship's thick ropes from their mooring and the ship slipped into the harbor. Passengers stood on the deck, waving, some with handkerchiefs pressed to their faces. The crowd assembled to see them off waved back, calling out their wishes for a safe journey..

Danielle's eyes welled with tears. Would she ever be on a ship sailing away from France, she wondered? Were her parents at sea by now? Sailing in dangerous waters, where British warships lurked? How long would she have to wait to hear from them?

Jean turned to her and gave her a appraising glance. With his thumb he wiped a tear falling down her cheek. "Danielle, I'm sure the Betons and Serge will be fine. Your parents, too. These ships zigzag the seas, keeping away from the British fleet. Now, let's get back to work." His hand touching the small of her back, he led her away from the dock.

The following week the Chagalls, Peggy Guggenheim and the artist, Max Ernst, departed for Spain and Lisbon where they would leave for New York. When Max Ernst's baggage was packed and he was ready to depart, Varian, Jean and Danielle went to the villa to say goodbye. It was a fresh spring morning, and purple bougainvillea and golden lilies were in bloom. Peggy Guggenheim was with Max. Danielle assumed they were lovers. Max held out a heavy sack to Varian. "It's gold," he said. "I can't take it with me. I'm hoping you can use it for the Centre—and do your trick with the bank in New York."

Varian took the sack and nodded. "We'll deal with it."

After tearful farewells, Peggy and Max climbed into the car that would take them to the border, squeezing next to the driver in the front seat. The back seat and trunk were stacked with carefully wrapped paintings. Danielle knew that the very wealthy Miss Guggenheim planned to fly her art collection with her on Pan American Airlines to New York.

Varian sighed as he entered the villa. "I'll miss all those clowns!" He hefted the bag of gold in his hands. He turned to Jean. "And what will we do with this until we can sell it on the black market."

Jean shrugged. "Bury it!"

"Where?"

"Right here in the garden. You said you were moving back in here now that Breton and Serge have left. I'll see what I can find out about gold dealers. I'll talk to Dmitri. And you still have those sacks in the safe. I could bury those also. Sooner or later Inspector Cardon and his gendarmes will look behind the poster and discover your safe."

Varian agreed to Jean's plan, and he and Danielle returned to the Centre. When Danielle entered the office, she eyed Lili Duchamp, their newest staff member, who was interviewing an elderly man. Lili's café au lait eyes were sympathetic as she listened to the client. Her auburn hair brightened the room. Lili was married to their other new staff recruit, Jaques. They both had thrown themselves into the work with intelligence and enthusiasm.

After Lili had finished her interview and the client had left, Varian called her into his office. He also summoned Danielle. "I've been thinking about the villa," he said. "I've decided to move back in. I know, Lili, that you and Jaques are new to Marseilles and need a place to stay. And Danielle, now that Marian has left, you're alone in your apartment. I've lost three tenants since the Bretons and Serge have left—four counting Max Ernst—when he wasn't with Peggy. So I'd have rooms for you, if you"d care to join me. Fredi lives there, too."

Danielle felt her cheeks flush with pleasure. "Varian, I'd love to live in the villa. It's so lovely—but I don't have much money, as you know. . ."

"Don't worry. I'll charge you less than you were paying Marian. It's just one room after all."

"Varian, I gratefully accept," she cried.

Lili was smiling broadly. "Yes, M. Fry. We, too accept your offer. You are too kind."


Jean continued to rent his small room near the Vieux Port. It was quiet and unremarkable, a good place to work. And work, he did. Not only did he write copy for the Bulletin, and help Fredi, but his tasks at the Centre were formidable. On a warm day in May, the week after the ship for Martinique sailed with their famous clients, the Fittcos walked into the Centre.

Jean was in Varian's office when over the sound of clacking typewriters he heard Hans' voice—then Lise's. Astonished, Jean rushed toward them and gave them both warm embraces. Immediately, he noted their solemn expressions. Although Hans appeared healthy and fit, his tanned face was shadowed. The slight, pretty Lise looked frail and tense. "Is something wrong? Was anyone caught?"

Hans pulled a handkerchief from his pocket and wiped his forehead, pushing back the dark lock of hair that had fallen over his brow. "No one was caught. But the Fittco route is kaput. We were ordered to leave the region."

"Ordered to leave? Who ordered you?" Jean asked.

"Pétain. The Germans. No foreigners are permitted to remain near France's borders. We had to leave. The mayor of Banyuls warned us. He knew we were German. We're here in Marseilles to arrange our papers. To get out of France. And we need money. And a visa."

Varian had emerged from his office and had stood listening to the exchange between Hans and Jean. He stepped forward and shook Hans' and Lise's hands. "We owe you two a great deal. I only wish we'd been able to get you an American visa. Our State Department is sometimes heartless. They don't know what heroes you are. And our Committee wants only famous artists, writers or scientists."

"But we know you're heroes!" Jean exclaimed. How unfair it was that after risking their lives helping other people get to America, the Fittcos had been denied a visa.

Varian looked troubled. "We'll try to get you a visa to Cuba or Panama. And what about passports?"

"Our old Czech ones don't work anymore, but the French—and I can't believe it—the prefecture is issuing refugees identity papers in lieu of a passport—which can be used for visas. Suddenly, they're eager to get rid of us."

Varian nodded and ushered Hans and Lise into his office, Jean heard him ask if they needed a place to stay, that he could squeeze them in at the villa. Hans thanked him and said that Lise's brother had made room for them at his rented cottage in Cassis, just outside Marseilles. "But we need a visa!"

As Varian closed the door to his office, Jean turned and exchanged looks with Fredi, who had been listening closely to Hans' bombshell announcement. He realized, of course, that the Fittco route was finished and another way over the mountains would have to be found. There were still English soldiers and downed airmen who needed to be smuggled to Spain and clients on the Gestapo's list who couldn't apply at the prefecture for visas. He and Fredi both knew that they would soon be scouring the city for information about new escape routes. And there was the gold to exchange on the black market. And their work for Frenay. Jean looked longingly at Danielle. And what to do about Danielle! Would she leave soon for Cuba or Panama?

# Chapter Twenty-one

## Gold

*May-June, 1941*

The air was balmy and the newly opened roses perfumed the garden. It was Sunday, late afternoon, and Danielle, Lili and Jaques were relaxing on the terrace of the Villa Air Bel sipping glasses of wine. The week before, the three had settled into their rooms on the ground floor. Varian's suite was upstairs and Fredi had a guest house in the garden. Danielle was delighted with her new digs, although she missed Jean, who would be gone for a few more days. Last week Varian had sent him on a quest to find safe a house in the Var region in the mountains of Provence. He would rent it for the refugees who couldn't get out of the country.

As Danielle sipped her wine, she thought of her family. A month had passed since she had watched them climb onto the train that would take them to Spain. She knew she wouldn't hear from them for another month, at least. Varian had received a postcard from Val mailed from New York only the week before. The passage across the Atlantic could take ages, since many of the the ships that sailed from Lisbon made stopovers in the Azores. Furthermore, in order to avoid warships their route would be circuitous.

She set down her glass on the rustic table and turned to Lili, who sat quietly watching the birds flit in and out of the branches of the plane trees. She wondered about Lili's family. They had all been so busy at the Centre dealing with clients—and then moving to the villa, that they hadn't had a chance to find out much about each other. "Lili, you must be concerned about your parents in Paris."

Lili nodded, her shoulder-length auburn hair brushing her freckled cheek. "Yes, I am, but they said they were too old to start over, to move south. They write to me, but they can't say much about the occupation. My father works at the Banque de Paris in the fourteenth arrondissement. Maman spends her days standing in shopping lines. They say they're coping."

Jaques grinned, showing a crooked but gleaming white front tooth. He was a good looking man, broad-shouldered, compact. He was not tall, but his dark hair was thick and curly and his brown eyes expressive. "You know, of course, their letters are censored. I'd love to hear what they're really thinking."

"And Jaques, your family?"

"They're in Tours. Just on this side of the demarcation line. They're well enough. They write but they can't say much either. They always suspect their letters will be censored, even if they're in the unoccupied zone."

At least they weren't Jewish, Danielle thought, having to fear their parents and relatives would be dragged away to a detention camp. But Jaques and Lili were emphatically anti-Nazi, which had its dangers. Fredi had told her they had supported the Socialist Prime Minister, Leon Blum. Jaques had fought in the French army in the Ardenne. That's where he and Fredi met.

"Jaques, after the Armistice, in all that confusion, how did you find Lili?"

"When the war started we agreed that if the Germans invaded France, Lili would leave Paris and go to her aunt's outside of Lyons. We knew that as Socialists and Blum followers, she could be a targeted by the Germans." He glanced at Lili. "After the Armistice, I hid from the Germans, hitched rides, slept in barns—and finally made it to Lyons."

"You've no idea," Lili said, her eyes brimming, "how absolutely wonderful it was to see that grubby, unshaven husband of mine when he walked into my aunt's house."

Danielle could imagine how Lili felt. She thought of Jean and glanced at the couple. Above their heads a pair of yellow finches flew by. The setting sun turned the birds to gold. "Where did you two meet?" she asked, finally.

Lili smiled and shot Jaques a complicit look. "At the Sorbonne. Our first week there. He bumped into me and knocked me down!" She laughed. "Ten years ago. Hard to believe."

Jaques lifted his glass. "And we were married as soon as we got our degrees."

"And then you both went to work at the Quai d'Orsay?"

"Right. In the passport office."

Danielle sighed. "Too bad you didn't bring some passports with you!" She thought of the passports hidden behind the framed pictures in Varian's office. And the gold in the safe. Jean had told her he and Varian were going to remove the gold from the safe and bury it here in the garden with Max Ernst's stash. She turned her head a little to examine the patch of dirt that had been dug around the rose bushes. That's where Ernst's gold was buried.

The murmur of men's voices from inside the house startled her. As she recognized the voices as they came toward the French doors to the terrace she relaxed. Fredi's tall form filled the doorway and blond Charlie was right behind him. Fredi carried a rolled up newspaper under his arm. "Hey comrades. Having a party?"

"Sure. Come and join us," Jaques said, rising and embracing his wartime buddy.

Danielle laughed. "Fredi, you better not call us comrades. Remember Inspector Cardon? Which reminds me, Lili, Jaques, take care. Cardon and his gendarmes can sweep through this place and pick up anything they believe is suspicious. They arrested André Breton because they found an unflattering cartoon of Pétain in his room."

"We'll be careful. We know policemen." Lili said, a serious glint in her eyes.

Jaques reached onto the side table for two more glasses and poured wine for Fredi and Charlie. "Santé," they murmured, lifting their glasses. Fredi then picked up the newspaper he had placed on the table. "Bad news," he said quietly. "The Winnipeg was captured—with many of our clients on board."

Shocked into silence, the group stared at Fredi. Danielle finally spoke. "My God, that was the ship that Lise Fittco's brother and his family sailed on to Martinique. We finally got him his American visa."

"He's the physicist, right?" Charlie said.

Danielle nodded. "But this is disastrous. It means we can't trust the Martinique route. And, Fredi, does it say who captured the ship?"

"No. An unknown hostile vessel, that's all the article says. It's probably British, which wouldn't be so bad for the refugees. They'd be interned for a while. I guess it depends where they're taken."

Danielle shook her head. "It's so unfair. Lise and Hans worked so hard to get people out—and were successful—and now her brother has been taken away."

Fredi tapped his fingers on the open newspaper in front of him. "And something else. There's a notice here that all foreign-born Jews must register at the prefecture immediately. If they fail to register they can be imprisoned." He eyed Danielle. "They're not registering French Jews, at least."

"Not yet! And I won't register," Danielle announced firmly. She raised her eyebrows, her gaze sweeping around the table. "And at that point I'll trust you all not to turn me in. After all, we're all at risk. Any one of us can be marched off by Inspector Cardon, if he wanted to. We work for Varian Fry!"

Fredi reached for the wine carafe and poured everyone more wine. "To Varian!" he cried, holding up his glass.

"To Varian," they all repeated, laughing.

Charlie glanced around at the rose bushes and the birds in the plane trees. "Let's hope the good Inspector hasn't bugged the roses or those finches up there."

Danielle thought about the clicking sounds she'd heard on the telephone at the Centre office. They all knew they were under surveillance. That was what was so great about having the garden here in the villa. No one to eavesdrop.

At the Centre two weeks later Danielle opened the window next to her desk to let in the fresh morning air. A ray of warm sunlight slanted across her desk. She lifted her hair away from her neck and unbuttoned the top button of the canary yellow cotton dress that Marian had given her. Clients were waiting outside the door, which Charlie would soon open. Varian was in his office, but Lili and Jaques were the only other staff present. Jean wouldn't return from the mountains until the next day, and Fredi was scouting for guides to escort the downed airmen over the Pyrenees. Marcel was in Toulouse.

Suddenly, Danielle heard a clamor outside the door to the Centre. Someone screamed. Then the door burst open and Inspector Cardon and four gendarmes tramped into the room. Charlie trailed behind them. The clients who had been waiting to enter had disappeared. They'd scattered.

Cardon strode to the middle of the room, planted his thick-soled shoes on the floor, his short legs spread out like a prize fighter. He glared at the Centre staff—one by one. He held a document in his hand decorated with stamps and seals. "My men will search the premises," he snapped. Danielle's heart drummed in her chest.

Cardon eyed Jauques, then Danielle and Lili. "We have received reports that this organization is dealing with black market criminals. We also suspect M. Fry has been procuring forged documents. I must speak to him at once."

As if in response to Cardon's command, the door to Varian's office opened. "What's going on out here!" Varian cried. He quickly surveyed the scene then shot Cardon a steely stare. "M. Inspector" he said, ice in his voice. "You visit us again. What is it this time?"

Cardon held out the document in his hand. "I have a warrant to search your office. We have received reports that you are dealing both with the black market and with forged documents."

Varian took the paper Cardon held out to him and scanned its contents. "Very well. Go on with your search. You will find nothing."

Danielle stared at Varian, astonished. How could he remain so cool, so apparently unperturbed. Surely, this time the gendarmes would find the safe in the wall behind Varian's desk and force him to open it. The poster hiding it was too obvious. And the passports? That might be more difficult. Jean and Val had secured an extra cardboard backing on the paintings—where they could slide the passports without their being seen if the paintings were taken from the wall.

Cardon motioned to Varian and the staff to move to one side of the room away from their desks. Danielle watched as the gendarmes pulled open desk drawers, examined papers, searched filing cabinets. From inside Varian's office she heard files being dumped on the floor, drawers opened and slammed shut. Then a shout. "A safe! Hidden behind this poster!"

Inspector Cardon rushed into the office and a moment later called out "M. Fry, come here at once. Open this safe immediately."

Danielle felt faint. They'd find the gold. She exchanged looks with Charlie, Jaques and Lili. Charlie stood leaning against the wall, appearing relaxed and unperturbed. Was it a pose? Was he playing the part of a cowboy in an American western? In contrast, Lili's eyes were wide with fright, and Jaques' stood like a soldier at attention, tense and stiff.

The safe was directly behind Varian's desk. She could see through the open door as Varian twirled the combination right and left—and right again. He opened the safe and Cardon stepped forward. He reached inside and drew out three sacks. One by one he turned the sacks upside down and poured their contents on the desk. Paper money, francs, fluttered and settled in a pile. No gold. "This cash is for our clients." Varian said calmly. "We help them with their living expenses while we try to arrange their papers to emigrate. We receive donations—sometimes from clients or friends who are leaving the country." He slid Marcel's account book from the safe. "Our accountant keeps a record of our income and expenditures. You are welcome to examine it."

Danielle fixed her eyes on the cash, then on Charlie, who was smiling behind his hand. Varian was so cool. He lied so easily. But who had removed the gold? Jean and Fredi were not here. Nor was Marcel. It must have been Charlie and Varian—or Jaques. In the meantime, while Cardon flipped the pages in the account book, the gendarmes continued to search the rooms. One of the men lifted the paintings from the wall, gave them a perfunctory glance and re-hung them. While this was happening Danielle tried to copy Charlie. She leaned against the wall, pretending to be relaxed, but her stomach was in knots until the gendarme threw up his hands and said "nothing!"

Frowning, Varian shoved the francs back into their sacks. "M. Cardon, this invasion is unpardonable. You have interrupted our work, created havoc, and have insulted us. I shall complain to my Consul. This is an American relief organization, strictly humanitarian."

Cardon gave Varian a crooked smile. "M. Fry, you are skating on thin ice. A bientot, Monsieur," and he marched out the door to the Centre, the three gendarmes behind him.

Charlie closed the door firmly.

"Lock it, Charlie," Varian ordered, "but put up a sign for our clients that we're closed until tomorrow. It will take us that long to clear up this mess." Varian turned to Danielle, Lili and Jaques. "Obviously, we have no gold." He held his finger over his lips—then pointed to the walls, the phone. Danielle smiled. They would have to wait until they were at the villa to find out where and who had moved the gold.

And later that evening, sitting in the garden, Varian explained to Danielle, Jaques and Lili that he had, indeed, taken the gold from the safe and given it to Charlie to bury in the pine woods in the back of the property. "Charlie has arranged with Dmitri to buy Max Ernst's gold. In fact, I'm expecting Charlie any minute. He'll dig up Max's gold from the rose bed and take it to Dmitri tomorrow."

Danielle knew that Fredi had introduced Charlie to Dmitri and had been involved in the exchange of francs for dollars deposited in bank accounts in the States. She also knew that Charlie had helped Fredi with his intelligence gathering for Frenay.

After dinner they were upstairs in Varian's study gathered around his illegal short-wave radio. As the program was signing off, footsteps downstairs caused them all to freeze. Danielle stopped breathing.

Varian was reaching for the radio dial when a familiar voice called to them from downstairs. "Anyone home?"

It was Charlie. "Come on up, Charlie!" Varian called, looking vastly relieved. "We're listening to the BBC."

Charlie raced up the stairs.

The radio made it's screeching noises and the program was over. Varian switched it off and wound up the wire antenna which was strung around the room. He then wrapped the radio in a blanket and stowed it into a small metal trunk. He turned to Charlie. "We'll bury the radio as well as the gold." He picked up his heavy briefcase and handed it to Charlie. "We'll also bury our cash reserves. Cardon didn't find anything illegal in the office this time, but I'm sure he'll be back. He'd love to get his hands on our cash. He'll almost certainly come here to search the villa." He picked up the metal case and headed for the stairs. "Allons y, Charlie, lets find the shovel."

"It's in the gardener's shed." Charlie said, grinning.

Danielle smiled. Charlie was only twenty-one and was loving every minute of what he considered his exciting life. He was thrilled to be dealing with gangsters like Dmitri. She wished him luck. She turned to Jaques and Lili. "Be sure you check your room for anything Cardon might find suspicious. There's plenty of space in the back woods if you need to bury anything—papers, lists, passports. Victor Serge left some old suitcases in the box room."

Lili's complexion had paled. She shot Jaques a frightened glance. "I don't think we have anything—but, Jaques, let's go check. Just to make sure."

"Good idea," Danielle said quickly. All three then ran down the stairs to search their rooms.

# Chapter Twenty-two

## June, 1941

### Charlie

Wearily, Jean stepped from the train, relieved to be back in Marseilles. The city noises seemed comforting after the silent emptiness of the Var region where he had spent the last week. He was longing to see Danielle. He'd been lonely without her, but decided that before he joined her at the Centre he would go to his room to wash up and change clothes. He felt grimy with sweat and dirt.

When he pushed open the door to his apartment building, the concierge greeted him with a message. "M. Barrault, a phone call came for you from M. Fry. He wants you to meet him at the villa as soon as you return."

"The villa? Merci Madame." He felt a tinge of disappointment that he would have to wait longer to see Danielle. Was there something Varian wanted to discuss that he didn't want overheard by eavesdroppers? His proposed project in the Var would not need to be kept secret. Renting old farm houses for refugees and setting up a charcoal-making facility would be perfectly legal. The mountains in the Var were thickly forested and rugged—and remote. It would give the clients who couldn't escape a place to hide and work to do to earn a living. He'd been thinking that it might be a good place for

Danielle to hide—if the heat turned up on Jews—and if her American visa never came through.

Feeling refreshed in clean clothes, but still wondering why Varian wanted to see him so soon after his return, he approached the villa. In the bright sunlight the bougainvillea blazed like fire. The lilies were a shining gold. The housekeeper opened the door at his knock and informed him that Varian was upstairs in his study and was expecting him.

Rising from his desk, Varian greeted him warmly. He moved to a table in the corner of the room and motioned for Jean to sit next to him. He then reached for a carafe of water and poured some for them both. "And how did it go, Jean? Did you find a place that might work?"

"Indeed." Thirstily, Jean sipped his water. "I rented an old farm for next to nothing. The property is surrounded by thick woods. I think it'd be ideal for your project. And I visited nearby villages—ancient, very remote. A perfect hideaway. People there are friendly and have no love for the Germans."

"Excellent. Let's go ahead with the plan. Maybe I'll go up there myself next week." He sipped his water. "But Jean, that's not why I asked you here. I need you to do something for me." He paused, as if marshaling his thoughts. "We had a visit from our friend Cardon yesterday. He did a thorough search."

Jean felt a stab of alarm. "Did he find the passports?"

"Fortunately, no. They lifted the paintings off the wall, but didn't spot the extra backing. But one of the gendarmes discovered the safe and I had to open it."

"Did the bastard take the gold?"

"I'd already brought the gold here to the villa, planning to bury it—like Ernst's stash. But I know Cardon is after us. He will certainly return both to the office and here to the villa for further searches. Last night Charlie buried both the gold and the short-wave radio in the pine woods. We also dug up Ernst's gold from the rose beds. I'm expecting Charlie to come here in an hour or so." He pointed to the briefcase next to his desk. "Charlie has an appointment with Dmitri at two o-clock and will hand over Ernst's gold. To be exchanged for francs. I want you to watch his back. Keep out of sight, but keep an eye out for him."

"D'accord. No problem. I'll babysit."

An hour later, Jean was following Charlie's trail. He sat five seats in back of Charlie on the trolley to the Canebiére. Walking to the Vieux Port he kept about ten paces behind him, his eyes darting from side to side, scrutinizing each person Charlie passed by. Holding his briefcase firmly under his arm, Charlie kept up a steady pace. He appeared calm, but Jean knew he would be experiencing that heightened sense of alertness, that he, himself, knew so well.

When Charlie arrived at the door to the restaurant where he was to meet Dmitri, Jean stopped at a newspaper kiosk and picked up Le Temps. As he held out the few coins for the paper, he kept his eyes trained on Charlie's blond head. Suddenly, just as Charlie was about to walk into the restaurant, Dmitri appeared. He'd popped up from an outdoor table where he'd been sitting in the shade of the canopy. Jean watched as Dmitri leaned toward Charlie and said something into his ear. Abruptly, Dmitri then turned away without accepting the briefcase and entered the restaurant.

Charlie immediately strode away from Dmitri along the quai. As he turned he shot Jean a quick glance, but didn't stop. Jean tucked his newspaper under his arm and followed, startled by this unforeseen move. Before Charlie had walked ten paces, two gendarmes lurched from the shadow of a doorway and grabbed Charlie by both arms. Jean swore silently to himself. Shit! The kid had been set up. That bastard Dmitri. Barely breathing, Jean inched closer and heard one of the men demand to see what was inside the briefcase. Charlie opened it. The gendarme rummaged in the bag and held up a heavy sack. Peering inside, he held it out to the other gendarme. "Gold coins, Imagine! Don't you know it's illegal to keep gold?"

"Yes, but. . . It was given to me by Max Ernst, the artist, before he left for America. It was a gift. A gift to me."

The gendarmes grabbed Charlie's arms and marched him along the quai, muttering about telling his tale at the Evêche.

Jean was stunned. He considered his next move. He had to find Varian immediately. Charlie was an American. Consul Fullerton should be informed of Charlie's arrest. If Charlie—or the Centre

Américain—were caught dealing with the black market they would all be in grave trouble. He hurried to the Centre office.

Danielle jumped up from her chair when he rushed in. He gave her a quick hug. "Is Varian here?" he blurted, breathing hard.

"No. He's still at the villa. He wanted to see you. But you look awful. What's happened?"

"It's Charlie. He's been arrested. With Ernst's gold. I think he was set up."

Danielle reached for the phone and dialed the villa.

As soon as Varian heard Jean's tale of Charlie's arrest, he assured Jean he would contact the American consul immediately. An hour later Varian and Jean met with Fullerton. From what Varian had told him about the chief consul's attitude toward the Centre staff, particularly Varian, Jean didn't have much faith in the man's willingness to intercede on Charlie's behalf. But to Jean's amazement, he did just that. The consul listened carefully to Jean's description of the arrest. He then picked up the phone and called Cardon. "Charles Furst is an American citizen," the consul said sternly. "The boy merely accepted a gift from a friend and was carrying it to his flat. The police had no right to arrest him."

Charlie was kept at the Evêche overnight, but was released the next day. Jean was waiting for Charlie in an outer office of the Evêche as the gendarme led him from the holding room where he had spent the night. His skin was gray and shiny with sweat, his clothes were rumpled and his eyes bleary. Jean asked to speak to Inspector Cardon, but the gendarme snapped that he was out of the building. Jean watched as the clerk returned Charlie's belongings. Not the gold, of course, but he handed Charlie the empty briefcase. Charlie hefted it and gave a pale version of his grin. He signed the paper placed in front of him. "You are free to go," the gendarme said, "but the judge will hear your case in two weeks. Report here July 6 at ten o'clock."

The gendarme had barely spoken before the two men were out the door. Jean clapped Charlie on the back. "You're in luck, Charlie. Did you hear that the consul went to bat for you? If he hadn't you'd be sweating it out in the cellars."

Charlie rotated his shoulders as they hurried away from the Evêche. "I don't feel lucky, believe me. That bastard Dmitri set me up, I'm sure."

"So what do you think happened? I saw him say something to you and then you turned away."

Charlie turned to Jean, his eyes blazing. "He told me the police were on to us—the exchanges—and to get out of there vite, pronto! But I only took two steps and the gendarmes grabbed me. They were waiting. And Dmitri just faded into the woodwork."

"Yeah, I saw. And there was nothing I could do except find Varian. Varian and I went to talk to the consul. I was astonished when that guy actually picked up the phone and talked Cardon into letting you off." By now they had reached the Canebiere. "So, Charlie, what do you want to do now? My advice is to get the hell out of the country. Do you have your passport?"

Charlie fixed his eyes on Jean. "Yeah. It's in my room. I hope. Unless the cops were there."

"Let's go look." Jean looked behind them to check they weren't being followed. He didn't see anyone suspicious. When they arrived at Charlie's apartment building, he pushed the buzzer and the door opened. He waved to the concierge, who was knitting on her chair behind the window. "Any messages?" Charlie called out.

"No messages," she said, shaking her head.

They ran up the two flights of stairs, and Charlie opened his door with the key that had been returned to him by the gendarme. The room was a mess with its unmade bed and clothes scattered on the floor, but there was no evidence of the chaos created during a police search. Charlie headed for his bed and lifted the mattress. "I know this is a dumb place to hide things, but it's convenient." He slid the green booklet from under the mattress and held it up triumphantly. He then picked up his toilet kit from the washstand and emptied it. Lifting a flap from the bottom of the kit he pulled out a wad of banknotes; both francs and dollars. He counted it. "It isn't enough to get me to Madrid." He gave a tired laugh. "I'll have to ask Varian for help."

"He's at the Centre, but as you know most of his cash is buried at the villa." Jean peered around the room. "You'd better pack a musette. You might have to hike over the mountains."

"I know. I figure I'll go to Toulouse to get my transit visa for Spain, but I don't dare ask for an exit visa. I'll need money for the guide."

"You're not getting a Portuguese transit visa? So you can leave from Lisbon to the States?"

"No. I'm not going home. I'm going to the British Embassy in Madrid and volunteer for the British air force. I want to join the RAF."

When Jean and Charlie entered the Centre office, Danielle stared at Charlie in dismay. He wasn't smiling and his eyes were puffy and darkly shadowed. His chin was covered in a blond stubble and the remainder of his face was gray and damp. "Charlie," she cried, it's so good to see you!" She immediately felt how inadequate her greeting had been, but what could she say? He'd taken on a heroic task and lost. That damned Inspector Cardon. She rose from her chair and gave both men hugs.

Jean asked if Varian was in his office.

She went to his door, knocked and opened it. "Varian, it's Charlie and Jean. He's out of jail."

Varian rushed out and shook Charlie's hand. "Come in, Charlie." and he motioned for him to go inside. He pulled out a chair opposite his desk. "Sit down, boy, you look—well you look like hell."

Charlie shot him a tired smiled, but his eyes weren't smiling. "That's how I feel."

Varian then beckoned to Jean and Danielle. "Come in. You may be needed. And shut the door, Danielle." Pointing to the walls, he reached behind him to turn on the radio, adusting the volume. Leaning close to Charlie, he spoke in a low voice. "So what's the story, Charlie. Are they letting you go entirely?"

"They want me back in two weeks, " Charlie said quietly. "But. Varian, I want to get out of here. I know it will look bad for the Centre, but they'll put me in jail. I know. That Cardon is out to get us."

"I know, Charlie." Varian said, "And you're right. You must go. What can I do to help."

"Well," Charlie hesitated, then attempted his normal grin, "I need dough. I'll have to go the Carlos route over the mountain and that takes money for bribes. I have a little, but not enough."

Varian nodded. "No question, Charlie. I owe you." He turned and turned the radio dial to another, louder music program. He then opened his safe. "We keep enough here for clients, and you, young man, are now a client." He shuffled some notes onto his desk. "I'm giving you both francs and dollars." He opened his desk drawer and pulled out some packs of Lucky Strikes. "And some of these for bribes." He looked up at Charlie. "So what is your plan? Or do you have one?" He glanced at the radio, still blaring with orchestral music.

"It's all I thought of last night when I tried to sleep on that table." He leaned closer to Varian. "I'll go to Toulouse for a Spanish transit visa. I have my American passport. Cardon kept my identity permits, but my passport will be enough to get me to Toulouse, I hope."

"What about a Portuguese visa? For the ship from Lisbon?" Varian's voice was so low Danielle could barely hear him.

Charlie spoke quietly but forcefully. "i won't be going home. I want to join the RAF—so I'll head for the closest British consul or embassy." Varian nodded. "I see. Well, Charlie, I wish you luck. You know you can't get an exit visa. You'll be on the black list."

"I know. That's why I have to go over the mountains. Like the airmen. I went with Fredi a couple of times to meet Carlos, so I'm not entirely green."

"Good. So when will you leave?"

"As soon as I say goodbye to your all. I'll head for the gare. There's a train for Toulouse in another hour."

Varian rose and shook Charlie's hand. Jean and Danielle followed Charlie into the main room. Danielle put her arms around Charlie's neck and kissed him. Tears welled in her eyes, but she pushed them back. He had to go.

Jean waited by the door as Charlie said his farewells to Lili and Jaques. "I'll watch your back, Charlie," he whispered. "You might be tailed."

"Thanks, Jean. O.K. See you all after we've won the war!" and the two men went out the door.

# Chapter Twenty-three

## Varian

### June, 1941

And the work at the Centre continued. As Danielle was typing a visa application for a  client, she couldn't stop thinking about Charlie. She missed Charlie's happy go-lucky grin, but she felt sure, at least almost sure, that he would make it into Spain and even the RAF. Jean had watched him board the train to Toulouse. Fredi and Marcel had returned from their last trip with the British airmen on the Carlos route, and they told her it was running more or less smoothly. They thought Charlie would make it. "Charlie's smart. And lucky!" Fredi assured her.

The big news blasting on French radio that morning was the jolting report that the Germans had invaded Russia. That was all anyone was talking about. What did it mean? Jean had told her he thought it was great news—that the Germans couldn't fight on two fronts. The Brits would be pleased, more or less. Imagine, Russia and Britain would now be Allies.  Danielle cast a glance around the office. There was a buzz in the room. Their clients were excited by the news and clung close together, whispering to each other, puzzled, perhaps hopeful.

She glanced at their gaunt faces. The stream of refugees that flowed into the Centre seemed never ending. Most of the clients didn't fit the New York committee's guidelines. In fact, the famous artists and writers on the original list had almost all been taken care of. Danielle fretted over those ordinary people, like herself, who weren't considered special enough to received the precious American visa.

And Varian was in trouble with the Committee. They'd ordered him to return to the States. They'd received reports he'd been involved in illegal activities for the refugees. Varian had confided to her that his passport had expired and the consul had refused to issue him a new one unless he were to use it to leave the country. He'd requested a replacement director, but so far the Committee hadn't found anyone to send. If Varian left what would they do? Nobody could replace him.

The Centre was also short of money. Danielle was convinced that Dmitri had betrayed Charlie. She was terrified he'd betray Jean. She knew that yesterday Jean had carried $6,000 worth of francs to the villa, the francs he'd received from Dmitri before Charlie's arrest. Jean had buried the money in the pine woods along with the radio and illegal documents. She'd also seen the parade of gendarmes that patrolled the street outside the Centre, frightening their clients.

As she was finishing the application, the sound of tramping feet on the stairs stopped her in mid sentence. Four gendarmes burst into the room, demanding to speak to Varian. Danielle held her breath. What now? Fredi, without saying a word, slowly rose from his chair, knocked and opened Varian's office door. Two of the gendarmes barged in. Varian remained seated in his chair and gazed at them coolly. "What is it this time, Monsieurs?"

The tallest of the men stepped closer to Varian's desk, tapping it with his stick. "We demand that you hand over the francs worth six thousand dollars you obtained from the black market!"

"I don't know what you're talking about." Varian's tone was sharp, icy.

The gendarme held out a paper covered with red ribbons and seals. "We have a warrant to search the office."

Danielle's eyes darted around the main room, checking on the clients, who sat frozen in their chairs, frightened to move, their eyes cast down. The constant searches and raids were devastating for these people. The thought of a German defeat by the Russians fled from their minds. Danielle' heart was beating so loudly she was afraid the gendarmes would hear it. How did the police know about the francs worth $6,000? It had to be Dmitri who betrayed them. Now she was certain. First the gold, now this.

Varian stood up and motioned to the gendarmes to proceed with their search. "You've done it before. Go ahead. I'll open the safe, unlock my desk." He lifted the poster from the wall that hid the safe, dialed the combination, then took a key from his pocket and unlocked the desk. The police found the safe empty except for 500 francs, and when they pulled out the drawers to Varian's desk found nothing incriminating.

Danielle was not surprised. But what shocked her was the man in motorcycle clothes who at that moment tramped into the Centre. "Varian Fry!" he snapped.

In a tired voice, Varian responded. "Yes. I'm Varian Fry."

The motorcyclist strode into Varian's office. He thrust a document into Varian's hands. "You are ordered to report to Inspector Cardon at the Evêche. Immediately! Now! We have a car waiting outside for you."

Varian reached for his fedora, turned to Fredi, who had been standing, as if on guard, with folded arms and straight back behind Varian. "Fredi, take over, please."

Fredi, his expression impassive, spoke calmly. "OK, chief, Take care."

It was closing time at the Centre and Varian still had not returned. Fredi locked the door and shrugged. "I'm not sure what we should do. I called the villa and Varian's not there. And the duty officer at the Evêche wouldn't tell me much—except that Varian's name wasn't on his list of arrests."

Jean stood at the window, watching the street outside the building. "The police have left." he said. "Let's get out of here." They all descended the stairs and when they reached the street, Jean leaned close to Fredi and said quietly, "Fredi, you have that guy, that policeman in your group. Why don't we try to find him. Ask him if he knows anything."

Fredi nodded. "Let's give it a try." He glanced at the others—Danielle, Lili, Jaques, and Marcel. "And why don't we all meet at the villa. We have to make a plan."

Although the sun had gone down, it was still light when Fredi and Jean walked onto the terrace at the villa. Danielle and the others had gathered around the outdoor table, sipping wine, their faces dark with apprehension. They spoke in low voices, talking about Russia and the war news to keep from worrying about Varian. When Danielle spied the two men loping toward them, she jumped up and ran to them. "Where is he? What did you find out?" She searched their faces, trying to discern if they'd brought good news. They were not smiling. Her chest tightened.

"We think he's with the consul," Jean said bleakly.

"He was at the Evêche for two hours." Fredi said. "Then he was taken to the American Consulate. The police left him there and that's all my guy knows."

Danielle picked up the carafe and poured glasses of wine for the two men and refilled the others'. "Maybe they're forcing Varian to leave the country," she murmured. Then she heard footsteps tapping across the tiled floors inside the house.

The group all turned as one, to stare at the tall French doors leading to the terrace. It was Varian, slow-moving, ashen-faced. They all rushed to him, talking at once, pleading with him to tell them what happened.

In a flurry they all assembled at the table. They helped Varian into a chair and poured him some wine. Lili pushed a plate of grapes within his reach, but he didn't eat. They waited for him to begin his tale. He took a deep breath, removed his glasses, and picking up the napkin Lili had placed before him, polished the lenses. "Both Cardon and Fullerton order me to go home. Cardon suspects me—and this agency of a variety of crimes—dealing with the black market, arranging forged documents, etc etc. He has no proof, I'm sure, but someone has been speaking into his ear. Maybe Dmitri. He spoke about Charlie. It was obvious he didn't believe Charlie's story."

"Do you think he knows Charlie left town?" Fredi asked.

"No. He told me Charlie would be heard by the judge on July 6. He acted as though he was doing me a big favor not tossing Charlie in jail. He says that even if I'm innocent, or Charlie's innocent, it's more expedient for him to lock us up than to let us go. He'd rather jail an innocent man than let the guilty ones go free, which is not exactly what the French laws in the past have stated."

"But he'll let you go? He didn't arrest you?" Fredi asked.

"Because I'm American. He doesn't want to offend the consul, apparently. But Cardon wants me to leave immediately. Fullerton had my passport ready, the newly issued one plus all the necessary visas stamped into it. So they're in on it together."

"So will you leave us?" Danielle asked, close to tears.

"I'm afraid so, but I won't go home immediately. I've persuaded Cardon and Fullerton to give the Committee time to find my replacement. But Cardon won't let me stay in Marseilles. I can take a holiday, he says. Go to St Tropez." He gave a wry laugh. "So, Fredi, Jean, all of you, you must run the Centre on your own. Fredi I want you to be in charge. OK? Until they send someone to take over."

Fredi nodded, his blue eyes dark with anger. "I'll try," he said, quietly.

"Actually," Varian added. "I want to go up into the Var region, Jean, to check out the farmhouse you rented. I'd like you to go with me. Danielle, too, if you wish. For a few days. You can get some ideas of how it might work to have some of our clients up there—safe from police raids—and with a way to earn a living. And maybe do a little farming as well as the charcoal manufacture and wood cutting."

Danielle smiled. "I'd like that, Varian." She glanced at Jean for his reaction. Jean's eyes glinted with approval. "A great plan, Varian. You'll like it up there. It's a wilderness, but beautiful. And you'll be out of Cardon's reach."

Varian frowned. "Oh, but I've forgotten something extremely important. He reached into his inside jacket pocket and pulling out a yellow telegraph envelope. "It's from the Committee. I stopped at the telegraph office on my way here. I'd expected to hear from the Committee about my replacement, but this came instead." He opened the envelope and fished out a half-sheet of thin yellow paper striped with lines of paper tape. He shot a glance at Danielle, hesitated, then read aloud: "The American Rescue Committee is pleased to report that we have obtained Cuban visas for Hans and Lise Fittco and Danielle Berger.

The documents should arrive at your office in two weeks." He held the small yellow sheet in his outstretched hand toward Danielle. Danielle, you might consider traveling with the Fittcos. Think it over."

Danielle's chest was so tight she could barely breathe. Stiffly, she reached for the telegram, staring at Varian. Thoughts tumbled in her brain, twisting and turning. She locked eyes with Jean. How could she leave him? And this work at the Centre. Cuba?

Varian reached for his wine, glanced at Danielle, and sighed deeply. "This has been quite a day. Eventful. Russia invaded, me arrested and ordered to leave, and Danielle hearing about her visa." He gave a wan smile. "How's your Spanish, Danielle?"

That night, after a quiet dinner on the villa terrace, Danielle excused herself and left for her room. Jean followed, closing the door behind them. Danielle sank onto the edge of the bed and peered up at Jean. I haven't been able to stop thinking about that Cuban visa," she said, slowly.

He sat next to her on the bed and put his arm around her shoulders. "You know you should go with the Fittcos, don't you?"

She gave him a long look. "Do you want me to?"

"Yes, I do. I don't see an alternative. Danielle, I love you. If I could keep you safe, right here in my arms, I wouldn't let you go, but that can't happen. It's too dangerous for you here."

"But it's dangerous for all of us—you too, with the work you're doing."

"But that's beside the point. You're a Jew. They could haul you off to a camp and I'd never see you again. Danielle, I want to protect you. I want to ask you to marry me, but until this war is over, until I can be Gino Baroli again, it's not possible. I'm here in France with a fake identity and forged documents. Being married to me could even be more dangerous for you. You must leave when the visa arrives. After the war we'll find each other, and if you're willing, we'll be married. Would you wait for me, Danielle?"

"Jean, I want to marry you and I'd certainly wait for you, but I don't want to leave. I could go up to the Var to the village there. You said it's remote. I don't look Jewish. I could even go to Mass, wear a cross. It won't be forever!"

Jean buried his face in her neck. "Oh, Danielle, if only this war were over!"

# Chapter Twenty-four

## The Bulletin

### June, 1941

Early the next morning, Jean gave Danielle a hug, kissed her warmly and left her packing a few things for the following day's journey to the Var. He knew she'd not stop pondering over her fate. Their talk the night before had been disappointingly inconclusive. If she remained in France—even in a remote mountain village—he knew she would be gambling with her life. He wanted her to stay with him always, but he knew she ought to leave when the visa arrived.

Since Danielle had moved to the villa, he spent most nights in her bed. Danielle's villa-mates, including Varian, were not shocked about the lovers sleeping together. These were precarious times. Bourgeois attitudes toward sex had to be abandoned. Lili had even taken Danielle in hand and made an appointment with a doctor who had fixed her up with the French cap. Much to his relief. Condoms were not always easy to find and this was no time to bring children into the world. If only they could be married, but that couldn't happen until he became Gino Baroli again.

As he walked through the dining room, Fredi called out to him from the table where he was drinking coffee. "Jean, will you be at the

Centre today? Varian isn't going in, you know. He's up in his room packing."

"No, actually. I'm going to my room to work on the Bulletin before we leave for the Var tomorrow. Then I have to take the copy to the printer. Maybe late afternoon I'll come in." Jean eyed Fredi's coffee thirstily, but knew he didn't have time to dawdle. He would make coffee in his room.

Fredi set down his cup. "The reason I'm asking is that I'd arranged to bring the guy I told you about—to the Centre—the one who used to write for Humanité in Paris, Alain Montret. I sounded him out. He told me that after the Stalin/Hitler pact he was deeply troubled. You know how the Party line called for appeasement and collaboration. He resigned his Party membership. Alain hates fascism. He fought in Spain. When we talked a couple of weeks ago I thought he might want to help you, but he didn't commit himself. He still felt a certain loyalty to the communist ideals. Now that the Russians are on our side—he said he no longer feels ambivalent—and the Party line has changed, of course. He told me late last night that now he was sure he wanted to join our movement."

"Humanité, huh? Hard line communist? You know how I feel about that, Fredi. Can you trust him?"

"Yeah, I trust him. We fought together in the Ardenne. And I know how you feel about the Party. But Alain has had second thoughts."

"OK, why don't you bring him around to my room this morning. Instead of the Centre."

"Fine. See you later."

Jean wasted no time settling at his typewriter. There was plenty to write about, and his fingers flew on the keys. The report of the German invasion of the Soviet Union had been a bombshell—and shockingly good news. How could Hitler fight two fronts successfully and occupy most of Europe at the same time? His troops were fighting the British in North Africa. They'd already been repulsed by the Brits at Tobruk. Now the British were in Syria and Lebanon and had counter-attacked the German troops in Egypt.

And most important for the resistance movement, it meant the French communists would slough off their skins of ambivalence and flock to the cause.

A knock at the door propelled him to his feet. "Who is it?"

"Fredi, and my friend, Alain Montret." Recognizing Fredi's voice, Jean took the chain off the door and opened it.

After the initial introductions and greetings, Jean put a kettle of water on his tiny alcohol stove. "We'll have some ersatz coffee. It's not too bad." As he spooned the mixture into a coffee pot, he shot rapid looks at Alain, who had dark hair and eyes and was of medium height. Jean guessed he'd be in his late twenties. He noted that Alain's shoulders were sturdy under his dark blue open-necked shirt and his arms were well muscled. He looked more like an athlete than a journalist. The man's khaki pants were shoddily patched at the knees—certainly not sewn by a woman.

Fredi quickly drank his coffee and then left the men to their work. Jean described the Bulletin to Alain, its goals, and how it needed expanding. "We hope people will read it and be inspired to resist the Germans—and their French right-wing puppets. We report news that is not published or broadcast in our muzzled press and radio. The BBC is a good source. Also tidbits we pick up on the street, docks or railroad yards."

Alain gave him his full attention. He read Jean's draft of the morning's copy. "I like what you're doing. And I think I can help. I've brought you some pieces I wrote."

"Good!" Jean scanned the columns Alain handed him. The man wrote clearly, although his pieces followed the Party line. "You write well. But I have a question—your politics. We've tried to avoid dogma. We want to tell the truth, but at the same time inspire people to resist the German fascists and the French collaborators. We're writing propaganda, of course. But we're not communists."

Alain met Jean's look. "When I wrote for Humanité I was still a Communist Party member, although after what I witnessed in Spain I was beginning to have doubts about its methods. I'm not a Stalinist, if that's what you want to know. I couldn't stomach the brutality. Too many of my comrades were disappearing."

"What about now. Are you still a Party member?"

"No. After the Hitler/Stalin pact I resigned from the Party. It sickened me to be an ally of Hitler."

Jean felt a surge of relief. The man sounded OK. And Fredi trusted him. He clapped Alain on the shoulder. "You've answered my question." He smiled. "I can put you to work immediately. Tomorrow I have to go up to the Var region with my boss at the Centre. I might be away for a week. You could make this room your studio, if you like. We publish twice a month, so I'd be back to work on the next edition."

Alain peered around the tiny space. "OK. It's a quiet place to work. Do you have any ideas for the next issue."

Jean nodded. "I have a file of possible subjects, but it depends on what happens in the news. We'll need to find out what we can about the invasion of Russia. We won't be able to trust the official German reports." He scooped up the typewritten pages on the table. "But now I need to take this copy to the printer. Do you have time to come with me?"

"Absolutely."

# Chapter Twenty-five

## The Var

*July-August, 1941*

When the trio, Varian, Danielle and Jean, stepped out the door of the gare at St Raphael, first showing their papers to the officials on guard, they felt a soft breeze from the sea. Danielle breathed deeply of the briny air. It smelled of sand and salt and seaweed. She could feel the skirt of her turquoise blue dress fluttering around her knees. She placed one hand on the crown of her straw hat to hold it in place, and slung her lightly packed musette over her shoulder. Her spirits lifted. It was such a relief to be away from Marseilles and Inspector Cardon's surveillance. She could shake off the habit of fear.

She glanced at Jean, then Varian. Varian had left most of his belongings stored at the villa and carried only a small suitcase. Jean's musette was stuffed. She took hold of Jean's free hand. "I feel like we're on holiday!"

Jean squeezed her hand, the gold flecks in his eyes glinting in the sunlight. "Wait 'till you get to Chateaudouble, an 11ᵗʰ Century gem. It's perched on the edge of a deep gorge, surrounded by forests."

Varian pointed to a bus parked some distance from the entrance to the St Raphael gare. "That might be our bus."

Danielle knew that Varian would be with them only until he'd checked out the farm Jean had rented. St Raphael was on the coast between St Tropez and Cannes. Varian planned to return to the coast for a much-needed rest in St Tropez—free from the eyes and ears of Inspector Cardon and his gendarmes.

They hurried to the waiting bus, and after being assured by the driver that it went to Chateaudouble, they boarded. Danielle found herself checking to make sure they were not being followed. The bus was crowded with people who appeared to be locals. Sitting in front of her were two sun-browned women carrying baskets covered in embroidered napkins. Danielle took a deep breath. They were truly free from surveillance.

As they were boarding, she had noted the furnace in the back of the bus that she'd been told burned charcoal. The smell of smoke and burning wood was strong inside the bus. Varian had dreamed up the charcoal-making project for his refugees when he realized what a market there was for the product. Most formerly gasoline-powered vehicles now used charcoal or coal. Danielle shot a look at Varian, who sat across the aisle from where she and Jean had taken their seats. What an admirable man. He believed so ardently in his rescue mission. How sad it was that the committee in New York were so unsupportive of his efforts. They couldn't understand how disastrous it was for refugees when they were sent to detention centers. People died there of disease and malnutrition and loss of hope. She turned to Jean, who sat beside her and grasped his hand. For the next few days she vowed not to think of detention, going to Cuba, or being watched by the police. And she would assume that her parents and David had arrived safely in America.

Jean leaned toward her and kissed her on the cheek. "The road will go up the mountain quickly. We'll be in Chateaubouble in about an hour."

They had already left the outskirts of St Raphael and were riding through a thick forest. The gravel road was narrow and winding but in fair condition. The bus began a steep climb, but forged ahead, its engine popping in back, The road ran along the edge of a deep gorge. Across the gorge, above the thickly forested slope, a ridge of rock outcroppings rose like a castle wall. A stream of clear water flowed on crushed yellow and white stones at the bottom of the gorge. Danielle squealed as the bus bounced around a hairpin curve, throwing her against Jean. Jean put his arm around her waist, laughing as they were tossed from side to side.

When they reached the village, the driver stopped the bus next to a high stone arch that formed an opening in the remains of an ancient wall. "Chateaudouble," he shouted. The women in front of Danielle rose from their seat and with their baskets over their arms stepped down to the cobbled street and through the arch that led to the village.

Danielle, Varian and Jean collected their belongings and followed the two women through the arch, while the bus chugged away on its route to other villages. The cobbled street was bordered by buildings of pale yellow sandstone capped by red tiled roofs. Pots of red and pink geraniums rested on ledges of the light green or blue-shuttered windows and doors. It was mid-day and only a few people were in the space next to the Mairie, which Danielle recognized by the tricolor flapping in the breeze above its door. Four elderly men sitting in the shade of a plane tree looked up from their newspapers and stared at the strangers. The bench where they sat overlooked the gorge and its wall of rock and the forest beyond. Danielle smiled at the men. "Bonjours" she said.

Two of the men smiled back and touched the brims of their caps. "Bonjours," they replied. Their faces expressed curiosity, but their glance was not hostile. Danielle looked at Varian in his jacket, tie and fedora—carrying a suitcase. He was obviously a city man, belonging to an exotic species. Jean, in his khaki pants, open-necked shirt and beret, wouldn't appear so strange to these men.

When they passed a bakery and noted its empty shelves. Jean sighed. "No bread here, either. I'm afraid. But let's see if the little shop next door has anything we can pick up to take to the farm."

Varian set down his suitcase. "Let's go first to the inn you told us about. I need to get rid of this bag. And how long is the walk to the farm, Jean?"

"About a mile. Maybe we can hitch a ride with someone with a wagon. We can ask at the inn."

The only inn in the town was up the narrow, sloping street a few meters from the Mairie, and Jean had told them it contained the town's only bar and café. He'd stayed in one of its five rooms when he was here searching for property. The innkeeper greeted Jean as if he were an old friend. "It's good to see you again, comrade." He eyed Danielle—then Varian with curiosity.

Jean shook his hand and made the introductions. "We need three rooms, M. Derain." Jean had already confided that here in the village they would need to observe the proprieties, but that wouldn't stop him from visiting her later.

Derain plucked three large iron keys from pegs on the wall behind the counter and led them up two flights of stairs to their rooms, first to Danielle's. He opened the shutters to let in the fresh breeze that smelled of pines, grass and cow dung. Danielle peered out the window at the jumble of red-tiled roofs that spread out below. She noted that most of the building's stone walls were plastered in a pale yellow stucco. To the right, built high into a rocky outcropping, rose the ruin of one of the towers of the old château, undoubtedly why the town was named Chateaudouble. Beyond the town, on the horizon, rose the forested mountains topped by jagged rock outcroppings. How very lovely it was. She exchanged looks with Jean, who was smiling at her.

Derain handed them their keys. "I hope you will be comfortable. Dinner is served at seven o'clock, lunch at one."

Jean told Derain they'd take dinner, but not lunch. He then asked about transportation to the farm. Derain directed them to a supply shop down the cobbled street, and there they found a farmer with a horse and wagon who was willing to take them to the farm.

As the horse jogged along the crushed-stone track, shaded by beeches and chestnuts, Jean explained to the farmer about their plan to open a charcoal manufacturing operation at the farm. "We have refugees who need work and a place to live. The mountains here are thickly forested. We think it's a perfect place to make charcoal for fueling cars and trucks—and buses."

The farmer listened carefully to Jean. "And from whose land would you cut the wood?"

"I have talked to one or two people who are willing to sell the trees they cut when they clear their fields for planting. They seemed to think there were others who would be willing to have the logs removed from the property—for a small charge, of course."

"That should work," the farmer said, after a moment's thought. By now they had arrived at the gate to the farm and the three passengers hopped down from the wagon. They thanked the farmer and walked up the path toward the structures they could see from the road. Jean pointed to the two-story building of pale yellow stone. "The farmhouse," he said. He fished a key from his pocket. "And over there is the barn." He pointed to the stone structure with a wide double door and a shuttered opening above it. Both structures were roofed with red tile. A weed-covered field stretched out at the side of the buildings and another cleared piece of land lay behind. Surrounding the fields was a thick forest of pine, beech and chestnut. Danielle took a deep breath. The air smelled of grass and old leaves—and a faint whiff of hay and manure.

Danielle felt a surge of excitement as Jean unlocked the house's thick oak door. He shoved it open and stepped inside. "Come in. It's dusty and needs some work. But what do you think?"

As Danielle and Varian slowly entered, Jean hurried to the windows and opened the shutters to let in light. The large room was empty of furnishings, but a stone fireplace on the wall facing the windows was equipped with an iron rod on which hung a large smoke-blackened pot. The plaster which partially covered the stone walls was black with soot, but the light pouring from the door and windows glowed on the red tile floors. A rustic sink and wooden counter sat under a window opposite the fireplace. Danielle could imagine the room with a large table in the center and curtains at the windows. Jean pointed to a steep wooden staircase in the corner. "Upstairs are three rooms. And under this door in the floor is the root cellar." At the foot of the stairs Danielle saw the trap door. A good place to hide, she thought. Jean then led them into two adjoining rooms, which were empty but clean, and when he opened the shutters, were filled with sunlight.

Varian wandered around the rooms smiling broadly. "This should be quite comfortable, Jean. Our refugees can easily put together some plank tables and benches. They'll need cloth to make mattresses, but I saw plenty of dried grass and hay out in that field. It may be too late to plant vegetables, but if they get busy with the charcoal they could barter with the other farmers—or use cash if they sell the charcoal."

"And there's plenty of room in the fields to set up the charcoal colliers." Jean added.

Danielle turned to Varian. "Would CAS be able to come up with money for a cow? Or a horse and wagon to transport the charcoal?"

Jean gave her a troubled look. "Danielle are you really thinking of become a farmer, joining our clients?"

She gave him a long look. "I can think of worse things. It could work, you know, and the people in town are friendly."

Varian stared at her. "Danielle, Cuba would be safer."

Three weeks later Danielle was at her desk at the Centre typing a report Varian had given her a few minutes earlier. Two weeks had passed since she and Jean returned from the Var. She smiled to herself, remembering how light-hearted she'd felt there. The days and nights had been an idyll, a romantic interlude in a time of chaos. But at this moment she was worried about Varian. He'd returned from St Tropez only the night before and was now in his office. He'd arrived at the villa late at night and had remained in his room while his staff left for the Centre. He hadn't spoken to any of them about when he planned to leave France. He'd rather abruptly handed her this handwritten report addressed to the Committee and had told her he needed it immediately. Perhaps, she thought, he planned to take it with him when he left for America. The report spelled out the Centre's activities, both the numbers of refugees helped to leave France and those who were given funds for living expenses. He'd also described the establishment of the charcoal factory.

She then thought of Jean, who had left a week ago for Chateaudouble with a group of refugees and Alsatians—ten men between the ages of eighteen and thirty. They would be setting up living quarters on the farm as well as obtaining wood for the colliers. Jean had inspected a charcoal manufacturing operation outside of Marseilles and had persuaded one of its workers to go with them to help them get organized. Jean had described the process to her and had drawn a picture of the way the logs were arranged in a pyramid—and burned with a mixture of dirt and straw covering it—and vents for air.

The door to Varian's office suddenly opened and Varian called to her. "Danielle, could I see you a moment, please?"

She jumped up and entered his office, giving him a questioning look. "Sir?"

He tapped at a stack of mail on his desk. "I've just been through these. There's a letter from the Panamanian consul for you. They've given you a visa."

"Panama!"

"And Danielle, I haven't asked you what you decided about going to Cuba. Have the Fittcos left yet?"

Danielle nodded. "They left last week. From Cerbére. We haven't heard from them but assume they're OK."

"And you?"

She hesitated. "Varian, I want to wait a while. There's work for me to do here."

He gave her a studied look, then a wry smile. "And you don't want to leave Jean, I fear."

She nodded and he handed her the Panamanian letter. "Think it over carefully, Danielle. It won't get any better here, you know. Vichy is cooperating fully with the Nazis."

Angry voices and the sound of boots stamping on the stairs outside the open door to the Centre caused them both to freeze. Danielle's heart pounded. Another search? Then she heard Fredi shouting at the two gendarmes who were bursting into the Centre. The gendarmes then barged into Varian's office and held out a paper under his nose. "We have a warrant for your arrest. You must come with us to the Evêche immediately. We have a car waiting."

Varian sighed and reached for his hat on the peg by the door. He turned to Danielle. "I'll need that report, Danielle." He then looked at Fredi. "You're in charge, my friend. It would seem that Inspector Cardon is serious about my deportation."

The two gendarmes held an ashen-faced Varian by both arms and led him out of the office.

Danielle was soon to learn that Varian had guessed correctly. Cardon was indeed serious about Varian's deportation. Varian was kept overnight at the Evêche, and the next afternoon a police officer was assigned to escort him to the Spanish border. He was allowed to go first to his office, where a stunned staff watched him silently stuff papers into his briefcase. Danielle handed him the report he had asked her to type. "Thank you, Danielle," he said in a low, exhausted voice. "I will be carrying this to America to give to the Committee." His gaze went from Danielle to Fredi and the others. "You have all heard. I am being deported. Officer Bouley will escort me to Cerbére on the three o'clock train." He turned to Officer Bouley. "And would it be permissible for my Deputy Director, Frederique Chardin, to ride with us in your car. I need time to give him instructions concerning his running the Centre after I leave."

The officer gave his consent and he, Fredi and Varian left the Centre. Varian for the last time.

# Chapter Twenty-six

## Fredi

*January, 1942*

Danielle hopped off the trolley and raised her tattered blue umbrella. The sky was the color of eggplant and the rain fell in sheets. In the dim early light, she inspected the street in front of the Centre office. No cars were parked on the curb occupied by newspaper-reading men in plain clothes and the doorway was clear. The windows of the café next to the Centre were steamed up, which meant that nobody could be watching the comings and goings at the Centre.

Five months had passed since Varian was forced to leave the country, but the Centre had continued functioning. They were under constant surveillance, but they'd managed to arrange the escape of over two hundred refugees. Just last week a few of their celebrity clients departed for Lisbon. Among them was Wanda Landowska, the harpsichordist. Landowska was Jewish.

Danielle tightened her jaw. And she, Danielle Berger, was still here. Her Cuban and Panamanian visas were carefully hidden at the villa. Her parents had written from California, assuring her they'd pull as many strings as they could to get her an American visa. Actually, since the Americans had been attacked at Pearl Harbor the month earlier, and America was now at war with the Axis powers, the American consulate had been issuing more visas for Centre clients. Jean had told her the consulate was also now cooperative about wiring information to the British that he and Fredi were gathering about train schedules and ship sailings. Frenay's resistance movement had grown and was now called Combat.

As she closed her umbrella and mounted the stairs to the office, she thought of the project in the Var. She'd been up there two weeks earlier, and in spite of the winter rains, she found the charcoal factory thriving. The operation was made up of twenty workers. Most of the men were single, sturdy and in their twenties and thirties, and there was one woman, the wife of one of the workers. Danielle visited the farm every two weeks to bring new orders. She was no longer so nervous on the train. She took the local and boarded at one of the suburban stops. Police almost never checked papers at the small stations. So far she'd had no problem getting new orders. Some of their customers came to the farm to collect the charcoal themselves, but the colliers had acquired a horse and wagon which they used to haul their sack-loads of charcoal to nearby villages on market day. There they would contract with trucks or buses to carry the charcoal to larger towns.

Now she reached the top of the stairs where a line of rain-dampened clients waited for the office to open. She greeted them with a smile and glanced at her watch. "Five more minutes Monsieurs, Madames," and she entered the office. Lili and Jaques had arrived before her, but neither Fredi or Marcel were present. She knew Jean would be in later. He would be meeting one of Corelli's people to pick up francs in exchange for sums deposited in American bank accounts, as he'd done with Dmitri. Corelli was a sworn enemy of Dmitri and was not adverse to taking away his rival's business.

After exchanging brief greetings with Jaques and Lili, and just as she was depositing her umbrella in the umbrella stand, the door flew open. It was Marcel. His auburn hair was plastered on his head, and drops of water slid down his face. His eyes were smoldering. "They've got Fredi!" he shouted.

The three staff members stood in a shocked silence.

Marcel was breathing rapidly. "I saw them take him away. He was in the café next door. He was at a table with a man I don't know." He took a deep breath. "I just had opened the door—to go for coffee—

when I saw two men in plain clothes grab him and a long canvas case that was on the floor next to Fredi—then push him toward the door. Fredi glanced at me as he went past but didn't speak."

Jaques stared at Marcel, his dark eyes flashing with alarm. "So who were they? The men who grabbed him? Cardon's men—or Gestapo?"

"They weren't German. They spoke local French. One of the men seemed familiar. Maybe I'd seen him hanging around here, but I'm not sure."

Danielle finally found her tongue. "What did the man at Fredi's table do then? Did he seem shocked—angry—try to escape?"

"He showed no emotion. He just calmly tossed back his coffee. Then he dropped some coins on the table and sauntered out the door."

Lili touched Jaques' arm. "Is there anything we can do? Or anyone to call?"

Marcel shrugged. "What <u>can</u> we do? The American Consul won't help him. Everyone in this agency is suspect."

"Maybe Jean will know," Danielle said, bleakly.


A few moments earlier, Jean had hopped off the trolley and was opening his umbrella, when from the corner of his eye spied two raincoat-clad men shoving Fredi into an unmarked car. Then he'd noticed a tall man coming out of the café. The tall man watched the car pull away from the curb before striding off down the street. He was wearing a brown fedora and a raincoat. His face was not visible, but from the way he walked Jean was sure he recognized the man. He was the contact sent to them by Copeé—a member of Combat—Frenay's organization. His name was Paul Barnier. So what was going on? Did Barnier have the gun he'd promised Fredi—for Combat?

By the time Jean reached the sidewalk, Barnier had disappeared. Then Jean noticed Marcel rushing out the café door and going into the Centre. Jean stood by the door watching the street before entering the Centre. It was still raining hard and few pedestrians walked by. The windows to the café were steamed so he couldn't see the interior. He gripped the straps of his musette. He'd buried most of Corelli's 70,000 francs at the villa—an unpleasant job in the rain. His shoes were still encrusted with mud.

Giving a final scrutiny to the street around him, he entered the Centre, wondering what was happening to Fredi. Had he been set up? Was Barnier a Gestapo or Abwehr agent? Doubled? Would Fredi keep his head under interrogation? Jean's stomach churned. Combat's network would be tested. They were all in danger now.

A few clients stood outside the open door to the office, and as Jean entered he saw that the staff was all occupied with clients. He stood inside the door, watching Danielle, who acknowledged his entrance with eyebrows raised, her eyes troubled. He hung up his coat, and carrying his musette, walked behind Danielle's chair. He touched her shoulder, and leaning toward her whispered into her ear, "they got Fredi. I saw Barnier. It's a setup." He then entered Varian's empty office and closed the door.

# Chapter Twenty-seven

## More Changes

### May, 1942

Sunlight was pouring through the open window next to Danielle's desk. Her task that morning was to prepare a report to send to Varian. As she inserted a sheet of paper into her typewriter, she thought about Fredi. Four months had passed since his arrest. In the meantime Jean had taken charge at the Centre and had brought Alain Montret onto the staff. So many of their people had left: Val, Marian, Charlie, and Varian—and now Fredi in jail. Danielle approved of Alain. She liked his sturdiness, his toughness. She glanced at him across the room as he interviewed a client. He'd added another skill to the Centre's collection. He owned two cameras and had set up a small darkroom in his tiny apartment. He photographed clients if they needed forged identity cards.

Nobody had heard from Fredi directly. All Jean had been able to find out he learned from Fredi's policeman informant. Fredi was still in jail at the Evêche, Cardon's turf. They received frequent letters from Varian, who had been most upset about Fredi's arrest. The report she was preparing for Varian would be mailed to him by the American consulate in the diplomatic pouch, thus avoiding censorship. The new Consul General Benton was more cooperative than his predecessor. In fact, he had apologized to Jean for the consulate's unfriendly behavior to Varian. "In the nine months since you left," she wrote, in the report, "we've been able to send four hundred people—legally—out of the France. We've evacuated twenty-two refugees who were on the Nazi's black list Furthermore twenty refugees are working in the Var at the charcoal factory." They had also sent twenty-seven British airmen back to England, but she was reluctant to put that information in the report.

She was interrupted in her work by the entrance into the Centre of a man she had met several times before. He was a refugee worker from Geneva, a French-speaking Swiss, a colleague of Varian's. Bernard Barel was his name. He was in his early forties, had a narrow, handsome face and lively brown eyes. His movements were quick and graceful. He was a skier, of course. She rose and shook his hand. "M. Barel, it's good to see you. What brings you to Marseilles?"

After an exchange of pleasantries, Barel came to the point of his visit. "I have news for you. I need to speak to Jean. Is he here?"

"Yes, he's in the office," and Danielle pointed to the open door and led Barel to Jean.

Jean burst into a beaming smile when he spied Barel. He strode forward and shook his friend's hand. "Bernard Barel! Great to see you. Ça va?"

"Ça va! And I have good news for you." He held out a paper sack, opened it and indicated that Jean should look inside. "Here's 5,000 francs for the Centre. It's just a beginning. From now on we can transfer francs from Switzerland for you. You won't have to deal with your usual sources any longer."

Jean's eyes lit up. "Fantastic! How did you manage it?"

"it's nothing to do with me. Our banking regulations and Vichy's eased up—a tangled web, believe me."

Jean took the sack from Barel's hand. Danielle watched the expression of relief cross Jean's face. Dealing with gangsters was both dangerous and unpleasant. The only one who had enjoyed the transactions was Charlie. Jean closed the door to the office and placed the sack of money into the safe. "Bernard, let's go down to the café for coffee or a glass of wine." He pointed warningly to the phone and the walls. "It's a nicer place to talk. Danielle, why don't you take a break. Come with us."

After they settled in a quiet corner of the café and the waiter had served their coffees, Barel leaned forward in his chair. "I have something else I need to tell you about. I know the acrobatics you've had to perform to get your refugees into Spain—and to get visas. Dangerous, heartbreaking work." He took a sip of coffee before continuing "We're setting up a new escape route into Switzerland—at the frontier at Saint Gingolph. You might consider it an option."

"But," Jean blurted, "the Swiss have been turning refugees away—back into France."

"Yes, but recently at Saint Gingolph they've been placing them in detention centers. Some get through to Lausanne or Zurich. They'll be better off there than in French or Spanish camps. The Jews here in Vichy are in extreme danger."

He glanced at Jean—then Danielle. "We believe it will get worse for the Jews—here in Vichy as well as the occupied zone. Laval, as you know, has just been appointed Minister of the Interior and has power over the police. We have heard reports that Jews are being taken from the detention camps and loaded onto to trains to Drancy, in Paris—by French policemen. From there they are being sent to Germany and points east. The Nazis have a quota they insist the police fill."

Danielle felt the blood drain from her cheeks. Laval was a notorious anti-semite. She cast a quick glance at Jean. His olive skin had taken on a green cast. A stone settled in Danielle's heart.

As soon as Bernard left the café, Jean fixed his eyes on Danielle's. They were as blue as the Provence sky, and her blonde hair fell to her shoulders in soft waves. She didn't look Jewish and she hadn't registered as such. Could she pass? It's possible—but. . ,"Danielle, cherie, I must find out what's happening at the camps. The closest one is at Aix, Les Milles. I want to see for myself." He glanced at his watch. "The train for Aix leaves in half an hour."

Danielle frowned. "Let's hope Barel is wrong, that the story is a horrible rumor."

He gave her a steady look. Danielle continued to deny the truth. Could he keep her safe? "Let me assess the scene at Les Milles. It's possible that Barel is repeating a rumor. But frankly I doubt it. I want to see first hand what's happening. Then I can write a report to the committee in New York. I'll be back as soon as I can." He kissed her on the cheek and rose from his chair. "Courage, ma cherie." He dropped some change on the table and left the café.

When he arrived at Aix he took a bus that went in the direction of the camp. When he saw the camp's tower in the distance, he signaled for the driver to stop. He stepped down and walked toward the tower, the hot sun beating down on his head. Sweat slid down his back. As he peered ahead, he noted the train tracks that ran about fifty yards from the road that edged the fence surrounding the camp. He could smell the stench from the latrines within. As he drew closer to the entrance to Les Milles, he noted the freight train standing before the high metal gate. Then he heard children crying, women screaming, men shouting in protest. In the midst of the chaos he spied a line of gendarmes dragging struggling people toward the freight cars and pushing them inside.

Jean stood by the gates and watched. Helpless. Stunned. These police were French—not German. He guessed there may be a hundred men, women and children being forced in to the cars. Jews, of course. A sign on the car said: Capacity, 8 horses, twenty men. He stared in disbelief as a gendarme pushed a pregnant woman carrying a wailing toddler toward the car. She stumbled and fell, clutching her child. The policeman yanked the child from her arms and pushed it into the car. The woman screamed. The gendarme pulled her onto her feet and shoved her screaming through the wide door into the train.

And there was nothing he could do. He turned away, sickened, the gorge rising in his throat. He'd read about such scenes happening in Germany, but here in France? Then a wave of rage propelled him away from the gates. He had to do more. The Americans had to know what he'd witnessed. And Combat must be informed. He would immediately find Simone.

And Danielle. Suddenly, he could envision her being dragged, pushed, thrown into a cattle car. She must leave France immediately. He would insist!

That evening Danielle and Jean were alone at the villa. Lili and Jaques were visiting friends in Cannes, and Marcel was in Toulouse dealing with the airmen. The couple sat silently at the table on the terrace, lit by two lanterns containing stubby candles. They had just finished eating their meager dinner of lentil and carrot soup. Danielle peered into Jean's shadowed eyes. Since returning from Aix he had barely spoken. He'd grasped her in his arms, but seemed unable to speak about what he'd seen. He'd told her only that French police were forcing Jewish refugees at Les Milles into a train headed for Paris.

Danielle sighed. "Jean, why can't you tell me more about what happened today? Was it so unspeakable?"

He slowly turned and gave her a long, tormented look. "It's just... it's just that I can't find words to tell you how helpless I felt—how frozen, impotent—when I watched those women and children being shoved into freight cars—like garbage!" He pounded his fist on the table, causing the plates to rattle and the candles flicker. "And I don't know what to do about it. And I'm scared shitless for your sake. I just know that you must leave this godforsaken country immediately!"

Danielle reached for his hand. How could she tell him? She couldn't leave immediately. "Jean, I have to tell you something. It's about my visas."

"For Cuba and Panama?"

She nodded—then took a deep breath. "They've expired."

He jumped up from the table, his eyes wild with shock. "Expired! Good God, Danielle, how could you let that happen? Why didn't you tell me? Let me see them. Maybe you're mistaken."

"They're in my passport. Hidden in my room. Come with me if you want, but I'm certain. They've expired!" With rapid steps she entered the villa and headed for her room. Jean followed. Within moments she removed a large envelope she'd taped to the back of a mirror and handed it to him. He withdrew the passport, flicked open the pages and eyed the two documents inserted there. He studied them slowly then handed them back to her. He sank onto the bed and put his head into his hands. "I don't want to believe it. You didn't show me. You didn't tell me. What were you thinking of!"

She sat next to him and leaned her head on his. "Jean, I didn't want to leave. I want to stay here and fight. I'll go to the Var. There's room for me at Chateaudouble. The villagers know me already. I can work from there."

He lifted his head and stared at her. "Danielle, you don't know what you're talking about. You should have seen how brutal those police—those French police—dragged those poor souls from the camp to the freight car. They were packed in like cattle being sent to the butcher."

Danielle turned away, unable to keep back her tears. Maybe Jean was right. She'd been foolish. But she'd truly believed she could pass as a gentile. And everyone working for Combat was in danger. What difference did it make she was also Jewish. And she was in love with Jean and hated the Nazis. But now Jean was furious with her. She covered her face with her hands and sobbed.

Jean reached out to her and held her tightly, as she cried on his shoulder. "I'm sorry, Danielle, It's just that I'm so afraid for you. Maybe your parents can come up with an American visa."

Danielle lifted her head and fished a handkerchief from the pocket of her skirt. "They've tried twice. And twice the request was rejected."

Jean sighed deeply. "Well, maybe a third time?"

The sounds of a closing door and footsteps crossing the floor caused them both to jump to their feet. Then they heard Fredi's voice boom out. "Anyone home?"

"Good God, it's Fredi," Jean cried. "They've let him out! After four months!" He rushed out of Danielle's room and down the hall to the front room. "Fredi, I can't believe it! You're alive."

Danielle, mopping the tears from her face followed in his footsteps. Jean embraced Fredi, whose clothes hung on him loosely. "You look terrible, but they let you go!"

Fredi gave a wan laugh. "Yes. The judge dismissed the charges. So here I am. Alive, more or less."

"Fredi, let's go out on the terrace. I have questions." Jean pointed to the walls. As soon as they were outside Jean turned to him. "You were interrogated repeatedly, I heard. And did they find out about your connection to Combat? Or our false passports and money laundering at the Centre?"

"No. I stuck to my story. I knew nothing about Combat and our work at the Centre was strictly humanitarian. Eventually they believed me. Interrogation after interrogation."

Jean's stomach tightened. Had Fredi been turned. Had he talked? "They used torture?"

"Not really. The inquisitors were French not Gestapo—a few punches, but sleep deprivation, filth, cold, bad food, rats, fleas. Don't get too close to me!" He laughed weakly. The judge finally decided that Barnier was a provocateur, attempting entrapment, that I had not intended to purchase a gun, that I knew nothing. I think they decided Barnier was an Abwehr agent, which didn't please the judge. But I'm exhausted."

Danielle touched Fredi on the shoulder. "Fredi, I'll fix you something to eat. We have some soup. And wine?"

"Wonderful. Then I need a bath and some sleep." He waited for Danielle to leave the room before he continued. He sank into a chair by the terrace table. "And, Jean, I must get out of Marseilles, go underground. I need a new identity and forged papers. I won't get a second chance. I'll need your help."

Jean stared into Fredi's tired blue eyes, thinking that he'd get Fredi his papers but he'd keep an eye on him. "I'll go to Simone tomorrow."

"I should leave tomorrow as soon as I can get papers. OK, Jean?"

"OK, old comrade. Simone will contact your man who does false papers. What name will you use?"

"Felix Couvet. I'll keep my own initials. And birth place, Alsace, because of my accent."

"Do you have a safe house to go to?"

"I'm thinking of Cap d'Antibes. My aunt has a cottage there."

Jean glanced toward the terrace door, thinking of Danielle, that she should use the Var farm as a safe house. Soon. "Good. And you must stay away from Marseilles. Cardon would like to see all of us stashed away in those damp cellars."

Fredi leaned back in his chair and looked up at the sky. "It's wonderful to see the sky again. All those stars." He then gave Jean a sharp glance, his voice like steel. "And Jean, did you question Coupeé, the man who introduced me to Barnier?"

"I talked to Coupeé, and I'm pretty sure he's loyal. He thought Barnier was one of us. He was fooled, too. Barnier disappeared, of course."

"I know. He wasn't around to give evidence. The judge was pissed off at him. My informant at the Evêche told me the guy was Abwehr. He was good, I'll say that."

As Danielle came through the door carrying a tray holding a steaming bowl of soup and a carafe of wine, the two men stopped talking. Fredi turned to her. "Danielle, you're an angel. That soup smells heavenly!"

"It's not bad—not great—but it's food and you look like you could use it."

"Indeed I can!"

Watching his comrade wolf down the soup, Jean wished he could discuss their group's latest activities, but until he felt certain about Fredi's loyalties, he'd keep mum. "Fredi," he said, "I want to hear about your interrogations—how you kept to your story—what they asked. I might find myself in the same situation some day."

Fredi looked up from his soup and gave a deep sigh. "Not now, Jean. Tomorrow maybe. Now I want to eat. Then sleep. All night in a room without a light shining. All night without being awakened by some fllic,"

"Sorry, Fredi. You're right. We'll talk about it tomorrow.

The next day at sundown Jean remained a few steps behind Fredi as he made his way toward the bus station, keeping a sharp lookout for a tail. So far none had appeared. Early that morning Jean had contacted Simone and found the artist who created the false documents. In the meantime Fredi had dyed his hair with some cast-off hair dye left by one of Varian's tenants, and found an abandoned pair of his glasses. Alain had photographed Fredi in his disguise and had rushed to the room he used as a studio and darkroom to develop It. The forger completed the work before dusk. Now Fredi planned to take the bus to a suburban stop where he would board the train to Cannes. The local train stations were normally not manned by police.

They soon reached the square where the buses collected. Four charcoal-powered buses were parked at a series of curbs. Fredi headed for the ticket office, handed the agent a few coins, and turned toward the second bus. He stopped before mounting the vehicle's steps, glanced at Jean, their eyes connecting briefly, and entered the bus. Jean felt himself relax. It was inconceivable to think of Fredi as a traitor. He was a pro. And clever enough to stick to his story during interrogation. All the same, he'd need to be watched. Too much was at stake.

Jean reversed his steps, heading for the Centre, now casting his mind on the problem of Danielle. He felt a surge of anger when he thought of her expired visas. Why couldn't she have told him they were about to expire? She didn't trust him! She knew, of course, that he would try to force her to leave. He hadn't realized how stubborn she could be.

Jean shrugged. There was no point in being angry with her. She wanted to resist the Germans, fight for France. He felt the same, of course, but he was a man, a soldier. Danielle was a beautiful young woman. Wars were fought by men. The women should be protected, be safe. Then he thought of the women he'd seen being shoved into the box car and his heart tightened. Jewish women in France were not safe. Could Danielle get away with pretending to be Christian? She wasn't a practicing Jew. She was agnostic—just as he was. They'd discussed religion, and neither had considered their differing religious backgrounds a problem. Tonight they must talk.

# Chapter Twenty-eight

## Sam

### *June, 1942*

The next morning, soon after Jean had arrived at the Centre, he received a telephone call from Sam Baxter at the office of the Unitarian Service Committee. Jean knew Sam as a friend of Varian's. Sam requested that Jean come to his office, that he had something important to discuss. Wondering what the man had on his mind, Jean shrugged, told Danielle he'd be back in an hour and walked out onto the street. By habit he surveyed the area for gendarmes or plainclothesmen. None appeared. He gave a wry smile. They were late this morning.

A brilliant sun was already shining down on the city. Jean carried his jacket over his shoulder as he trudged down the two blocks to the 's office. He thought of his talk with Danielle the evening before. She'd agreed to consider moving to the farm in the Var, but she didn't want to be pressured. Jean sighed. He hadn't known how stubborn she could be.

When Jean arrived at the Unitarian office, Sam, a rotund man Jean guessed to be in his thirties, emerged from his office. His handshake was firm and his voice had a metallic ring. His French was fluent, but when Jean answered him in English, he responded in an American accented English similar to Varian's. "Sam Baxter here," he said, smiling. "I've been wanting to meet you. I've heard about your good work at CAS. And elsewhere."

Jean didn't know how to reply. From whom had this man heard of him? Varian? Did Sam know about the Bulletin? Or his other work for Frenay? "Yes, we've been able to continue our work—even without Varian."

"I'm glad you're holding it together. We miss Varian. An amazing man. He's helped hundreds of refugees—if not thousands. And I think the way he was treated by the State Department was deplorable. But Jean, I have something else I want to discuss with you, Would you mind taking a walk with me?" He smiled. "I need some exercise."

Feeling more than a little trepidation, Jean agreed. The two men crossed to the shady side of the street and strolled one block to a small square, speaking about the plight of their refugee clients. Sam pointed to an empty bench under a palm tree, and they both sat down. "I won't beat around the bush," Sam said abruptly. " And I'll be brief. I've called you here because I have a proposition to make. I know you are in contact with Combat. I know about your Resistance work. Now we want you and your group to gather intelligence to pass to the Americans. For the Office of Strategic Services,"

"For the Americans?"

"Yes. We're on the same side, Jean. We're fighting fascism. Like you, we hate Hitler."

Jean stared at Sam, stunned into silence. The Americans? He'd never considered working for anyone other than the French.

Sam gave him a sympathetic look. "I know you're surprised by my proposition, but hear me out. Officially we Americans have been in this war since December, but five months before that Roosevelt created an intelligence organization, which has recently been re-named, the Office of Special Services, or OSS. Roosevelt appointed Bill Donovan to be its head. He's cooperating with the British secret services."

"And de Gaulle?" Jean asked.

Sam's face clouded, but he nodded. "Yes, certainly, although de Gaulle has competition with Giraud and Darlan—but that's not our concern at the moment. Although it would be useful to know how the people here feel about de Gaulle."

"What kind of information are you looking for?" Jean said, finally.

"We need to know French attitudes toward Vichy, the mood of the workers. We need train schedules, ship arrivals and departures, location of manufacturing plants, the economy in general. Anything that could help the Allies."

Jean took a sharp intake of breath. It sounded as though the Americans were planning covert activities—or bombing raids. He didn't know what to say. He needed to think about Sam's request. He wished he could talk it over with Fredi, but that was impossible now Fredi's loyalty was in question.

Sam's sharp blue eyes were searching his face. "I have one more thing to add. We are well funded. We can pay you for your expenses and supply you with equipment you might need. Cameras, weapons, etc. And we have an arrangement with the American Consulate here in Marseilles to act as a liaison."

Jean stared at him. "Sam, I need a day or so to think this over. OK?"

"OK," and he rose and the two men shook hands. Sam's hand was dry and firm. Jean could feel his own hand damp with sweat. What should he do?

# Chapter Twenty-nine

## The Farm

*June, 1942*

The air cooled as the bus chugged up the steep, curving road to Chateaudouble. Danielle turned her face toward the open window and peered into the gorge below. The sun glinted on the water that flowed over crushed yellow stone at the bottom of the gorge. The sight soothed her nerves and she felt the muscles in her neck loosen. She glanced at her musette in the rack above her seat, which contained a sheaf of charcoal orders and a change of clothes. Although she was on a routine visit to the charcoal project, she would be staying a few days. It was a relief to get away from Marseilles. Cardon's men continued to watch the entrance to the Centre, and police rode by the villa on their bicycles two or three times a day. And Jean wanted her to move to the Var. He thought they all should move out of the villa.

"We need to be less conspicuous," he'd said last night after dinner alone on the terrace. "And Danielle, there's something else I need to talk over with you."

She had frowned, believing he'd continue the lecture about leaving France or going to the Var. He held up his hand. "No, Danielle, this isn't about your plans. This afternoon I got a call from one of the men at the Unitarian Service Office, an American, called Sam." Jean then proceeded to describe the astonishing conversation he'd had with the Unitarian. They'd been asked to pass intelligence to the Americans.

"For the Americans?" she'd responded. "But we already take our information to the American Consulate."

"This is different. This would be spying for their intelligence organization, the OSS. And I feel a little strange about that. Spying for America. Not French Resistance—or de Gaulle. We'd always intended the consulate to send our stuff to the British and Free French."

"What did this Sam want us to find out?"

"He wants the usual stuff—train schedules, factory production, ship arrivals in the Rhone area—anything, he said, that would help the Allies. He also needs information about French attitudes toward the Nazis and Vichy, or if they're followers of de Gaulle—or of Giraud or Darlain. And furthermore, he'd give us money for our expenses."

Danielle digested this information, feeling a frisson of excitement. "What about your work for the Bulletin?"

"Alain is helping me with that. And he has a friend he's going to bring in, a writer. I think we could manage. So, Danielle, tell me what you think we should do?"

"I don't know what to say. The money part is good. Frenay has had trouble getting money to you. And the Americans are so committed and energetic. Think of Varian. It's something to consider."

"I know." Jean had risen from the table and was pacing the terrace.

"Jean, I'd say go ahead if you can get enough recruits. We have the Swiss escape route that Barel has organized for our Centre clients. And the charcoal factory."

Jean leaned on the back of his chair. "And Alain and I have had men contact us who want to join the Resistance. We have a couple of men in our group who work at the post office—and another at that airplane factory near Aix. There's no reason why we can't give our information to the Americans as well as Frenay and Combat. Let's do it. I'll tell Sam tomorrow while you're in the Var. It will take a while to get organized."

Now the bus had reached Chateaudouble. Passengers were reaching for their bundles and baskets preparing to get off the bus and walk through the arch. As Danielle grabbed her musette, she couldn't stop thinking about the Americans and the OSS—and how pleased she'd been that Jean had included her in his decision-making about the American's offer. It wasn't always like that. The other evening with Fredi she'd noted how the two men had stopped talking when she'd returned to the terrace after being gone for a few minutes. So often they didn't include her—telling her she didn't need to know." Now, of course, Jean hadn't been confiding in Fredi. He was still worried Fredi had been turned under interrogation. She didn't want to even consider Fredi could be a traitor—but all the same, they had to be cautious. Would they ever know for sure?

Descending from the bus, she slung her musette over her shoulder and walked through the arch. She passed the Mairie, smiling at the old men on the bench overlooking the gorge. "Bonjours," she called out. They touched their caps and greeted her warmly. She glanced up at the ruin of the old château, its stone tower presiding over the village. The sky was blue, the sunshine warmed the skin on her bare arms, and the streets smelled faintly of farm animals. It was good to be here, she thought, smiling to herself. It was such a relief to be free of fear. She then searched for a horse and wagon that might pass the charcoal factory, but none appeared.

Shifting the musette on her shoulder, she turned onto the dirt road that led to the farm, just a mile away. It wasn't long before she smelled the faint odor of wood burning. Then she spied the columns of smoke rising into the sky. The colliers were at work. When she approached the entrance to the farm, she counted ten shoulder-high smoking mounds. Four men, whose faces and bare arms were smudged gray with ashes, guarded the mounds. She called out to them, and they swooped toward her, clamoring their greetings, begging for news from the city.

The youngest of the workers, a sixteen year old named Luc, relieved Danielle of her musette. "Let me carry this for you. And you must be thirsty. Come. Maman will be so glad to see you," and he escorted her to the farm house, which was far enough away from the colliers to be free of smoke. As they approached the house, three chickens and a strutting rooster were pecking in the dirt by the front door, and Danielle noted that the geraniums planted on either side of the doorway were in bloom, their blossoms a bright red. How far away the fevered atmosphere of Marseilles seemed, that world of desperation, spies and fear.

"Maman!" Luc called. "Danielle is here."

A woman wiping her hands on a blue apron emerged from the house and embraced Danielle, giving her the three times kiss on her cheeks. "Danielle, come in, come in. Let me get you something to drink. It's so warm today. And how are you and tell me all your news!" Words tumbled from her as if she hadn't spoken to a soul in days. Danielle knew she was the only woman here on the farm and was hungry for feminine conversation. Her name was Louise Godet and she was the wife of Paul Godet, both from Alsace, where they'd been forced to sell their farm when the Germans annexed the region.

As Danielle sipped her glass of cool well water, she admired the new curtains at the windows sewn from unbleached muslin and edged with crocheted lace. "Louise, your new curtains are lovely. Did you do the crochet work?"

Louise nodded, smiling broadly, her blue eyes as bright as the summer sky. "In the evenings here by the fire. At least we have plenty of wood."

"Right." Danielle reached for her musette that Luc had placed on the plank table. "And I've brought new orders from town for charcoal."

Louise lifted the pitcher of water and filled Danielle's glass. "You must go to the barn and see how much the men have produced." She then pointed to the row of jars on the shelves next to the sink. "And I've made jam from the blackberries I picked in the meadow. And we're getting honey from our beehives. And chanterelles from the forest. I've been selling them at the local market. You must take some back to Marseilles when you leave."

"Wonderful, Louise!" Danielle sighed. It was a different world here in the Var, but now she must attend to the books, which was not her skill, although Marcel had been giving her accounting lessons. When she gazed out the window at the forested landscape, for a moment her hands itched for a paintbrush—or her drawing pencil—but only for a moment. This was not the time for art.

# Chapter Thirty

## Endgame

### June, 1942

The day after Jean's conversation with Sam, he sat in the Centre staring out the window.  On his way here he'd stopped at the Unitarian office to tell Sam he'd accept his offer.  Sam had made a date with him for the following week to go over methods.  Jean's heart was still thumping with excitement and fear.  Working for the American spy agency was a step above their amateur sleuthing he'd been engaged in these last months.

Jean stretched his shoulders.  He must get to work.  Marcel had left the account book on his desk and it was time he checked it.  The outer room was filled with grim-faced clients, most needing money to survive.  Thank God for Bernard Barel, who had been faithfully sending couriers with packets of francs.

The sound of boots tramping on the stairway outside the office, brought Jean to his feet.  He recognized that sound.  Cardon's men. Would they be searched again?  Cardon just didn't give up!  Jean walked into the room where the clients eyes were riveted on the doorway.  The door burst open and four gendarmes and two plainclothesmen rushed into the room.  Cardon was among them.

Two of the gendarmes rounded up the terrified refugees and herded them out the door. Cardon stood before Jean, his legs spread, his arms folded over his barrel chest. "I have a warrant to search the premises. I know you are providing your clients with forged documents. And spreading propaganda. Open the safe, please." he commanded.

Jean opened the safe and Cardon peered inside. He pulled out a sack, which he then emptied on Jean's desk, which Jean knew it contained 5,000 francs. Cardon shoved the money back into the bag and handed it to one of the gendarmes. Jean protested. "You have no right to seize that money! It was sent to us from the Centre office in New York—a humanitarian organization."

"We shall see, Monsieur," Cardon said coolly. I continue to suspect that your so-called humanitarian organization is engaging in illegal activities."

One of the plains clothesmen called to Cardon and handed him a sheet of news print. Cardon glanced at the paper then looked up at Jean triumphantly. "I knew it! Look! Subversive propaganda."

Jean took the sheet in his hand, examining it carefully. It was not a Combat publication, Where did it come from? Had Cardon's men planted it? "M. Cardon, this has nothing to do with us. Someone has left it here. One of our clients, perhaps."

"A likely story, Monsieur." Cardon called to the men in plain clothes and pointed to the four staff members. Escort these men to the Evêche at once. They are under arrest. And you," gesturing to the gendarmes, "seize the typewriters and all the paperwork you find and take it to headquarters. Then seal the door. This organization is now shut down. Permanently!"

Lili, who had turned pale, stood stiffly by her desk. Cardon strode toward her. "And you, Mme, leave the premises immediately. Go home!" and he sauntered out the door.

Lili grabbed her bag, shot Jaques a stricken look, and wordlessly left the room.

As the gendarmes were collecting the typewriters, emptying desk drawers, Jean, Alain, Marcel and Jaques were hustled down the stairs. A police van was waiting for them by the curb. Jean saw Lili emerge from the building when he was being shoved into the  police van.

Jaques had also seen his wife. He called out to her. "Go to the farm! Now!"

Jean then poked his head out the door. "Tell Danielle to stay there!" He watched as Lili, hurried up the Canebiére, holding a handkerchief to her eyes.

The next day, after endless interrogations, the four men were released, their charges dismissed. As they trudged down the steps of the Evêche, Jean's damp shirt clung to his skin. It was close to noon and the late June sun was hot on his bare head. He glanced at Jaques and Marcel. Then at Alain. Their faces were streaked with sweat and grime and their eyes were red from lack of sleep. They'd spent the night in a holding cell that contained only a table and two chairs. Now were they waiting for him to tell them what to do next? But what should they do? He was too tired to think straight. Silently, all four began to move as fast as possible away from the Evêche and Cardon's gendarmes.

When they reached the Canebiére, Jean turned to his companions. "The Centre is finished here in Marseilles, you know. They let us go this time, but I don't think we can keep on talking our way out of jail much longer."

Marcel turned to Jean. "Did you ever figure out who the idiot was who left that propaganda piece on the table?"

"No. It could have been one of the clients. It wasn't ours, and Cardon didn't have evidence that it was. Maybe he planted it! He had to let us go, but he's adamant about closing the Centre. He's been waiting for an excuse."

Jaques sighed. "Well, let's go to the villa and clean up. Then I'll catch the bus to the Var. Lili will be frantic."

Marcel touched Jaques' shoulder. "I think I'll go with you."

Jean nodded. Danielle would also be frantic. "Not a bad idea for all of us. Lay low for a while. But lets go to the villa and dig up the stuff we've buried there. Let's hope Cardon's men aren't on guard. Then we should pack up and move out. It's time we go underground." As he spoke, a trolley that would take them to the villa rumbled to a stop. Without further comment the four men quickly climbed aboard.

When the men approached the villa they moved cautiously, checking the road for signs of parked vans or patrolmen riding by on bicycles. "It seems clear," Jean murmured, "but let's search the house before we begin digging. And make sure Mme Sorel and Annette don't see what we're doing." Jean trusted both the housekeeper and the maid, but it would be safer if they didn't know about the buried objects in the woods. "Alain, why don't you stay outside and watch the road for Cardon's men. OK?"

"OK." Alain sat on the stone bench by the front door and lit a cigarette as the other three entered the house. They searched the many rooms, greeted Mme Sorel, and concluding the house was safe, moved into the garden and fetched the shovel in the shed. As they headed for the pine woods they were stopped by Alain, who was running after them, breathing heavily. "Two gendarmes are parked across the street," he said, panting. "They kept staring at me, but stayed in the car. After a few minutes I stubbed out my cigarette and strolled into the house. They're still there."

"Shit!" Jean said, "Alain, go back inside. If they question you, keep them talking. Jaques, Marcel, let's go!"

The three men sprinted into the woods, desperately trying not to make noise. They stopped not far from where they knew their stash was buried, hiding behind a clump of flowering yellow broom. After a few agonizing moments, Jean rose and crept toward the pine-needle covered spot where they must dig. "Let's hurry. Jaques, will you stand guard? Whistle if you hear anything."

Jaques gave a silent salute and sauntered into the villa's garden. Jean and Alain took turns digging up the sack of gold, the suitcases containing francs and the short wave radio. It didn't take them long. They quickly divided up the francs into four portions, shoving it into the musettes and briefcase then covered up the holes with dirt and pine needles. "Now we wait," Jean whispered, crouching behind the trunk of a huge pine.

They waited for almost an hour before Alain and Jaques came running into the woods. "They've gone!" Alain cried. "Let's get the hell out of here."

Jaques volunteered to carry the gold to the Var. Jean kept the radio, realizing he needed it to listen to BBC news reports for the Bulletin. They left the villa, walking briskly, alert for tails, but feigning nonchalance.

The next day Jean and Alain sat side by side on the crowded bus headed for Chateaudouble. The bouncing of the bus on the rough road kept Jean awake, although he was bone weary. Since they were released from the Evêche the day before he and Alain had not stopped moving. Had they remembered everything? After they had dug up their buried treasure, Jaques and Marcel had quickly packed their things and left for the Var. Jean moved out of both the villa and the small room he had been renting for so long. Alain had helped him move the precious typewriter, the radio, the bicycle, some of Danielle's things and Jean's own meager pile of personal belongings to the new room he had rented on the outskirts of town. Alain had found a room nearby to set up his darkroom. The moving process had been nerve-wracking. Constantly alert, fearing they might be watched by Cardon's men, they'd taken circuitous routes to their new quarters.

Now as the bus swerved around a narrow curve, Jean thought of Danielle, hoping Jaques and Marcel had been able to calm her fears. Then he considered Fredi, or Felix, as he was now called. The more he'd pondered about Fredi, the more he wanted to trust him. The people who worked with him all worshiped him. The police informant at the Evêche had assured Jean that Fredi had not been tortured. He'd been interrogated time after time, "but the French police aren't the Gestapo," he'd said firmly.

He had wanted to talk to Fredi about the work for OSS and his next meeting with Sam. He wondered about the methods Sam had said he'd talk to him about. And was it now time to change his own name and acquire new papers? This had been his first arrest, and he wasn't charged with a crime, but would he be on the Gestapo list now? If he were, he'd need to change his identity and move again, since he'd registered with the concierge as Jean Barrault. He also must contact their Swiss connection, Barel, to tell him they'd continue rescue activities for the refugees. They would go underground now that the Centre had been shut down. He owed it to Varian and the desperate refugees. Concerns swept through his head. Would he be smart enough to deal with these challenges? He'd have to be!

A cooling draft of air blew through the open window at his side, chasing away the smell of smoke from the bus's charcoal-burning engine. He eyed the rocky outcroppings rising steeply across the gorge.

A glimmer of late afternoon sunlight flashed on the yellow and white rough stone. He took a deep breath of the fresh air, then turned to Alain, whose bent head bounced with the bumps in the road, and who was fast asleep.

When Jean pushed open the farmhouse door, Alain behind him, Danielle and Lili let out cries of welcome. Both men were caught in tight hugs and barraged with questions. Exhausted, they did their best to recount the events of the previous forty-eight hours, all the while consuming the wine and chestnut bread smothered in honey pressed on them by Louise Godet.

That night Luc Godet gave up his upstairs room to Lili and Jaques and moved into the barn with the other charcoal workers. Jean joined Danielle in her attic room under the eaves. He fell asleep the moment his head touched the pillow, but at dawn he awoke, and with a feeling almost of disbelief, realized Danielle lay next to him. He reached for her, drew her close. The sun was up well over the mountain when the lovers descended the stairs to breakfast.

Jean was surprised to see Fredi at the table. At first Jean hadn't recognized Fredi with black hair and glasses, but when he called out a hearty greeting, Jean knew his voice. A smiling Jaques and Lili lifted their cups of coffee and sang out their "bonjours." Louise immediately went to the stove for the coffee pot and poured two more cups for the late-comers. Marcel had already left for Toulouse. The sharp, incessant sound of wood chopping indicated that work was well in progress in the woods outside the farmhouse.

"Fredi," Jean said, "it's wonderful to have you here. We've got to talk."

"It's Felix, remember!"

"OK, Felix. But before we talk, let's have breakfast—and I can get used to your new look."

While they ate and drank their coffees Jean and Felix exchanged stories of their recent exploits. Although Jean did not want to broach the subject of the OSS and the Americans until he talked to his group about Fredi, they could discuss how to continue Varian's work. "You were in jail when Bernard Barel dropped into the Centre." Jean described the new method of obtaining funds for their refugees and

Barel's suggestion about sending their clients into Switzerland through the frontier at Saint Gingolph.

Jaques turned to Jean, then Fredi. "Should we make this farm our new headquarters? Can we deal with our Centre clients from here, get them to Switzerland, arrange to pick up the money Barel offered to provide us with?"

"Possibly. It might work." Jean replied. "I've rented a room near Marseilles, but I can travel here easily enough. It' takes only about two hours. We could use the rented room as a safe house while I'm here at the farm."

Alain leaned forward. "I've rented a room too, near Jean's, but I can come up here and work with the other men when I'm not writing for Combat, but we'll need new work permits."

Danielle set down her coffee cup. "We can be registered with the local mayor and the prefecture as workers here at the charcoal factory. Any of us could be traveling about to get orders for our farm. The mayor is anti-fascist, and will pave the way for us at the prefecture. The mayor's an admirer of de Gaulle. I'm sure he'll cooperate."

"Good idea, Danielle," Jean said. "And we need new residence permits, ration coupons and travel passes."

Fredi, who had been quiet until now, lifted his head. "I need to be near the coast, but I can meet you all here. And I have a source for ration coupons. But I don't know what Marcel will do. He has a girlfriend in Toulouse and might decide to stay there."

Jean nodded, thinking that Marcel would probably continue his work helping downed airmen cross the Pyrenees into Spain. As Fredi spoke Jean watched him. Even with the glasses Fredi's eyes were true blue, reflecting honesty. He'd been a close friend so long that Jean couldn't help but trust him. He'd talked to Alain about his suspicions and Alain, also, refused to believe Fredi would betray them—and their cause.

Danielle was speaking and Jean turned to her to listen. "It's going to be different, that's for sure. We'll be split up now that the Centre is closed. No more coffee together at the café downstairs from the Centre."

Lili touched Danielle's hand. "Instead we can rendezvous in this kitchen."

# PART THREE

## RESIST

# Chapter Thirty-one

## Clandestine Tasks

*November, 1942*

The sky was dark with clouds and a chill wind blew from the north as Danielle pedaled Jean's bicycle toward the village. She was on her way to catch the bus and train to Marseilles. She would be meeting Jean at a café at a suburban stop near the city. They'd made the date five days earlier before he left for the Rhone. She tried not to think about the task she would be performing today. It was too frightening. She'd think about the farm instead.

With one hand she tugged at her flapping scarf, tucking it into the collar of her coat. She thought about the newcomers the farm had absorbed. Five were Jews who had evaded police deportations. Fredi had sent four more men who were refusing Laval's order to report for work in Germany. Until they could organize to fight the Nazis they were working as colliers and woodsmen. They'd built a makeshift shelter in the woods behind the barn. They were a lively lot—some were communists.

Vetting these men hadn't been easy. Jean and Alain had interrogated each one several times, listening carefully for contradictions in their stories. They all knew that as the Resistance grew, the Germans would try to place infiltrators in their midst. Jean had been adamant about the repeated interrogations. It was a matter of life or death. So far, the newcomers seemed to be legitimate resisters. Furthermore, Jean had finally concluded that they need not doubt Fredi's loyalty. It had been five months since Fredi's release from prison, and he'd shown himself to be a hard-working, risk-taking resistance fighter—a patriot who would die before betraying his country and comrades. When Jean confided to her that he no longer suspected Fredi of treachery, she'd felt her heart lighten. She'd never believed that Fredi could betray them. He loved France too much.

At the bus stop Danielle chained her bike to a rack and locked it carefully. The bike was a valued item at the farm. Draguignan, a town larger than Chateaudouble was only fifteen kilometers away and was a good place to shop.

When Danielle boarded the bus headed for St Rafael, she exchanged greetings with most of the passengers. Since she'd moved here five months ago she'd become acquainted with many people in the village—especially those who rode the bus to buy or sell their produce at the daily markets in Draguignan or St Raphael. She'd also learned which villagers not to trust, the pro-fascist, admirers of Vichy, the collaborators. The mayor had warned her of whom to beware.

An hour later, as she approached her train stop on the outskirts of Marseilles, her stomach tightened. Her task today would be terrifying. It would be the third time she had acted as courier for the OSS. At the café Jean would hand over the information his group had gathered in the Rhone. She would then carry the report to Consul Benton at the American consulate, and he would arrange for the information to reach OSS. She had an appointment with Benton at half past one. Since Jean had been arrested, and was known by the police as the man in charge of the suspicious Centre Américain, it was risky for him to carry material for the OSS while he was in Marseilles. He could be stopped by the police, and If intelligence information were discovered in his possession, the entire network could be in jeopardy.

Fredi had suggested that she would be a wiser choice to carry the intelligence reports to the American consulate. He and Jean had considered Lili, but since Lili was helping Jaques organize the escape of Centre clients to Switzerland, Danielle insisted that she be the courier. Jean had objected strenuously, but she finally convinced him she had an excellent cover to be in Marseilles—her job collecting charcoal orders. And as for going to the American consulate, she could claim she had come to inquire about her visa application.

Now, at this moment, as the train began its screeching deceleration, she wanted to tell Jean she'd changed her mind. She felt paralyzed. She couldn't move. But when the train finally lurched to a stop, she forced herself to rise from her seat, walk through the corridor to the end of the car and descend the steps. Her limbs moved automatically. She slung her musette over her shoulder, and strode toward the café. Jean was waiting for her.

He rose from his table at the back of the café, and enfolded her in a tight embrace, "I was afraid you might decide not to come," he said, seating her at the banquette, sliding next to her, touching her hand. She placed her musette on her lap. Jean's musette was squeezed between them. She knew it would contain the intelligence reports she must carry to the consulate. The two musettes were identical.

After the waiter brought their coffee and took their lunch orders, Danielle unbuckled her musette and pulled out a sheaf of charcoal orders. She handed them to Jean, who pretended to go over them carefully. He then tucked them into his musette and replaced it on the banquette. In the meantime, she had fastened her musette and placed it next to Jean's. She knew that when they left the café she would pick up Jean's musette instead of her own. Jean would carry hers. The charcoal orders in the musette would be the cover to show the police if they stopped to search her. Jean will have placed the intelligence material in a concealed pocket in the bag.

When they left the café, Jean stopped and buttoned his coat, all the while eying the street in all directions. Danielle also glanced behind them at the closed café door. No one followed. She then checked her coat's inside pocket for her wallet stuffed with identity documents and money—and the letter from the American Consulate confirming her appointment for this afternoon. If stopped by the police for a document check—or to buy tram or train tickets, it was safer not to need to open her musette.

Jean made a final check of the street, then put his arm around her shoulders as they walked toward the tram. He spoke in a low voice close to her ear. "Now we can talk."

She replied in almost a whisper. "Did you get what you wanted for the report?"

"Yes,   And I think the Americans will be pleased with what's in that bag." He paused a moment, waiting until they'd passed a couple walking in the opposite direction. "It has notes and photographs of much of the Riviera shoreline. And the German defense installations. And the docks at Toulon—and manufacturing plants and railroad lines."

Danielle's pulse quickened. Photographs? "Jean," she murmured, "Won't photographs be bulky, easy for a gendarme to feel through the bag?"

Jean shook his head. "It's film," Danielle, "rolled up tightly in a toothpaste tube. That's what I needed to tell you.  There's a small zippered toilet kit in the bottom of the bag—with a toothbrush and the toothpaste inside. You'll just need to hand over the kit as well as the envelope of papers."

Danielle gave a nervous giggle. "I hope Consul Benton won't think I'm suggesting he needs to brush his teeth!"

Jean grinned and shook his head.

"And, Jean, why did you photograph the Riviera?  Didn't the OSS ask for information about the Rhone?"

"Yes, they did, but they also wanted a description and pictures of the entire coast.  We're  guessing that the Riviera could be a site the Allies are considering for an invasion of France.  What's more, we believe the invasion of north Africa is imminent—Algeria, we think. Sailors have told us they're seeing more British and American shipping sailing the Mediterranean.

By now they had walked the two blocks to the tram stop.  She was surprised to see Alain standing on the corner among four other people apparently waiting for the tram. but before she could greet him, Jean leaned toward her and murmured, "pretend you don't know him. He's going to watch your back. He's less well-known by the police than I am. When the tram arrives, get aboard and remain as near the front as possible—like before. He'll be in the rear. OK? He'll stick with you until you're back in Chateaudouble. And I'll see you tonight at the farm. Take care, Danielle." At that moment the tram trundled down the track and stopped at their corner. Jean gave her a quick kiss, and along with the other passengers. she boarded the tram.

Luckily, she found a seat in front by the window. As the tram entered a busier section of Marseilles, more and more passengers boarded. People stood in the aisle jostling each other as they hung onto the overhead straps. Danielle stared out the window, careful not to make eye contact with anyone. She was aware of Alain's presence in the back of the tram, but didn't turn her head to look for him.

At last, the tram clanged to a stop at the American Consulate. Danielle shouldered her way through the crowd and descended to the street. Eying the guards posted around the consulate, her heart pounded crazily. She stopped herself from glancing back to see if Alain were following her, and tightening the knots of her resolve, she walked briskly up the building's stone steps. When she reached the top, a gendarme stopped her. "Papers," he snapped.

She forced herself to remain calm and shot him a beaming smile. Reaching into the inside pocket of her coat, she drew out her brown leather wallet. She handed over her identity card, work permit and residence card.

"And what is the reason for your visit here, Mademoiselle?" he asked, glancing from the pictures on the documents to her face, then once again to the documents. He then leaned to one side and eyed her musette.

"I'm here to see Consul General Benton about my visa," she replied matter-of-factly, praying he wouldn't ask to search her musette.

The gendarme frowned. "But Mlle, the visa section is in Montredon."

Danielle kept her voice steady. "Yes, I know." she said, with another pleasant smile. "I made my application there, but Consul Benton has something he wants to discuss with me. I have an appointment," and she pulled an official-looking letter from her pocket and handed it to him.

The gendarme gave the letter a perfunctory glance, then with a brief nod, he returned her papers and gestured politely toward the door. "Entrez, Madamoiselle."

Jean peered down the road that passed the Chateaudouble gate. He was waiting for the six o'clock bus from St Rafael, waiting for Danielle to arrive. He paced from one side of the gate to the other, unable to stand still. He'd decided to meet her here. It would be dark soon. If she wasn't on this next bus, he didn't know what he'd do. He was sure of one thing, from now on he would insist that someone else act as courier. It had been Fredi's suggestion that she carry the information, and in the corner of Jean's mind that shard of mistrust hadn't been totally dislodged. He couldn't bear to think Danielle being arrested. The vision of the woman being shoved into the freight car at Les Milles never left his mind.

A whining noise from down the road caused him to stop pacing. The bus trundled up the road, trailing smoke from its charcoal furnace. It screeched to a stop and the door wheezed open. A man in wooden clogs hopped out, then a woman carrying a basket—and finally Danielle with her musette. She looked pale and weary, but she gave him a triumphant smile as he rushed to take her in his arms. He released her and held her at arms' length, peering into her sky blue eyes. "Danielle, you don't know how glad I am to see you!" He kissed her again, then waited for the bus to leave and to make sure all the other passengers had walked off. "So how did it go?"

She shrugged, laughing. "No problem! And Jean, wait 'till I show you!"

"Show me what?"

Removing the musette from her shoulder, she opened it and held it out for him to eye its contents. "From the OSS via Consul Benton." She lowered her voice. "50,000 francs—for our resistance people. And Benton wants me to tell you how pleased he is we're working for the OSS. He says he's met General Donovan, the head of OSS, and admires him enormously. And he also told me there's an OSS section in Switzerland—where the money comes from."

Jean stared into the bag—then wrapped his arms around both Danielle and the musette. "Good work, Danielle! I can't believe it! Wait 'till I tell the others." He suddenly thought of Alain. "Alain didn't come with you?"

She stepped back and fastened the buckles of the musette. "He needed to work on the Bulletin. But he stayed with me until I climbed onto the bus. I told him about the money—and Benton. He was thrilled."

Jean glanced toward the stone wall where his bike was chained. He moved toward it and twirled the dial on the combination lock and wheeled the bike toward Danielle. "It's getting dark. Let's go home." He held the bike steady while she climbed onto the rack behind him, sitting sidesaddle, her arms around his waist. He could feel her warmth through his coat. He suddenly felt like singing. Danielle was safe and the OSS gave them money.

# Chapter Thirty-two

## Occupation

*November, 1942*

A blanket of smoke lay over the collier field, and the sound of axes cutting wood echoed in the forest beyond. Jean was hitching the farm horse to the wagon when Danielle came running toward him, yelling hysterically. At first he didn't understand what she was trying to tell him, but when she finally caught her breath and blurted out her message, the news hit him like mortar fire. The Germans had crossed the demarcation line and were occupying the south of France,

"It's on the radio." she said, her eyes wide with shock. "It's official. Pétain just spoke. And he ordered the French soldiers to remain in their barracks—to avoid provoking the Germans."

Stunned, Jean barely grasped what she had said. The Nazis were marching into unoccupied France? He shook his head, as if he could shake away the devastating news. They'd all been feeling so ebullient about the Allies invasion of North Africa yesterday, but now this?

Danielle was shivering. "When do you think they'll reach us?

"Did the report say where they crossed the line?"

"Only that they were on their way to Vichy and Lyons."

He hesitated. What size army would Hitler send? His troops would be engaged in the east and now in Africa. He looked into Danielle's troubled eyes. "I doubt if they'll come to Chateaudouble. But they'll certainly head for Toulon to capture the fleet. And Marseilles, of course. All the ports. It'll take a some time to move their heavy equipment."

"Jean, what are we going to do!" she cried, her arms hugging her chest.

He grasped her shoulders and searched her stricken face. "We'll just have to be very, very smart. Stay out of their way. But keep on resisting."

"Jean, I'm not brave enough." Tears brimmed her eyes." You were right. I should have gone to Cuba when I had the chance."

He pulled her towards him, holding her close. "You'll be safe here on the farm. The war won't last forever. Hitler hasn't been able to take Stalingrad from the Russians, and now that the Americans have landed in North Africa he'll be in trouble there too."

Suddenly, the horse nickered noisily and stamped a front hoof. Jean released Danielle and eyed the mare. He unbuckled the harness and grasped her halter. "I'll take Marron back to her paddock. I'll go into the village tomorrow. Nothing will get done today. Everyone will be in shock—even the fascists. And I'll pass on the bad news to the workers here. Danielle, did Jaques and Lili hear Pétain speak?"

"Yes. They're in the kitchen now. So is Alain. And Luc."

"Good. I'll join them in a few minutes. We need to talk—plan what to do."

Danielle's eyes were still dazed, but her tears had stopped. "I'll ask them to wait." She gave a wan smile. "They'll be glued to the radio for more news."

A few days passed before the Germans reached the southern coast. Danielle waited nervously for the gray and green uniformed soldiers to appear, but as Jean had said, it takes time to move an army. Fredi had arrived the day after the news of the occupation was broadcast. He'd been in Toulon where the French fleet was anchored. He and a group of his resisters were camped on a hill above the city.

Danielle, Jean and the other former CAS staff and the Godets met in the farm kitchen with Fredi the evening he arrived. Fredi had brought five young men who were avoiding the order to work in Germany. Laval had announced that all men between the ages of twenty one and thirty must report for transport. Only essential farmers and those working in war plants were excused. At the moment the new arrivals were billeted in the barn with the charcoal workers. "We'll make a camp here," Fredi said, "like the other Maquis camps that are forming in the mountains." Fredi paused. "If none of you objects."

Danielle glanced at Louise, wondering if she would object to Fredi's suggestion about the camp, but although her face was pale with anxiety, she remained silent.

Jean was eying Fredi. "Shouldn't we put the camp further into the forest? And how do we feed them all?"

Fredi hesitated. "You're right, of course. We should find a spot a mile or so away—beyond the cleared field. The charcoal factory can be a cover, of course. The men can work here when they're not training."

"Training?" Danielle said.

"To fight Germans, Danielle. Guerrilla warfare," Fredi replied calmly. "And as for food, we'll try to find. . .support, shall we say?"

Danielle realized he meant that he or Jean would contact the OSS or Combat for weapons and supplies. And money. The problem would be how to make contact with their handlers. Simone would know how to contact Frenay, of course, but Benton at the American consulate would be recalled—now that Vichy France was under Nazi control. Germany and the United States were at war. And what would happen to the other Americans, like Sam, the OSS agent? Would he be interned? Or would he go underground? And what about their Swiss connection, Bernard Barel? And would Jaques and Lili be able to help more refugees get to Switzerland?

Louise had moved to the radio on a table next to the fireplace. She turned the handle, winding it vigorously. She then twisted the dial and the sound of distorted orchestral music blared from cloth covered loudspeaker. When the music stopped, an announcer read a short statement. "The French Armistice Army has been ordered to disband immediately. All weapons are to be turned over to the Germans."

Fredi groaned. "And those idiot army officers will do as they're told. They'll obey orders!"

Jean sighed. "Let's hope a few patriots will be smart enough to hide their weapons. Sooner or later the Allies will invade France. Then we should be ready to kill those fucking Nazis."

A week went by and still no German or Italian soldiers appeared on the road to Chateaudouble. It was mid-November and as Jean rode into the village on his bicycle he felt the chill wind penetrate the cloth of his thin jacket. He was headed for the post office to check for mail. Sam had said he would get a message to him addressed to Chateaudouble poste restante. Of course, Jean had no idea what had happened to Sam now that America was at war with Germany. Fredi had returned to Toulon to continue his information gathering for Combat about the fleet. Would Admiral Laborde order the ships to sneak away before the German troops arrived? Jean had agreed to meet Fredi in Toulon the following day. OSS would most certainly want a man on the ground to report what happened to the fleet.

Jean had concluded that Fredi was straight. All the same, Alain and he had questioned Fredi's newcomers extensively. Jaques and Alain had marched the recruits into the forest to search for a good camp site—and a flat, cleared field hidden from the road that might serve as a drop zone. Some of Fredi's recruits were former soldiers in the French army and could help with training. They would need weapons and ammunition if they wanted to prepare the men for an insurrection—or sabotage. A few weeks ago Sam had promised he could arrange a drop. The OSS would parachute guns and money. Jean had no idea how they would communicate with the air crew, since they didn't have a wireless. He needed to confer with Sam as soon as possible.

Chateaudouble was quiet. As Jean wheeled his bike by the Mairie, he was shocked to see that the French tricolor was no longer flying over the door. Instead the Italian red, white and green tricolor hung there, flooding his heart with mixed emotions. He'd been raised with that flag. He'd loved his country until it had been taken over by Mussolini's fascist thugs. Radio reports had not been clear about the area the Italian Military would control. It would seem that this part of the Var, at least, would be ruled by the Italians. And not the Germans?

He glanced at the space by the Mairie overlooking the gorge, where normally old men sat smoking their pipes. The bench was empty. He scrutinized the square and the street in both directions. No sign of military uniforms. Or of the locals. Everyone waited.

Where had this flag come from? Jean entered the Mairie. The mayor had become a friend. They could speak freely. The clerk behind the desk looked up from his work but did not smile. "Bonjours", Jean said quietly. "You have a new flag."

The clerk scowled. "It arrived yesterday. Delivered by a French clerk from the Var Department office in Draguignan. With the orders to remove the French tricolor. Apparently, the Var will be in the Italian sector, Marseilles and the Rhone, German."

"More military road blocks, checkpoints, documents, random searches."

"Right," said the clerk, his shoulders bent. "But better the Italians than the Germans. The Italian soldiers have warm hearts. The Germans have ice blocking their veins." He let out a deep sigh. "Poor France."

"Yes, poor France." Jean moved toward the door. He wouldn't disturb the mayor. Not today. Enveloped in a cloud of gloom, he forced himself to enter the post office. At the poste restante window he asked the clerk if there was mail for him or others at the farm. The clerk handed him one postcard. "That's all today, Monsieur. A card from Grenoble."

Jean gave a wry smile. "And what does it say?"

The clerk grinned. "I don't remember, Monsieur."

As Jean left the post office, he quickly read the card. It was addressed to him: *I'll be in Grenoble on bank business December 7 to 10. I have a client there who you might want to meet. A prospective customer. I'll be at the Hotel La Gambetta. B. Barel.* Jean tucked the card into his coat pocket, wondering what Barel meant to tell him. A customer? What type of customer? For the charcoal factory? He'd certainly get himself to Grenoble—next week, after he returned from Toulon. It wouldn't take long on the bus. Jaques had stayed there just a week ago with some Centre clients on their way to Switzerland. He wondered if Grenoble would be in the Italian sector.

The clerk in the Mayor's office was right. Italian soldiers were not like the Germans—or even the Duce's Fascists. Many were country boys who came from large, warm families. They could be dealt with. All the same, he'd need to be careful. As Gino Baroli he was an Italian fugitive, an escapee from a Milan prison. although it was unlikely that his true identity would be uncovered. It had been six years since he fled Italy for the International Brigade in Spain. Not unless by a fluke someone from Milan or Genoa recognized him. Danielle was the only person here who knew his story.

Jean climbed on his bike and pedaled toward the farm. He needed to pack a few things for his task in Toulon tomorrow—like his camera and binoculars, which he'd need to conceal carefully. Would the Germans be assigned to capture the fleet? Or the Italians?

# Chapter Thirty-three

## Toulon

*November, 1942*

It was the roar of motors that woke him. The distant rumble grew louder. Jean sat up and peered into the darkness, and Fredi, who had been sleeping next to him in the barn, jumped to his feet. "The attack's started! I hear tanks!"

Throwing off the blanket that reeked of cow manure, Jean quickly pulled on his boots and jacket and reached for his musette. He followed Fredi out the barn door and scurried down the slope to the low stone wall that defined the farmer's land. From there they would have a sweeping view of Toulon and the harbor. Jean glanced at his watch. He could barely see the dial in the starlight. It was 4:30 in the morning. With icy fingers he unbuckled his musette and grabbed the binoculars. He and Fredi had chosen this spot the evening before, soon after they arrived at the farmhouse. The farmer, André Colbert, was a trusted member of Fredi's group of resisters.

It was too dark to make out the ships in the harbor. A half-moon dipped low on the horizon and the eastern sky had not yet lightened. The sounds of the moving armored vehicles now came from both the east and west of Toulon. Two days earlier the German tanks and half tracks and heavy artillery had rumbled down the highway from

Marseilles. By yesterday afternoon they had encircled the city. The Colbert farm was perched on the mountain that rose steeply from the coast, and was just above the army's encampments.

The two men knelt on the ground behind the low wall, their elbows propped on the cold, lichen-covered stone. Jean shivered. He raised the binoculars to his eyes but could see only blackness. He lowered the glasses, and straining his eyes, tried to make out the outlines of ships in the harbor. A few lights flashed through the misty darkness and a necklace of lights, which he assumed were the headlights on the tanks and half-tracks, moved slowly down the highway.

Fredi spoke quietly into his ear, his tone intense. "If only Laborde had obeyed the order to set sail for Algiers. Now it's too late. Look, the tanks are heading for the arsenal. That god damned fucking Pétain."

"D'accord!" Jean breathed, his jaw clenched. Directly below their perch he could see the arsenal. Last night Fredi had told him that some of his men worked there. One was a wireless operator—and coder. He'd told Fredi last week that he'd de-coded messages from Algiers. He'd learned that Admiral Darlan, the Commander of Vichy French forces in North Africa, had defected to the Allies. He then heard that Laborde met with the Secretary of the Navy, Admiral Auphan and Pétain. Auphan told Laborde to lead the fleet to North Africa immediately, but Laborde said he'd set sail only if Pétain gave the formal command. Pétain refused.

Now Jean frowned "But surely Laborde will scuttle the ships before he lets the Germans or Italians get them!"

"From what I hear, I think he will, but God knows what will happen in the next hour."

Jean continued to stare at the docks and noted that the eastern sky was getting lighter. "Look, Fredi, that line of tanks and artillery has halted at the arsenal gates." Fredi focused his own binoculars on the arsenal. Jean studied the view. Beyond the tiled roof tops on the slope below he could make out the several clusters of buildings within the arsenal walls. Next to the arsenal were the cement enclosures harboring the big guns that defended the coast from allied ships. Jean then swept his gaze to the eastern section of the Toulon shoreline and spied another column of vehicles approaching what he knew to be Fort

Lamalgue. The armored vehicles were all marked with the German cross.

As the sky grew lighter the ships in the harbor and at the docks became visible, Jean focused his glasses on the docks below the Fort. A line of twelve submarines was moored to a floating dock in a neat row. "Two half-tracks and three tanks have entered the Fort grounds," Jean announced. Almost immediately the tanks began firing at the closest submarine. The other submarines began to slip into the harbor away from the dock.

Fredi was watching the arsenal. "But look, Jean, there's some confusion at the arsenal. Tanks are riding in circles around the buildings."

Jean snorted. "Maybe they're lost!"

The shooting had stopped at the Fort, and more submarines pulled away from the dock. Suddenly, one of the ships further out in the harbor, a battleship, fired its big guns at the tanks. The tanks returned fire, and the flash of gunfire continued for several minutes. Suddenly, it stopped. Life boats were lowered from the ship. Jean could see sailors climbing down the netting to the boats. Soon after, an earsplitting explosion sent black smoke and fire from the battleship into the sky. The ship was sinking. "They're scuttling," Jean cried. Almost immediately another ship burst into flames and began to sink.

Jean grabbed his Leica from the musette, quickly adjusted the aperture and shutter speed, peered through the view finder and clicked the shutter. He continued to snap pictures as one by one the fleet of seventy ships burst into flames and slid into the harbor's murk. The flames and black smoke that obscured the harbor, combined with the tears that filled his eyes, soon forced Jean to lower the camera. He turned to Fredi, who was staring at the scene with horror. "All those beautiful, powerful ships—lost," he murmured.

Danielle was in the farm kitchen peeling potatoes, helping Louise prepare dinner for the men. Danielle thought about Jean. He'd left for Toulon three days before and she was feeling extremely anxious. They hadn't had any news from him or Fredi—or about the fleet—or whether the Germans or Italians had tried to capture it. Very little news was being broadcast on French radio, and the short wave radio for BBC news was with Alain.  She was always scared when Jean was off doing his resistance work, but now she was deeply frightened for him—now that the Germans and Italians had occupied all of France.  The Gestapo were vicious torturers.  Cardon was nasty but he obeyed French laws.

She reached into the bottom of the sack for another potato.  Now she shifted her worries to their food supplies.  The sacks of potatoes and onions that remained in the root cellar were almost empty.  They had plenty of chestnut flour and honey, but the new recruits needed something more nutritious if they were expected to work and fight.  Fredi had already used much of Benton's money to supply the men at the encampment in the woods with blankets and canvas.  They needed a steady supply of cash to buy food and equipment for all the men— the charcoal workers as well as the Resistance trainees.

Maybe Barel would have money for Jean when he went to Grenoble next week.  She wondered about the mysterious customer Barel wanted Jean to meet.  If nothing came from Barel or Sam, the charcoal factory would need more orders.  Since the news about the German betrayal of the Armistice agreement, she'd remained on the farm.  It was too risky for her to go to the coast until the new situation had been surveyed by Fredi or Jean.  Someone else would need to take over.

When Jean had told her about the Italian troops being in control of their region of France, she'd felt somewhat relieved.  The Italian's attitude toward Jews was not like that of the Germans.  The Italian military in charge of the previously held zone  near the border with Italy had ignored the German's demands to ship Jews to concentration camps.  She prayed they would continue that refusal now that they were in control of more territory.

A clamor of voices outside the farmhouse caused her to drop the potato she was peeling and fix her eyes on the front door.  Immediately, the door burst open and Jean and Fredi swept in, half-carrying a man dressed in a French sailor's uniform spattered with scorch marks.  His left arm was wrapped loosely with what might be a tablecloth.  He groaned as the two men lifted him over the threshold and carried him to the daybed in the corner of the kitchen.  They eased him onto the bed and Fredi gently propped the sailor's head on a pillow.  Danielle noted the beads of sweat on the man's brow that began to trickle down his cheeks. Grimacing with pain, he gingerly placed his injured arm across his body

Danielle turned questioning eyes upon Jean. She then realized another sailor was standing in the doorway. Fredi beckoned him to enter. "Jean Marc, come, warm yourself by the fire." The sailor stepped inside and moved stiffly toward the huge fireplace. Louise, who was stirring a pot that hung over the hot coals in the fireplace gave the sailor a searching look, but stepped aside.

Jean touched Danielle's shoulder. His face was streaked with dirt and his green eyes were half-closed with fatigue. "We'll need a doctor for our burned sailor, here. Is Luc here?" he said, turning to Louise."

"He's in the barn, fixing the horse's harness. Do you want him?" and she reached for the shawl that hung on a hook by the door.

Jean nodded. "Tell him to take the bike and find Dr. Lamonte. Lamonte will come, I'm sure. Tell Luc it's a burn—and the man's in pain—a French sailor."

As Louise went out the door, Danielle stared at Jean. "What happened?" she cried. "Did the Germans capture the fleet?"

"No, thank God," Jean answered, "Laborde gave the order to scuttle. The entire fleet is lost. But the Germans didn't get it—and we think a couple of submarines got away."

The sailor by the fire gave Danielle a long, weary look. "And most of the crews got off the ships before they burned—and sank."

Fredi picked up a chair and set it by the fire and beckoned the man to sit. "Jean Marc," he said, addressing Danielle, "is a wireless operator—and a coder, and he's one of my informants. He was in the arsenal throughout the confrontation. He transmitted the order from Laborde's flagship to scuttle. He got out before the Germans entered his building."

Jean Marc nodded, Then he gave a wry grin. "The sentry at the entrance to the arsenal held off the German tank commander by insisting he didn't have the correct papers to enter. For once those asses and their worship of permits and signatures was a blessing. It was hilarious, really. It gave me time to radio Laborde's order to all the ships. Scuttle, scuttle, scuttle. And the crews to evacuate."

The burned sailor then spoke up, his voice hoarse and weak. "And we signaled with flags!" He took a deep breath and he gave a short laugh. "And our Captain wouldn't give the Germans permission to board our ship when they snapped out the usual request. And while they argued, we opened the ship's valves and set off the demolition charges. That's when this happened." He lifted his arm slightly, then winced.

Danielle gave the sailor a sympathetic look, wishing she could help him. Then she wondered how he found Fredi and Jean. Were they in the midst of this inferno? "Jean, where were you and Fredi while all this was going on?"

Jean gave her a wan smile. "We were safe on the mountain above Toulon—with our weapons: binoculars and camera. At a farm belonging to a man who is one of Fredi's resisters. We watched the ships explode and slide into the sea. It broke our hearts, but we were not in danger. And the Germans didn't capture the fleet. Jean Marc knew about Fredi's safe house, and helped Valjean to climb up to us. He was in pretty bad shape. His arm is badly burned. Fredi's farmer drove us up the mountain road with his horse and cart. He took us to another farm and that farmer brought us here—with his horse and cart."

Danielle searched the faces of the four men. They were unshaven and smudged with dirt and ash. Valjean, the burned sailor, was in pain. Suddenly, she pulled herself together. They must all be hungry and thirsty. She strode to the larder and brought out two bottles of wine, a round loaf of chestnut bread, and a large pork sausage and a sharp knife. By the time she'd collected plates and glasses, Jean, Fredi and Jean Marc were seated at the table and Jean was slicing the sausage. Valjean, she noticed, had closed his eyes, and was perhaps asleep. It was all so sad. So very, very sad.

# Chapter Thirty-four

## Grenoble

### December, 1942

The bus rumbled along the winding road toward the snow-covered Alps, a trail of steaming smoke billowing behind it. The road ahead was wet with rain, and the tires of the bus hissed as they splashed through puddles. Jean figured they should arrive in Grenoble in another hour. Jaques had given him directions to the Hotel La Gambetta, advising him how to avoid police searches at the bus depot. The ride so far had been uneventful. Each time the bus stopped to pick up passengers, Jean scrutinized each person carefully, but nobody suspicious had entered. There'd been only one military road block just before entering Gap. A French policeman and an Italian soldier with a rifle slung over his shoulder entered the bus and examined documents. The search had been routine and quick. The gendarme had given his papers only a perfunctory glance and handed them back. The soldier had eyed him sharply, but continued down the aisle.

Jean was experiencing a charge of excitement thinking about his meeting with the mysterious customer Barel had written about. Barel knew their people needed support, and Jean didn't truly believe the customer merely wanted to order charcoal from the farm, but who could it be? Jean's thoughts then shifted to the events of the last week— when Marcel suddenly appeared at the farm. Fredi and he had been meeting in the kitchen with Jaques, Lili, Alain and Danielle. They'd been discussing the possibility that they might need to change their resistance strategy since the German/Italian invasion. The sailor, Jean Marc, took part in the discussion. Jean and Fredi had agreed the sailor was to be trusted and had welcomed him as a future Maquis fighter. They'd also accepted Valjean, the burned sailor, who Doctor Lamonte had been treating.

When the door opened, Fredi stopped speaking and they all stared in the direction of the open door. The wind whistled and a gust of damp air blew into the warm kitchen. Three huddled figures then stumbled into the room. Jean recognized the first intruder as Marcel. A blanket-wrapped woman and a young girl huddled behind him. He hadn't seen Marcel for over a month.

Jean and Fredi jumped to their feet and rushed to the door. "Marcel!" Jean cried. "What's happened!" Marcel and his companions stamped their feet and shook their coats of rain, leaving puddles on the linoleum. Fredi slammed the door closed and drew Marcel and the women toward the fireplace.

Danielle stepped forward and helped them remove their wet, rain-soaked wraps. Marcel, his face white with cold, put his arm around his companion and pulled her close—as if, Jean thought, he needed her warmth. "This is my friend, Marisol Dupré, whom I've told you about." Marisol nodded to them, still shivering, her gray eyes heavy with fatigue. "And this is Chantal, a girl who worked with us." The others murmured quiet greetings and Marcel continued. "You asked me what's happened." He glanced at Jean—then Fredi. "The O'Leary route has been blown." His voice was flat, expressionless.

Danielle was staring at him. "The O'Leary route?"

Jean knew what Marcel meant. O'Leary was the code name for the leader of a circuit of resisters—a chain of men and women—from Belgium to the Pyrenees—who had been aiding downed airmen and Resistance workers to reach Spain. Some links in the chain must have been caught. Betrayed, he guessed, by some Nazi sympathizer. Jean turned to Danielle. "It's a network of patriots who help airmen get to Spain."

Fredi had pushed a bench toward the fire, and touching Marcel's shoulder, guided him to sit. Marisol and the girl, Chantal, sat next to him. "Tell us, Marcel," Fredi prompted.

"Four of our people in Toulouse were arrested by the Gestapo. Two were women. We know what the Gestapo does to their prisoners. We also know that sooner or later the prisoner will talk. It means, of course, that those of us who were known by the prisoners must escape before we are caught in the Gestapo's net. The German armies have only been in the south for a few weeks, but undercover Gestapo agents must have been watching us for some time. When the army arrived, they pounced." He sighed, holding his hands out toward the blazing fire. "So we've gone into hiding. Chantal is Jewish. She was a courier for the line. Replacements will have to be found for the arrested ones—and us. O'Leary is shrewd and he'll repair the line and get back into business, but we'd like to join you here." He gave Fredi a searching look. "I think we can be useful. Marisol is a nurse. Chantal could assist her. I was a soldier in the French army, as you know", he said, addressing Jean. "I fought with Fredi in the Ardenne. Maybe I can help training the new recruits—or. . ." and he shrugged. "I can help Danielle keep the books."

Now, Jean glanced out the bus window and realized they had turned onto a major highway. He stopped thinking about Marcel and forced himself to concentrate on the job at hand. This road had to be the Route Napoleon, the road that Napoleon had taken from Elba when he returned to France. Now he must keep a careful watch for Italian solders and more road blocks. As Jean kept his eyes trained on the landscape he noted a river flowing next to the road. The Isére, he thought. A gracefully arched bridge spanned it, reflecting in the water. Soon, white stuccoed buildings bordered the road, and perched on a mountain beyond, were dark fortifications of stone. They had arrived in Grenoble.

Jaques had advised him to get off the bus at Blvd Gambetta before reaching the depot. He would then avoid the police or Italian military document inspection. The bus would be on Blvd Joffre, Jaques had told him, and would cross Gambetta as it approached the center of town. The hotel was only one block north. Jean was watching for the tan uniforms of Italian soldiers—and especially for the peaked cap and black shirt of Mussolini's Centurians. He had experienced the Blackshirt's brutality in Milan and had no wish to have it repeated.

Two of the passengers in front of him rose and reached for their bags on the rack above them. They walked to the front of the bus, spoke to the driver, and at the next stop light the driver opened the door and they hurried down the steps. Jean was watching the street signs painted on the corners of buildings. Finally, he saw it. Blvd Gambetta. He prayed that a stop sign would occur soon, which indeed it did. He quickly reached for his musette, asked the driver to open the door, and stepped onto the snowy sidewalk. So far so good, he thought. He peered around for signs of uniforms, but only a few bundled up civilians carrying shopping bags walked by. He soon reached Gambetta—and the hotel—and strolled through the door. Sitting on a wingback chair in the lobby, an Italian officer was reading a newspaper. Under his tan uniform Jean could see the collar of a black shirt.

With his heart pounding, Jean located the reception counter and moved toward it. The sight of the Blackshirt had shocked him deeply, but he forced himself to breathe slowly. Were the Blackshirt officers billeted here? This man would not be an undercover agent—not in his uniform, but his presence in Barel's hotel was most unwelcome.

The reception clerk looked up as Jean approached. Jean spoke in a steady voice. "I have an appointment with M. Bernard Barel who's staying in this hotel." He held out his identity card. Could you tell me his room number, please?"

The clerk glanced at his registration book, picked up the telephone, and asked for room 320. Jean could see the hotel operator, a woman, through an open door behind the counter. She plugged the cord into a switchboard and made the connection. "M. Barrault is here to see you sir, shall I send him up?" the clerk said. He then nodded and pointed to the stairway. "Room 320—two flights up."

Jean fixed his eyes on the stairway, avoiding eye contact with the Italian officer. When he reached the third floor, he took a deep breath to calm himself. He knocked at 320 and the door opened immediately to a smiling Bernard Barel. Jean entered the room then stood rooted to the floor with shock. Rising from a chair in the corner, dressed in a pinstriped suit, was his friend, Val, who'd worked for Varian, and whom he'd known in Spain as Johann Hirsch. He'd last seen Val in

Marseilles two years before. He'd been climbing aboard the train to Toulouse, Cardon's gendarmes on his tail. Before Jean could shout out Val's name, Val caught him in an embrace and whispered into his ear. "My nom de guerre is now André."

Jean stepped back and stared at Val. It was unbelievable. He found himself laughing with pleasure. "What a surprise!" He turned to Barel and shook his hand. Val then pointed to the phone, the walls and put his arm over Jean's shoulder. "We must get some fresh air—and it's almost lunchtime." Barel and Val struggled into their overcoats and they hurried out the door, Barel locking it carefully behind him. When they walked through the lobby, Jean noted that the Blackshirt officer was no longer there.

# Chapter Thirty-five

## Val/André

### December, 1942

A weak sun shone down from a bright blue sky, and Jean, Val and Barel tramped along the snow-dampened sidewalk to the tram stop. Barel left them there. "I'll meet you both at seven at the hotel for dinner. I should be finished with my bank business by then." He walked away just as the tram came to a stop. As he mounted the tram steps, Jean thought about the Blackshirt officer. He hadn't asked Barel if the Italians were billeted at the hotel. The thought of being surrounded by those thugs while he ate caused his bowels to churn.

The tram was crowded, but the two men found seats across from one another. Jean forced himself to stop thinking about the Blackshirt. Instead he wondered about Val. He noted his friend's tanned skin, his fit, erect figure. His face had developed sharp angles and furrows around his mouth, but he looked good. The image of Val in Marseilles two years earlier flashed into his mind once more—of Val dressed in shabby dungarees turning to wave as he stepped onto the train with the visa for America sewn into the lining of his jacket. The last Jean had heard about Val's whereabouts was from Danielle's father who had met Val on the University of California Berkeley campus where they were both teaching. What had Val been doing since then? And why was he here? As they'd left the hotel, Val had quietly suggested to Jean that they find shelter at a friend's ski chalet on the hillside above Grenoble. "We can talk there," he'd said, grinning.

The air was fresh and bracing as the pair climbed a steep but cleared path to a stone chalet overlooking the city. As they walked, they exchanged brief stories about their colleagues at the American Center. Val asked about Danielle and somehow knew she was still in France. "And Charlie Furst," Val said, "remember him? I had drinks with him in London a few weeks ago. Well, he hiked over the Pyrenees and got himself to Gibralter. He signed up for the RAF and flies Spitfires. And survives!"

"I thought Charlie would make it, but we all worried about him." Jean said, remembering Charlie's carefree bravery.

Val then told Jean he'd talked to Varian on the phone a few times, and Varian had sounded depressed. "The Committee didn't treat him well. I can't figure it out. He'd done such a fantastic job—got so many people out—and even set up your charcoal factory." He'd given Jean a sharp look. "I know about that, you know."

"How?" Jean replied in surprise.

Val took hold of his arm. "I'll tell you. As much as I can. But let's be drinking some brandy. It's a long story."

As they approached the stone building, Val lowered his voice. "The couple who take care of the house are both trusted members of the local Resistance." A man with iron-gray hair answered Val's knock. Val introduced him to Jean as Francois. Francois guided them into the chalet and lit a fire in the large room smelling of wine and spices. Nodding toward Francois, Val switched from French to English and explained that the house belonged to a friend of a friend. The friend was posted in Geneva and worked for Bill Donovan. "You know who Donovan is?"

Jean nodded. "The head of the Office of Strategic Service. My friend Sam mentioned him."

"Ah yes, Sam—we'll get to him in a minute." Val reached for the brandy bottle that stood on a well-stocked side table and poured a good measure into two snifters. "So this owner, a Jew who escaped to Geneva, offered us the use of his chalet as a safe house."

"Us?" Jean asked, wanting verification of what he was beginning to comprehend.

"The OSS. Eighteen months ago I joined the American army. Almost immediately, I was asked to volunteer for intelligence duty. As you know, I speak German, French, Italian and English fluently—and some Spanish. My German and French without a foreign accent. My name got to Donovan and here I am." Val swirled his brandy and took a sip.

Jean stared at his old friend, then took a big swallow of his own brandy. So Val was with OSS? But why was he here in Grenoble?

Val set down his glass, rose from his chair and moved toward the warmth of the fire. He gazed into the flames as he spoke. "I know you want to know what I'm doing here and why I'd arranged to meet you. I'll tell you what you need to know."

Jean gave a short laugh. "Jesus, Val, you've got me hanging on every word. Get on with it, man!"

Val grinned. "OK. Let's say I know you've been working for OSS. Sam was your handler. I know that Danielle had acted as courier for your group. Consul Benton told me in London. A plucky girl, indeed. I also know that you have a bunch of men hiding out in the woods near your farm—and they need training in demolition, weapons, and how to prepare a drop zone to receive their supplies."

Jean's heart was beating faster. Maybe Val would arrange for drops of equipment—like boots, warm clothes, weapons—and especially a wireless

Val continued. "The British have been working with Maquis groups not far from here, but we think your resisters further south could use some help. We heard from Benton about the charcoal factory Varian had started, and when some smart officer actually read my file, they sent me here to find you. We expect that when the Allies invade France we'll need French fighters to knock out trains, bridges and munition dumps—mess up German transportation, communication, and engage in guerrilla warfare."

"Do you think the Allies are considering the Riviera as a landing site for the invasion?"

"Probably. I'm sure Hitler considered that possibility when the Americans invaded North Africa, which probably was one reason he took over the south of France."

Jean sipped his brandy, attempting to absorb Val's astonishing information. He then set down his glass and gave Val a searching look. "Val, are you planning to come with me to Chateaudouble"

"Indeed I am. Do you mind?"

Laughing, Jean jumped up from his chair. He clapped Val on the shoulder and shouted, "Old comrade, I'm delighted! When do we leave?"

"Tomorrow. First there's someone else you need to meet." He glanced at his watch. "I'm expecting her in half an hour."

"Her?"

"Our local contacts have a circuit of couriers. Many are women, some quite young. French and Italian officials don't expect women to be engaged in dangerous tasks. We need to make arrangements for messages to get to my friend in Geneva."

"But the border is closed now." Jean had been puzzling over how to get his film of the scuttling of the fleet to the Americans or British now that Consul Benton had been recalled. He guessed that the "friend" was Alan Dulles.

"We have ways to get around that. And at this point you don't need to know more that how to make contact with your courier. That courier will pass the message on to someone else. There are two main methods of sending intelligence material now. It can be carried over the Pyrenees into Spain—mostly by smugglers—or cross into Switzerland—by various means." Val set down his brandy glass and moved toward the desk by the window. He opened a drawer and fished out a postcard with a picture of Mont Blanc on it. He tore the postcard into two pieces. He put the large portion of the card into his wallet and held up the other. "This piece is for our courier. When we send someone to meet her, he or she will present her with this." He then placed that piece of the postcard into his jacket pocket.

Jean had watched the maneuver with keen interest. Then he heard a knock at the door and the voice of the caretaker. Within seconds a girl dressed in a short green coat and knit cap entered the room. Jean noted her ankle socks and brown oxfords and her round rosy cheeks.

She didn't look more than sixteen. Val greeted her warmly and the girl gave him a sunny smile. "Odile, what a pleasure to see you! I want you to meet a good friend of mine, Jean. Jean, your courier, Odile."

Danielle was bent over her accounting books at the cluttered kitchen table. Jean had been away for three days, He'd said he'd be back today, but it was late afternoon, and, as usual, Danielle was worried about him. She was trying to keep busy. She frowned. "Merde!" she mumbled, shaking her fountain pen. The pen had dried up. Sighing, she rose from the table and moved toward an open set of shelves next to the window where she kept her supplies and the ink bottle. As she glanced out the window, she let out a sharp cry of pleasure. She saw Jean trudging up the path. He'd returned from Grenoble—safe—and someone in a dark overcoat was with him. She ran to the door and rushed out to throw her arms around Jean. He hugged her close, and when he released her, she looked up at his companion, who was carrying a small suitcase.

"Good God," she cried, "it's Val!" How could it be!

Val gave her a tight hug, almost lifting her off the ground. "Except you must call me André. The papers for Jean Valleron were torn up and tossed into the sea in Lisbon long ago. Now I have a Swiss passport. I'm an economist, and work for the bank of Geneva."

"But, Val—André—what are you doing here in the Var?" She couldn't believe her eyes. "Have you seen my parents? Have you come from Berkeley?"

"Not for a while, Danielle, but it's a long story. And it's cold out here."

"Yes, of course, come inside to the fire." Val picked up his suitcase and Danielle linked arms with both men and escorted them into the farmhouse. The two men stood by the fire a moment before removing their coats. Val then set his suitcase next to the table in the center of the room. Danielle was watching him closely. "Val—sorry—André tell me please, how did you find us?" She stared up at him, noting his tanned face, the lines around his dark blue eyes. "The last time I heard about you was from my father, who said you were in Berkeley on a fellowship."

"Yes, that was well over a year ago, Danielle. Since then I've been traveling." His smile was warm. "And I missed you all so much I found a way to come back!"

Jean moved to the kitchen counter and reached for a carafe of wine. "Let's sit down and have a drink." He brought out three glasses and set them on the table, scooping Danielle's papers into a pile.

She closed her account book, gathered the papers and placed them on her supply shelf. As she returned to the table, she saw that Jean was giving Val—André—a questioning look. André then turned to her, a shadow crossing his face. "Danielle, I've spoken to Consul Benton in London. He told me of your bravery, your work for OSS. It's a dangerous business, but you know that. And that's why I'm here. I'll be working with all of you here for a while—to get your men organized, supplied—ready to fight Germans."

It took Danielle a few seconds to absorb what Val had just said. He was also working for the Americans? It was hard to believe. "And will you actually get us money—and a wireless?"

"Indeed. I've brought money with me." He pointed to the suitcase he'd placed on the floor at his feet. "It's hidden carefully. And yesterday afternoon I sent a coded message by courier to my commanding officer that says I'd made contact with you and to expect to hear from us when we were ready for a drop."

"We don't have a radio operator in Grenoble?" Jean asked.

"Not yet, but the Brits do. They're willing to cooperate but our receivers' codes and frequencies are different from theirs."

Danielle was puzzled. "If we don't have a radio how will we know when the drop will happen?"

"Do you have a short wave radio here?"

"Yes, it's upstairs."

"I'm sure you've heard those nonsensical phrases the announcer repeats over and over. On BBC French news."

"You mean—like the 'brown cow knocked over the bucket'

"Right. And I wrote out such a phrase in my coded message. After we tell them we're ready, we listen for that phrase on BBC. That means we should prepare the site. When the message is repeated, the following night there will be a drop. If the weather is bad, they'll try the next night."

"So what's our phrase?"

Val laughed. "I'll tell you when it's time."

Jean was frowning. "When you said you'd sent a message by courier—was that Odile?"

Val hesitated. "No. It wasn't."

"Odile?" Danielle said, glancing from Jean to Val.

Val answered. "Odile is a young woman, a Grenoble resister, who acts as a courier. Women are good at getting through check points—as you know, only too well, Danielle. Odile will carry messages for this group. We've agreed that on Wednesdays our courier will meet Odile in Sisteron—on a bench in front of the Town Hall—at noon. She'll be eating her lunch. If the weather is not good she'll be at the café opposite."

"And you, Danielle," Jean interjected, "will stay here on the farm. Someone else will take the film and messages to Odile. Lili, perhaps? As a cover she can be selling charcoal—like you've been doing—or visiting a relative."

Danielle's first reaction was to object. She wanted to be an active resister. Although she was afraid of the Germans, the Italians didn't frighten her nearly as much. But then, she hadn't asked Jean about the presence of the Italians in Grenoble. "Jean, do you really feel it's dangerous for me to leave the farm?"

Jean spoke forcefully. "Yes! Absolutely. There were Blackshirts at the Gambetta Hotel. They scare the shit out of me, Danielle. They're almost as bad as the Gestapo. I had rather unpleasant encounters with a couple of those thugs in Milan. The Italians may be more tolerant of Jews than the Germans, but don't bet on it."

Val picked up his wine glass. "Danielle, we need you here. There'll be plenty to do, believe me." He lifted his glass, as if in a toast. "To the barricades, my friends!" Jean and Danielle held up their glasses and tossed back their wine. "To the barricades!"

# Chapter Thirty-six

## The Camp

*March, 1943*

Was the clearing ready? Jean stood on a slight incline bordering the field where they'd been working. Trees had been cut, the trunks and roots dug out, the surface tamped smooth. The field was flat, and 100 meters long, but on both sides rose rocky ridges dotted with stunted pine trees. It was conceivable that a twin engine bomber could land here, but he'd hate to be the pilot who made the attempt. As a drop zone, though, it ought to work.

Thrusting his hands in his jacket pockets, he trudged along the track to the camp. Standing next to the camp kitchen shelter, he saw Val, Fredi and Marcel huddled in a tight circle, studying the sketch of the camp and field. Jean surveyed the surroundings with satisfaction. They'd accomplished a lot. Although they'd thinned the thick forest, there was enough of a canopy of branches overhead to screen the camp from the air. On one side of the central area stood a barracks about four meters long made of pine logs with a roof camouflaged with leaves and branches. Several meters down-slope from the barracks were the latrines. On the opposite side of the campgrounds, further in the woods, was a hut used as a first aid station. The nurse, Marisol, and

Chantal, the Jewish girl, bunked there. Behind the hut was a fast-flowing stream where the recruits could launder clothes and bathe.

Jean thought about how hard they'd all worked. For the last six weeks they'd been here from dawn to dusk constructing the camp for their eighty maquisards and clearing the field for the drop zone. In the evenings they'd listened to lectures and demonstrations Val and Fredi gave about techniques of guerrilla warfare and demolition. They were hoping that now the field was ready as a drop zone they would soon have weapons and plastic explosives they could use for training purposes—then for action. They also expected to receive a radio and a trained OSS operator.

Val and Fredi had been firm about guiding discussions away from politics. Many of the men were ardent communists. Others were for de Gaulle. Fredi was a charismatic leader, Jean had concluded, and the group listened to him. "First we rid the country of the Nazis—then worry about who will lead us," he preached.

Val had been away for a week. He returned only the day before. He hadn't disclosed the purpose of his absence to Jean or the others, but Jean figured Val needed to confer with his superiors about their plan of action. He'd probably gone to Geneva to check in with Dulles and use the OSS radio to send and receive messages, but Val hadn't disclosed where he went or how he got there. Jean didn't "need to know".

Val had provided money to buy tools needed to build the camp and food for the men, although the charcoal business was doing well and its earnings had contributed to the project. Almost all the men took turns cutting wood and helping the colliers at the farm. So far, the Italian military hadn't discovered the camp. The charcoal production was a good cover. They had to thank Varian for that.

Now as Jean approached his three companions, Val called to him. "Jean, what do you think of Danielle's map and sketch?" He held one end of the curling sheet of paper and Jean the other.

Jean scanned the map. "It's good." Danielle had sketched the spots where the men would light the bonfires when they heard the plane's engines overhead. There would be three fires marking the angles of an isosceles triangle, the center of which would be the target area for the drop. The next few nights would be full moon, which was the time the pilots could see enough of the terrain to find the drop zone. If they missed this full moon, they'd need to wait another month for the next.

"Jean," Val asked, "have you spoken to the colliers about their fires?"

"I told them to wait until after the drop to start new fires, that you were expecting to hear a BBC signal tonight that the drop was a go. And that fires would mark the drop zone. They agreed they didn't need a bunch of parachutes coming down on their collier field."

Val rolled up the map and tucked it under his arm. "I told Danielle and Lili we'd come to the farm for lunch. We need to have a meeting." He then led Jean, Fredi and Marcel a few meters up the track that headed to the farm. Hidden in a shelter covered with canvas and tree branches, was an old Citroen that had been converted from burning gasoline to charcoal. One of their resisters, a mechanic, had modified the engine.

Now they all climbed in and Marcel drove the sputtering, rattling old vehicle up the narrow track to the farm, steering it skillfully when the wheels hit rough spots. It was Marcel who had spied the car parked on a narrow village street. It had belonged to a widow who didn't drive. She was sympathetic to their cause and was willing to sell the car for 500 francs and a few loads of charcoal for her stove.

Danielle and Lili were in the kitchen chopping carrots and mushrooms to put in the soup pot hanging on its iron hook in the fireplace. Lili was describing her last visit to Sisteron where she'd met Odile by the Town Hall at noon. "The sun was shining and Odile was sitting on the bench eating a piece of cheese. She's such a pretty girl— with curly black hair and rosy cheeks. We know each other now, so I didn't bother to bring out the postcard piece." Lili scooped up her pile of chopped dried mushrooms and dropped them in the soup pot. She wiped her hands on her blue apron, then tucked a strand of her red hair behind her ear.

Danielle reached for another carrot. "So how do you hand over the basket?" Danielle knew that hidden under the checked lining in Lili's two-handled basket were Fredi's intelligence reports—his account of the type and size of German and Italian military units his people had observed on the coast and their type of vehicles and weapons.

"After I took out my sandwich I set the basket on the ground in front of the bench. Odile has a basket somewhat similar which she'd placed on the bench beside her. When I finished eating, I got up to leave, we said our goodbyes and I picked up her basket and walked to the bus stop."

"Do you act like you're friends? Do you talk much?"

"Like acquaintances. My cover story is that I'm in Sisteron to see a sick friend of my mother's. Odile is visiting an aunt, which is the truth. My basket contained jars of honey and a bag of chestnuts. Hers had jars of strawberry jam."

Danielle tossed the chopped carrots into the pot. "And if the police ask you for the name of the sick friend, what would you say?"

"They gave me the name and address of a woman who's sympathetic to the Resistance. But thank God, nobody has bothered me. I guess I look like all the other women who are out shopping for food."

Danielle glanced at Lili, her slender form, her clear eyes, her bright hair, thinking that she made a good courier. No one would believe Lili was engaged in covert pursuits like carrying lethal documents to the Allies. Danielle remembered only too well how terrifying it was to carry intelligence material through searches and checkpoints. They all knew what they risked: capture, torture, execution. She stood by the fire a moment, watching Lili as she peeled an onion. "Lili, you went through checkpoints, right? Did the Italian soldiers question you?"

Lili turned to her, the knife and onion still in her hand, her eyes tearing a little. "The gendarmes questioned me. The Italian soldiers stared, but I don't think they speak French. It;s so scary I hate to think about it." She turned back to her onion.

"Are there many checkpoints?"

Lili stopped peeling, but didn't turn around to face her. "On the the highway at Sisteron the bus has to pull over—and they come aboard. Also at the bus station—though they haven't stopped me there." She lifted her knife and sliced the onion into small pieces, making sharp, loud sounds on the chopping board.

Danielle turned back to the pot, stirring the soup with the long wooden spoon, thinking of the dangers they all faced, wondering if they would survive. She was also experiencing a certain dissonance listening to Lili's account—envy of Lili, perhaps—wishing she could be more active, take more risks. At the same time she remembered the terror and was relieved she was safe at the farm. The sound of footsteps on the path outside the door brought her back to the task at hand, woman's work, cooking. She turned to Lili. "It sounds like our men have come for their lunch."

But to Danielle's surprise, when the door opened, it was Alain. "Alain, we didn't expect you!" She fastened her eyes on Alain's pale face, his unkempt appearance. "Alain, what's wrong? What's happened?"

Alain limped into the room. "I've come from Marseilles. It's Simone. The Gestapo picked her up. Nobody has heard from her. Her people are scattering, hiding, changing names, addresses. I've moved my darkroom, to Cannes. I need new documents, a new name. Is Fredi here? He must be warned."

# Chapter Thirty-seven

## The Drop

*March, 1943*

Luc had climbed into the attic with the short wave radio's aerial wire, stretching it up the stairs from the farm kitchen where its residents waited silently to hear the BBC broadcast to France. Jaques was rapidly winding the handle on the set, charging its batteries. Danielle gave a quick glance around the room. Everyone except Luc, the teenager, and Marisol, the nurse, were former members of Varian's staff. All were frozen in their positions around the radio. Alain, his face still pale, stood motionless, staring at the set. It was only an hour earlier that he had blurted the news about Simone's capture by the Gestapo to Fredi and Jean.

Fredi's eyes were half-closed and shadowed, and Jean's mouth was set in a grim line. All three would be picturing the Gestapo torture chamber, Simone its victim. And they'd be pondering over the danger they were in themselves, wondering what Simone knew about this camp—and it's location. Did she know? Maybe not. Jean and Alain hadn't been reporting to her since they started working for OSS, and they'd stopped writing for the Bulletin. Fredi stayed away from Marseilles and didn't report to Simone either, although he kept in contact with Frenay's informants in San Rafael and Cannes. He also had changed his name and carte d'identité several times, and since Val had been here he'd remained at the camp unless he was on a mission. Furthermore, Simone would not "need to know" about the camp, but whatever she revealed, they'd all need to be even more cautious than ever.

Danielle's attention was suddenly caught by the voice of the radio announcer who was reporting the latest war news. *The German army is still in full retreat from the Russian front. Today's communique from the war office states that the German army has also begun its withdrawal from Tunisia.* There was a brief pause before the program continued. The announcer then said, *We will now recite messages to the French people.* Val had told them the phrase they should listen for: *Thomas sends roses to Lili.* The BBC announcer fired out his messages as if from a machine gun. Some were ridiculous, Danielle thought, but no one was smiling. *Fifi the cat will catch a rabbit. The rain splashed in the gutter.* and finally, *Thomas sends roses to Lili*, repeated twice.

They all stood up and cheered. "It's a go!" Val cried "Tomorrow night. Now we must review our reception committee plans."

With a clatter of chairs and benches, the group assembled around the kitchen table. Val had taken his place at its head, the map of the camp and field spread out before him. "Jaques," Val ordered, "tomorrow morning, go to the Marquand farm. "Ask Marquand to bring his horse and wagon to the camp as soon as its dark. Tell him about the drop, that we need him to help us haul the cannisters and gear away from the drop zone."

Jaques nodded, his brown eyes bright with excitement. "Got it!"

"Luc, you will drive Marron and our wagon to the site. We'll need two wagons to clear the cannisters quickly."

Luc grinned. "Yes, sir!"

Val then turned to Alain. "After we pick up the stuff—and unload—the cannisters must be buried in the woods—away from the camp. Tomorrow morning round up a squad of men and some digging tools and look for a good hiding place. After the drop and after the gear has been loaded onto the wagons, haul the cannisters and parachutes to the place you've chosen for burial."

"Yes, sir," Alain responded, straightening his spine. He was a well-trained soldier, Danielle thought. He was forcing himself to move on. There was nothing he could do for Simone.

Val continued to rap out orders. Marcel would drive the radio operator to the farm in the Citroen. Danielle and Lili would prepare food and a place for the operator to sleep—and would ride with Marcel in the Citroen—to take the parachutist to the farmhouse and to run messages. Marisol would stand by at the drop zone with her medical kit—in case the radio operator were injured in the jump. Jean and he would be in charge of unloading the cannisters and organizing the removal of the weapons and other supplies to the spot they'd picked for storage.

"Fredi," he said, pausing a moment, "you're the leader of this group of maquisards. I think you should take command of the operation on the ground, organizing your men to prepare and light the bonfires, and to signal the pilot it's safe to continue the drop. And then greet the radio operator and hustle him away from the drop zone." Fredi lifted his head and stared at Val as if he were coming up for air. Val switched from French to English, and said, quietly, "Are you OK with that, Fredi."

Fredi gave a quick nod. "Sure."

Val suddenly stopped his onslaught of commands. He took a deep breath and reached for the glass of wine that Danielle had poured for him at the beginning of the meeting. "You know," he said quietly, in French. "I think we're ready. Let's make a toast." He lifted his glass. "Tomorrow night. Safe landings!"

The following evening the same crew gathered around the radio waiting for the signal indicating the bomber would fly that night. As Danielle listened to the announcer read off the meaningless jumble of words, she could barely breathe. Finally, the words they'd all been waiting for came from the cloth-covered speaker: Thomas sends roses to Lili. Again, the group let out a whoop of joy, and Danielle breathed freely. Jaques pulled Lili into his arms and kissed her firmly. "Who is this Thomas, Lili," he cried, laughing.

Val lifted his glass of wine. "We all know our tasks." He glanced at his watch. "It's half past eight. The plane will be taking off about now.

235

It's my understanding that the bomber they're using, the Whitley MkV, flies at a little over 200 miles per hour. The coast of England is about 600 miles from here, so it should take three hours or so for the plane to arrive. It will cross the Channel, and then face anti-aircraft fire as it enters France. It will be close to midnight when it reaches our drop zone, so we have time to get ready. We'll need to work quickly when we hear its engines. It has a range of about 1500 miles, so the pilot can't spend extra time flying above our field. He has to turn around and fly back to England. But you all know what you have to do." He fixed his eyes on Fredi. "Fredi, from here on, you take command."

Fredi held up his glass. "OK. And good luck to us all."

An hour before the plane's expected arrival time, all the participants were in place. Those maquisards who had no specific assignment at the drop zone, were on guard at the farm, on the road, and scattered around the camp. The two farm wagons and horses and their drivers were waiting on the crushed-stone track several meters from the field. Danielle and Lili sat up on the hood of the Citroen parked at the edge of the field. Marcel had propped himself against the thick trunk of a pine tree nearby. They all gazed up at the sky.

Danielle shivered with cold, excitement and fear. The round moon sailed overhead, casting an eerie, bluish light on the open field. The ground under the trees was deeply shadowed, black and mysterious. Danielle searched the sky and held as still as she could to sharpen her hearing. It was so quiet. Nobody spoke. The sound of a branch cracking or a heavy footstep was all that broke the silence. Then another tremor of fear chilled her spine. Would someone be watching them? She knew that the area was well guarded by their maquisards—and the village was over five kilometers from the drop zone—and the Italian soldiers were twenty-five kilometers further, but they could not be sure they were not seen. Someone might report seeing a plane painted black fly overhead. Or what if the pilot selected the wrong site for the drop?

She could see the pyramids of wood in the moonlight on the field, three of them, arranged in a triangle. At each pile stood two men waiting for the signal to light the bonfires. She could make out Fredi next to one of the stacks of wood, holding a long flashlight. She couldn't see Jean, but she knew he was at the side of the field hidden in the darkness of the trees.

After what seemed many hours, but was less than one, she heard the faint whine of an airplane engine coming from the northern sky. It grew louder. She slid off the hood of the car and clapped her hands over her mouth, to keep from crying out in excitement. Lili grasped her arm and they both stood motionless, listening, watching. Almost immediately the pyramids of wood burst into flame. The dark plane was almost overhead, flying low. Fredi was signaling the plane with his flashlight. In Morse code, she'd been told. The plane swooped over and there it was—a parachute opening, pale white in the moonlight, and then whoosh, thump, a man rolled over, then scrambled to his feet. Fredi rushed to his side and helped him tug off his parachute harness. Another man gathered up the cloud of white silk and harness and dashed into the shadow. Fredi hurried the man off the field, where Danielle knew that Marisol was waiting to check him for injuries.

The plane was circling, then a flock of parachutes opened, floating like dandelion seeds, one after the other man-sized cannisters thumped onto the ground. She noted three of the parachutes floating toward the tall pine trees next to the field. White silk was soon draped over the tops of the trees and she could hear branches crashing. The plane circled again and made another pass over the field, dropping more cannisters. Many, many. Finally, the pilot dipped the plane's long wings, circled and flew off into the northern sky.

Marcel, his wiry, tall form clothed in black, had climbed into the Citroen's driver's seat and started the motor just as Fredi and Marisol shepherded the parachutist to the car. He walked without their assistance, Danielle noted. and hadn't been injured in the fall. Danielle and Lili embraced him warmly and kissed him on the cheek. The boy gave them a bashful smile, showing white, even teeth. He couldn't be more than twenty, Danielle decided. Fredi beckoned him into the seat next to Marcel and quickly closed the door. He waved them off, and the two women jumped into the back. Marcel drove as fast as the old car would go on the rough track to the farm.

While they bounced along the road, Danielle introduced herself and Lili and asked the boy his name. She spoke in French. "My name?" he said, after a brief pause in hesitant French, "I am called Robert Derain." Lili began speaking a rapid French, asking him if there had been much anti-aircraft fire crossing into France. By his confused look, Danielle concluded he hadn't understood. She repeated what Lili had said in English, and appearing relieved, he answered in his flat American accent, "they shot at us, but they missed, thank God."

"You must have been really scared."

"You can say that again!" He turned to face her and she saw that his eyes were a sky blue and he had freckles on his nose.

By now they had arrived at the farmhouse. Marcel parked the car and they all piled out and entered the kitchen. Lili stoked up the fire and Danielle fetched the wine and four glasses. Marcel held out his hand to the parachutist. "Welcome to France, Robert," he said in English. "My name is Marcel and we are very, very happy to see you. But you must be hungry, thirsty, and do you need help getting out of that jump suit? André, our agent here, told me to dispose of it and your jump boots."

Robert grinned. "First I need to empty my pockets, and. . ." He then leaned toward Marcel, "and I need a john!"

"John?" Marcel murmured, and then he broke into a grin. "Yes, of course." He clapped Robert on the shoulder and led him out the door to the outhouse.

Danielle poured wine into the glasses and glanced toward the door. "Brave kid," she said, turning to Lili. "But he's here in one piece, thank God. Let's hope his radio landed safely."

Jean, Val and an excited squad of maquisards had finished unloading the radio, guns and boxes of ammunition. By the light of the moon and Fredi's flashlight, they'd counted thirty sten machine guns, fifteen M1 rifles, ten Walther P-38 handguns and two bazookas. From another cannister they'd unpacked ten carefully kapok-wrapped sacks of plastic and the same number of demolition devices and fuses.

"What are these trucs?" a young man asked, holding up one of the metal devices."

Val, who'd been examining the bazookas, turned to the boy. "When we blow up a train we put these on the track and attach them to a container of plastic explosive. The weight of the train engine acts like a trigger."

With raised eyebrows the boy gently replaced the detonator in its pile. The men then resumed stacking the weapons, placing each one lovingly in the underground bunker of logs and canvas that they'd built the day before. Fredi and Jean had selected a spot in the woods behind the camp fifty meters or so from the barracks. The bunker could be covered with planks of wood, scattered branches and leaves.

Jean turned away from the weapons stash, and picked his way through patches of moonlight and deep shadow to the center of the camp where a fire blazed, illuminating the remaining jumble of cannisters, kapok, and wood shavings where the wagons had been unloaded. Alain and his squad of maquisards were still in the process of burying the huge cannisters in the woods. Beyond the jumble lit by the fire, was a separate pile: sacks containing boots and blankets—and a suitcase. Jean knew the European-style leather suitcase contained the precious radio, which he would now take to the farmhouse. He lifted the case and examined its outside surface. The leather had been scraped in spots and the corners were dented. He could only hope that the radio itself had been carefully packed and was in working order, but the young operator would need to check it out.

Jean picked up the suitcase, which to his surprise was not unduly heavy, but decided he'd rather not carry it the two miles to the farmhouse. He could see Luc's wagon parked in front of the barracks. Jean called to him. A sleepy voice answered and within a few minutes Jean climbed onto the seat next to him, holding the bag in his arms. Luc tugged on the reins and Marron turned the wagon around and headed for the farmhouse.

Luc peered at the suitcase on Jean's lap. "Where will that guy run his radio—and where will you put him? Here in the camp—or the barn?"

"I don't know, Luc. Tonight he'll be in the attic in the farmhouse. After flying all those miles over enemy territory and jumping out of an airplane in the dark, the poor kid will be exhausted."

Luc glanced at Jean. "I'll bet! It must be so scary—but exciting. Maybe he could teach me how to run a wireless. I hope you put him in the barn."

Jean then thought about the discussions they'd had about where the operator should transmit his messages and where his quarters should be. Jaques had mentioned the farmhouse attic, but Fredi believed the camp would be safer. The Italian soldiers hadn't appeared yet, he'd said, but if someone from the village reported seeing parachutes or the low-flying Whitley painted black, they might turn up.

The candles were burning brightly in the farmhouse kitchen when Jean and Luc entered. The young radio operator, who was seated at the table spooning soup, glanced up as Jean moved toward him and clapped him on his back in a hearty greeting. They then shook hands and introduced themselves, Robert in a hesitant French. Jean felt a twinge of dismay hearing the boy stumble in French. Obviously, this young man could not pass as a native. Jean switched to English. "So! You landed OK. No broken bones! Great. And here's your radio." He set the suitcase at the end of the table. "Let's hope it works!"

Robert abandoned his soup and with dexterous fingers unfastened the suitcase buckles and raised the lid. Gently, he lifted out the radio, removing the protective packing material, and set it on the table. "It looks OK, but I'll need to try it out. It's one of the new models, a B2. I trained on it." He lifted a metal handle attached to the lid of the suitcase and inserted its end into the side of the radio. "I'll need someone to turn the handle to charge the batteries when I'm transmitting or receiving."

Luc stepped forward, grinning broadly. "I'll do it. It's like our short wave set. OK?"

Robert nodded and demonstrated how to turn the handle, which Luc copied with vigor. After several minutes a whining static buzzed from the set. Robert twisted the dials, then burst into a happy smile. "It's OK! It's small, but it'll work just fine when I put up an aerial."

Danielle smiled at him. "Robert, the sun will be up soon. You need some sleep. Let me show you to your room in the attic."

Robert nodded and dismantled the radio, placing it gently in it's case. "Yeah, I can hardly see straight." He followed her up the stairs, the precious radio in his arms.

Watching them, Jean let out a deep sigh. The first drop had been a success. Now they could fight Nazis!

# Chapter Thirty-eight

## The Italians

### May, 1943

The afternoon sun lit the treetops and rocky ridges as Danielle pedaled the bicycle up the road from Chateaudouble. Birds trilled overhead and pale green leaves sprouted on the chestnut trees, but Danielle could think only of the frightening news the mayor had just told her—that a detachment of Italian soldiers arrived in Draguignan the day before to be stationed at the old French artillery grounds. Draguignan was only sixteen kilometers away from the farm. Another larger detachment was now in Sisteron, the town where Lili met the courier, Odile. "An Italian official came to the Mairie two days ago," the Mayor said. "The official asked about the fires people had reported seeing in the direction of the charcoal factory. I assured him that your farm was a legitimate operation and was licensed. I showed him your licensing application."

When Danielle heard those words, her heart squeezed shut. The charcoal production was legitimate, but most certainly not the Maquis camp. She'd stared at the mayor. He knew, of course. She shook his hand, thanked him for his message, and climbed onto her bicycle.

Now she wondered how many people in the village knew about the Maquis. Probably most knew, but except for two or three families, the mood of the village was one of hatred for the Nazis and fascists. They were almost all champions of de Gaulle, although many of the villagers also hated communists, and would know about the many communists among the maquisards. But who had reported the fires to the Italians?

She thought about the camp of maquisards. They were drilled daily by Val, Fredi and the other former members of Varian's staff. They'd become Maquis leaders. Would Varian be shocked if he knew? For the last two weeks they had been preparing for a demolition raid on the railroad between Toulon and Marseilles. It was scheduled for the following night. A week ago Fredi had gone down to Toulon to check out the terrain along the railroad line. She'd need to pass on the mayor's information immediately to Fredi and Val. They'd want to send someone into Draguignan to have a look at the Italian encampment—how many soldiers and of what type. They'd need the information for their own safety, but also to inform OSS. It was just the type of intelligence the Americans and Brits asked for. Robert would transmit the information on his radio.

As Danielle grew closer to the farm, the air became tinged with smoke from the collier fires. At least the charcoal business was doing well. In fact, they'd bought an old truck and the mechanic at the camp had modified the engine to burn charcoal. Although officially it delivered charcoal, the maquisards often borrowed it. They all still used the wagon pulled by Marron, and they now had a cow, which produced plenty of milk.

Now she waved at the men hovering over their smoking mounds of wood covered with dirt. "Bonjour," she called.

"Bonjour, Danielle," they called back, cheerily. "Ça va?"

"Ça va," she murmured with a wan smile. She leaned the bike against the trunk of the oak tree next to the house and slung her musette over her shoulder. When she entered the kitchen, she was greeted by Robert and Chantal—in French. Robert's French was improving since he spent so much time with Chantal,

"Bonjour, Robert, Chantal." She set her musette at the end of the table and eyed Robert, who sat across from Chantal, who was shelling peas. On the table in front of Robert was a sheet of paper with rows numbers and letters penciled on it. "I see, Robert, you're still working on your codes."

He frowned, his pale eyebrows shadowing his sky blue eyes. "The kitchen table is a much better place to work than anywhere at the camp." He folded the paper and tucked it in his shirt pocket, buttoning it carefully.

"Of course!" she said, glancing at eighteen year old Chantal, whose hair framed her pretty face in dark curls. Robert found excuses to be near her—wherever she was. When Chantal wasn't assisting Marisol in the medical hut, she came to the farm kitchen to help cook. Danielle had grown fond of her. They were both Jewish, but Chantal's story was much sadder. While Chantal was in school, her parents had been picked up and taken to Drancy in Paris, then shipped on a train to Germany or Poland. Chantal hadn't heard from them since, of course. She'd then worked as a courier for the Resistance. Marisol had taken her under her wing after the O'Leary line was blown.

Now Danielle opened her musette and fished out a stack of charcoal orders. She sat at the table next to Robert, eying the the pocket where he'd stashed his codes, thinking he shouldn't be here at the farm. The Italian soldiers were too close. She wanted to blurt out the news about the Italians in Draguignan, but hesitated because of Chantal. She hated to frighten the girl. "So, Robert, did your transmission go through this morning?"

"Yes, indeed. I sent André's message without a hitch."

Danielle knew that Val—code-named André—had asked for more demolition materials and weapons. They were planning several raids on trains and munition plants. "And you will hear from London tonight?"

"I hope so. Just to acknowledge receipt of my message—unless they have something new to tell us." Although Robert was billeted at the camp, he transmitted his radio messages from ridges near the farmhouse. His transmissions and receptions were restricted to specific times of the day. He transmitted to London from 10 o'clock to 10:30 in the morning and received the London messages from 9 to 9:30 in the evening. Luc was his faithful helper, turning the crank to provide power.

Voices from the open door called out greetings. It was Jean, followed by Fredi. Jean touched Danielle's shoulder then stole a handful of peas from Chantal's pot. She laughed, but shoved the pot out of his reach. "No fair!"

Fredi swung the duffel from his shoulder and set it gently in the corner of the kitchen. From the careful way he handled the duffel, Danielle wondered if it contained plastic explosive. The thought chilled her. "Fredi, I hope that duffel doesn't contain what I think it contains."

Fredi shrugged. "For just a few minutes, Danielle. And it's quite stable, nothing really to worry about as long as it's not close to the fire." He then turned to Robert. "And did your transmission get through this morning?"

Robert nodded. "Yes, sir. As far as I know. I'll find out for sure tonight, I hope."

Jean placed a pitcher of water on the table he'd just pumped from the well outside the door. As he moved toward the dish cupboard for glasses, he glanced at Danielle's stack of charcoal orders. "Anything happening in the village?"

Danielle hesitated, but only for a second. The mayor's information couldn't be held back. Chantal would hear it soon enough. "I spoke to the mayor, and he gave me some very distressing news." She spoke slowly, repeating what the mayor had said about a detachment of Italian soldiers stationed in Draguignan and Sisteron—and of the official who had asked about the fires here at the farm.

Both Fredi and Jean stared at Danielle with shocked eyes. "Jesus," Fredi murmured. "Draguignan is only twenty minutes away by car. They could show up here at any time." He glanced at the duffel in the corner of the room—then at Robert. "I'll move my duffel immediately. And Robert, you must stay in the camp. Your French isn't good enough to be questioned. And I hope to hell you've hidden your radio carefully."

"I have, sir." Robert answered, rising from his chair. "And I'll return to the camp. Right away." After checking to make sure his pocket was buttoned, he gave Chantal a longing look, picked up his musette and marched out the door. Fredi loaded the duffel on his shoulder and followed Robert. Speechless, Danielle and Chantal watched them leave. Jean, still holding glasses in his hand, looked from Danielle to Chantal. "Merde!" he whispered.

The rattling Citroen descended the narrow road that edged the gorge. The afternoon sun lit the jagged rock formations that rose like a steep wall on the other side of the deep ravine. Marcel was at the wheel. Jean sat next to him. Fredi and Jean Marc, the sailor from one of the shuttled ships in the Toulon harbor, were in back. Besides the smoke from the charcoal burning engine, the car smelled strongly of fish. Jean wound down his window all the way. "Fredi, those trout are beginning to stink. Did Luc really catch them this morning?"

"So he said. Anyway, the stronger they smell the less likely the soldiers at checkpoints will investigate my pack."

"You hope!" Jean considered Fredi's pack. It contained the plastic explosive and a few detonators underneath a sack of six freshly caught trout—plus a brace of four rabbits, shot by Luc. Jean Marc carried the dismantled sten guns and the 9MM ammunition in his backpack under a large sack of tomatoes. Two Walther P-38 handguns and four knives with ankle holsters were in pockets cut into their seat cushions. All four of the men carried forged documents stating they were farmers. If questioned, they would claim they were going to the market in Cannes to sell their fish, rabbit and produce. They decided not to use the papers that describe them as charcoal makers. If they were caught blowing this train, they didn't want to put the charcoal factory people in danger—or the Maquis camp.

Fredi tapped Marcel on the shoulder. "OK, Marcel, pull over here. The turnoff to Draguignan is around that curve." He grabbed his pack, beckoned to Jean Marc, and giving a quick glance around, crossed the road and strode into the thick forest of pines and oaks that bordered the road. Jean Marc followed. They had discussed this maneuver the evening before after Luc and his mother returned from the market in Draguignan. Luc had reported that French police and Italian soldiers were questioning and searching people at the turnoff. On hearing this, Fredi decided that he and Jean Marc would carry the plastic and stens through the woods on foot and meet the Citroen beyond the checkpoint. From there Marcel knew how to follow the minor roads down the mountain to the coast to avoid searches.

A bus and two other cars were in the line waiting to go through the barrier. As they waited, Jean glanced at Marcel, whose worn, dark overalls looked authentically rustic. His old straw hat was frayed at the edges and his skin was tanned. They'd all been working like farmers and they looked it, but even so, each time Jean waited to hand over his forged papers the palms of his hands began to sweat. When their turn finally came, the young soldier peered briefly into the interior of the car, the gendarme gave their papers a quick glance, handed them to the soldier, who returned them and beckoned them through.

Marcel shifted gears and slowly drove away. "At least that's over," he mumbled.

Jean took in a deep breath and wiped his hands on his pants. "Right! I wonder if that kid could read French."

Marcel shrugged and continued driving. They both kept a sharp lookout for more soldiers and for Fredi and Jean Marc. When they were out of sight of the checkpoint, about 100 meters beyond it, Marcel pulled over to the side of the road. Across the narrow road, hidden in the thick branches of a chestnut tree, birds trilled. From the edge of the road Jean peered into the gorge where a steam flowed over yellow and white stones. The crack of a branch and the rustle of leaves caused him to snap to attention. It was Fredi and Jean Marc, their bags on their shoulders, pushing their way through the underbrush. Without speaking they clambered back into the car and Marcel drove off down the mountain, heading for the safe house above Toulon belonging to André Colbert.

They arrived at the farmhouse before dark. Marcel drove the Citroen into the barn, where Colbert had directed him. They unloaded the car and proceeded to organize their equipment. Jean pried out the handguns, the knives and ammunition from the batting inside the car-seats, then sat on the floor to assemble and load the stens. Jean Marc sat cross-legged beside him loading the Walther P-38s. Both the stens and the handguns took 9mm cartridges. After they were loaded the two men clicked on the safeties. Fredi lifted the packet of plastic from the bottom of his duffel and placed it carefully on a cloth he'd spread on the dirt floor. "When it's dark enough," he said, "we'll go. You'll need to follow me closely. There'll be no moon. I'll go over your tasks once more." Jean listened carefully.

"As I told you last night, our contacts in Toulon know the railroad schedule. The train we'll blow is expected to arrive at our target site around 9PM. It'll have left the docks twenty minutes earlier. When the engine hits the metal detonator it will set off the plastic. The engine will explode, catch fire and the cars derail. It's possible the train will be carrying tankers of fuel." He paused a moment, glancing at each of them, as if to impress on their minds the noise and heat and danger of the burning train. "Last week when I hiked down to the line, the best spot I found to place the plastic is where the tracks go over a trestle. It crosses a stream that rushes down a steep slope—making quite a racket—which should mask any noise we make pushing through the undergrowth. The trestle looks easy to climb. I didn't see any sentries, but we can't count on that. Dock workers warned Colbert that German soldiers often guard the trains carrying fuel or munitions."

Fredi then picked up one of the detonation devices. "Jean Marc, you and I will climb onto the track and place the detonators and the plastic. Jean and Marcel, you will stand guard at the ends of the bridge and whistle our signal indicating it's safe to set the explosive. Whistle the warning signal in case of danger. If a sentry appears you know what to do. You have your knives and your stens." Jean thought about the training Val had put them through. He had learned how to kill a man silently, slitting his throat. Could he actually do it? He'd killed before in Spain, but at a distance, with a rifle. Slitting a man's throat was something else.

They were interrupted by a knock on the barn door and the voice of André Colbert. "Come into the kitchen," he called, opening the door a crack. "My wife has cooked your trout —and some soup." Fredi covered their weapons with clean flour sacks and they followed Colbert into the farmhouse.

# Chapter Thirty-nine

## The Train

*May, 1943*

The barn was lit by a lantern propped on a rough wooden shelf. Jean tugged his dark sweater down over his shirt and pulled on a sailor's black cap. Fredi handed him a stick of charcoal, which he smeared on his face. Marcel and Jean Marc did the same. They then picked up their weapons, first strapping knives onto their ankles, carefully pulling down the cuffs of their dark pants. Jean and Marcel slung the stens over their shoulders, while Fredi thrust the Walther P-38 handgun into the back of his pants and hoisted the bag containing the detonators and plastic. Jean Marc tucked the pliers and a screwdriver into his back pocket and, the P-38 into his pants. They were ready to go.

Fredi stood at the barn door. "OK? Follow me and remember, keep low." Jean felt a shiver rush up his spine. His heart pounded wildly. He felt like a parachutist must feel waiting for the green light to shine before he jumped.

To his surprise, as soon as he began to move, crouching, creeping down the trail, following Fredi, he felt energized. His training took over. His breathing steadied. He concentrated on moving stealthily, carefully, one foot after the other. The weight of the sten on his back was reassuring, and as his eyes became accustomed to the darkness he became more sure-footed. Fredi was about two meters ahead of him and kept up a steady pace as he crept down the steep slope. Marcel and Jean Marc were close behind. Stars were thick overhead but dimmed on the horizon where the blue lights at the edge of the ruined harbor glowed. He could smell the oil-slicked sea.

Sooner that Jean expected, he heard the sound of a rushing stream on his right. Was this the stream that flowed under their trestle? The ground underfoot was now almost level. Fredi suddenly held up his hand and stopped. The railroad trestle was straight ahead. Jean turned to Marcel behind him and repeated Fredi's gesture. Marcel signaled to Jean Marc. They ducked down while Fredi crept forward. He returned within seconds and gestured silently for them to take their assigned positions.

About twenty meters on the other side of the the trestle a lower bridge crossed the stream for cars and trucks. Jean scanned the road in both directions, but no headlights appeared. He climbed down the ravine to the edge of the stream which he needed to cross, since Fredi had assigned him to guard the northern end of the trestle. The night was dark, but starlight reflected on a trail of white rocks that surfaced from the swiftly running water. Steadying his sten, Jean stepped onto the first rock. His heavy boots rapped noisily on the stone, He stopped, placing both feet on a wide, flat rock next to it, hoping the roar of the water had masked the noise of his boots. Without moving, Jean listened for sounds other than the water rushing over stone. Hearing nothing unusual, he continued crossing the stream.

On the other side of the ravine he crouched behind a boulder, giving himself a moment to calm his racing heart. He crept up the bank close to the railroad tracks at the end of the trestle, keeping low, forcing himself to breathe slowly. Then, with a jolt, he heard the sound of boots hitting gravel. He froze. He fastened his eyes on the tracks, peering into the darkness. Within seconds a soldier appeared from the shadows—in a tan uniform, an Italian, marching slowly along the side of the trestle—on guard—his gun slung over his shoulder, humming to himself. Shit, Jean thought. He'd have to take the soldier out.

Silently, Jean slid his knife from its ankle holster and crept closer to his prey, ducking behind a blackberry bush. He waited for the soldier, still humming, to pass by. When the man was no more than two meters in front of him, his back turned, Jean sprinted forward, wrapped his left arm around the soldiers neck, covering his mouth with his sleeve, bending the Italian's head sharply back. With a swift gesture of his right hand, Jean slit his throat and pushed him away, blood pumping from the soldier's neck. Kneeling beside the body, peering into his fellow-countryman's face, he realized the soldier was just a boy, a lad with curly dark hair. Jean eyed the boy's gaping, bloody throat which was no longer pumping. A wave of nausea forced him to turn away. Breathing raggedly, his jaw clenched, he wiped the knife on the grass and shoved it back into the ankle holster. He glanced again at the soldier and numbly pulled the Italian's body down the ravine into the brush beside the stream. He then dipped his hands into the cold, clear water to cleanse them of blood. His fingers rose to his forehead in an automatic gesture. An image had flashed through his mind of the font of holy water in his church in Genoa. He'd been about to make the sign of the cross. Instead, he took another deep breath, straightened his spine, and climbed up to the edge of the tracks, where he whistled an all clear signal to Fredi, Almost immediately, another whistle sounded from Marcel's position at the other end of the bridge. It was time for Fredi and Jean Marc to place the explosive. They had a job to do.

Now Jean kept his eyes sharply trained on the road beyond the tracks, watching for the slitted blue lights of army vehicles—and listening for the sound of motors. Except for the noise of the stream below the trestle, the night was still. He thought he heard the clink of metal on the tracks toward the middle of the bridge. He strained his eyes to try to make out the figures of Fredi or Jean Marc, but the shadows were deep. The fast-flowing stream below masked any noise they might make. Soon, he heard Fredi's whistle signaling the completion of their task. Now they all must flee, run up to the line of trees, which would be out of range of the explosion.

Jean slung his sten over his shoulder and slid quickly down the ravine, glancing briefly into the brush where the young Italian's body was hidden, checking to make sure it was not visible from the trestle. Assured the body was out of sight, Jean leaped from stone to stone across the stream, Breathing hard, he ran up the slope to the trees, retracing his steps, scanning the path for Fredi and the others. A short hissing sound caused him to look around. It was Marcel, on the other side of a thicket of willows a few meters on his right. Jean moved quickly around the willows and Marcel pointed to a tree a few meters ahead. "Fredi," he whispered. "It's done." He tapped his watch, which Jean knew he meant that it was time for the train to arrive. Jean continued up the slope, listening for the sound of the train approaching, glancing toward the track and the road as he ran.

Then he heard the long, high sound of a locomotive whistle followed by the deep roar of metal wheels on steel railroad tracks—and glimpsed a blue light traveling forward in the darkness. Both Jean and Marcel slowed their pace, but did not stop, knowing they were well beyond the reach of the explosion, but also realizing they had to escape quickly. They peered down at the trestle directly below them. Within minutes the train was approaching the bridge. It was on the bridge— and whoosh, the bang of the explosion and the flames that flew up into the sky caused Jean's head to pound and the breath to stop in his throat. With a rapid glance at the inferno below, Jean saw the brush next to the bridge catch fire as the engine fell into the ravine. The cars behind the engine toppled over, exploding in flames and he saw figures of men jumping from the car roofs, some on fire. Then he heard shots and shouting men. Soldiers in gray and green German uniforms were jumping from the rear cars and scattering, their guns pointing into the forest. Jean immediately scrambled up the slope, running for his life, tripping on roots and bumping into rocks. He could hear Marcel behind him. Fredi and Jean Marc were up ahead.

They continued running, gasping for breath. Jean had lost sight of Fredi, but Marcel was with him. Suddenly, Marcel tripped and fell flat on the ground. Jean stopped to help him up. Marcel winced. "My ankle." he whispered.

"Here," Jean murmured, holding out his arm, "I'll help you."

"No," Marcel answered. "Go on. I can make it. It's not so bad," and he hobbled up the trail. Jean went ahead, but kept glancing back at Marcel, who was moving too slowly. He could hear the soldiers rushing up the hill, getting closer, their torches flashing. "Marcel, crawl into those willows over there," he whispered.

"OK. But you go on," Marcel murmured, hoarsely.

Jean scanned the terrain. "I'll go up behind those rocks. See them?"

Marcel nodded and then crept into the brush, pulling the branches back in place. Jean ran up the slope to the pile of rocks and crouched in the shadows behind them. As he hunkered down, he made a quick scan of the slope above for a possible escape route. It wasn't good. The slope contained only a scattering of trees. He removed his sten from his shoulder, clicked the safety catch, and pointed the barrel through a crevice between the rocks. By now the soldiers' torches were visible. Five of them. It was too dark to see the men, but the lights were moving forward at a rapid pace. Jean was ready for action, his breathing steady. If they came closer, he thought, he could get them all, but he had to wait. The steel of the sten's trigger was cold on his finger. Now the men approached the spot where Marcel was concealed. One of the men swept a beam of light on the clump of willows. Jean held his breath. Don't move, Marcel, he wanted to yell. Don't move a muscle!

The soldier poked at the brush with his rifle then shouted loudly in German. He'd found Marcel. As he shouted, Marcel jumped up from the clump of willows, blasting the Germans with his sten. Three men fell, but a fourth and fifth let loose a volley of bullets into Marcel, who slumped to the ground. The two soldiers still on their feet bent down to check their fallen comrades. One was motionless, the other two were covered in blood but were moving. One propped himself up on his elbow. A surge of black hatred coursed through Jean's body. The urge to jump up shooting was almost impossible to resist, but he remembered Val's training. The guerrilla's job was a hit and run operation. And the sten had only a four meter range. And the Germans were at least ten meters distant.

Now the soldiers were helping the two wounded ones to their feet. They'd tied strips of cloth over the bleeding wounds and were half-carrying them down the hill. When they were out of sight, Jean emerged cautiously from behind the rocks. The sound of men shouting and the flashes of light now came from the direction far to Jean's left. If he hurried, he might make it up the slope before they spread out. He crept to Marcel's body, eying the fallen German closely. The German was dead, his face covered in blood. Jean then knelt beside Marcel and quickly felt for the pulse in his neck. Nothing. He, too, was dead. He then checked his pockets for any object that could identify their organization or the farm. He removed Marcel's wallet with his forged identity cards and picked up his sten. "Goodbye, my friend," he murmured. Numbly, he turned away and scrambled up the hill, the two weapons clanking on his back.

Danielle plucked a wild strawberry from the meadow grass and dropped it in the enamel bowl. The field behind the barn hid a treasure of the tiny fruits, and Lili, Marisol, Chantal and she were harvesting them. Lili would carry a precious basket of berries to Sisteron the next day with the photographs and information Jaques had ferreted out about the military detachment in Draguignan. Alain had developed the film in a shack he'd built at the camp. The chemicals he used had been dropped in the last delivery from the Americans.

Although Danielle felt a surface delight being in the sunlit field with the three women taking part in such a pleasant task, underneath lay a shadow of deep concern for Jean and the other three men. Last night was the night they'd planned to blow the train. If all went well they should be driving up the road soon. They'd stop here before they'd go to the camp. The colliers had taken time off from their charcoal burning to block off the wagon track that went from the farm to the camp. Now to reach the camp the maquisards stayed on the small dirt road from town that continued from the farm's turnoff to the next village. They'd cleared a trail entering the camp from the road, hiding the entrance with branches and rocks, knowing that sooner or later, soldiers would investigate their charcoal operation at the farm.

Danielle popped a strawberry into her mouth. It was so delicious, she let it linger on her tongue. They would keep a few for themselves, but very few. They would sell most in the market in St Raphael or Cannes. Lili would use them as soldier sweeteners and checkpoints in Sisteron—and as the "gift for her sick aunt".

She glanced at Chantal, whose mouth was pink with strawberry juice. The girl was chattering to Marisol, looking lithe and merry. In these last few weeks at the farm she had browned in the sun and opened up to them all—especially Robert, the American radioman— who was so smitten by the girl. Danielle smiled to herself. His French was almost perfect except for his slips into American slang. His accent was good. He'd explained that his mother was born in St Denis, near Paris, and had come to America as a war bride in 1918 to marry his father, an American soldier. She had spoken French with Robert as a young child, but had switched to English when he started school. Val no longer insisted he stay at the camp. At the moment Robert was up behind the rocky ledge above the farm transmitting to London with Luc's help.

A voice from the trail to the camp stopped her musings. She held her fruit-stained hand over her eyes to shade them from the sun as she looked towards the trail-head. It was Val carrying an axe over his shoulder. "Well, well," he said. "a lyrical sight, I must say." He smiled broadly. "Four lovely ladies in a strawberry field. And I've come to tell you some fabulous news."

The women stopped their picking and smiled gaily.

Val took a deep breath. "I came to tell you what I just heard on a German broadcast just now. On our camp radio."

The women all turned to him in expectantly.

"The Germans and Italians have surrendered in North Africa!" He held up his arms in a victory salute. "First Stalingrad—now North Africa!"

Danielle stared at Val. "My God," she exclaimed. "Is it possible we'll really beat them!?"

"It would seem so!" and he gave her a tight hug, smiling broadly. "We'll just have to keep hitting them! Harder and harder."

Chantal and Marisol hopped to their feet and with clasped hands twirled in a celebratory dance, shouting with glee, their strawberry baskets abandoned.

The sound of a charcoal burning engine chugging up the road caused the two women to stop dancing. Danielle and Val moved toward the front of the barn. Was it the Citroen? And it was, indeed. Jean was driving. He was safe! But then as he, Fredi and Jean Marc climbed out of the car, the shocking realization hit her that there should have been four men. Where was tall, stringy Marcel?

Marisol ran toward the men, who stood motionless and silent with blood-shot eyes and grim mouths. Chantal trailed behind her.

"Where's Marcel?" Marisol cried, her gray eyes wide with fright. Jean Marc looked away. Fredi eyed Jean.

Danielle scrutinized Jean's face. Something terrible must have happened. Jean's eyes expressed pain, his lips were tightly closed. "I don't know how to tell you this, Marisol." he said finally, He took a deep breath. "He was shot!"

"Captured?" Her voice was shrill, her face contorted. Danielle glanced at Fredi, then back to Jean.

Jean shook his head. "No, Marisol. I'm sorry. He's gone. Dead." He held out his arms to her and she fell into them, sobbing. Then suddenly she lifted her face, peering up at Jean. "And his body? Tell me, Jean." She turned to Fredi, then Jean Marc. "Tell me what happened, for Christ's sake!"

Danielle watched as Jean gripped Marisol's shoulders, holding her at arm's length. "He died bravely, Marisol. Quickly. After killing one German and wounding two others. I couldn't help him. I'm so, so sorry." He held her as she sobbed on his shoulder, tears falling down his cheeks. They all listened as he recited a story of the train, the Germans, the stens, Marcel's twisted ankle, and his own position out of shooting range. Over Marisol's shoulder he locked eyes with Danielle, who could feel her own tears flowing down her face, her heart a tight fist in her chest. Poor Marisol. How will she cope? And Chantal? Marcel was her savior. Now the girl was slumped on the grass weeping, her hands over her face.

A voice from the trail from the rocks above the barn caused Danielle to turn in that direction. Robert was running down the slope, returning from his radio transmission task. He hurried toward them—then stopped as he took in the scene of the tear-filled faces. He rushed to Chantal's side. "What's wrong, ma cherie," he said, sinking onto the grass beside her, lifting up her face. "What's happened!"

"It's Marcel," she said. "He's been killed. Blowing the train."

# Chapter Forty

## Events in Italy

### September, 1943

The fire crackled in the fireplace, a busy sound that matched the voices in the farm kitchen. Jean switched off the short wave radio and scanned the room, his eyes finding Danielle's. What wonderful news they'd just heard. The Allies had invaded Italy's mainland at Salerno and were pushing back the Italian troops. Mussolini had been arrested, and King Victor Emmanuel had appointed Marshal Badolgio the leader of a new government.

Danielle picked up the carafe of wine and re-filled glasses. "That report calls for a toast!"

Fredi lifted his glass. "Absolutely!"

"To the Allies!" Val called out.

"To the Americans!" Lili said.

Jaques' arm went around Lili's shoulders. "Yes, and to the Brits and the wonderful BBC for sending such good news."

They gathered around the table for their weekly planning meeting. Jean sat on the bench next to Danielle. "And now that Sicily's in the Allies' hands—and North Africa—and the Italians are weakening, the war may be won sooner than we hoped."

Val held up his hand. "The invasion of France has to come first, and we have to prepare the ground—and keep hitting the railroads and the phone lines and bridges. In these last four months you've done a great job, and you've done it well. We've lost only five men."

The image of Marcel's riddled body flashed through Jean's mind. He still felt guilt about that death. He'd been on several raids since that first train, and he'd killed more young Italian soldiers, which pained him deeply, but watching Marcel being shot—and doing nothing to help him, was a remembrance that burned like hell-fire.

Jean shook off that memory and paid attention to Val, who was unrolling a map and spreading it on the table. "Fredi, your next target should be here," and he tapped his finger on the map, "the bridge across the Le Cians. The Italian detachment at Sisteron gets its supplies from Torino over the Col de Lombarda. Blowing the bridge would force them to take alternate routes, using more fuel, taking longer. . ."

At that moment, the back door to the farmhouse opened and Robert dashed in. He held a silk cloth in his hand, which Jean knew was Robert's one-time-code key. On it were printed different decoding keys for his radio transmissions and receptions. After coding or decoding a message he would cut that key from the silk handkerchief-like square and burn it.

Robert was breathing rapidly. "André," he called, pausing for breath. "I need to talk to you. In private. It's important. A message for you."

Val/André jumped up from his chair, and excused himself. "This shouldn't take long, but Fredi, you continue. Robert, shall we step outside?"

Robert nodded and he and Val hurried out the door.

Jean glanced around the table, then lifted the carafe of wine and re-filled glasses. Fredi reached for the map. "It shouldn't be too difficult a job. Blowing that bridge. We could take the road going north that bypasses Castellane. There've been no checkpoints there for the last month."

The door opening caused them all to turn their heads. Val strode into the room, his eyes alive with excitement. Robert trailed behind him, looking stunned. "OK. The message is one you need to know. The news is startling. OSS says that Italy is surrendering to the Allies.

It's still secret. The Germans haven't been informed, but it's in the works. Furthermore, I've been recalled. I must leave tomorrow."

Val's listeners sat immobile with shock. Val resumed his place at the head of the table. Robert was cutting off a piece of his of silk with kitchen shears. Jean watched as the boy tossed the scrap of silk into the fire, but was pondering over what Val had just told them. The Italians were surrendering. He glanced at Val, then Danielle, and put his arm arm around her waist. "You know what that means for us here, Val."

"I'm afraid so. The Germans will take over the Var. No more nice Italian boys. Instead, Wehrmacht, SS Waffen troops. Gestapo. You can only hope the Wehrmacht is spread too thin to station many troops here." He turned to Danielle. "And if it's known we have Jews here, the SS will arrive to haul them off to the camps. And we know what happens there."

Jean felt Danielle stiffen under his arm. "You said the Italian surrender to the Allies should be announced within days."

"Right." Val locked eyes with Jean.

"So we'd have a brief window of time to prepare for the German arrival? This information comes from OSS. Not the Italians?"

"Apparently Badoglio and the King's emissaries kept their military out of the talks. The surrender negotiations were secret. Frankly, I'm surprised you're being informed."

Jean looked at Danielle, noting the fright in her blue eyes, her stiff shoulders. Nobody spoke. Jean turned to Val. "And you've been recalled?"

"Yes. I'm to leave tomorrow. And I don't know why they've called me in. Robert will remain here."

Jean hesitated, glanced again at Danielle. "Val, is there any chance you could get Danielle and Chantal into Switzerland?"

Danielle gave a short cry. "Jean, what are you doing?"

"I'm trying to save your life, that's what I'm doing. If Val can get you across the frontier you should go!"

Val gave Danielle a long, thoughtful look. Nobody spoke. Finally, he turned to Jean. "I believe I can manage that, but it's not without risks. Danielle, are you willing to take that risk?"

Danielle's eyes met Jean's, then Val's. "It's not that I'm afraid. I just don't want to leave—my comrades—and Jean."

Jean took hold of her hand in both of his. "But, Danielle, when the Germans arrive they would cart you away like refuse. And think of Chantal."

Danielle's stared at him. Although she didn't speak, he knew she was thinking about Chantal Stein, a girl with a Jewish name and olive skin—and what that would mean when the Germans came. After a moment's hesitation she turned back to Val. "But what about our documents? We wouldn't have time to forge new ones."

"You may not need documents to cross the frontier. And consider, Danielle, you could be of use to OSS in Geneva. Actually, this is something I've thought of before. In fact, I've discussed the possibility with my commander. You have first hand information about conditions here, the land and people in the Var, Riviera and Marseilles. And you're fluent in English."

Danielle bit her lip, shot Jean a tortured glance, then let out a deep breath. "OK. I'll go."

Val jumped up from his chair. "Good. Now you need to pack a few things—what you can carry in a musette—warm clothes to wear and sturdy boots. Robert, you go to Chantal and tell her she'll be leaving for Switzerland early tomorrow morning. We'll be taking the bus to Grenoble. Tell her to gather all her documents so I can look them over. We may need to tinker with them a little. I'll go back to the camp with you. Examine her papers, do my own packing." Before going out the door he stopped and touched Danielle's shoulder. "I'll see you tomorrow, Danielle. You're doing the smart thing, believe me."

Jean and Danielle stood arm in arm and solemnly watched him go out the door,

Later that evening Danielle sat on the edge of her bed, her documents in her hand spread out like a fan of playing cards. She still felt somewhat numb, in a daze. Her musette was packed. She'd laid out warm clothes to wear the next day and sturdy boots. The boots were men's boots dropped for the maquisards—in a small size. She wondered if she'd be hiking over the Alps. Val had never told them how he crossed into Switzerland from France. She glanced around this

259

attic room. Oddly, she'd been happy here, hidden away, being with Jean when he wasn't out on a mission.

The sound of footsteps on the stairs outside her room caused her heart to jump a beat. It must be Jean. She slid her documents into the outside pocket of her musette and pushed back the tears that threatened to fall. She was determined to be brave, not to make a scene, to help Jean feel less depressed about her leaving, about the Germans.

When Jean entered the room Danielle flew into his arms. They stood a while holding each other. Danielle was conscious of wanting to remember this moment, this feel of his body holding her tightly. She leaned back and looked into his eyes. The light from the candle reflected in his gold-flecked hazel eyes and shone on his olive skin. Would she see him again? Would they survive this war? "I do love, you, Jean, and I really, really don't want to leave you!"

"I know." He held her tight. "And I love you so much I want you to go, but it breaks my heart."

They made love that night slowly, as if they wanted to stretch the moment, prolong the pleasure. They promised they'd find each other after the war. They'd marry and live in a peaceful world free from fascism. Finally, they fell asleep, limbs entangled in the narrow bed. Danielle woke at dawn, Jean's arm heavy on her shoulder. She lay still a few moments, savoring his warmth, not wanting to move, but it was time for her to rise, to dress, to go. She could hear activity in the kitchen downstairs: someone pumping water, firewood being split with the hatchet. Then she heard a knock on her door. It was Chantal. "Danielle, André is here. We're leaving in thirty minutes."

It had been five days and five long nights since Danielle, Chantal and Val climbed on the bus for Grenoble. Jean sat in the farm kitchen, feeling depressed and lonely—and anxious about Danielle's safety. Had she arrived in Switzerland? Or had she been apprehended crossing the frontier—lacking the appropriate visas and travel permits. At least the German and Italian military seemed unaware of Badoglio's negotiations with the Allies. He'd spent the morning in Draguignan, checking out the Italian presence in the town. Tonight he hoped BBC would have some news about the surrender.

He glanced across the room at Jaques and Lili. Jaques was winding the handle of the short-wave radio. Lili was at the table working on the charcoal factory books, a task she'd taken over from Danielle. He hoped Robert would return soon. The boy had left an hour ago to set up his radio for his 8 o'clock reception from London. As if he'd heard Jean's wish, the door opened and Robert strode into the room, smiling from ear to ear. "It's a message from André." He held up the pad of paper he used to decode his messages. "The girls are safe in S." He clapped Jean on the back. "They made it! They're OK!"

# Chapter Forty-one

## The Jedburghs

### *May, 1944*

Jean sat on the barracks steps in the moonlight cleaning his M1 rifle. The moon was almost full. He'd just returned from another sabotage action on the coast, and he was still too pumped up with adrenaline to sleep. This time they'd hit a military supply depot near San Rafael. He reflected that he was now a hardened maquisard. He remembered the pain that lingered in his gut when his comrades were cut down in Spain—and at Dunkirk—and when Marcel was killed here on the mountain. He'd now learned how to bury his feelings of grief when he witnessed men being killed or wounded. They'd lost five young men in the last month. Tonight one had been killed and two wounded.

But Fredi had trained them well. They were disciplined and tough. They were now officially part of the Forces Françaises de l'Intérieur, the F.F.I., de Gaulles' name for the bands of resisters in the mountains and forests of rural France. Fredi, as commander, kept his maquisards busy with guerrilla training, sabotage and surveillance. Now of Varians' original group, only Jaques and Lili were billeted at the farmhouse. German soldiers had come to inspect their charcoal operation not long after Danielle and Chantal left. Fredi was ready for them. The trails to the camp were well camouflaged, and only those people working for the charcoal operation had remained at the farm. Jaques and Lili handled the business details. It was Jaques who dealt with the Germans. His fluency in German helped. Fortunately, his name wasn't on any of the Gestapo's lists, according to one of Fredi's informants at the prefecture in Marseilles.

Six months had passed since Val, Danielle and Chantal left the farm. Jean thought of Danielle constantly. As much as he missed her, it was a relief she was no longer here at the edge of danger. He'd memorized her parents' address in California. Danielle had promised she'd write to her parents as soon as she was in Switzerland. She'd tell them he'd be contacting them as soon as France was free of German troops. From time to time Robert would bring messages to Jean or Fredi sent from the OSS office in Geneva via London. He knew Danielle was working in the OSS office and would be well taken care of. At the same time he harbored a lingering sense of uncertainty when he thought of the other men she might meet and find attractive—and fall for. She was beautiful and intelligent and some dashing male American agent would surely try to claim her. He sighed. But he couldn't help but hope she loved him—and would wait for him until the war was over. If only he knew for certain.

The sound of boots scrambling rapidly down the rocky crags behind the camp caused Jean to glance up from his task. It was Robert. Robert called out to Jean as he came stumbling into the camp. "Where's Fredi?" he gasped "Something new! Get ready for parachutists." He waved the scrap of silk and a piece of paper in the air.

"Parachutists?"

"Yeah, but where's Fredi? The message is for him."

Jean pointed to the medical hut. "He's with Marisol. He's checking on the two men who were wounded in our operation tonight." As he spoke, Fredi emerged from the hut, his face still smudged with charcoal, and his body drooping with fatigue. Robert hurried toward him. "A message from Special Forces—SFHQ."

"SFHQ? That's a new one."

Jean was puzzled. Would that be a section of OSS?

With a glance at Jean, Fredi moved a few steps away while he read Robert's decoded message. Almost immediately, he returned to Jean. "New orders. From a different outfit—SFHQ. We should expect a drop of three army officers, British, American and French, during the next full moon. Jedburghs, they're called. They'll be in uniform and they'll be flying in from Algeria. SFHQ will transmit a message when the flight is scheduled."

"Jedburghs? In uniform? From three different armies? What's that about?" Jean said, jumping up, staring at Fredi, a surge of excitement tingling his nerves. "Something is up! Could it be the invasion?"

Fredi shrugged, peering up at the moon. "Whatever it is we'll learn in three or four days!"

And three days later Robert received the message saying there would be a plane coming from Algeria the following night. Three officers from three allied armies—American, British and French—would jump into their drop zone. The American was a non-com, a radio operator, the Brit a captain and the Frenchman a lieutenant. We should be prepared to collect several cannisters of supplies.

The entire camp buzzed in anticipation. Officers in uniform? From three Allies? Why? But the drop went like clockwork. By now the maquisards built the bonfires and cleared the drop zone without a hitch. Fortunately, none of the jumpers were injured when they landed. Before the men climbed into the Citroen they removed their jump suits, first emptying their pockets. Jean watched carefully as they stepped out of the suits. Would they really be in uniform? The first to kick off his outer suit was the young American in the battle dress and insignia of a US army Sergeant. On his upper sleeve was a winged patch. In the center of the patch's spread white wings was a red circle with the letters SF in light blue. The other two men were officers, a British Captain and a French Lieutenant—each wearing their army's battle dress and rank insignia. Each also wore the winged patch with the letters SF.

The men introduced themselves. The code name for their team was Nessie, the British captain told them first in English—then in a stumbling French. "I'm Captain Ian Cameron." He shook hands with Fredi and Jean. Jean noted the captain's blue eyes and sandy hair—and his tall athletic figure. Fredi introduced himself with his code name, Felix, speaking in his fluent English.

"I'm very happy to meet you," the captain said. "You are the commander here, correct?"

Fredi nodded then introduced Jean as his second in command. The French officer gave a quick bow and shook their hands. "Francois Belloc, Free French army,"

"Sergeant Billy Walker, US army." the young American blurted in English.

"Welcome to you all," Fredi answered in English—then in French. "But now let's get you to the camp." Fredi ushered them into the Citroen. The British captain rode in front and Jean squeezed into the back with the French lieutenant and the American radio operator.

Although Jean was bursting with questions about the new organization and what they planned to do here, and struggling with a shard of resentment about their possible takeover of their outfit, he stuck to asking about their flight and reassuring them that the cannisters of supplies would be well taken care of. The young American was anxious about his radio. "Although I have two extra crystals with me, so I could use your radio if mine is damaged."

"Fine," Fredi replied, as he drove them to the camp. "Our OSS radio operator will be waiting for us. He's been looking forward to meeting you. He's American, too—and about your age, I'd guess."

After the three men had been offered wine and rabbit stew, Fredi, Jean, Robert and the three parachutists gathered around a table in the large tent Fredi used as his headquarters. The tent had been dropped among others several months earlier when they had set up a second camp deeper in the forest. A candle-lit lantern hung from the tent's center pole over the table, casting dark shadows on the canvas walls. Fredi lifted his glass of wine. "Santé!"

"Santé!" they chorused.

Fredi looked from one man to the other, breathing rapidly, his eyes flickering with puzzlement. "Now, gentlemen, it's time you tell us about the Jedburghs and what you expect to do here. We're delighted to know our small group of two hundred resisters are considered worthy of attention."

Captain Cameron set down his wine glass. "I'll try to start at the beginning. Stop me if you have questions. The Jedburgh section of Special Forces was initiated over a year ago. It's a combined effort of OSS and SOE, but it's under the direction of Eisenhower's office, SHAEF. Teams of three from the British, American and Free French armies were recruited and trained in England. The Jedburgh's major goal is to support the French Resistance forces, the F.F.I, It's expected that after the Allied landings on French soil, the F.F.I. will fight the Germans from behind the lines."

Jean' heart leaped with excitement. The landings! The Allied invasion would happen at last. They'd get to kill those German bastards.

Fredi was staring at the captain in astonishment. "And your team of Jedburghs? Do you expect to be in uniform here—only fifteen kilometers from a German reserve garrison of 700 men—the command headquarters of General Ferdinand Neuling?"

"Possibly. We can wear civilian clothes if necessary. At least before the landings." Jean's heart quickened again at Cameron's casual mention of the word landings. Cameron continued. "Many other Jedburgh teams have been dropped all over France. Those here in the south of France fly from Blida, in Algeria. It's a safer trip than flying from London over German anti-aircraft on the French coast. OSS and SOE both have headquarters in Algiers and have joined forces in this venture. We will provide weapons, money, and work with your leaders to coordinate armed insurrections and sabotage."

Cameron was interrupted by voices at the opening of the tent. One of the maquisards stepped inside carrying a suitcase. Immediately, the American radioman stood up. "Excuse me sir, but that's the case that holds my radio. May I have a look?"

Cameron smiled, flexing his shoulders. "Of course, and if you don't mind, Felix, I think it would be better to continue this briefing later—after we've had some sleep."

Fredi rose from his seat. "Absolutely. You've had a long night. We've set up a tent for you and Lt Belloc. Sergeant Walker will bunk with Robert."

As the days passed, it became obvious to Jean that anyone listening to the BBC French radio would conclude that the allied invasion would occur soon. The chatter of nonsense messages inundated the network. The excitement in the camp mounted. Finally, Robert and Billy, who received messages from both OSS and SFHQ reported to Captain Cameron and Fredi that Resistance leaders throughout France should listen for the lines of a Verlaine poem: *The violins of autumn wound my heart with a monotonous languor.* The invasion would begin within twenty-four hours after that broadcast and F.F.I. bands should be prepared to attack and destroy roads, bridges, railroads and telecommunications—anything that would prevent the Wehrmacht from deploying its troops to the landing zone. Thousands of armed maquisards in hidden camps throughout the rugged alpine regions of France were waiting to attack.

Cameron, Belloc and Felix had discussed the possible sabotage targets at length. They finally decided on three operations in their territory. First, blowing the fuel dump in Toulon. Second, cutting the telephone wires from Draguingan to San Rafael in several places. Third, breaking up the train tracks from San Rafael to Marseilles.

"We can use five patrols of ten to twelve men." Fredi said. "We have enough rifles and stens and hand grenades to outfit 150 men."

Cameron nodded. "I'll request for drops of more M1's, hand grenades and bazookas. We'll need those after the landings."

Jean gazed at the map of France that Fredi had spread on the table. Nobody knew where the allied invasion would take place, but most speculated it would happen on the northern beaches: Calais? Could it be on their own coast?"

# Chapter Forty-two

## Operation Dragoon

*August, 1944*

Jean had pulled his sleeping bag outside his tent and placed it on the pine-needle covered ground. The evening was warm and he lay on his back, smoking a Lucky Strike—from one of the precious packs of cigarettes the Americans dropped from the sky. As he smoked, he listened to the detonations of bombs hammering the coast. He could feel his heart pounding as the bombs exploded. Flocks of huge planes droned overhead as they crossed the darkening sky. They'd been hitting the coastal fortifications day and night for the last week. The Allied soldiers would land soon—somewhere on their southern coast. He could only hope that this invasion would be as successful as the landings in Normandy. They'd heard that Patton's army had broken out of the beachhead and was deep in France. It was expected that Paris would be liberated soon.

Captain Cameron had told them the southern invasion was imminent, but the time and place had not yet been divulged. The entire Riviera coast from Marseilles to the border with Monaco was under air attack. The excitement was mounting. And the fear. As soon as the order was given, their group of 200 maquisards would storm Draguignan and occupy it. He thought of their plan. They'd mapped out their strategy, each squad's task, and they'd rehearsed the operation. The palms of his hands began to sweat as he recalled his own role. He would lead the attack on the police headquarters.

He looked up at the sky. It would be dark soon. Too late for the order to attack to come tonight. Maybe tomorrow? He took a deep breath of cooling air, thinking that if this Allied landing was successful the war in France might soon be over. Imagine. Thousands of F.F.I. maquisards were waiting in the mountains ready to swoop down and attack the German troops as soon as the order was given. OSS was coordinating the partisan attacks. Could it be true? That France would soon be free? That he'd be alive to hold Danielle in his arms? He stopped himself from going in that direction. It was tempting fate to believe he'd be that lucky.

He was interrupted in his reflections by the voices of Cameron, Fredi and Billy as they hurried through the camp. Jean rose from the pine needles and called to them. "Any news?"

Fredi turned. "Jean, I was trying to find you." Excitement filled his voice. "The order came through. Tomorrow we partisans attack. The invasion will begin at dawn the following day—August 15th. It's called Operation Dragoon."

Jean was not the only one who didn't sleep that night. A restless murmur of moving bodies and whispers rustled amongst the pines. The sounds of the coastal bombings in the distance matched their skipping heartbeats, but the next day the men exuded excitement and bravado. Jean's breathing was rapid as he oiled his handgun and cleaned his rifle. His squad of twelve men would carry either stens or M1s. Jean remembered only too well that the stens had a short firing range, but Cameron had assured him that stens do their job in close combat—like inside the prefecture.

The men moved into their positions in the early evening. They would attack at midnight. Jean considered the terrain. Draguignan, a town of 10,000 or so, was located in a bowl-like valley surrounded by forest-covered hills and mountains. Rough tracks entered it from several directions, but checkpoints were located only the main roads to Grasse, San Rafael or Le Muy. The German garrison of about 700 infantry troops was two kilometers north on a field once occupied by French artillery. The officers were billeted in town.

The maquisards hiked through the woods, carrying their rifles and stens, fanning out, encircling the town. Jean and some of his squad approached the town in the horse-drawn wagon, Luc holding Marron's reins. They were all dressed like farmers or charcoal workers and their weapons were hidden. Their signal for the attack was to be the church bells striking twelve o'clock. They should all be in their assigned position by that time.

As Jean waited in the wagon under a canopy of pines next to the road, he listened to the roar of airplanes as they flew overhead. Then the bombs exploded. Draguignan was thirty kilometers from the coast, but in the quiet of the evening, the detonations seemed closer. He thought he could hear the distant thud of artillery. The air smelled of smoke, and a red glow on the horizon could come from forest fires—started by the bombings? And had the neighboring maquisards assembled to attack the German coastal positions begun their assault?

Jean glanced at his watch. It was almost midnight. Their own assault would begin within moments. At the sound of the church bells the guards at the checkpoints had to be taken out or captured. It was believed the police might be quite willing to surrender, but the Germans had to be killed—quietly, in the manner in which the maquisards had been trained. Four men had been assigned that duty.

When the bells stopped ringing Jean called to his men to assemble their weapons. He then commanded Luc to drive the wagon down the road toward the checkpoint. When they reached it, he spied the two bodies in gray and green uniforms sprawled on the ground—both with slit throats, The maquisards had done their job. Had the gendarme surrendered?

Fifty meters beyond the turnoff, Jean jumped down from the wagon, his M1 slung over his shoulder and his Walther P38 in his hand. The three men who'd been hidden in the wagon joined him, their stens under their arms. In the shadows of doorways he recognized five more of his men. He glanced up at the upstairs windows of the houses bordering the street, noting the shutters slammed shut. The street was eerily quiet. He and his men stayed close to the shadowed walls as they moved toward the central square and the police headquarters, the prefecture. Opposite the prefecture was the Town Hall, where he could see shadowy figures creeping toward it. Fredi was leading that squad. They knew it would be guarded by two German soldiers. Fredi and one of the maquisards would silently kill them. Next to the Town Hall was a café that Jean knew was a popular spot for German officers to gather when they were off duty. They all wore sidearms in holsters on their leather belts. Jean strained his eyes to see if Jean Marc's squad was moving toward the café. To his relief, he noted the men crouching behind the stacks of outdoor tables and chairs in the front of the café. They were ready.

And so was he. Now he signaled to his men with the low whistle they had agreed upon. Barely breathing, they crept up the prefecture steps, fingers on the triggers of their weapons. Jean kicked open the door with his foot, his handgun held in both hands, aimed at the gendarme seated at a desk. "Put your hands on your head." Immediately, two of Jean's men, brandishing their stens, rushed the man and grabbed hold of him. The gendarme spluttered his acquiescence, trying to convince them he was on their side. Jean snatched his keys from the man's belt and tossed them to another of his squad. "Lock him up," Jean ordered. In the meantime, as had been rehearsed, all but three of his squad searched the premises for the night-duty police, whom they captured and locked into the cell with the first captured policeman. The prisoners would be released later.

After a thorough search of the building, leaving four men to guard the prisoners, Jean and the remaining four of his men then descended the prefecture steps, their eyes darting from side to side, sweat beading on their foreheads. On the coastal horizon the sky was orange-red. Smoke obscured the stars. Sounds of bombing and gunfire thudded in the distance. Jean beckoned to his men. They crept to the café, which was quiet. Suddenly, Jean Marc burst out the café door, three of his men behind him. "They're all at the garrison," he shouted. "The officers were ordered to be with their men. They expect the invasion. They're preparing to move—to counterattack."

The owner of the café was gesturing wildly in the direction of the garrison. "You must stop them!"

By now, Fredi, Lt Belloc and his group were clustered in front of the Town Hall. Lt Belloc, dressed in his French uniform, pulled a tricolor from his musette. Trampled on the ground was the Nazi's hated red flag, its swastika ripped into pieces. Next to it, were the bodies of two

German soldiers, blood pooling under their heads. Belloc helped one of the young maquisards attach the tricolor to the flagpole over the door of the Town Hall. Jean noted the emotion in Belloc's face—exhilaration and pain.

The sound of footsteps on cobblestones caused Jean to stiffen. With relief he saw it was the uniformed Captain Cameron. Cameron ran toward them, followed by his squad of maquisards and five civilian men carrying hunting rifles. "Draguignan is under our control," Cameron said, grinning. "Fifty of our men are patrolling the town and guarding the entry points. The German guards have all been killed. Jean, what about the police?"

"In jail!" Jean replied.

Jean Marc then stepped forward, his blue eyes filled with alarm. "We're in control of Draguignan, but the German Infantry Corps, is on alert. The officers billeted here were ordered back to their headquarters. By now they must know we've occupied the town."

Fredi turned to him. "Twenty of our men are at work blocking the roads to the garrison with tree trunks and piles of crushed rock. The Germans have trucks and three half tracks, but no tanks. And we've destroyed their telephone lines."

Cameron shifted his rifle and glanced at his watch. "Our truck with the bazookas and hand grenades will be here within minutes. We'll leave a few men here to guard the Town Hall and the prefecture. The rest of us will proceed—on the double—to the periphery of the garrison."

Jean shoved his Walther P38 into his belt, held his M1 under his arm and beckoned his men to follow at a run. Fredi and Jean Marc rushed ahead with their squads, while Cameron stood in the square waving to the truck that was roaring down the narrow street. As Jean's squad left the central square and loped up the street bordered by stone houses and apartments, Jean scanned the shuttered upper windows as he ran. The distant thuds of battle, and the clatter of boots on the cobblestone resounded in the silence. It was as if the people behind those closed windows were holding their collective breath. But the takeover of Draguignan had gone smoothly. The German garrison would be a different story.

It was well after four in the morning before all the maquisards were in their positions. Jean and his squad lay sprawled on their stomachs behind a stone wall opposite the garrison's main entrance. Behind them, bordering the wall, was a row of umbrella pines, which Jean hoped would provide shadows to make them less visible when the sun rose. He eyed the road that passed the garrison. He knew it was blocked in both directions. Fredi had ordered it earlier. The entrance to the garrison was guarded by four sentries protected by chest-high sand-bagged enclosures spaced four paces apart. Fredi and Captain Cameron had concluded that the sentries could not be silently killed. The maquisards would need to surround the garrison undetected. Although he couldn't see or hear them, Jean knew that armed with hand grenades, stens and M1s, the maquisards had crept into their positions surrounding the compound. The distant sounds of bombardments would mask the crackle of twigs or the rustle of grass as they moved into place. All garrison exits would be covered.

Although they were hidden behind a tree trunk, Jean knew that two men were aiming a bazooka at the main gate. Another bazooka was positioned at a side exit with Captain Cameron in command. Lt Belloc and the civilians from Draguignan were crouched behind an outcropping of rocks at the side of the garrison. Behind them was a cleared field, once part of a dairy farm.

And now Jean waited, heart pounding and palms damp with sweat. He listened to the sounds coming from within the high stone wall surrounding the compound. He heard what he concluded was the sound of a generator. Lights flashed, perhaps from flashlights or truck headlights. Men's voices shouted commands or curses. Would they wait for dawn to form their columns?

An hour went by. Jean shifted his position. His body was stiff and his eyes ached with the strain of watching. He flexed his shoulders, and checked his men. They, too, were restless. He peered up at the eastern sky that was now gray not black. He glanced at his watch. Five o'clock. Suddenly, from the south, flocks of bombers roared overhead heading for the beaches thirty kilometers away. Within minutes bomb after bomb exploded. lighting up the horizon. Jean felt the shock waves at each detonation. From the coast flashes of light pierced the sky and deep blasts of what sounded like naval artillery split the air. Next, a horde of fighter planes swooped through the sky like a swarm of angry bees. The noise was deafening. His heart pounding, Jean clapped his hands over his ears, but found himself wanting to laugh. The Allies had arrived like Furies from hell.

During the bombardment lights had been extinguished within the garrison. Now a siren blew, and Jean could hear the sound of boots running on pavement. When would they move their columns? Were they waiting for the bombardment to stop? The bombing continued for over an hour. Suddenly, the explosions and rattle of machine guns stopped and the fighters zoomed out of sight. After a few moments of silence, low-flying bombers droned above. Soon the pale sky was filled with billowing parachutists floating toward the ground, landing somewhere out of sight. A crashing sound of breaking branches above his head caused Jean to aim his rifle into the canopy. The top of the tree was draped in white silk, and a paratrooper in a green and black jumpsuit was struggling to cut himself loose from a tangle of parachute lines. Jean threw a quick glance at the sentries guarding the gate. Only two were in their enclosures and they were aiming their guns toward the field where the parachutes had disappeared.

Luc, who crouched next to Jean, crawled toward the tree on his elbows and scurried up the trunk. When the white-faced paratrooper held out his knife in a threatening gesture, Luc made a thumb's up sign. "Nous sommes Resistance!' Luc whispered. "Bienvenue!"

The paratrooper burst into a smile and whispered back,"American! 551$^{st}$ Airborne, Hi!"

Luc reached out to the soldier, helping him disentangle himself and yank down the parachute, which they dropped on the ground. Then they both slid down the tree trunk and flopped onto the ground behind the wall. As the soldier reached into his musette and began to assemble his Thompson machine gun, Jean noted the palm trees painted on the American's helmet. Jean felt as if his heart would burst with gratitude. A savior had dropped from the heavens. Smiling broadly, Jean clapped the soldier on his back and murmured a greeting in English. Then, holding his finger over his lips he pointed at the garrison opposite. "Germans," he whispered, "700 of them. We're the Maquis, only 200 of us. We're very, very happy to see you!"

A roar of motors and the grinding sound of gears being shifted from within the garrison, caused the men crouched behind the stone wall to grasp their weapons and freeze. Jean beckoned them to keep their heads down while he rose to his knees and gave a quick glance over the wall. The sounds of engines grew louder and the gate to the entrance was slowly opening. Jean dropped down and unhooked a hand grenade from his belt. His men clicked off the safety on their rifles. The American paratrooper, who had finished assembling his gun, was ready to fire.

Moving slowly, Jean peered once again over the wall. Emerging through the gate was a monster half track, a personnel carrier. A helmeted soldier manned the armored machine gun mounted on its body. The carrier's tracks crunched on the road's crushed rock. Jean ducked down and pulled the pin from the hand grenade. He jumped up and with all his strength threw the grenade at the carrier. Simultaneously, the machine gun swiveled toward him and spat out a round of bullets. Jean fell to the ground just as the grenade exploded. Before he blacked out he heard another roaring explosion. The bazooka.

# Chapter Forty-three

## Danielle and Jean

### October, 1944

The train had just crossed the border from Switzerland into France. Tears brimmed in Danielle's eyes as she watched the tricolor above the border station flowing in the crisp autumn breeze. The blood-red Nazi flags had been removed—destroyed, she hoped. The Germans occupying much of France had retreated toward the Rhine. 100,000 had been captured. German troops were still fighting in Alsace and the Ardenne, but southern France and Paris had been liberated. She gazed up at the high peaks and glaciers that loomed on both sides of the valley. She was still in the Alps, but her very own French Alps.

She glanced at the documents she still clutched in her hand: her French passport and her travel papers issued to her by the OSS office in Geneva, where she had been working. Her boss had finally decided to send her into France. She tucked the papers carefully into the inside pocket of her coat, which also held the precious radio message she'd received a month ago from Robert about Jean. She slid the piece of paper out of her pocket and read it yet again. "Jean took a couple of bullets in the shoulder at the battle at Draguignan, but is OK. Jaques and Lili are taking care of him at the farmhouse. Say hello to Chantal."

The message was signed, POPEYE, which was the code name Robert had chosen to call himself.

As soon as she'd received Robert's message she asked her boss for help in returning to France. He told her she'd have to wait until they were certain the southern region was entirely cleared of German troops. She would have asked Val for help, but he was in Italy on a mission. The Germans were still occupying northern Italy.

She had no way of communicating with Jean. There was nobody she could ask in her office to send a personal, unofficial message to Robert in Chateaudouble via London OSS. Mail and telegraph service had not yet been restored. Telephone lines had been cut and removed by the Resistance. Was Jean recovering from his wounds? Had he been treated with sulfa? She knew that Fredi's maquisards had been supplied with sulfa before Operation Dragoon, but now that the fighting had stopped, they were no longer receiving war materials. They were expected to disband or join de Gaulle's Free French army and march with the Allies into Germany.

When the OSS officials concluded that the south of France was free of German troops, she was given permission to travel to the Var and was provided with the requisite documents. Now she would go by train to Grenoble, then take the bus to Draguignan and Chateaudouble. Her heartbeat quickened when she thought that by that evening she would walk through the farmhouse door and wrap her arms around Jean. Would he be on his feet, his arm in a sling—or would he be sick and feverish? Or will he have completely recovered and no longer be there? That was a shocking thought. By tonight she would know. She wanted to know so much.

As the train approached Grenoble, she thought of the brave people she had met there with Val. Resistance members had guided her and Chantal over the Alps into Switzerland. Val had his own special method of crossing the border, which he told her she didn't need to know, but he'd taken them to a safe house and turned them over to people he trusted belonging to the local Resistance. "They're experienced," he'd said. "They smuggle refugees over the border regularly. They're good at it."

She thought of Chantal, who she'd seen just yesterday. She'd promised Chantal that if Robert was still at the farmhouse she would give him her address in Geneva. She would tell him that a good Jewish couple had taken Chantal in and was sending her to university. "But tell him I really want to hear from him. Soon!" she'd said.

Now in Grenoble, Danielle left the train and found the bus that she needed to take for Chateaudouble. As the bus traversed the town, she was elated to see the French flags flying everywhere and people on the sidewalks walking briskly, as if they felt lighter, happier, now that their ruthless conquerors had been vanquished. She looked for young women with shaved heads that she'd heard about, but she saw none. Perhaps they were ashamed to be out on the street. She felt sorry for those girls. Maybe they slept with German soldiers to get food for their families. Food would still be scarce, of course. And gasoline. She noted the few cars on the streets, and most of those were charcoal burning. Would the charcoal factory at the farmhouse still be in operation?

Then she thought about her parents—and her aunts and cousins who had disappeared. She'd been able to correspond with her parents since she went to Geneva. The letters would be delayed and some didn't arrive, but they had been in touch. Her mother had written that the whereabouts of her aunts, uncles and cousins was unknown. She hadn't heard from them since they'd arrived in the States. She didn't know if they were hiding somewhere in the country or if they'd been taken away like the other Jews they knew had been sent to German concentration camps. Soon, she hoped, mail would go through to Paris and she would write to non-Jewish friends. Danielle's mood darkened. So much was unknown.

When she finally reached Chateaudouble she found a farmer with a horse and cart who was willing to take her to the farmhouse. It was dark by the time she hopped off the cart at the entrance to the charcoal factory. The farmer lifted down her suitcase and wished her luck. She stood a moment and gazed at the mounds of wood and mud that dotted the clearing. Beyond them shone the candle-lit windows of the farmhouse. Her breathing quickened. Will Jean have changed? Will he still love her?

She didn't knock on the door. She placed her hand on the latch and pressed the lever. The door slowly opened and she stepped inside. Sitting at the table in the center of the room were Jean, Jaques and Lili. Jean's arm was in a sling, just as she had imagined. His shoulder was thick with bandages. "Bon soir" she called, laughing, dropping her suitcase, closing the door behind her. All three turned and stared at her, their eyes wide with astonishment. Simultaneously they jumped up from the table and rushed toward her, calling her name, exclaiming greetings. With one arm, Jean pulled her close and gave her a long, hard kiss.

"But Jean" she said, pulling back, not wanting to hurt him. "Your shoulder. Robert told me you were shot."

Jean laughed, kissing her again. "I'm fine, Danielle. No pain! It's so fantastic to see you walk into this room. Have you come from Geneva?"

Jaques and Lili embraced Danielle warmly, kissing her three times on the cheek, preventing her from answering Jean, their voices ringing with excitement, helping her take off her coat, leading her to the table, pouring her a glass of wine. Jean's left arm slid around her waist. She peered up into his eyes, his eyes that flickered with specks of light. Eyes that told her he still loved her. He hadn't changed. At least, not much—except for the fine creases at the corners of his eyes and mouth, and his face was leaner, harder? He'd been in battle.

Jaques lifted his glass. "To all of us and absent friends!"

Danielle raised her glass, but the words absent friends sounded an alarm in her head. She thought of her aunts and cousins—but also her companions here. Now she must ask difficult questions, but Jean spoke first. "Robert gave us a message from Val saying that you were in Geneva—and then Robert told us he'd sent you a message about my wounded shoulder."

Danielle nodded. "And I have a message for Robert from Chantal. Is he still here?"

"Yes, but just for a few more days. At the moment he's up on the ridge waiting to receive messages from London."

"And is Luc still turning the handle?"

For a moment nobody spoke. Lili stared into her wine glass and Jaques shot Jean a questioning look. Jean removed his arm from her waist and took a deep breath. He touched her hand. "Luc was shot at Draguignan, killed, soon after I got hit in the shoulder."

Danielle's throat tightened. "But Jean, this battle of Draguignan, why was Luc there?"

Jean sighed. "I wish he hadn't been there, but he was seventeen, old enough to shoot and he was a good shot. Good enough to be a sniper. I didn't see what happened, but they told me about it when I came to. Our group had occupied Draguignan the night before the invasion—and then we surrounded the garrison. We wanted to stop them from their counterattack. Remember the garrison?"

She nodded. When she left it was manned by Italians. The Germans would have taken it over.

Jean continued. "When the first half track drove through the gate, I hit it with a hand grenade, but the machine gunner got me at the same time. I passed out, but Luc then climbed the tree back of us and started shooting with his M1. He hit five men before they spotted him. They killed him. Knocked him out of the tree." Jean took another gulp of wine.

Silence filled the room. Jaques finally spoke. "But, Danielle, with the help of American paratroopers—and they lost 400 men while landing—we beat the Germans into submission. They surrendered."

"Yes, I heard, Jaques. You all did a great job. But what a loss for the Americans." She then turned Jean. "And who else did we lose?"

"Four maquisards. I don't think you know them. They joined us after you left."

"And Fredi? Alain?"

"Fredi's OK. He's in Draguignan. He's liaison officer between the Allied Command and the prefecture of the Var, dealing with security and documents. People need identity cards, travel permits."

"And Alain?"

Jean gave her a pained look. "The Gestapo picked him up in San Rafael. In July, a month before the Allied invasion. We don't know what happened to him. If he's still alive—and hasn't been sent to Germany—he might turn up. We haven't had news about Simone, either."

Danielle caught her breath. Her insides were crumpling. She closed her eyes. France was almost free of Germans, but at such a cost. How tired she was—exhausted. She rested her head on her hands.

Jean placed his arm over her shoulders. "Danielle, it's too much to bear, I know—and you're exhausted. We haven't even let you wash up, rest a bit. Let's get you upstairs."

She lifted her head and tried to smile. She then dug a handkerchief from her skirt pocket and blotted her eyes. "I'm sorry. Yes, it was a long trip—and seeing you, all of you, was so wonderful, and knowing the Germans have gone, no SS, no Gestapo, no Jews being thrown into cattle cars, and that we can breathe again—but then hearing about Alain and Luc and all those brave American paratroopers—and the maquisards. . ."

Jean glanced out the dormer window in the attic room which used to be Danielle's but was now his. The moon was full and a shaft of bluish light lit Danielle's lovely face. She was sound asleep. He smiled. His shoulder was hurting. Making love with just one arm had been a puzzle, but they'd managed. How he loved her. How magical she looked in that narrow bed with the moonlight on her face. He felt as if his heart might burst with happiness.

But what would happen now? He knew the war for him was over. The doctor had told him it would be weeks before his shattered clavicle would heal completely. No more soldiering. So what would he do next? First of all, he needed to get his identity straightened out. He needed a passport or an identity card in his own name so he could marry Danielle legally. But how? He was born in Genoa, but the Germans still occupied northern Italy. How much longer would the Germans hang on? And even if they surrendered, the country would be in a mess. Birth records could have gone up in smoke. He didn't know if the Italian Embassy was functioning yet. Eventually, the Paris embassy would be the place to go. But the fact that he'd escaped from prison and was a fugitive could complicate matters considerably. How long would it take for his case to be cleared?

Perhaps he could get a temporary identity card here in France. Fredi had said he'd try to find out if that was possible. The only person who could vouch for his identity was Val, but Danielle had said Val was on an OSS mission in Italy. They had known each other by their true names in Spain. In Marseilles they both had used a nom de guerre and forged papers. Maybe someone in OSS could help him. He gave a quiet laugh. They could forge an Italian passport in his name.

He fastened his eyes on Danielle, who had turned on her side. He could no longer see her face. He carefully slipped into bed beside her.

Her hair smelled of lavender. When she awoke in the morning, he made love to her again and barely felt the pain in his shoulder. After breakfast they wandered into the meadow behind the barn. The sun was shining and the air was soft and mild. Jean sought Danielle's hand and led her to sit next to him on a silvered tree trunk. "Autumn arrives late in Provence. Not like Paris." Jean said quietly.

"No, not like Paris." she repeated.

He lifted her hand and kissed her palm. "Shall we go to Paris? I've been thinking I could get a reporter's job there—maybe with Combat. It's no longer an underground paper for the Resistance, but maybe Frenay will remember that I wrote for Combat in Marseilles. And that you did the art work. He's in Paris, I hear."

She sighed. "Paris. It will have changed. So many friends and relatives have been killed or deported. My aunts, my cousins. My parents want me to come to California. We've been able to write to each other since I went to Switzerland. They believe it will be easier now to get me a visa."

"But Danielle, it wouldn't be easy for me. I fought in Spain for the International Brigade. The American State department thinks we were all communists, and love Stalin. They believe their next war will be with Russia. They wouldn't let me in. Stay with me here in France, Danielle. You will marry me, won't you?"

"Danielle touched his cheek. "Yes, Jean, I'll marry you. As soon as you're Gino Baroli again." With his one good arm he drew her close and they kissed, quite solemnly, as if cementing the pact. Danielle pulled back and locked eyes with his. "Have you thought about asking OSS for papers?"

He laughed. "Yes, I have. They can forge anything. Val could help me if we could get in touch with him."

"Let's talk to Robert. I haven't seen him and I promised Chantal to give him her address in Geneva."

He jumped up from their perch and held out his hand. "OK, let's find him. He's at the camp." As they walked through the forest toward the camp, Jean described the Jedburgh team that had helped plan the occupation of Draguignan and the attack on the German garrison. "They were flown out a week ago from Nice—returned to London.

They weren't told where they would be sent next, but they thought the team would be split up now that France was just about liberated."

Danielle squeezed his hand. "I'm sorry I didn't get to meet them."

"But I'm so glad you were not here, Danielle. So many Jews who had been safe in the Italian zone were taken away when the Germans came. We did what we could. Jaques and Lili got two families to Grenoble—and the local Resistance people smuggled them into Switzerland."

Danielle sighed. "Chantal and I met those Resistance people. I told you about them." She suddenly stopped and picked up a chestnut that lay on the path. "Jean, I've been thinking—even if we can't get married at the registry until you get your identity changed—let's have a wedding. We can get Fredi to do a ceremony and have a party at the farmhouse."

Jean laughed, picked her up and spun her around. "Wonderful idea. And in the meantime I can ask everyone possible to help get me my papers—legal or forged—but as far as we ourselves are concerned, we'll be married. Then as soon as the doctor says I'm well enough we can go to Paris. I'll write to Frenay and Combat this afternoon. The mail should be going through by now. OK, Danielle?"

"Oh, yes, OK." she said, laughing, pirouetting on the path. "How good it is to be alive!" As she twirled, she felt a stab of guilt like a knife piercing her heart. She stopped and shot Jean a stricken glance. "How could I say such a thing when so many, many are dead—or disappeared. And the war isn't over. Hitler is still alive. The killing goes on. Why was I spared?"

He touched her cheek. "I know. We can't help but feel guilty. But we did survive. We were lucky. And now we move on. We're free." He gave a wry laugh. "Well, more or less. If we can scare up some documents."

She breathed a deep sigh, then took hold of Jean's hand. As they continued their walk down the path, she said, "I wonder if there'll ever be a day that we don't need identity cards and passports and visas and travel passes to go from one country to another."

Jean shook his head. "Never."

# Bibliography

Eisner, Peter, *The Freedom Line, The Brave Men and Women who Rescued Allied Airmen from the Nazis in World War II*, Harper Collins, 2004.

Fittco, Lise, *Escape Through The Pyrenees*, Northwestern University Press, 1991.

Foot, M.R.D., *Resistance, European Resistance to Nazism 1940-45*, McGraw-Hill, 1977.

Foot, M.R.D., Langley, J.M., *MI9, Escape and Evasion 1939-1945*, Little Brown & co, Boston, 1980.

Frenay, Henri, *The Night Will End, Memoirs of the Resistance*, Abelard-Schuman Ltd, London, 1976.

Fry, Varian, *Surrender on Demand*, Colorado: Johnson Books, 1997.

Irwin, Will, *The Jedburghs, The Secret History of the Allied special Forces, France 1944*, Public Affairs, Perseus Books, 2005.

Jackson, Julian, *France, The Dark years, 1940-1944*, Oxford University Press, 2001.

Marino, Andy, *A Quiet American; the Secret War of Varian Fry*, St Martin's Press, NY, 1999.

Marks, Leo, *Between Silk and Cyanide, A Codemaker's War 1941-1945*, Simon & Schuster, NY 1998.

Ottis, Sherri Greene, *Silent Heroes, Downed airmen and the French Underground*, University Press of Kentucky, 2001.

Smith, Richard Harris, *OSS, The Secret History of America's First Central Intelligence Agency*, Lyons Press, 2005.

Sullivan, Rosemary, *Villa Air-Bel, World War II, Escape and a House in Marseille*, Harper Collins, NY, 2006.